PENGUI

THE
LAVENDER KEEPER

Fiona McIntosh is an internationally bestselling author of novels for adults and children. She co-founded and ran an award-winning travel magazine with her husband, Ian, before becoming a full-time author. Fiona now roams the world researching and drawing inspiration for her novels. She also trains emerging writers and is a columnist for News Corp's Escape supplement. She lives in South Australia.

www.fionamcintosh.com

FIONA McINTOSH

THE LAVENDER KEEPER

PENGUIN BOOKS

PENGUIN BOOKS

UK | USA | Canada | Ireland | Australia
India | New Zealand | South Africa | China

Penguin Books is part of the Penguin Random House group of companies
whose addresses can be found at global.penguinrandomhouse.com.

Penguin
Random House
Australia

First published by Penguin Books Australia Ltd, 2012
This edition published by Penguin Group (Australia), 2013

Cover design by Marina Messiha © Penguin Group (Australia)
Text design by Cathy Larsen © Penguin Group (Australia)
Cover photos: Sunset over lavender fields by Guy Edwardes/
Getty Images; Lavender field by Andrew Sharpe, sharpeimages.co.uk
Typeset in Fairfield by Post Pre-Press Group, Brisbane, Queensland
Printed and bound in Australia by Griffin Press, an accredited ISO AS /NZS 14001
Environmental Management Systems printer.

National Library of Australia
Cataloguing-in-Publication data:
McIntosh, Fiona, 1960-
The lavender keeper / Fiona McIntosh.
9780143568438 (pbk.)
A823.4

penguin.com.au

Dedicated to the Crotet family:
Marcel, Françoise, Laurent, Severine and especially to Louis –
a maquisard at sixteen years old – with whom we shared a meal
and friendship one summer's afternoon in Provence.

PART ONE

PART ONE

I

12 July 1942

Luc loved this light on the lavender in summer, just before sunset. The field's hedgerow deepened to glowing emerald and finally to dark sentinels, while the pebbly rows between the mounds of purple blooms became smudges of shadow. The lavender spikes, so straight and tall, never failed to mesmerise him. His gaze was drawn to the bright head of a wild scarlet poppy. No wonder artists flocked to the region in summer, he thought . . . or used to, before the world went mad and exploded with bombs and gunfire.

The young woman next to him did up the top button of her frayed summery blouse. Stray wisps of her long red hair fell across her face to hide grey-green eyes and her irritation. 'You're very quiet,' Catherine said.

Luc blinked out of his reverie, guilty that he'd briefly forgotten she was there. 'I'm just admiring the scenery,' he said softly.

She cut him a rueful glance as she straightened her clothes. 'I wish you did mean me and not your lavender fields.'

He grinned and it seemed to infuriate her. It was obvious Catherine was keen for marriage and children – all the village girls were. Catherine was pretty and much too accommodating, Luc thought, with a stab of contrition. There had been other women in his life, not all so generous, but Catherine obliged because she wanted more. She deserved it – or certainly deserved better. She knew he saw others but she seemed to have a marvellous ability to contain

3

her jealousy, unlike any other woman he'd known.

He brushed some of the tiny purple flowers from her hair and leant sideways to kiss her neck. 'Mmm,' he said. 'You smell of my lavender.'

'I'm surprised I haven't been stung by the bees as well. Perhaps we should consider how nice a bed might be?'

He sensed she was leading up to the question he dreaded. It was time to go. He stood in a fluid motion and offered her a hand. 'I told you, the bees aren't interested in you. Ask Laurent. The bees are greedy for the pollen only.' He waved an arm in a wide arc. 'It's their annual feast and they have a queen to service, young to raise, honey to make.'

She didn't look, busy buckling the belt that cinched her small waist. 'Anyway, Luc, it's not your lavender. It's your father's,' she said. She sounded miffed.

Luc sighed inwardly, wondering whether it was time to tell her the truth. It would be public knowledge soon enough anyway. 'Actually, Catherine, my father has given me all the fields.'

'What?' Her head snapped up, as the expression on her heart-shaped face creased into a frown.

Luc shrugged. He wasn't even sure his sisters knew yet – not that they'd mind – but his annoyance had flared at Catherine's hostile tone. 'On his last trip south he gave them all to me.' He knew he shouldn't enjoy watching her angry eyes dull now with confusion.

'All of them?' she repeated in disbelief.

He opted for a helpless grin. 'His decision, not mine.'

'But that makes you a main landowner for the whole Luberon region. Probably even the largest grower.' It sounded like an accusation.

'I suppose it does,' he replied casually. 'He wants me to take full responsibility for cultivating the lavender. It has to be protected, especially now.' He began to amble away, encouraging her to start the walk home. 'My father spends more time in Paris with his other businesses than he does down here . . . and besides, I was raised in Saignon. He wasn't. This place is in my blood. And the lavender has always been my passion. It's not for him.'

She regarded him hungrily. Now she had even more reason to secure him. But the more she demanded it, the more he resisted. It wasn't that he didn't like Catherine; she was often funny, always sensuous and graceful. But there were aspects of her character he didn't admire, and he disliked her cynicism and lack of empathy. As a teenager he could remember her laughing at one of the village boys who had a stutter, and he knew it was her who'd started a rumour about poor Hélène from the next hamlet. He'd watched, too, her dislocation from the plight of the French under the German regime. For the time being her life was unaffected, and it bothered Luc that her view was blinkered. She never spoke about dreams, only about practicalities – marriage, security, money. Catherine was entirely self-centred.

'I can't think about anything but making these fields as productive as I can. These aren't times to be planning too far ahead,' he continued, trying to be diplomatic. 'Don't scowl.' He turned to touch her cheek affectionately.

She batted his hand away coldly. 'Luc, Saignon may be in your soul but it doesn't run in your blood.'

When things didn't go Catherine's way she usually struck back. Hers was a cruel barb but an old one. Luc had been an orphan and most of the villagers knew he was an interloper. But he might as well have been born to the Bonet family – he had been only a few weeks old when they took him in, gave him their name and made the tall, pink stone house in the village square his home.

His lighter features set him apart from the rest of his family, and his taller, broader frame singled him out in the Apt region. All he knew was that his ageing language teacher had found him abandoned and had brought him to Saignon, where Golda Bonet, who had recently lost a newborn child of her own, welcomed his tiny body to her bosom, and into her family.

No one knew where he had come from and he certainly didn't care. He loved his father, Jacob, his mother, Golda, and his grandmother, Ida, as well as his trio of dark-haired sisters. Sarah, Rachel and Gitel were petite and attractive like their mother, although Rachel was the prettiest. Luc, with his strong jawline, slightly hooded brow, symmetrical square face and searing blue gaze stood like a golden giant among them.

'Why are you so angry, Catherine?' he asked, trying to deflect this attack.

'Luc, you promised we would be engaged by —'

'I made no such promise.'

He watched her summon every ounce of willpower to control herself; he couldn't help but admire her.

'But you did say we might be married some day.'

'I responded to *your* offer of marriage by saying that "one day we might". That is not an affirmation. You were spoiling for an argument then, as you are now.'

Her large eyes were sparking with anger, and yet again he watched her wrestle that emotion back under control.

'Let's not fight, my love,' she said affectionately, reaching to do up a couple of buttons on his shirt, skimming the skin beneath.

But he did not love Catherine . . . nor want a wife in this chaotic world they found themselves in. If not Catherine, then Sophie or Aurelie in nearby villages, or even gentle Marguerite in Apt would grant him a roll in the hay – or the lavender.

'What are you smiling about?' Catherine asked.

He couldn't tell her he was amused by her manipulative nature. 'Your flushed cheeks. You're always at your prettiest after —'

She put a hand to his lips. 'Please, make an honest woman of me.' She smoothed her skirt. 'We don't even need an engagement; let's just be married and we can make love in a bed as *Monsieur* and *Madame* —'

'Catherine, stop. I have no intention of marrying anyone right now. Let's stop seeing one another if it's causing you so much grief.'

Her expression lost its mistiness; her eyes narrowed and her mouth formed a line of silent anger.

'We are at war,' he reminded her, a plaintive tone in his voice. 'France is occupied by Germans!'

She looked around her, feigning astonishment. 'Where?'

Luc felt a stab of disappointment at her shallow view. Up this high, they were still relatively untroubled by the German soldiers, but his father's letters from Paris were becoming increasingly frantic. The people in the north – in the occupied territories – were suffering enormous economic and social pressure, and those in the capital were bearing the brunt of it.

'So many of those who fled here at the invasion have already gone back north,' Catherine said, sneering. 'All the Parisians have returned. You know it! They're not scared.' She gave a careless shrug. 'It doesn't really affect us. Why should we worry?'

'They've gone back,' he began, quietly despairing, 'because it feels so hopeless. Their homes, their friends, their livelihoods are in the Occupied Zone. They ran south fearing for their lives; they've since decided to learn how to live among the Boches.' He spat on the ground at the mention of the Germans. 'The northerners have no choice. It doesn't mean they like it, or that we have to support the Germans.'

'You'd better not let Gendarme Landry catch you talking like that.'

'I'm not scared of Pierre Landry.'

She looked up at him, shocked. 'Be careful, Luc. He's dangerous.'

'You're the one who should be careful pandering to his

demands. I know your family gives him a chicken once a month to stay on his good side.'

Catherine glanced around nervously. 'You're going to get yourself into trouble if you keep talking like that. I don't want to be shot for denouncing the Marshal.'

'Marshal Pétain was a hero in the Great War, but he was not up to the job to lead our nation. Vichy is surely a joke, and now we have the ultimate Nazi puppet leading us. Laval more than dances to Hitler's tune; in fact, he's destroying our great democracy and adopting the totalitarian —'

She covered her ears and looked genuinely anxious. Luc stopped. Catherine was raised as a simple country girl who figured obedience to the Vichy government's militia was the best way for France. And in some respects, perhaps she could be right – but only if you were the sort of person who was content being subservient to a gang of avaricious and racist bullies who were dismantling France's sovereign rights. A *collaborator*! The very word made his gut twist. He didn't know he had such strong political leanings until he'd begun to hear the stories from his father of what it was like to experience Paris – Paris! – being overrun by German soldiers. The realisation that his beloved capital had opened her doors and shrunk back like a cowed dog before Hitler's marauding army had brought disillusionment into his life, as it had for so many young French. It had seemed unthinkable that France would capitulate after all the heroics of the Great War.

His acrimony had hardened to a kernel of hate for the Germans, and on each occasion that German soldiers had ventured close to his home, Luc had taken action.

It was he who thought to blockade the spring, said to date back to Roman times, which fed the famous fountain in the village. By the time the German soldiers, parched and exhausted, had made their way up the steep hill into Saignon, the fountain was no longer running. All the villagers watched the thirsty soldiers drinking from the still water at the fountain's base, smiling as the Germans drank what was reserved for the horses and donkeys of the village. On another occasion he and Laurent had stopped the progress of German motorbikes by felling a tree onto the road. A small win, but Luc was thrilled to see the soldiers, scratching their heads and turning tail.

'One day I'll kill a German for you, Catherine,' Luc promised, unable to fully dampen the fire that had begun to smoulder within.

'I hate it when you talk like this. It frightens me.'

He ran a hand through his hair, realising he was behaving like a bully; she had no political knowledge. After all, if the Luberon kept its collective head down and continued to supply the German war effort with food and produce, this rural part of Provence might escape the war unscathed.

'Listen, I'm sorry that I've upset you,' he began, more gently. 'How about we —' He didn't get any further, interrupted by a familiar voice calling to him.

Laurent appeared, breathless and flushed. He bent over, panting. 'I knew where I'd find you,' he gasped. Laurent glanced shyly at Catherine; he was continually impressed at Luc's way with the local girls.

'What is it?' Luc asked.

'Your parents.'

'What about them?' Immediately Luc's belly flipped. He had a recurring nightmare that his family were all killed – his parents, grandmother, and his three sisters – in some sort of German reprisal for his bad thoughts.

'They're home!' Laurent said excitedly. 'I was sent to find you.'

'Home?' Luc couldn't believe it. 'You mean, Saignon?'

Laurent looked at him as though he were daft. 'Where else do I mean? In the village right now, kissing and hugging everyone. Only you are missing.'

Now Luc's belly flipped for different reasons. He gave Catherine a slightly more lingering kiss than could be considered perfunctory. 'I'll see you soon, eh?'

'When?' she asked.

'Saturday.'

'Today's Saturday!' she snapped.

'Monday, then. I promise.' He reached for her but she slapped his hand away.

She glared at Laurent, who quickly walked a little way off. 'Luc, tell me this. Do you love me?'

'Love? In these uncertain times?'

She gave a sound of despair. 'I've been patient, but if you love me, you will marry me, whether it's now or later. I have to believe in a future. Do you love me?' It came out almost as a snarl.

His long pause was telling. 'No, Catherine, I don't.'

Luc turned and walked away, leaving Catherine stunned, her face hardening into a resolve burning with simmering wrath. 'Your family's money might give you your proud, arrogant air, Luc – but you're just as vulnerable as the rest of us,' she warned.

Laurent's face creased with concern at her words. He cast a despairing look at Luc's back before turning once again to Catherine. 'Will you let me see you home?'

'I'm not helpless, Monsieur Martin,' she said, in a scathing tone.

Laurent's cheeks coloured.

She shrugged. 'As you wish.'

Laurent kept his silence as they made their way back up the hill. He didn't even look around when his shirt got caught on an overhanging branch. He heard it rip, but didn't care about anything right now, other than walking with the woman he had loved since he was a child.

The scene with Catherine was already forgotten; the dash home had cleared Luc's head and by the time he'd made it to the top of the hill, he was feeling relieved that he'd finally spoken plainly to her.

It was young Gitel who saw him first. 'Luc!' she yelled, gleefully running towards him and launching herself into his arms.

He gave a loud grunt. 'What are they feeding you in Paris? Look how tall you've become!' he said, instantly worrying at how petite she seemed. He swung her around, enjoying her squeals of delight. Gitel was nine and Luc loved her exuberance, but she was small for her age and her eyes were sunken. Luc did his best to indulge her, and his elder sisters were always warning him that the way he spoiled Gitel would ruin her perspective on life. He'd scoffed, wondering how any youngster could grow up in Paris since 1939 and not have a skewed view of life. Luc didn't believe any of them could cosset Gitel enough and wished he could persuade his parents to leave her in Saignon. But she was bright and eager to learn at her excellent lycée in Paris. She possessed an ear for music, a sweet voice and a love for the dramatic arts. Her dream was to write a great novel, but while Luc urged her to write down her stories, their father pushed her to keep up her science, her mother insisted on teaching her to sew, and her sisters despaired of her dreamy nature.

'Have you been practising your English?' Luc demanded. 'The world will want to read you in English.'

'Of course,' she replied, in perfect English. 'Have you been keeping up your German?'

It was his father who had insisted he learn German. He urged that the language would be useful in the lavender business in years to come. Luc had not questioned his father's wisdom but had kept his German secret from the villagers.

'*Natürlich!*' he replied in a murmur. Luc kissed the top of his sister's head. 'Do you think old Wolf is any less relentless? I suspect your Miss Bonbon allows her junior students to get away with far more.'

Gitel was giggling. 'Bourbon,' she corrected.

He gave her plait a tug and winked.

Gitel's expression changed. 'Papa's not happy. We had to make a mad dash from Paris. He's barely let us pause to sleep and we weren't allowed to stay in any hotels. We slept in the car, Luc! Mama is exhausted.'

Luc caught his father's gaze and immediately saw the tension etched deeply in the set of his mouth, buried beneath a bushy, peppered beard. Jacob Bonet was instructing the housekeeper while amiably continuing a conversation with one of the neighbours. Luc knew him far too well, though, and beneath the jollity he saw the simmering worry in every brisk movement.

A new chill moved through him. Bad news was coming. He could sense it in the air in the same way that he could sense the moment to begin cutting the lavender, whose message also came to him on the wind through its perfume. His beloved saba insisted the lavender spoke to him and him alone. She invested the precious flowers with magical properties, and while her fanciful notions amused Luc, he hadn't the heart to do anything but agree with her.

He watched her now, hobbling out to help with all the possessions that the family had brought south, from his mother's favourite chair to boxes of books. Saba was muttering beneath her breath at all the disruption, but he knew she must be secretly thrilled to have everyone home. It had been just the two of them for a couple of years now.

His grandmother's hands were large for her small, light frame – even tinier now that she was eighty-seven. And those hands had become gnarled and misshapen with arthritis but they were loving, ready to caress her grandson's cheek or waggle an affectionate but warning finger when he teased her. And despite the pain in her joints, she still loved to dance. Sometimes Luc would gently scoop her up like a bird and twirl her around their parlour to music; they both knew she loved it.

'The waltz was the only way a young couple could touch one another, and even through gloves I could feel the heat of your grandfather's touch,' she'd tell Luc, with a wicked glimmer in her eye.

Her hair, once black, was now steely silver, always tied back in a tight bun. He couldn't remember ever seeing her hair down.

He watched the little woman he adored throw her hands apart in silent dismay as Gitel dropped a box.

'Don't worry, Saba. It's only more books!' Luc came up behind the tiny woman and hugged her. 'More hungry mouths to cook for,' he said gently, bending low to kiss. 'Shall I trap some rabbits?'

She reached up to pat his cheek, her eyes filling with happiness. 'We have some chickens to pluck. More than enough. But I might want some fresh lavender,' she whispered and he grinned back. He loved it when Saba flavoured her dishes with his lavender.

'You'll have it,' he promised and planted another kiss on the top of her head.

His elder sisters gave him tight, meaningful hugs. He was shocked at how thin they felt through their summery frocks, and it hurt to watch his mother begin to weep when she saw him. She was all but disappearing – so shrunken and frail.

'My boy, my boy,' she said, as if in lament.

It was all terribly grim for a reunion. 'Why are you crying?' He smiled at his mother. 'We're all safe and together.'

She waved a hand as if too overcome to speak.

'Go inside, my love,' Jacob said in that tender voice he reserved for his wife. 'We can manage this. Girls, help your mother inside. I need to speak with your brother.'

'Let me —' Luc began, but his father stilled him with a hand on his arm.

'Come. Walk with me.' Luc had never heard his normally jovial father as solemn.

'Where are you going?' Sarah complained softly. 'We've only just arrived.'

Luc smiled at his eldest sister, trying his best to ignore the way her shoulders seemed to curve inwards, adding to her hollow look. 'I'll be back in a heartbeat,' Luc whispered to her. 'I want to know everything about Paris.'

'Be careful what you wish for,' Sarah warned, and the sorrow in her tone pinched Luc's heart.

2

Luc fell in step with his father, who now appeared brittle enough to snap. 'It's so good to have you all back, but if we'd known, we could have made arrangements.' He laid a hand across the older man's shoulders and not even his father's clothes could conceal the blades, hard and angular, that jutted beneath.

'No time,' Jacob admitted brusquely. 'Where's Wolf? I sent him a message ahead.'

'We were planning a meal together tonight anyway. Saba is cooking his favourite.'

'Good. I need to talk with him.' His father sighed and looked up. 'I used to run up this hill.'

Luc had registered his father's far slower tread. 'Are you well, Papa?'

His father looked down and Luc was astonished to see his lip quiver. 'I don't know what I am, son. But I am glad to see you.' He linked arms with Luc. 'Now, help me up this wretched hill. I would see my favourite valley from our lookout.'

They said no more, walking slowly in comfortable silence as Luc guided his father through the tiny alleyways of the village, chased by the smells of cooking and echoes of people's chatter through open shutters, ascending all the time to the great overhanging cliff. The sun had set by the time they reached the summit, but the evening was still bright enough in the Provence summer. Night wouldn't claim the village for hours yet. Luc helped his father to sit, making him comfortable on a small outcrop of rock, trying to mask his confusion.

Jacob Bonet stayed wordless for a long time. He was not quite seventy and had been a businessman for most of his life, even though he'd begun as a lavender farmer. Jacob didn't have the same affinity for the land that Luc had. Lavender had been the source of his family's wealth but Jacob had used his inheritance and savings with skill and daring. By the time Jacob had been Luc's age, he no longer had much to do with his family farms, and had managers supervising them. He could have sold them, but Jacob had been sentimental and kept them going. How glad Luc was that he had. Lavender had become highly profitable as the perfume industry had grown. But Jacob's work was all about accounting and investment, not hard toil in a field. At seventy he shouldn't be this frail, Luc thought with despair.

It was only now, looking at one of the people he most loved, that Luc was able to see how traumatised his father appeared. Jacob's skin had a ghostly pallor and was stretched too thin over what had become an almost skeletal frame.

Luc felt guilty that his own body was so strong, muscular – even tanned. 'Living in Paris has not been kind to our family,' he remarked.

'I have to educate your sisters, Luc. There's nothing for your sisters here in Saignon. Can you imagine Sarah or Rachel not being able to use their bright minds? And Gitel? She needs what Paris offers.' His father looked down. 'We all do. It's where my business is done.' Then he lowered his head. '*Was* done.' Jacob closed his eyes and inhaled. 'What do you smell?'

It was a question he'd asked many times during Luc's childhood but Luc hadn't tired of it. He dwelt in the memory of far happier times overlooking this picturesque valley, with its patchwork of fields and orchards, olive groves and the tall stands of cypress deep blue in the dusk.

He cleared his throat to rid it of the sour taste that had gathered. 'Lavender, of course,' he answered. 'And the thyme is strong this evening. As well as rosemary, mint and just a hint of sage. Oh, and Madame Blanc's stew is already simmering in her pot.'

'Mmm.' His father nodded. 'Heavy on the marjoram this evening.'

Luc smiled. 'You didn't bring me up here to discuss herbs.'

'No. I just wanted to cling for a moment to the illusion that nothing has changed, that life is still simple and secure.'

'Papa, tell me what has brought you here in such haste?'

The bell of Saint Mary's tolled gravely in the distance. It was a twelfth-century Romanesque church that had been greeting pilgrims journeying to Italy and Spain since the Middle Ages, which accounted for its size and grandeur in their tiny village.

Jacob took a pipe from his pocket and tapped out the spent ash on a nearby rock. It was only now that Luc noticed a piece of yellow fabric, sewn onto his father's jacket sleeve and shaped as a star. He was astonished to realise that it had the word *Juif* inked onto it.

'What the hell is that?' Luc asked.

'We've been wearing this now for a month or so, son.' His father shrugged. 'The decree came into effect in early June. Wherever we Jews are, we have to wear it.'

Luc stood, anger flaring. 'They've already removed our people from every civil service position, from industry, from trade —'

His father finished for him. 'Law, medicine, banking, hotels, property, even education. Benjamin Meyer has never recovered from losing his teaching position at the university. But it's been steadily getting worse. All the confiscations of goods, all the humiliations add up. I've managed to protect our girls from the worst of it, but even I can't keep them safe now.'

'You have come home for good, then? We shall keep the family safe here.'

His father smiled sadly. 'I'm not so sure about that, my son, not with the new *Schutzhaft* in place.'

Luc stared at him. It felt like an icy fist had suddenly clenched around his gut. '*Schutzhaft?*' He knew what the word meant – detention and protection – but it didn't make sense.

'It's the Gestapo's generous way of keeping us Jews safe. Protective custody, it's called, but it's simply a front behind which they can hide as they drag us all off for imprisonment.'

'Detention?'

'It's not just the Nazis. Our own French administrators are to blame too.'

'The General Commissariat for Jewish Affairs was always —'

His father spat on the ground between where they sat, shocking Luc into silence.

'They're a corrupt and avaricious mob!' Jacob snapped. 'Vichy has embraced anti-Jewish ordinances with glee and is so anxious to prevent everything it confiscates from us from falling into German hands that most of our friends from the Occupied area are now destitute or being carted off to detention camps.' His father gave a sad laugh. 'And we've made it so easy for them. Like obedient sheep we've done everything asked of us, from going to the sub-prefectures and registering our names, the names of our parents, our children, our addresses. They have a complete record of every Jew in Paris. All of France, probably, for all I know.'

'It's just a list,' Luc began.

But Jacob grabbed his shirtsleeve. 'It's not just a list, son. It's information. And information is power! I have run my own business since I was nineteen, and information is the key. It's why I've given you the lavender-growing business. I want you to learn early, understand what it is to be in charge, to learn the very thing I'm telling you now. Money makes you feel invincible, but it is a brittle shield, as you can see; my money is no true protection when you really need it. The real power is information; the authorities have all the might they need because we have meekly given them the means to find us, how many children we have, their names, even their photographs. They have confiscated our properties, our paintings, our silver, the chairs we sit on and tables we eat at. And no one fights them!'

Luc waited. His breath felt as ragged as his father's voice sounded as Jacob continued. 'It is information that kept us alive. I knew it was vital to get out of Paris, that something truly bad was coming, because I listened and paid the right people to inform me. I warned others; they didn't all believe me and will pay a terrible price. And still they can hunt us. Hunt us like the vermin they believe we are.' The old man's voice broke and he put his face in his hands.

Luc swallowed. It was all so much worse than he'd feared.

'Can you believe it?' his father asked. 'Detention camps for honest, god-fearing citizens patriotic to France, who have fought for her and whose sons have died for her. They're now being interred in shitholes like Drancy!'

Luc had never heard his father talk like this. But there was no more anger in Jacob's voice. Luc realised his father was only now allowing his sorrows to surface.

'It began in the eleventh arondissement; they rounded up thousands of Jews and took them to Drancy . . . that was its official opening, you could say, last year. But there's worse coming. Mark my words.'

'Why didn't you tell me?' Luc asked, shocked.

His father shrugged painfully thin shoulders. 'What could you do? I needed you here, carrying the burden of our farms. A lot of people count on us for their income.'

The words, though true, felt hollow to Luc. 'The girls, they . . .?'

'Sarah just wants to attend university and study the history of art. She wants to lecture.' He gave a small, strangled sound. 'They won't let a Jew near a class any more! Rachel knows what's happening but won't discuss it in front of your mother and refuses to play her music. Gitel . . .' He gave the saddest of smiles. 'We need her to remain ignorant for as long as possible. It is only going to get worse.'

'Stop saying that, Papa. We can keep the family safe here, I promise you.'

Jacob gave a tutting sound of despair. 'Stop dreaming, Luc!'

Luc felt the sting of the rebuke. He didn't know how to respond, but there was no doubting Jacob Bonet's information. His family's religious background made everyday life of Occupied Paris now impossibly hard to stay safe.

His father drew on the pipe and closed his eyes momentarily, enjoying its comfort.

'So the apartment in Saint-Germain is . . .?'

'Acquired,' his father replied somberly, not opening his eyes. 'The Germans love the Left Bank. We've been staying with friends for the last few months.'

'What?'

'I didn't want to worry you until we knew more.'

His father was normally the most optimistic of men but he sounded so beaten that genuine dread crept into Luc's heart.

'What day is it today?' Jacob asked.

'Saturday.'

'A fortnight gone already.'

Luc frowned. 'What happened two weeks ago?'

'Well, you're aware that the Commission for Jewish Affairs has sanctioned all the German initiatives with barely a blink of conscience?'

Luc nodded, but didn't say that he had failed to grasp that it was as determined as Hitler in discriminating against Jewish people. As critical as Luc was of the Germans, his loathing had increasingly been directed more at the French *milice* in the region. They were far more visible, far more demanding of the people of the provinces than any soldiers. The German soldiers he'd seen were mostly lads with pink faces and clean chins and a ready grin. They were as unlikely as he to look forward to killing.

His father continued. 'Shops must carry signs stating that they are Jewish-owned; the Reich has been imposing hefty taxes on Jews. We've been forbidden from buying our groceries in certain places. Parks are now off limits. It's no longer safe for Gitel's friends to be seen playing with her. But until now we've been relatively safe so long as we obey rules and keep to ourselves.'

'And now?'

'Now property belonging to Jews is being confiscated as a matter of course. Families are being evicted. It's unthinkable, although I shouldn't be so surprised, given the rumours we're hearing from Poland.'

Luc frowned. 'Evicted and then what?'

'They're being rounded up, Luc.'

'Rounded up?'

'A lot of our men who fought in the Foreign Legion at the beginning of the war have already been deported to build the railway in the Sahara. I suppose we should have paid more attention to last year's announcement that Jews were no longer able to emigrate.'

'But, Father, to where? Why would you want to leave?'

Jacob Bonet turned to his son and smiled gently. 'I let you all down. I should have got the girls away when I had the chance in 1939. But you were all still so young and your mother would have died of a broken heart if I'd sent her away. But I should have packed

21

them off on a ship to America. Instead now all they have ahead of them are places like Drancy.'

'Drancy isn't interested in our family,' Luc growled.

'Do you really think the Gestapo has finished with the Jews? Drancy is surrounded by barbed wire. There are now five of its sub-camps around Paris. Last year they slaughtered forty inmates there in retaliation for an uprising. They despise us, want us gone. And by gone I don't mean from Paris or even Provence. I mean oblite-rated.' Luc's heart skipped a beat as his father's voice faltered. 'They will hunt us down, north or south. There is nowhere for us to flee. I have tried, my boy, believe me. I, Jacob Bonet, cannot even bribe safe passage for my daughters out of Europe. The doors of France are closed and our so-called head of government has happily thrown away the key. Laval's determination to follow the totalitar-ian Nazi regime will see every last Jew rounded up and thrown into camps. But there is talk that these camps like Drancy and Austerlitz are simply holding prisons.'

The hair at the back of Luc's neck stood on end. He didn't want to ask but still the question tumbled from his lips. 'For what?'

'For the master plan,' his father murmured, clutching his pipe tightly. 'I have heard that there is to be a concerted series of arrests as early as next week in Paris. No one is safe; no Jew will be spared. At first they only arrested gypsies, then foreigners – but that was a smokescreen. France has begun deporting its Jews east to work camps, but the rumours are that those not of use to the German war machine will simply be killed.' He looked up and fixed Luc with a fierce gaze. 'Except you.'

'Me?' Luc's voice cracked in surprise. 'Yes, as a farmer I'm considered part of essential services, but —'

Jacob gave a dismissive noise. 'I didn't mean . . .' but his voice trailed off and he sighed heavily.

Luc's frustration rose. 'Papa, this is all hearsay. The

rumour-mongers at work, surely? I mean, what would be the point to this obliteration you speak of?'

Jacob looked at Luc as though he were simple. 'To rid Europe of its Jewish population, of course. I know that some have already been transported from Drancy to a place called Auschwitz-Birkenau in Poland.'

'A new work camp?'

'It may well be a work camp but it is also a place of death.' Jacob held up a hand to prevent Luc jumping in. 'Just a fortnight ago I saw an article smuggled into Paris that ran in *The Telegraph* about mass murders of Jews at Auschwitz. It's a respected British newspaper and the news had been sent by the Polish Underground to its exiled government in London. The Nazis are now killing Jews systematically and in the tens of thousands. They'll begin with the old, the infirm, the very young, the sick, the needy – making sure the fit and the young work until they can't work any more, and then they'll be exterminated too.'

Luc stood, bile rising in his throat. 'Stop, Papa!'

'Pay attention! This is not hearsay. This is fact. Genocide is underway.'

They faced each other; Jacob angered in his despair and Luc simmering with rage at the fate befalling his people.

'Jacob?' enquired a new voice.

'Ah, Wolf,' Jacob said, turning with a smile to greet his old friend as he crested the hill.

Despite having one leg shorter, Wolf was tall and heavily built with a knitted waistcoat straining across his round belly. He was the opposite in looks to Jacob Bonet, with thinning, wispy hair that had once been a reddish-gold escaping from beneath the straw hat he habitually wore. Like Jacob, Wolf wore a loosened tie and an ironed shirt, now slightly dampened and unbuttoned at the collar. He was breathing heavily at the effort of climbing the hill but he gave them both a broad grin. 'Heavens, Jacob. Is that really you?' he wheezed as he limped towards them.

'It is,' his father replied, standing with difficulty. 'Here, let me bid you a proper welcome.'

The two men embraced and stood back to look at each other, Wolf much taller, his eyes glistening with emotion.

'The years are taking their toll, my friend,' Wolf admitted, clearly shocked. 'Beware the evening breeze coming down from the Massif. It will blow you over.'

'You worry about yourself, old man!' Jacob said gruffly, with obvious affection.

Wolf kissed Jacob's cheeks. 'It gladdens my heart to see you.'

'I wondered if we'd make it here in one piece.'

'All the women are well?'

Jacob nodded. 'For now, Wolf, for now.'

Luc helped them both to sit side by side.

Wolf glanced over at him. 'How are you, my boy? *Alles ist gut?*'

'I don't want to speak German!' Luc retorted. 'I don't ever want to speak it again.'

'Listen to me,' Jacob growled. 'Speaking German might save your life!' He turned to Wolf. 'Has he been practising?'

'Practising? Luc can curse like a local.'

His father frowned. 'How come?'

'He slips down to Apt all the time.'

'I didn't see any soldiers there.'

'They come and go,' Wolf said. 'They prefer L'Isle sur la Sorgue for obvious reasons.'

Luc hadn't seen L'Isle sur la Sorgue since just before war broke out across Europe but he knew from his own family trips that the town was beautiful. It took its name from the pretty River Sorgue, whose tumbling, chilled waters fed a spring that traditionally attracted the wealthy on holiday. Now the town was full of loud, hard-drinking Germans on leave.

Heaven alone knew how Jacob had got the family down south without running into bother with soldiers or how he found enough petrol, but Luc didn't dare ask. Even tucked this far away from Paris, he knew how hard it was to cross from the German Occupied Zone into Vichy France. Money still carried some weight, no doubt.

'Have you spoken with German soldiers directly?' asked Wolf.

Luc shrugged. 'I listen a lot. When I speak I mix French in to make it clumsy. I sound like anyone else from around here.'

'Good,' his father replied. 'You've never introduced yourself? None of them know your name?'

Luc felt bewildered by the intense questioning. 'No. I have no desire to be friendly with the Germans. Why are you asking?'

'I'm trying to save your life,' Jacob replied.

Luc's gaze fell. As true darkness closed in, the tiny village below began to illuminate itself. Beyond that the larger town of Apt sprawled like a star-dusted piece of velvet. He loved it here; the longest he'd ever left was to do his obligatory military service six years earlier. Unlike many of the other young men, the time away from home hadn't given him a wanderlust; if anything, it had intensified his passion for the lavender fields of his home.

'Don't worry about me, Papa. Let's just concern ourselves with Maman, Saba and the girls.'

His father's next words were so chilling that Luc could barely take them in.

'It is, I fear, too late for them . . . for us,' Jacob replied in a soft voice. 'But not for you, Luc.'

He regarded the two older men. His father had fought bravely for the French Legion during the Great War, and Wolf, with his crippled body, had fought on the other side, only to relinquish his

German citizenship after the defeat and flee to France. They were both survivors. How could they adopt such a beaten attitude?

'Too late?' he finally repeated. 'We can hide, we can —'

'We can try, but it will always be different for you. The time is now,' Jacob said, unnerving Luc. 'I . . . I have something to confess.'

Luc blinked. Of all the things his father could have said, this was the most unlikely. 'Confess?'

Jacob realised his pipe had gone out, muttered a low curse and began the slow process of relighting the tobacco. There was silence, save the puffing sound of Jacob sucking on the pipe expertly, drawing air through the bowl until the leaf caught and began to smoulder again. Soon the mellow, comforting aroma of his tobacco filled the air around them, combining with the cooking smells of the village, and Luc felt a momentary sense of peace.

Luc reached into his pocket and took out a stub of candle that he habitually carried; Jacob tossed him the matches and soon they were weakly illuminated, the tiny flame giving his elders an ethereal glow. He hadn't imagined it – they both looked hesitant . . . no, fearful.

'What is it?' he asked.

They appeared to sigh as one.

'What?' Luc repeated. It was a demand now as he felt a strange fear penetrate his chest.

'Luc,' his father finally said, 'my beloved and only son.' He felt his throat tighten. The air felt thick with tension and an owl hooted mournfully from somewhere nearby. 'We have lied to you.'

3

The two old men talked haltingly, and as one paused or hesitated, the other would take up the story. They punctuated their tale with affectionate reassurances, sharing long-secret memories of 1918, a year, Jacob said, in which two wonderful events had occurred – the Great War ended and Luc had come into their lives.

They talked until Luc vaguely registered the bell tower chiming the hour again, but his thoughts were swirling, his life suddenly a mess. Beneath the familiar sound of their voices, Luc tried to gather his wits but realised he was sitting in a vacuum of thought, hearing words but unable to truly absorb them.

'Luc?' Jacob asked.

The bell finished its sombre toll at eight. Saba would be tutting over her stove by now.

'Luc?' his father tried again. He sounded anxious.

A storm was gathering in his mind; he could feel it beginning to pound at his temple. He ground his jaw, dreading asking the question. Nevertheless he was compelled. 'What is my real name?'

Jacob hesitated.

Wolf answered for him. 'It is Lukas.'

Luc grimaced, closed his eyes. How could three letters of the alphabet turn his world on its head? And how could those same three letters change a simple name he liked into one that had instant connotations of evil?

He drew a deep breath to steady himself. 'And my real family name?'

Wolf cleared his throat. 'Ravensburg.'

Luc stood abruptly and walked away, no longer thinking, only reacting. If someone had just plunged a knife into him, it couldn't have hurt more.

He was German.

Did it all make sense now? His fairer looks, his bigger build? So was this the reason his father had insisted on him learning the language until it was so ingrained he sometimes dreamt in German?

'Who knows this?'

Jacob gave a small cough. 'Your mother, grandmother, Wolf, obviously. Your sisters know nothing, other than that you are adopted. I cannot disguise that from anyone.'

Wolf rushed to continue. 'Your birth parents were good people. Your father was a man called Dieter; he was younger than you when he was killed at the Front in 1918. Your mother, Klara, was younger still but she loved him. I knew her briefly – she was beautiful and fragile, and terribly weak during your birth. She lasted barely days, but long enough to fall in love with you.'

'The heavens are certainly having fun at my expense,' Luc said darkly.

'Don't talk like that, son,' Jacob said.

'Son? I'm no son of yours,' he said, shaking the large yellowed German birth certificate Wolf had produced. 'I've been a pretender all of my life!'

Luc had his back to them both, staring out across the valley, beyond Apt, looking west to Avignon to where he knew the Germans gathered in numbers. He thought of their strong bodies, their sense of invincibility, golden hair and shining teeth, their smart uniforms and polished boots. He thought about how one of the Apt girls on a trip with her parents into Avignon had spoken of the men in black: paramilitary soldiers of the Schutzstaffel, strapping German SS in smart uniforms with distinctive insignia on their lapels, armbands, shoulders.

The shock was now giving way to anger and he had a momentary vision of himself killing faceless but laughing men in uniform; he couldn't tell if they were soldiers or local *milice* – they were all the enemy; all responsible for this pain.

It seemed Wolf understood; he was as much a father to Luc as Jacob was, and had always been able to read Luc's heart. As if listening in on Luc's bleak thoughts now, the old man reached out to touch Luc on the arm.

'There are ways to strike back.' He gestured at the document in Luc's fist. 'You look German, you talk and swear like one, you *are* German,' he emphasised, touching the birth certificate. 'Use that to help yourself . . . to help France.'

Luc turned to look at him, confused. 'What are you talking about?'

It was Jacob's turn. 'Listen to me, Luc. Look at me!'

Luc's gaze slid unhappily to his father's face.

'I can try to understand how this feels. If we could have spared you, we would have. What does it matter where you came from? You are French in your heart, you are Jewish in spirit and —'

Luc cut across his father's words like a blade. 'And I possess the killing soul of my kin!'

A slap echoed around, bouncing off the tiny natural amphitheatre that the rock face provided. The sting of it arrived seconds after, and it was only then that Luc realised that Wolf had struck him. There was passion in the blow.

'Don't you dare! Do you think your true father had a bad soul? I read his letters – he was just a young, lovestruck youth, doing his military service, obeying his orders and dying for his country. He didn't want to kill. Few soldiers do. Dieter wanted to be with his wife, his son. And the woman who brought you into this world? God forgive you for tarnishing Klara's memory. She was a young, frightened mother alone, and she begged me to make sure I taught you to think of her kindly. She wanted you to know that she loved you more than her own life. She was eighteen, Luc! She knew she was dying but I never once heard her grieve for herself. Her thoughts and prayers were only for you and for the soul of Dieter.'

Luc swallowed and looked down. He couldn't bear to see the disappointment in Wolf's eyes. He didn't want to think of these young strangers as his parents, loving him, their dying thoughts of him.

Wolf's anger wasn't spent. 'Do you think I have a killing soul, Luc? I am German. Or have you forgotten?'

Luc kept his eyes down, shamefaced.

'Your conceit astonishes me. This filthy, ugly war is not about you!' Wolf continued. 'People are dying all over Europe. Your story is but one among millions. But you are that one among millions who may survive this war because of your parentage, because of the Bonets who have raised you and loved you and given you their name. Don't you dare spit in their faces now! They didn't tell you this for fun, but for your own protection.'

Wolf turned away, wiping his mouth of the spittle that had flown from it with a trembling, liver-spotted hand, and Luc saw him, perhaps for the first time, for the seventy-six-year-old man he was.

Luc glanced over at his father. 'I'm sorry.'

'For what?' Jacob asked, sounding surprised.

'For not being your real son.'

Jacob looked up, his eyes misting, and Luc's heart felt close to breaking as he watched his father struggle laboriously to his feet, waving a helping hand away from Wolf. He limped to Luc, gazing up to look him in the eye.

'You are my real son – real to me, to your mother, a grandson to your saba, a brother to your sisters.' He held out his arms and Luc, without thinking, wrapped his father into a hug and wept.

———————

Luc let Wolf and Jacob go ahead of him as he took a detour. He'd promised his grandmother some lavender, and he ran to the nearest of their fields to snatch some purple-headed stalks. The night was balmy and Luc was treated to wafts of perfume. The fields were telling him that it was just days now before he would need to prepare for harvest.

There would be far fewer workers to help this year, and Luc had heard that the Germans might be calling up able men from France to assist the German war machine. He grimaced at the thought, while his cheek was still warm with the sting of Wolf's slap.

He went back over what the old men had finally revealed, after nearly a quarter of a century of secrecy. During the Great War, Wolf and his wife, Solange, had lived in Strasbourg, close to the German border in Alsace. Wolf had been too old to fight at the Front, and his limp prevented active service anyway. He was a linguistics professor at Strasbourg's university, where he taught amongst other languages, Old Norse. As easily as changing clothes, Wolf had swapped from speaking German to French in his everyday dealings.

Despite his position, Wolf wanted to distance himself from Germany. He decided to leave Strasbourg once the war had ended. Just before departing, he and Solange had come across the heavily pregnant Klara Ravensburg, alone and in labour, trying to make it into France from her village in the Black Forest; she too was running away from Germany, a country that she blamed for killing her beloved Dieter. The day after the war ended Klara had received the full devastating news of Dieter's accidental death. He had died in friendly fire just hours after the ceasefire. 'Her mourning was just beginning while people were still drunk in the streets from celebrating,' Wolf said in his gentle voice.

With Klara's mother long dead and her father and brothers all killed at the Front, her heartbreak pushed her over the brink. In a stupor, without any belongings, she had walked out of her village and just kept going.

It was just chance and good luck that she'd collapsed in front of Wolf's wife. 'Solange took her into our home, bathed her, dried her, even handfed her – for she could do little for herself – combed her hair and sang her off to sleep,' Wolf had explained to Luc.

A baby boy was delivered amidst the chaotic and celebratory atmosphere of the Armistice. Luc was born on a chilly, drizzly, late November day in 1918 as Europe began to fully grasp that the Great War was over. Klara died soon after from complications.

Wolf and Solange left Strasbourg three days before Christmas, planning to head far south into the warmer climes of France with the baby. As Luc recalled the story, he was struck by the madness of their plan. A middle-aged couple, winter, a newborn? What was in their heads? But the Armistice made people reckless, full of hope for a brighter future.

'I was moving on instinct,' Wolf had admitted. 'You were not our child but no one cared during that time. No one wanted someone else's newborn, few questions were asked . . . Everyone just assumed you were our grandchild. I had to get Solange and you away; I wanted you raised as a Frenchman without any attachment to Germany.' Wolf shrugged. 'And it all worked out – at least for nearly twenty-five years. Now, it's your German heritage that may save you.'

Tragedy had struck soon after the fledgling family left Strasbourg. A week after they fled Solange was dead also, knocked over by a bus when Luc was but weeks old.

Until this evening Luc had always believed that Wolf had found him in a barn in eastern France. Clearly his mother had abandoned him, and that had always made it easier to accept his adoption. And yet, in his quiet moments, Luc had wondered at the details. He'd stopped asking questions in his teens, though, as it became obvious the only story he would get was the one he had already been told.

Now Luc had learned that the old man had walked away from his prestigious university and brought with him a baby. Wolf had put as much distance as he could between himself and his past, filled with grief for his wife and Luc's mother.

Fate had brought Wolf together with a grieving Jacob and Golda Bonet, wealthy French, travelling with their dead infant daughter back to Provence in the depths of the January winter of 1919. Pity and kindness had been shown for the grandfather and grandson, and it was in that train carriage that Wolf had broken his silence and admitted the truth to the Jewish couple. A pact was made, a new baby came into the Bonet family, and Luc's heritage was hidden as a new background was fabricated.

Wolf had decided that Luc had a better chance of a normal life within a younger family, but he couldn't bear to be parted from the baby. And so he'd stayed on in Provence, working at the university in Avignon and retiring to a hamlet not far from Saignon. Luc had never known a time without his beloved Wolf.

But how could Luc hold a grudge against his family, the people who had shown him such love, and especially in his greatest hour of need? Luc looked at the lavender in his hand; his saba would be waiting. And this was a family reunion. He was the only son; he needed to defend them. 'Warian,' – protect, in Old Frankish – he murmured to himself, and then raised his eyes to the heavens. Wolf had taught him well – now he even thought in different languages.

Germany had killed his real parents. It would not have the parents he loved also. *Over my dead body*, he thought to himself.

4

Luc's footsteps resounded on the cobbles of Saignon and he waved to the priest emerging from the church as he strode down the streetlit lane. He had a perfect view of the Bonet home ahead, an imposing triple-storeyed building that sat directly behind the central fountain.

The house was cloaked by evening now, but of an afternoon its pale ochre colour glowed warmly beneath the summer sun and the grayish blue of its shutters and window boxes made a typically bold Provençal contrast. Perhaps he took its simple, exquisite prettiness for granted. And it was only on the rare times he'd been taken to Paris that he'd seen how very lacking in colour a big city was; how lacking it was in the purples and pinks, greens and yellows, oranges and blues of Provence.

To Luc, the Luberon was like a laughing country girl with generous hips, loose hair and the scent of a garden, wearing a colourful dress and a blush at her cheeks. Meanwhile, Paris – oh, Paris was a chic woman with a slightly bemused expression, slim-hipped with perfectly cut clothes in conservative dark grey. But she was coquettish – her grand boulevards lined with plane trees, her fabulous gardens and daring monuments, her romantic street lamps. Oh, yes, Paris was more than capable of being playful, yet her demeanour never anything less than graceful. He loved both these women and it hurt his heart to hear that Paris was now draped in huge swastika flags; that those same romantic streetlights were extinguished, and that Adolf Hitler was dressing her in a fearful red and black ... the colours of carnage.

Luc was so preoccupied that he nearly walked into the baker. '*Pardon*, Monsieur Fougasse. Forgive me. I was dreaming.'

The grizzled-looking man shrugged beneath a flour sack on his shoulder. 'We all need dreams, Bonet.' His voice was surprisingly gentle. Fougasse was a solitary figure. His wife had died early in their marriage and they had been childless. Several of the village women had tried to catch Fougasse's eye but he kept to himself. He certainly worked hard, baking for many of the villages that didn't have their own boulangerie.

'You're working late, *monsieur*,' Luc remarked.

'There are always people to bake for.' Fougasse gave a typical Gallic shrug. 'Someone has to make sure the children get their morning *tartines*.'

'I might reserve a few of whatever treats you bake tomorrow ... My sisters are home; they need fattening up.'

'I noticed. They will need more than cake to cope with what they may have seen; there are bad reports coming through from Paris.'

'Reports?'

Fougasse gave him an unflinching look.

How could Fougasse, a baker in the isolated alpine region of southern France, know anything about what was happening in the capital?

The baker turned back into his shop. '*Bonne nuit*, Bonet. My best regards to your family. I will cook some treats just for your sisters. Take care of yourself.'

Luc was bemused. '*Bonne nuit*, Monsieur Fougasse.' He nodded with a smile but the baker had already disappeared.

Luc continued down the lane, his mind a tangle of warring thoughts and sorrow. Today had been the most unpleasant of his life, but his father was clearly counting on him to carry on. He could see Jacob and Wolf ahead.

Shutters were open on the houses flanking the lane, the residents hoping to catch any vague breeze, but they would have to be closed soon. Hot or not, curfews meant no light must escape the village after ten. Luc caught snatches of conversation, grumbles, laughter, children's voices and the sound of Madame Theroux's new baby whimpering. The *milice* had come through and confiscated wireless sets several months earlier, so the familiar sound of the radio could rarely be heard these days. Luc had been working late in the field when the *milice* had swooped, but even so he'd found it hard to take the threat seriously. The *milice* were French, like them, and no one felt any fear of their own people.

But these French were in league with the country's Nazi overlords. Waving government papers and bullying the seemingly timid villagers, the police had collected wireless sets from everyone, regardless of wealth or position. The villagers, keen to avoid trouble, dutifully handed theirs over.

However, like a couple of other wily families, Luc's grandmother had seen fit to hide their good set in the cellar, and with eyes lowered, gnarled hands trembling, she had offered up their old, crackly wireless on a wheelbarrow. Since that time, Luc and his grandmother regularly tuned into the BBC. The height of the Luberon gave them a clear signal to hear the dulcet tones that only Luc understood. And while he was not as confident in English as he was in German, Luc could translate well enough, whispering the gist of what he heard to his saba, who hung on his every word. Luc would sit on the floor, liking the earthy smell of where they kept their preserves and some of the fruit and root veg they grew. Saba would put her hand on his strong shoulder and they'd sit like that – connected – and listen to the curious *messages personnels*, both of them delighting in some of the odd French phrases and sayings that were clearly coded messages.

Together they had shared the rousing broadcast from London by the exiled French former war minister, Charles de Gaulle, urging the French to stay strong, to resist the Germans in any way. 'France is not alone,' he had declared, and then the call – *'Vive la France!'* – had resounded in Luc's ears long after the broadcast had ended.

So far, however, Saignon had been mostly left alone by the *milice* and the Germans. Life carried on much as it always had, with farmers permitted to remain on the land to help the German war effort.

Saignon was fortunate in what it produced: cherries in spring that France devoured; lavender in summer that Europe's perfumers couldn't get enough of; grapes harvested in autumn for the wine that certainly kept the Germans happy; and in winter . . . true gold in the shape of olives that would produce the precious and famed oil of the region. Most families would rather give up their wine to the Germans in war tithes rather than their olive oil.

The swallows had gone to their roost for the evening. Their frantic activity had given way to the music of a Provençal summer evening – the chirrup of cicadas. Luc sighed as he glanced up towards the glowing moon in a purplish sky. An ignorant man would imagine all was well in the world.

As Luc entered the square he was reassured to see a few men drinking quietly in the bar after a long day in the field. While life on the surface of Saignon ticked along since the advent of war, sadly nearly half of the village's men were now prisoners of war. Defeat had been so unexpected for France and came so swiftly, as the German war machine ignored the Maginot Line and swept brashly through the Low Countries in 1940, catching hundreds of thousands of French soldiers unaware.

In the chaos of the Occupation some of the men had managed to escape and return to their families. They were already back in their farming routines, rising at five to tend to animals, even earlier in summer. There was, however, talk of conscription, and their freedom might be short-lived. The Vichy government was soon to introduce *la relève*, asking the men of the Free Zone to volunteer their services to work in Germany. Although it was draped in the notion of being voluntary, there was no doubt it would fast become compulsory. For every fit Frenchman who volunteered, three French prisoners of war would be released. Laval was selling his concept hard, using guilt to coerce men to leave their homes and do the right thing for their fellow men.

Luc knew families would be torn apart as a result of Laval's scheme. And he hated the French police and the *milice* that was complicit in the blackmail. They both might as well have worn swastikas on their uniforms. No, he would do nothing to advance the German war effort – even though he knew some of the villagers were probably talking behind his back; he was young, fit, unmarried. He was the perfect choice to do two years' work in Germany if pressed, but he was beginning to realise that the Germans wanted no man with a Jewish surname entering their borders.

After his two years' military service he'd avoided conscription because he was considered a primary producer of a valued crop that made France wealthy.

Lavender was the key base ingredient for the flourishing perfume market. America would gladly take all of what Luc could produce in essential oil, but he chose to sell most of it to the perfumers at Grasse, north-west of Provence. They paid the premium for the true lavender *fin*, harvested by hand over just a few weeks when the flowers were at their optimum to yield a smooth, almost sleepy bouquet that would amplify other floral oils.

And it was not only the French who needed Luc; the Germans wanted lavender farmers producing plentifully for the plant's antiseptic properties. They couldn't get enough of it to the frontlines, where wounded men were in dire need of the oil's magic.

Luc nodded and smiled as he passed the men, a few of whom called out to give his parents their respects. Word had travelled fast that the Bonets had returned.

Marcel approached, a lanky, dark-headed man with an earnest look. 'I hear Rachel is back . . . and the whole family,' he said casually.

Luc flicked at Marcel's shoulder with the stalks of lavender. 'I'll let her know you asked after her.'

Marcel would be a good match for Rachel. She would not have to work; she would be well cared for and, war permitting, would be able to fulfil her dreams of writing or music, if not teaching.

Marcel slapped Luc's back in return as he walked on. 'I'd appreciate that, Bonet.'

Luc didn't look back but simply lifted a hand. By the time he reached the house, Jacob and Wolf had already gone inside, satisfied. He was still rattled – the secret of his birth felt too overwhelming to consider all at once – but was glad he'd had some time to calm down. Now he had to hold himself together. For his father's sake.

In the family house, the mouth-watering smell of chicken stew enveloped Luc like a comforting blanket as he entered through the back door, straight into the parlour. Saba liked her family to eat at the scrubbed pine table, often decorated with a simple vase of flowers. However, this evening the pine table was laid with their fine linen, and even finer crockery.

Golda looked small and spent. He kissed her and lingered with a reassuring hug. He winked at his two elder sisters but there was no response. They were both withdrawn. He could only imagine what they had seen in Paris. He winced at the yellow stars he noticed were dutifully sewn onto the sleeves of their jackets that hung on the wall hooks.

Sarah was serving wine but her gaze had followed his. Now

their eyes met. She shook her head as if to warn him to not mention the yellow stars.

'I thought you were never coming!' Gitel exclaimed. 'It's so good to be home.' She flung her tiny frame into his arms, squeezing him hard.

'Hungry?' he threw at her with a grin.

'Ravenous,' she admitted, and he could believe it. No nine-year-old should feel like a sack of bones, he thought.

'Coming, coming,' their grandmother replied from the stove. 'Help your sisters, Gitel. Your father's water glass needs topping up.'

Luc went to the kitchen. Ida looked smaller than ever as she hovered over her pot.

'Ah, the *lavande*. Thank you. We need its magic to improve your parents' humour. I shall burn some tonight to ward off evil.'

'Magic,' he repeated in an ironic tone. 'Prayer not enough?'

'Don't mock me, child.' She shook the stalks. 'If not for this, they'd be demanding you go and join all the other fools in Germany.'

'Those other fools don't have much choice. But if I were to go, I'd have a whole country of new, very blonde women to —'

She glared and stopped him saying any more, pulling the flowers off the stalks before inhaling their fragrance and tossing them into her simmering stew. 'I pray for all our young men, believe me. Ah, can you smell that?'

He bent over and sniffed the steam rising from her pot. 'Wonderful.' It was her rich, creamy chicken stew – everyone's favourite – flavoured with garlic and herbs from the garden, her homemade mustard, and enriched with a few dollops of cream from Monsieur Benoit's cow. He knew no other person who used lavender in their cooking.

'Always keep the lavender safe and it will keep you safe, my beloved boy,' she muttered.

He turned and went back to the parlour, smiling softly at her faith in his flowers.

'Marcel asked me to say hello to you,' he whispered to Rachel. 'You know he's in love with you.'

She pushed him away affectionately but he could see her genuine pleasure. Nonetheless, the family was struggling to embrace the happiness of the moment. Luc looked around at the long faces and, setting aside his own worries, he leapt to the old gramophone. On a rare visit into Marseille the previous winter he'd paid a small fortune for it on the black market but not regretted a franc. He didn't understand what 'Begin the Beguine' meant, but he didn't care. The music transported him.

'Dance with me, Rachel,' he said, daring her to have fun.

'What?' she said, taken aback. She was the prettiest of his sisters, normally vivacious with a laugh that could set an entire room of people off. Rachel only ever saw the good in people. It made her current mood seem all the more devastating for Luc. But he would tolerate no sadness tonight – not here, not in this house, not even in himself. He would lead the way out of the gloom.

Luc dropped the needle onto the vinyl and the velvety sound of the clarinet announced the start. He clicked his fingers and bobbed his head in time with the mellow brass section. Then he turned with a cheeky look to Rachel.

'Luc,' Rachel warned, but he was already weaving a dance step back towards her. Gitel clapped and giggled while Ida began swaying and humming by her stove. Jacob watched intently.

Luc opened his arms, beamed at Rachel and allowed the music to carry him away on its happy notes. Right now all that mattered was Artie Shaw's swing sound and seeing Rachel laugh, watching Sarah's big dark eyes glitter again. Even Golda seemed to have lifted herself out of her curious stupor, as though the music had finally awoken her. A tremulous smile crept onto his mother's face as Rachel laughed.

'Luc!' Rachel called again, but she was lifted easily and swung around, her long dark hair flying out.

'Hush!' he said. 'Pretend I'm Marcel and dance.' He felt her relax into his arms as she let him lead her around the parlour.

Luc caught Sarah's eye and she gave way to a helpless giggle. He gave Rachel a wide flourishing twirl that had her shrieking as he bent her backwards, safe in his strong arms.

Gitel was hopping around. 'My turn! Please! Oh, now look. Papa and Maman are dancing!'

Luc's heart nearly burst with pleasure to see his father, eyes twinkling, leading his wife around the table and then slowly, gently waltzing with her, cheek to cheek like young lovers. They were in their own little world. Ida watched them from the doorway with a teary smile.

Gitel was flitting around her parents, trying to form a threesome.

'Hold on,' Luc said. 'I'll put the song on again.' He didn't want the magic to end.

'Well, Ida,' Wolf called to the eldest in the room. 'If you don't mind a limping partner, how about shaking a leg with me?'

Ida pulled off her apron to the claps and cheers of her grand-children. Then all eight of them were dancing. The music had broken the dark spell. If just for this evening, the family would laugh and love again.

They swapped partners and Luc bent low to dance with his mother.

'When did you grow so big, son?' she asked tearily.

He didn't want to mention that it was she who'd shrunk. 'Since the war, Maman. God has given me long arms to wrap around you . . . to keep you safe,' he said. She felt frail enough to break.

'We have to protect Gitel,' Golda whispered.

'You have nothing to fear.'

A tear escaped, rolled down her cheek. 'Papa said he and Wolf have told you —'

Luc shook his head. 'Don't, Maman. Nothing changes. I have no other family but this one.' He danced out the song with her silently, letting the music wash over him.

When the needle began to scratch in silence, Jacob spoke. 'Let us break bread and give thanks that our family is together again.'

With Ida hovering, Luc lifted her pot onto the table and felt relieved that the mood was lightened. Jacob ladled food onto plates, and talk of Paris quickly turned to the harvest that would begin soon.

'Thursday, I think,' Luc suggested. 'I believe it will be one of our best,' he added.

'To Thursday,' his father said, lifting his glass and beaming. 'To you son, our lavender keeper.'

'*Jeudi!*' everyone echoed. Another season, another harvest . . . they were celebrating hope more than anything.

Only Golda didn't smile. Her gaze kept darting around her family as if she couldn't believe they were all there.

Gitel took her mother's hand. 'You can stop fretting now, Maman. We're back in Provence and, besides, my friend Miriam said the Germans are only interested in taking away the foreign-born Jews. So we're safe,' she assured her.

Her sentence, full of the naïve invincibility of a nine-year-old, burst whatever balloon of hope had begun to lift their spirits.

'I've changed my mind,' Luc suddenly announced. He was determined to get his family away from all threats, and nowhere was safer than their lavender fields. 'We start harvesting on Monday. Everyone has to be involved. Maman, Saba, I hope you're ready to cook up a storm. We won't have any extra labour this year. It's down to us. I'll spread the word. We're going to be busy firing up the Cygnet!'

5

Excitement on the first harvest day always spilled throughout the village. The lavender fields needed little tending – the lavender grew wild without watering, and the real work was at harvest time. The pressure to harvest or not was enormous. The local beekeepers always begged for the start date to be delayed, while the perfumers, wartime or not, were desperate for the oil.

Luc's childhood friend, Laurent Martin, came from a long line of beekeepers, and his family was essential to Luc's. Without the bees, the lavender fields would not be pollinated, and without the lavender, the Martin family would not be able to make their living.

Laurent had a theory that happy bees could improve Luc's yield by ten per cent, which Luc rolled his eyes at, and yet he always found himself delaying the harvest by a few more days to keep Laurent happy. But not this year.

Laurent caught up with Luc in the lavender fields before the birds had even begun their morning warm-up.

'Is it true? You're harvesting today?'

'I'd hardly be joking about something this important.'

'My bees aren't ready.'

Luc, towering above his friend, laughed. 'They never are.'

They were as different as two men could be. Luc was tall, with thick fair hair he kept neatly trimmed, and a broad white smile that came readily, while his closest friend didn't stand much taller than

Luc's shoulder. Laurent's hair was oiled, black and lustrous, and he'd grown a dark moustache because he thought it made him appear more debonair. Laurent had always looked like a boy next to Luc and now in his mid-twenties, despite his strengthening jawline, he had yet to enjoy the popularity he dreamed about with women.

It was a shame, Luc thought, for Laurent's dreamy disposition meant he could rattle off a poetic line that would melt most women's hearts. But despite his passionate nature, Laurent was shy and possessed none of Luc's dash or presence.

'You're eleven days earlier than last year,' Laurent moaned.

'I know, but today's the day,' Luc replied.

Laurent snatched at a stalk of the lavender. 'Even I can see this isn't fully in bloom.'

'These are unusual times.'

'More unusual than last year? What's changed? We're still at war. France is still occupied. People are still dying.'

'Perhaps all the more reason to get the oil extracted.'

'To save Germans from infection?'

Luc sighed, his expression troubled. 'It's my family, Laurent. When you see my sisters perhaps you'll understand. The harvest will keep them away from the authorities, and being high up here in the perfumed fields is enough to lift anyone's spirit.' His face softened. 'I'll help you move your hives to another grower's field.'

Laurent gave a low sound of dismay.

'Let it go – just this year, please.' Luc wanted to tell Laurent what he'd learned about himself. But now was not the time.

'All right, all right,' Laurent said, waving a hand at him. 'On one condition.'

'Name it,' Luc said, squinting across his field, trying to work out the best spot for the fire to heat the water for the Cygnet.

'Are you going to ask Catherine to marry you?'

Luc laughed. 'No. Is that the condition?'

Laurent scowled. 'The condition is that you promise to stop seeing her.' At Luc's bemused look he added, 'Until you're out of the picture she's not going to hear my proposal.'

'I'm out of the picture,' Luc assured, raising his hands in defence.

'I need your word now. Stop – you know . . . being with her?'

Luc felt a spike of surprise and guilt; he'd not realised that Laurent was so sweet on Catherine. 'You should have said something before.'

'Would it have stopped you?'

'Yes. I'm not heartless.'

'Catherine may not see it that way. In fact, I could name a number of girls who wouldn't see it that way.'

'I'm honest. I don't lie to any of them.'

'Maybe that's true. But, don't you think women *want* to be lied to sometimes?'

'No. Catherine's angry with me because she's not getting what she wants.'

'That's because she's only had eyes for you. But if you ignore her, perhaps she'll notice me.'

Luc rested a hand on his friend's shoulder. 'Listen . . . I'm sorry. I give you my word. I'll never lay a finger on her again, other than to give her a congratulatory kiss when she's your bride.'

Laurent brightened. 'I shall pay her a visit this evening. I – I think I might be in love . . .'

Luc smiled. 'I don't love her like you do. Let me be honest – I don't love her at all.'

'Why not?'

'It's not Catherine.' Luc ran a hand through his light hair. 'I think I'm incapable of it.'

'What . . . loving someone?'

'No, I love my family. I love you, even! But loving a woman

like you do . . .' He shook his head. 'The fact that you've waited for her. No, the fact that you've waited so long and still love her. It's so . . . so selfless,' he said. 'I think if I was in love with a woman I couldn't bear for her to even look at another man.'

'Then I hope your love is never tested in that way.'

'I'm sorry,' Luc replied and meant it.

'You can be an insensitive, arrogant bastard,' Laurent said, without any heat. 'But you're the only person I completely trust.'

'Trust is everything these days.'

'Do you trust Fougasse?' Laurent asked suddenly, the change in topic catching Luc unawares.

'The baker? Why wouldn't I?'

'I don't know. But I've found him watching me recently.'

'Watching you. How?'

'Furtively.'

'Do you owe him money? Does your family?'

'No,' Laurent said, indignantly.

'Perhaps he believes you should have volunteered.'

Laurent gave a snort. 'He should understand we need the beehives.'

'Have you said something about him behind his back?'

'I barely know the fellow.'

'Then maybe he too wants Catherine,' Luc said theatrically.

'Don't be a fool. Everyone knows Fougasse still visits his wife's grave every evening.'

Luc looked down. 'Yes, and that's the sort of love I'm talking about. I can't see myself ever loving someone like that. Look what it's done to Fougasse. His life revolves around visiting and tending that grave. Don't become like that, Laurent. Promise me.'

'You shouldn't be frightened of love, Luc. It's all we have to look forward to in life, especially now. If you have that, you have everything.'

'How do you know it's everything?'

'I know my heart . . . and it's full.'

Luc grimaced. 'Aren't these the worst of times to be in love? While I'm looking at Marcel, with his doe-eyes for Rachel, I'm hearing talk of the conscription. He'll be called up for sure. Third son. No chance.'

Laurent looked suddenly miserable. 'Then I suspect I will too. And my father's not as old as yours. They'll deem him fit. It's all right for you, Bonet. No one's going to let the French perfume market fail.'

'We can't grow lavender without your bees, Laurent. But listen, you'll run away if they come after you. We make a promise now; neither of us will fight for Hitler.'

Laurent gave a rueful sigh. 'I'll probably be shot. The *milice* are crawling all over the place just looking for an excuse to flex its muscle. Haven't you seen Gendarme Landry swaggering around with his new pistol?'

'That bastard Landry. I'm hearing his name too often.'

'Keep out of his way, Luc.'

'You're the second person to warn me. Perhaps I need to get in his way.'

Laurent grabbed his shirt. 'Don't be a fool. I've heard what's been happening in Paris. If for your family alone, keep your temper and stay out of that piece of dirt's way.'

Luc released his friend's fist. 'Don't worry about me.'

'You think you're invincible. But the Germans will shoot you as easily as spit on you.'

'Someone has to stand up to them some time,' Luc said, turning away.

'Where are you going?' Laurent called.

'To get the Cygnet. Are you helping with the cutting?'

'You know I always do. My family's coming too. We'll move the hives.'

'Thanks. I've asked Monsieur Fougasse to send up some breakfast for the workers. Everyone should arrive by dawn. Will you wait here for him?'

'Yes. It's going to be a hot one. The sooner we get going . . .'

'We should enjoy it after the last winter.'

'I hope to never live through one like that again.'

'I hope it's worse!' Luc said, and Laurent looked at him as though he was losing his mind. 'The harder the winter, the safer we are in Saignon. No one will come up here when it's snowing . . . if there are any German soldiers left after the Russian winter.'

'Enough talk of winter! Let me enjoy summer, my bees, your lavender fields, my lovely Catherine.'

The Bonet's lavender fields were wild, and although Luc didn't want to admit it, he knew cultivation was the future. But cultivated lavender meant a drop in quality, and the wild lavender of the alpine region was the only way to maintain the French perfume industry's reputation. Cultivators had already begun planting fields of hybrid lavender that grew at the lower altitudes and which had an almost double yield – but of a far more astringent oil. They would be producing the antiseptics, soaps, detergents in years to come. But Luc knew that his *Lavandula angustifolia* – the purest wild lavender that grew from only 800 metres in the Luberon – would always be the magical essence that the perfumers would covet.

Luc's early start to the harvest had taken the villagers by surprise but no one was going to knock back Bonet money. Alongside the few local workers came the Bonet family, and it was an emotional sight for Luc to see them being pulled behind the donkey Caesar in a little cart with the food. Gitel skipped alongside, a fresh glow about her. Ida and Golda were deep in conversation, but

Sarah and Rachel were not talking, their cheeks so hollow and their shoulders all but poking through their blouses. The girls of the south were so healthy and sun-kissed by comparison.

That morning Golda had tasted real coffee from their meagre remaining stores for the first time in an age, and had wept, having been reduced to drinking a form using chicory.

'Everything is rationed, but now Jews have reduced rations,' Jacob had explained to Luc. 'Gitel hasn't grown in a year. She's not getting enough milk or meat. I have to buy everything on the black market.' He shrugged in his habitual way. 'Everything is available for a price, even good coffee, but your mother insists we make do like everyone else.'

Jacob appeared stronger today. His silhouette against the rising sun looked taller, straighter, and Luc felt a rush of nostalgic pleasure to see him wearing his white straw hat with its distinctive red band. Jacob had worn it throughout Luc's childhood in the fields.

Now the apprentice was ready to show the teacher how much knowledge he had acquired. Luc welcomed the five male workers – remembering years gone by when the fields would be full of many more. And there were even a handful of women – ready to prove they were as capable as men. The Vichy government had initially asked employers in the provinces to sack female workers so they could remain home and have children, but these women were boldly flouting the directive.

Luc handed out equipment, including the small sickle used to reap the stalks. The men were also equipped with a trousse; the canvas sack tied to their backs made it easy to toss the cut flowers over their shoulders in a fluid motion.

A soft, welcome breeze caressed them, but Luc knew that today would be hot and dry and within an hour or two they'd have only the breathless sun for company. For now it was exquisite to enjoy this moment at dawn, as the sky began to lighten rapidly, fingers of luminous blue reaching overhead and slicing through first light. The wind had stirred the lavender and the field was scenting the air. Luc could almost convince himself that all was well in his world. Almost.

'I'm expecting 250 kilograms per man per day,' Luc began. 'And I'll pay double to anyone who reaches 300, with a further bonus if you can achieve that daily.' His challenge was met with murmurs of approval and slaps on the back. 'But first, eat! There's fresh brioche. And I almost forgot, the first man with a full sack gets a bottle of cognac.'

The workers cheered and the family clapped, laughing. Even Golda was wearing a faint smile as she was helped down from the cart by Sarah.

He glanced at his father. Had it really been two years since his father had walked these fields? The family had fled south from Paris in the summer of 1940, as the Germans advanced, but they'd returned fairly soon, like most of its inhabitants. What else could they have done, with children to educate, exams to sit, all of his father's businesses to be administered from the city?

'You look very pretty, all of you,' Luc said, grinning at his sisters' cloth bonnets. Their aprons were starched white and their skirts and blouses were kept long for protection from the fierce sun.

'Give me a *faucille*,' Sarah said, pointing to the smaller sickles among the many used for harvesting the lavender. 'It takes a woman to do this job properly.'

Luc grinned. 'Is that so?'

'It's the way it was. I bet I can collect more in my apron than you can in a sack.'

'I'd take that bet – but I have to get the fire going.'

'You're just scared,' Rachel said, joining in, and Luc felt his spirits lift even higher.

'I'll give you a head start,' he said, waving a sickle at them.

'I'll busy myself with preparing the still. And when I'm ready I'll cut and beat what the two of you can achieve in one hour.'

'Off you go then, little brother,' Sarah teased. 'And we'll be waiting for you. See you in the field.'

And as Luc watched his workers reap his precious blooms, he imagined how one day the people of France would cut away the ties that bound them to the Reich.

Luc's father owned the region's best copper still. The Cygnet, as it had been christened by Jacob twenty years earlier, with its delicate swan neck, would now work non-stop for the Bonet family until their fields were fully harvested. Luc loved its burnished, shining presence in the fields and its portability made it the envy of all the growers.

As the first vat of water began to simmer in the Cygnet, Luc noticed Gitel watching him closely. 'Gitel, do you understand how this works?'

His sister grinned sheepishly before admitting, 'No. But why don't you teach me?'

'This clever piece of equipment is an essentier,' Luc said. 'As pressure builds in the top half where the flowers are now steaming, they yield their precious oil, which will shortly be carried in the vapour.'

A few workers nearby began to listen. They all looked hot already.

'The steam will force its way into here,' Luc said, tapping the barrel, 'where there is cool water and a coiled tube.

'The steam, arriving into this barrel and passing through the cool water via the coiled tub, can't help but turn back into liquid. Any moment now it will drip out of the condenser's spout into this small pot at its base, as a blend of water and oil.'

Gitel's eyes sparkled with pleasure, and just at that moment – as if on cue – the first drips of the precious liquid plopped into the pot.

Amid a cheer, the workers gathered to take a break, sip some much-needed water and watch the first of the season's essential oil arrive. Luc dipped his fingers into the oil's surface and rubbed his thumb through the glistening liquid. He closed his eyes and inhaled the fragrance – heady, velvety, powerful.

At midday Luc called a halt and everyone settled beneath the few trees nearby that acted as a windbreak. They offered welcome shade to enjoy the food laid out – ham, paté, a goats' cheese omelette and fresh bread, washed down with watered wine or cider. Strawberries from Ida's garden were a treat. For a while, even Jacob seemed to lose his furrowed brow and Luc allowed himself to believe that Provence, with its bright colours and its plenitude, might just give his father hope for the future.

6

It had been a long day, more than twelve hours in the field, when Luc finally called a halt. The workers straightened for the last time, wincing as they stretched their spines and massaged tired muscles.

'We'll do the top field tomorrow,' he told them as his father entered the final tally in the accounting book against the last man's name.

The family watched the workers all drift away down the rocky hillside towards the village.

His father sucked on his pipe. 'A very good day. I'm impressed, Luc.'

Luc nodded. 'I don't even need to know the tally to see it. At this rate, we may fill four pots from the fields, and Saba will have enough of her precious aromatic water to daub on all the people and animals of the village.'

Wolf smiled. 'I have to admit – and I don't care what you say, Luc – last winter, Ida's lavender oil surely helped my rheumatism, and old Philippe's horse was cured of that strange swelling on his leg.'

'Well, watch out. She's got fresh supplies now. She'll be using it for everything from indigestion to lack of energy.'

'That little boy of the Rouens' – his fits and seizures are less frequent.'

'He could be growing out —'

'The lavender water might also work. You shouldn't be so sceptical.'

Luc put up his hands in mock defence and tucked a spray of lavender into his shirt pocket. 'I'm not, Wolf. The power of the lavender has been drummed into me since I was old enough to understand.'

Laurent's breezy voice called to them. 'Messieurs, the ladies are ready.' He pointed to the cart laden for its descent into the village.

'Thank you, Laurent,' Jacob said, and gathered up his writing materials. 'See you at the house,' he called to Luc, linking arms with Wolf and carefully making his way to the cart.

'I can help you with the equipment if you want. What can I do?' Laurent offered.

'Hold this,' Luc said, pointing to the neck of the Cygnet. 'We have to dismantle this first.'

They were so engrossed in the task that they didn't see Fougasse arrive back with Caesar ten minutes later.

'Hello, Bonet, Martin.'

They both looked up. Luc wiped his mouth with the back of his hand. 'Fougasse.' He nodded. 'Thanks for bringing the donkey back, but we could have done that.'

'I know,' the baker replied. He gave the donkey an apple core. 'A good day?'

Luc nodded. 'An excellent yield.'

Fougasse looked out across the valley. 'On a day like today one could pretend we aren't living in the madness.'

'After listening to my father, I can honestly say *we* aren't living in the madness. Paris is the crazy place.'

'Yes, you're right there.'

Luc paused, unsure whether to continue. 'Did you want to talk with me, Monsieur Fougasse? It's just that —'

'Both of you, in fact.' The baker sighed softly. 'It is a delicate matter, Bonet.'

Luc felt vaguely unnerved. There was something in Fougasse's steady, dark gaze that made him feel unsure.

'May we sit, Monsieur Bonet?' Fougasse said, gesturing at a rocky mound nearby. 'Best we're not seen,' he said, looking back down the hillside to the village.

Laurent sat, intrigued, but Luc wasn't so sure. 'What's this about, Fougasse? As you can see, I'm really —'

'Sit, Bonet,' the older man said. It was not an invitation.

Luc sat down slowly. 'It is harvest time, Fougasse. Every minute seems to count.'

'I understand.' The baker seemed uninterested in Laurent and only had eyes for Luc. 'I will take only a little of your time. I hope I am not wrong, but I sense anger and patriotism in you.'

'For France, you mean?' Laurent replied while Luc stared, astonished. The baker's remark was unexpected.

'Of course,' Fougasse replied, rubbing a dark, unshaven chin but not taking his hard gaze from Luc.

'Monsieur Fougasse, we are French! We are patriots! We hate the Boches.' Laurent dropped his voice. Habit had taught him to only think these thoughts, not say them, and he looked guilty at saying words that carried all manner of punishments.

Luc cut him a disapproving glance. 'Your point?'

The baker blinked at last. 'I am Maquis.'

Laurent gasped, but while Luc was surprised he was not shocked. It made sense that this man was an active resister when you looked at his life. He was single and self-contained, he never said much, and while he was friendly enough to all in the village, Luc knew him to be private – secretive, in fact. He was a strongly built man but known for his gentle voice and seemingly meek ways. Looking at him now, though, there was little that was meek about the baker.

Fougasse was taking a dangerous risk in declaring himself. Resisters rubbed shoulders daily with collaborators throughout the country but nowhere was the secrecy more pronounced than in the country. In the villages of France the resister would offer warm salutations to the collaborator from the neighbouring hamlet, perhaps even break bread or share a drink with him. Neither would know each other's persuasion, and secrecy became paramount if you were a resister.

Clearly Luc and Laurent's willingness to plug up springs, fell trees, and hamper the German soldiers and French police had caught the attention of these men. The secret group of renegades had formed initially to avoid any so-called voluntary work in Germany but had soon become part of the active resistance. In the Luberon it was difficult to be found if you knew your way around the hillsides. The locals knew the foothills and goat tracks better than they knew the main roads of the towns. These men became ghosts – rarely seen in the villages, barely heard from at all.

Men were disappearing all over France to join these renegade groups but in the south-east they were called the Maquis, after the scrubby terrain of their region. To belong was to be a maquisard, and to wear the badge of French patriotism. The group started out as loose collections of a few individuals in the hills, but increasingly it was becoming more organised. Luc felt his heart lift with pride each time he caught a rumour about another act of sabotage against the Germans. Sometimes they were petty and simply held up proceedings by a few hours; on other occasions they stopped the Germans from following through on orders. Killings were rare but not unheard of.

A thought flashed in Luc's mind. 'The note was from you!'

'Note?' Laurent repeated.

The baker nodded ruefully. 'I shouldn't have. It was incriminating, but I felt very proud the day you stopped the fountain flowing. It made my heart sing to think Fritz drank from the same water as our horses, our donkeys, our cattle.'

'It was more of a prank,' Luc admitted.

'Clever, though.'

Luc shrugged. 'I'd seen how all our girls smiled coyly whenever the German soldiers looked their way . . . and they are always looking their way,' he said, sounding disgusted.

Fougasse gave a mirthless laugh. 'I enjoyed the prank. And the second time you sent them back where they came from.'

Laurent grinned. 'I wanted to make it more dramatic but Luc said we had to keep it fast and simple, right?'

Luc nodded silently while Laurent continued. 'Luc knew of a tree that was dying. He said if we pushed it over, it would look real, as though it had simply fallen. Took three of us to get it down in time.'

'Effective,' Fougasse said. 'And clean. No one suspected anything.'

'You've been keeping close tabs, Monsieur Fougasse,' Luc remarked. 'And yet I have not been aware of you.'

'Sometimes it is because of our visibility that we are invisible,' he replied cryptically.

'Out in plain sight, eh?'

'Exactly. For me it works.'

'You don't trust anyone,' Luc said.

'I want to say no one, but I trust you enough to reveal myself.'

'Why?'

'Why trust you? Or why reveal myself?'

Luc's eyes crinkled at the edges. 'Both.'

'I know your families well, and apples don't fall far from their trees.' He gave a slight incline of his head. 'I fought alongside Jacob Bonet in the Great War. He was a good man, a brave man. He looked after us youngsters.'

How many times had Luc heard similar tales?

'He saved my life once. I have never forgotten it, though we never speak of it. So now I am obliged to save yours.'

'Save my life?' Luc asked, amused.

Fougasse didn't reply. The answer was in the set of his jaw.

Luc took a breath. 'Why reveal your secret?'

'I told you: to save your life. Or at least try. I can protect you more than your father can.'

'What are you talking about?' Luc felt wearied after a long day and keen to spend time with his family, have a bath, drink some wine.

'Become a maquisard – both of you,' Fougasse said bluntly. 'We need fit young men who refuse to bow to the Germans or to Vichy's new rules and regulations.'

'Us?' Laurent said. 'What can we do?'

'Stand against those who oppress us. If we're meek, our enemies don't even need to kill us; we make ourselves their slaves. Have you any idea of the scale of the German requisitions? It's not just food. It's equipment, and horses will be next. They're stealing our very livelihood. Without our animals, how do our farmers plough their fields to grow the food? Paris is starving but almost everything we grow is being sent to Germany. Meanwhile French babies die.'

The baker sighed. 'Forgive me. I do not mean to lecture. But this is important. Especially for you, Luc.'

'Why Luc?' Laurent asked. If he was offended, it didn't show.

Fougasse raised an eyebrow. 'It's his appearance. What's more, I presume you know he speaks German.'

Laurent's expression became guarded. 'We are lifelong friends. Of course I know! I should like to learn how you do, though.'

Fougasse turned to Luc. 'Your father has told me everything.'

Luc rounded on him. 'What do you know?' he growled.

'I know about you.'

'What's he talking about, Luc?' Laurent asked, a confused look on his face.

Luc pointed at the baker. 'Monsieur Fougasse, your secret is as safe with me as I trust mine is with you. But I do not need saving. I can look after myself, and what's more, I have a family to take care of.'

'It is too late for them, Bonet.'

'What?' Luc said, abruptly standing. 'Too late? What are you talking about?' He suddenly became aware of three strangers who had appeared behind him. His eyes widened at the beekeepers' nets they wore to hide their faces. 'Who are you?'

Fougasse nodded unhappily, and at his signal the strangers pounced on Luc and Laurent. There wasn't even time to yell. Big, hard hands clamped across their mouths and they were forced onto their bellies.

'I ask your forgiveness, Bonet. This is not how I would wish to conscript you,' Fougasse said. 'But I have no choice, if I wish to save your life as I promised your father I would.' And from his pocket he produced Luc's birth certificate. 'This is all you need from your home. I deeply regret that you cannot help your family but I am acting on your father's orders. We do not hold your ancestry against you, but now is a very good time to prove your patriotism to France.'

Luc roared his anger but the hand on his mouth muffled all sound.

The church pealed the hour. Eight. The cicadas began to tune up, and above the drone of a lone bee, Luc could hear the voices of village children playing and a vehicle groaning up the makeshift road.

Luc stopped struggling. A car?

'Hush now, Bonet. Let your eyes tell you everything you need to know.'

Below them Luc saw a van rumbling into Saignon village.

He twisted beneath the men and glared at Fougasse.

'That is Landry and no doubt someone from the SS,' the baker said, his face leaden with regret. 'They have come to arrest your parents, sisters and grandmother.'

The callused hand pressed even more firmly over Luc's mouth.

Fougasse continued. 'Somebody from the village contacted the authorities in Apt and reminded them that a Jewish family had returned to Saignon last week, fleeing from Paris. The snitch even suggested that the family was inciting hatred against the Germans.'

Laurent managed to speak. 'Rubbish! The Bonets are important to the village. No man would do such a thing.'

Fougasse shrugged. 'No man, maybe, but a woman perhaps,' he replied. 'Catherine Girard has brought this on your folk.'

Luc bit his captor's hand and his mouth was released. 'Prove it!' Luc snarled.

'Take the other one,' said Fougasse curtly, with a nod to his companions.

Laurent, struggling, was carried away. One man remained. Luc was shocked to see he carried a revolver.

'I regret this,' Fougasse said. 'I am doing this because your father asked me to. Come, you need to bear witness. Can I count on you to remain silent?'

Luc nodded.

'If you give us away, we are all dead, Bonet, including your friend. You do not want our blood on your hands.'

Luc stared grimly back at Fougasse, who seemed satisfied with Luc's silence.

They moved quietly and swiftly to a point where they had a clear view past the fountain to Luc's house.

Men had spilled out of the van. Among the uniforms of the French police, Luc could see a different uniform; it was the colour of a grey dove but worn with boots that were impressively tall and shiny.

'Gestapo?' Luc wondered.

'Worse. SS,' Fougasse confirmed. He pointed to the rooftops. Luc frowned. 'Follow me. It's the only way we can get closer. Are you sure you can do this, Bonet?'

Luc stared at him, his jaw working, his expression intense.

'I have to trust you to be silent. To reveal us is to give our lives uselessly to a German bullet.'

'That's my family!'

Fougasse regarded him, his expression not without pity. 'It is too late for them now.'

Luc couldn't respond. His mouth was open, his eyes felt glazed. He was suddenly unable to move.

'But you can avenge them,' Fougasse finished.

Luc's knees buckled. He crouched; he needed to think, needed to have a plan. He needed a gun, damn it! But the baker was well ahead of him.

'Don't even consider it now,' Fougasse warned. 'I promise you, I would have warned your family, but we only had moments. I would sooner kill you myself than break my oath to your father. Now, this is a tragedy, I know, but this is your reality. Your family is going to be taken away and there is nothing you can do about it other than get yourself killed and probably me and a few others in the bargain. Hear me . . . you cannot save them. But you can get your revenge.'

Luc didn't want to hear it, didn't want to accept it. The whole notion of doing nothing to help the people he loved was alien. Saba? They were taking away a harmless old woman?

'Why are they doing this?' Luc croaked.

'There is no reason. Your family has done nothing wrong other than to be Jewish.'

'Give me a gun. You don't have to —'

'Stop.'

'I'll involve no one else,' he gabbled his promise. 'I have to . . . my sister is just nine, my mother's heart . . . Rachel is in love. Fougasse, Sarah's going to be a doctor to help the people here. Why don't you understand? My grandmother is eighty-seven!' He was clawing at the baker in his desperation, his cheeks wet with tears. He couldn't remember the last time he'd cried.

'Luc,' Fougasse finally said gently. 'You must promise me that you understand there is nothing you or any of us can do to prevent your family being taken from Saignon today. The SS has the power and the authority. If you try and fight back now, they will send more men – soldiers – and they will take reprisals on the whole village. I have heard what they do, and it is more ugly than even your worst nightmare. They will not only gun down your family in front of you, but they will kill women and children in ways they find amusing. They do not care.'

Luc held his head in his hands. 'You want me to watch my family being taken away and just do nothing?'

'Yes, for anything you do will result in death for them, for yourself, and for many more. I can promise you that.'

Luc shook his head. Uncontrollable tears dripped down his face. 'I don't care about my own life.'

'But your father does. He wants you to survive. But I will promise you revenge, Luc. Can I trust you?'

Luc nodded, feeling trapped. This was just short of blackmail.

In a state of denial, he followed Fougasse around the back of the village until they were at the rear of the bakery. Soon they were at the top of the baker's small house and climbing out a window onto the rooftop. Fougasse pointed to areas that Luc should beware of in case tiles loosened. They disturbed some pigeons that took off but it was a familiar sound and Luc was sure no one would look up.

Fougasse finally turned with a forefinger against his lips, urging Luc forward. His expression was all sorrow. Luc wriggled along on his belly and then lifted himself up onto his elbows. What he saw made his previous meal feel as though it were roaring back up his gullet.

Gitel was crying, clinging to Sarah, who had encircled her arms around both Gitel and Rachel. Jacob was holding Golda, whose eyes were closed; she was praying and weeping at the same time. They were being harangued by none other than Gendarme Landry; Jacob was trying to reason with him but Landry was man-handling him, swaggering up and down the line of the family. And then Luc's tiny grandmother was dragged out of the house. Ida was the most vocal of all. While the others cowered, she gave as good as she got. Luc could hear her every shrill word, as she cursed and waved her frail arms.

It was Landry who silenced her, striding up and punching the old woman with a full fist in her midsection. Luc gasped as he saw his beloved saba double up. In her hand she had been clutching a spray of lavender, which she'd tried to curse them with. The flowers dropped from her grasp as she staggered first and then fell to her knees. The girls screamed, Gitel wet herself where she cowered, and villagers who rushed to the elderly woman's aid were threatened by Landry.

Luc was so shocked he couldn't have made a sound even if he'd wanted to.

Landry pointed at Jacob, who was permitted to help his mother-in-law, lifting her gently to her feet and into his embrace. Ida was quiet now, curled over herself by the side of her praying daughter.

It was so silent that Landry's words could be heard clearly.

'There is a son. Where is he?'

One of the German officers addressed Catherine, who was standing nearby. Luc only now noticed the flame-haired traitor.

Had she done this out of spite? Whatever her reason, he drew the smallest satisfaction at realising she looked as shocked as any of the other villagers. Luc watched her shake her head, mumble some words. He couldn't believe she had done this to them. *A woman scorned.*

'Where is Luc Bonet?' Landry demanded, even louder.

Catherine began to weep now. She pointed a shaky finger towards the hills, towards his fields.

Luc was so numb he struggled to speak. 'What will happen to them?' he whispered to Fougasse.

'Jews are being rounded up everywhere.'

'Non-French Jews, I was told,' Luc said.

The baker shook his head sadly. 'Any Jew.'

Luc dropped his shoulders. *Let it be a nightmare*, he begged. *Let me wake!* 'Where will they be taken?'

'Camp des Milles, a transit camp for Jews.'

'Transit to where?' He grabbed Fougasse's shirt.

'Drancy, most likely. Outside Paris.'

'So I can get to them, I can petition for my father. He is an important and senior man in —'

Fougasse made a hissing sound. 'You do not understand yet, Bonet? No one will see them. No one gets out. There are no privileges, no matter who you are. Monies, property, belongings – everything is confiscated. Bank accounts frozen. They belong to Germany now. And your family? There is nothing you can do for them except pray.'

'There is always a way,' Luc said beneath his breath. 'Let me go.'

Suddenly he had a rope around his neck. Fougasse's shadowy companion had crawled up behind him and slipped it on.

'He will throttle you before he lets you give us away.'

Luc could feel his eyes bulging as his breath was constricted.

The rope was relaxed slightly and he gasped, sucking air into his heaving chest. He realised there was no choice, and that his future, whether he wanted it to or not, lay with the maquisard and his cause.

'They'll go down into Apt first,' Luc groaned in a choked whisper. 'I want to see them.'

'Impossible,' Fougasse said, shaking his head.

'Then I will not go quietly with you,' Luc said. 'Have your friend choke me now.'

They stared at each other, neither blinking. After a tense silence, Fougasse finally relented. 'Let's get down the mountain before they do,' he whispered hoarsely.

Luc laid his cheek down against the warm terracotta roof and could feel the damp of his tears soak into the tiles. Earthy smells assaulted him as he closed his eyes, just for a moment in silent prayer; the tang of bird droppings and the musty aroma of drying leaves added to the decay of a long dead and desiccated rodent. But on the evening breeze he caught a gentle whiff of lavender being drawn down the hills and pushed through the alleys of his village . . . and that brought him hope.

He prayed his grandmother could smell it too.

The sight of his family being taken kept repeating in Luc's mind. He hated that he could replay it in such exquisitely painful detail. He hoped Catherine was haunted forever by this scene and the darkness of her foul deed.

Luc almost gagged to recall it, and swallowed the involuntary motion. He had to find them. Had to do something, no matter what Fougasse said. He'd rather die than desert them. What was he doing here? He'd been forced by Fougasse to wait at a tiny café in the back streets of Apt with the silent companion, whose name he had still to learn. He had to content himself with a weak but bitter coffee made from barley. They'd insisted he wear a beret pulled low to cover part of his face while Fougasse dropped into the local gendarmerie.

The baker returned just as Luc was sure he was going to explode and start flinging chairs and tables around. He felt so helpless.

'They're not holding them here even briefly,' Fougasse said. The words were blunt but spoken softly.

'What?' Luc said, beginning to push his chair back.

Both men growled at him. 'No scenes, Bonet,' Fougasse warned. 'I told the gendarmes that your father owed me money and I was chasing him. They could tell me only that the SS officers took control at Apt and they continued on to the internment camp at Aix.'

Luc stared at him blankly. *Aix-en-Provence!* It felt as though his family were suddenly beyond his reach.

'There's more,' the baker said, looking down. 'You might as well hear it all.' Luc couldn't imagine it could get any worse. He waited and watched Fougasse's expression darken further. 'My sincere regrets. Your grandmother died on the way down the mountain.'

Luc stared uncomprehendingly at Fougasse, who did not look away. He wondered whether he'd heard correctly. He felt breathless, as though a great weight had suddenly pressed onto his chest. The memory of his grandmother being punched flashed again into his mind. A tremble passed through him and then strengthened – it wouldn't stop; he was shivering in summer. Luc leant his elbows against the table to try to steady himself, and then put his head in his hands.

His companions shared uneasy glances.

'Breathe, Luc! We must be careful. The town is crawling with soldiers, and there's Gestapo and SS around too. This is not a clever time for us to be seen at all, let alone together.' Fougasse touched Luc's shoulder. Luc shook it away. 'The gendarmerie knew your family and were as shocked as we were, but they can do nothing.'

Luc groaned at the thought of his grandmother. No long goodbyes, no tears. Her life stolen from them by a Frenchman's fist.

'I'm going to be sick.' He shook off their arms and ran around the corner. He wasn't sure how long he stayed there, breathing in deep draughts. Soon he became aware of someone behind him.

'We must go,' the baker said gently. A wet handkerchief appeared. 'Here, wipe your mouth. Pull yourself together.'

'I can't,' Luc moaned.

'Shhh. You must not draw attention to us.'

'Then go away,' Luc growled, spitting to clear the sourness.

'I gave your father my word that I would protect you. Our word is all we have to give between patriotic men. Stand up now, and find your courage.' Fougasse waited.

Luc's cheeks were burning with rage. It was all right for Fougasse; he had no one to love and no one loved him.

'It is easy to accuse me of that,' Fougasse said and Luc realised he had spoken aloud. 'But it doesn't change the fact that you are not the first to lose someone you love to this war. I am sorry for you, truly, but you can keel over in this gutter or you can find a new courage and fight back, as your father hoped you would.' Fougasse stopped suddenly, an alarmed look on his face, as Luc heard the sound of boots. Instinctively he straightened. Soldiers. They laughed as they passed and threw some wisecracks at him in poor French.

Luc stared at the broad, straight backs of the young men walking away, their green uniforms clean and proud, the sound of their polished boots taunting him.

'Is she here?' he asked.

'She'll be buried tonight.'

'Can I take her back, bury her in Saignon?'

'*Non!*' Fougasse looked angry. 'Absolutely not.'

Luc swallowed hard. 'Then I will see her.'

'You cannot —'

'I will kiss my grandmother goodbye.' He glowered.

The baker relented. 'Follow me.'

———

Ida had been left in an old storeroom at the back of Apt. It was empty for the moment, awaiting the autumn when the harvest of apples, pears and plums would tumble in by the cartload. Luc wanted to do so much more for Ida but for the first time in his life he felt totally helpless. His father had been right. All the money, the status, the respect in the world couldn't help his family in their hour of need – not against this sort of persecution.

He steeled himself to look upon his grandmother. She was on her back, and the lovely silver hair had come loose from its bun and lay in wisps around her face. He wished he had a comb to neaten it. Fougasse left him alone with her, keeping a tense lookout over the storeroom. He knelt by her side, unaware of the tears that dampened his cheeks or the silent sobs that tightened in his chest. Today he had wept twice in as many hours. Shock, he knew, was helping him; it prevented him from looking beyond the tiny, frail body to the larger pain of the loss of his whole family. He didn't want to think about where they were, or how frightened they must be. He didn't want to see his father's desperation, his horror at the treatment of his children, his wife.

Ida embodied all of that sorrow in her stillness. His tears splashed onto her hand as he took it, clasping her stiffening, arthritic fingers to the unshaven cheek she would never pinch again. Her earrings and necklace had been taken but he noticed her rings were intact, stubborn beneath her swollen knuckles. Her wedding band was her most precious keepsake of her husband and she kissed it each night before bed. Seeing it safe gave Luc relief to think that his grandmother would not be separated from her beloved husband, even in death.

He reached into his shirt pocket and pulled out a small spray of lavender he had put there earlier.

'Here, Saba. Carry this with you,' he whispered and tucked it into her palm, folding her fingers around the flowers, squeezing them shut, before he kissed her hand and then bent to kiss her cheek.

As Luc pulled away, laying her hand gently back on her chest, he felt a bump in her cardigan pocket. He knew what this was: her precious seeds.

He gently pulled out the familiar silken pouch that she carried around. Inside were lavender heads, drying and dropping seeds that she would, from time to time, cast around her. The old girl would sow lavender wherever she found herself. The pouch was bulging. He pushed it into his pocket and made an oath he would always carry it. He would be her lavender keeper.

He took one final look at his dead grandmother, smoothing her hair back from her face, and as he did so, all of his anger at the war and its hardships – at his family's humiliations – seemed to gather tightly in his chest, along with the death and destruction. The numbness at losing his family was the final blow to a pain that had been building. Yesterday, it was the revelation of his birth and the melancholy that it had stirred; today, his family. The swastikas, the *Sieg Heil*s, the arrogant smiles of the Germans, the pandering approach of too many French who had decided that collaboration was the only way to protect France . . . all of it began to gather and pound in his heart and at his temple in a new, brooding rage.

Then Luc thought of de Gaulle's rallying words and how they

had affected his grandmother, made her eyes sparkle with mischievous pleasure. That was surely what she wanted now . . . for Luc to stand up and be counted as a fiercely proud Frenchman who refused to pay homage to Hitler and his swaggering soldiers.

And finally Luc thought of the lavender and whether his fields of blue would ever flourish again.

All of these thoughts melded as he looked at Ida's face in repose. His heart began to harden, filling with dark stones of hatred. Luc knew that when he left this place, he would walk out a different man.

Outside it was low light, just enough left for them to disappear into the mountains.

'Can you can lead us in the dark?' Fougasse said.

'I know the way blindfolded,' Luc said, his voice a monotone. He didn't move.

'Are you ready, Bonet?'

'Yes, I am ready,' he said to Fougasse, turning. 'And I am now Maquis.'

PART TWO

PART TWO

7

London, July 1943

Lisette Forester usually enjoyed her fifteen-minute walk home from work at Trafalgar Square to her tiny tenement flat, not far from Victoria Station. It was a bonus if she could make it home without having to duck into one of the London Underground stations to avoid the air raids. But even when it was necessary, she didn't fuss; she took the view that the bombings were so far out of her control it didn't bear even thinking about. She watched some people panic and scream, fleeing for relative safety, while others froze. She sympathised with the latter – they were usually those with others depending on them, and she could see the anxiety in their faces; the terror not so much for themselves but for their loved ones. Lisette had no one waiting for her at home and few would mourn her passing. Over time this knowledge had turned her inwards, and without her meaning to, it had disconnected her from most to the point where she knew some considered her cold.

Yet if another could walk in her shoes they'd realise she was a passionate woman, full of drive but lacking a target to aim for. She worked as a waitress, doing one day a week at the French Canteen, frequented by de Gaulle's followers, but most of her shifts were at the Lyons Corner House at the corner of The Strand and Trafalgar. She had toyed with taking a job at Fortnum & Mason but at Lyons there was the variety of serving everyone from film stars to Whitehall civil servants. And so Lisette became a 'Nippy', as the Lyons

Corner House waitresses were known, because of the speed at which they wove their way through tables serving customers. She liked her stylish uniform, which began with a loosely pleated black dress. A starched square apron was tied in a neat bow at the back, preventing even a glimpse of thigh, and was completed by a crisp white Peter-Pan collar with matching detachable cuffs and an even stiffer pleated white mitre-style hat. Her dress was studded with thirty pairs of decorative pearl buttons from neck to waist. Unlike some of the girls, who wore kitten heels, Lisette chose comfort with flat, black lace-ups. These days she, like most of the girls, wore short socks, without the access to stockings. She was embarrassed when the management used her in one of its promotional photographs. Lisette couldn't see the point of smiling while Britain was at war, yet the photographer insisted she look happy and welcoming as she balanced a tray with a pot, tea cup and saucer in one hand and her order notebook in the other. Management was delighted with the result and even gave her a bonus for her help.

Lisette liked to return home via the Admiralty Buildings, passing the army barracks as she strolled through St James's Park, around Buckingham Palace and back into Eccleston Bridge Road, where her flat was situated. The position was perfect. She enjoyed the atmosphere around Victoria with its constant movement of people and troops through the busy station, whose forecourt she often cut through. It was sad to see all the railings removed from the flowerbeds and around the parks, even the royal palace, but she knew the metal was needed to make bullets and shell casings.

And now parts of the great parks were being dug up to grow vegetables to feed Londoners. Kensington Gardens was growing impressive rows of cabbages, while Hyde Park had its own piggery! The distinctive *Dig for Victory* posters were everywhere and there was even an anthem on the wireless urging people to find new ways to cook with bland provisions.

People were responding with what Lisette was assured was the traditional British grit, turning their gardens into allotments. She was trying to grow some tomato plants in pots on her wide window ledges, but she wasn't having much success. In fact, she'd forgotten to water them this morning so perhaps it was a good thing she'd had to come home early today. Nevertheless a fresh frown of irritation creased her face.

What was this about? Lisette's boss, Miss Mappleton, had insisted it was all above board. She had waved the gentleman's card in Lisette's face and insisted she go straight home to meet him at the appointed time.

Flat number nine was up in the gods via an open stone staircase but she'd so loved its romantic views across the West End rooftops that she'd moved in the day she saw it. She'd shared with her friend, Harriet, whose father had found the flat for them; he worked for the railways and had access to British Rail accommodation. But since Harriet was now a casualty of Hitler's bombing raids, Lisette lived by herself, and no one had come to claim the flat back for the railways.

Lisette's inheritance had made her more than comfortable but she never spoke about it; she barely touched the money, in fact. She didn't want to live in the empty house in Sussex that was her inheritance, nor did she want to live with her grandparents in Hampshire. And she had quickly tired of the pity she constantly received at losing her parents. Living in the capital, having to find work and coping alone would make her stronger. She was happy in her own company and was rather enjoying life now that she had some good shifts and a regular income. Plus there was that nice airman, Jack, who had asked her out twice. She hadn't accepted yet but if he asked again, she planned to say yes.

Lisette had only been sharing the flat for nine months when war was declared. She soon found herself daubing the windows she adored with black paint and wondering whether her little home would topple in the Blitz. It hadn't; she'd been here three years now, and it was the Docklands and East End that had so far borne the brunt of the Luftwaffe's mass aerial bombings.

Day and night plucky Londoners had rallied their 'Blitz spirit' and defied the terror of those raids without respite. Nearly six thousand dead as a result after a fifty-seven-day period of relentless bombing. The Brits carried on, tightening their belts as food rationing intensified and still believing that a pot of tea solved a lot of sorrows, although most were indignant that the government had forbidden production of ice-cream. When Buckingham Palace was bombed Lisette sighed with relief that the West End now shared the heartache of the destruction. So, it seemed, did the stoic Queen Elizabeth, who remained in London as a show of strength and support to her people.

Now Lisette smiled faintly as she watched her visitor, who had introduced himself as Mr Collins, seated in the only armchair in the flat. She was perched on a small cherry leather ottoman she'd picked up on the King's Road. Behind her guest the blacked-out windows looked like two dark eyes but she'd opened the charcoal curtain on the one other window that overlooked the backyard below, allowing daylight to seep into the room. She watched her visitor sip his tea from a heavily gilded Limoges cup with its handle vividly painted with garlands of roses. Perhaps by today's conservative tastes it was rather garish but she loved the near translucent porcelain. Lisette knew she hadn't quite mastered the art of tea-making to English standards yet; privately she didn't understand the attraction. If he'd asked for a coffee, she might have been persuaded to dip into her meagre stocks and show him how a good cup of French boiled coffee would wipe away that grimace.

He put the porcelain cup back onto its saucer, its contents barely touched. 'Miss Forestier —'

'I prefer Forester, if you don't mind. I'm trying to anglicise my life as best I can.'

'Of course. Forgive me.' The man cleared his throat politely. She decided he looked like a fat blackbird chick with his round shape and dun-brown garments.

'However, it's your "Frenchness", that has brought me here. I would very much like it if you would agree to meet a colleague of mine. I can't tell you his name because . . . well, because it's a secret.' He gave a short tight smile. 'Miss Forester, it has not escaped our notice that you speak several languages . . . and that you speak them flawlessly.'

She blushed. 'How do you know this?'

He sighed. 'We've had you under what you might call surveillance for several months.'

Lisette blinked in confusion. 'Surveillance?'

He nodded and had the good grace to appear embarrassed.

'What do you suspect me of?' she asked, almost breathless with shock.

'Oh, no, no . . . good grief, no, Miss Forester. Nothing like that! Quite the contrary, in fact. What I mean is we've been admiring your skill with language. You are superb.'

Now she didn't know whether to be flattered or just plain relieved. She frowned more deeply. 'Why are you watching me?'

'It was by accident, really. You were serving a colleague of mine at Joe Lyons. She noticed that you moved to another table where some guests were speaking in French, and it was obvious to her that you understood what was being said.'

'How is that possible?'

Her visitor took a breath. 'She's an observer of people, Miss Forester, and noticed that you smirked at something they'd said.

'A few days later you served another colleague of mine, an English man. But on this occasion he spoke to you in French.'

'I see.'

'And he had brought another colleague with him whom he introduced as Swiss. You took it upon yourself to speak quietly in German to that man. I must confess to you, the Swiss visitor was English – a plant, you could say – but your German was spot on. What's more, you were clearly comfortable in the vernacular.'

'Mr Collins. It's true that I speak several languages; I also have some French dialects to my credit. Language is my specialty. It's why I work at the French Canteen and at Lyons, although I refrain from using German, for obvious reasons. I remember that Swiss man. He was very polite. What is this all about?'

'Miss Forester, we could very much use your services. The, er . . . the War Office needs as much information as it can gather. Someone with your linguistic skills is a rare prize we cannot ignore.'

It finally dawned on Lisette that the authorities were hoping she'd agree to learn wireless operation or something similar. She felt a thrill of excitement that she might finally be involved in Britain's war effort. If she was going to risk her life in London, she might as well risk it for a good cause.

'How do you feel about that?' he asked, leaning forward.

'Well, Mr Collins, as my granny says, we must all do our bit.'

'Oh, indeed,' he said, nodding. 'May I set up an appointment for you to discuss this further?'

'Yes . . . but I would need to speak with —'

'Miss Mappleton? That's all taken care of. Can we say four p.m., tomorrow, then?'

'That quick?'

He nodded. 'No time like the present, Miss Forester. Do you know the Hotel Victoria? It's not too far.'

'Northumberland Avenue, isn't it?' she said.

'Very good. Room 238. Could you be there a little earlier?'

'Yes, if you wish, and providing my shift has been cleared.'

'Please don't fret on that account,' Collins said, standing and giving Lisette a vague bow. 'Thank you for the tea,' he added and looked away quickly from his still full cup. 'I'll look forward to seeing you tomorrow.'

Lisette showed him to her door and then raced around, bathing, changing, primping her hair and becoming quietly excited at the prospect of working with people who were actually helping to change the course of the war. Lisette hoped with all her heart that she'd one day take down a message from one of the spies who courageously sent back messages from France. Maybe that's why they needed her? To translate messages from French men and women working in the field?

The following day at three, knowing it was far too early to leave but unable to sit still, Lisette walked slowly to Northumberland Avenue. She wore her cream blouse and new chocolate-brown cardigan that had cost her ten clothing-ration coupons. She'd left her face scrubbed clean but at the last minute decided to smudge a soft-pink lipstick lightly across her lips – a gift from her dad before he died. As she'd looked at her reflection she thought it was as though he was sending her a good-luck kiss.

She arrived at the hotel at three-forty. A woman was waiting in the lobby for her. 'Miss Forester?'

'Yes,' she replied, admiring the woman's thick, dark hair and chiselled features. She could have been French with those looks.

'Early. That's what we like. I'm Vera Atkins.' They shook hands and Vera kept Lisette walking as she murmured to a woman behind the hotel desk.

'This way,' Vera said, leading her up two flights of stairs and through various corridors until she tapped lightly on a door. She ushered Lisette inside. 'Have a seat. Captain Jepson will be here immediately.'

It didn't look like a hotel room, but rather a sitting room. Another door opened and in walked a lean man in his early forties. He had an oval-shaped face and genial eyes. His long nose led down to a mouth that seemed to be suppressing amusement.

'This is Captain Selwyn Jepson,' Miss Atkins said.

Lisette shook Jepson's hand. She was grateful that he didn't crush her hand as so many uniformed men were apt to do. 'Good afternoon, Miss Forestier,' he said.

'Forester,' she corrected.

'Ah, Collins did mention that. Thank you for seeing us,' he said, and moved into rapid-fire French. 'You live alone.'

She shifted into French as well. 'Yes.'

'Why?'

'Why not?'

He twitched a smile. 'No friends?'

'Plenty.'

'Is that true?'

Lisette held his gaze, and realised she couldn't stare him down. 'I prefer to keep my friendship group small.'

'Why?'

'I've been in Britain only since 1938; I haven't had a chance to develop many relationships since . . . well, since getting here.'

'No boyfriends?' It sounded like an accusation.

'No one special.'

'Do you like living alone?'

'Captain Jepson, is this relevant?' She only now noticed that Vera Atkins had left the room.

'May I call you Lisette?'

She nodded. She could hardly refuse.

'Lisette, presumably Mr Collins mentioned that we are looking to recruit you.'

'He did, but I don't see how my living arrangements —'

'We are at war, and we must know everything – we are handing over our trust to each other.'

'I understand. Well, I have very few friends, I have no boyfriend, and yes, I enjoy living alone because I can't bear other people's noise and mess.'

'Are you fanatically tidy?'

'No. I cope just fine with my own mess.'

'So you're messy?'

'Not at all. I am living in rental accommodation. I can't afford to be messy in case the Railways do a check.'

'That's your friend's flat, isn't it?'

She was surprised. 'Yes, Harriet Lonsdale.'

He nodded as if he already knew. He shifted into Italian. 'Tell me about your parents.'

'Your accent is terrible,' she said to him in the same language.

He laughed. It changed his whole demeanour. 'I know. That's why I couldn't possibly be a spy.' And then his gaze narrowed. She felt speared.

His words floated in her mind. Then they seemed to settle, resound more clearly. *Spy?* What?

'You're recruiting me to spy?'

'How does that make you feel?' he asked, switching back to French.

'Nervous.'

'That's good. If you'd said excited or happy, I'd have worried. How would you feel about returning to France?'

She sat back in her chair, speechless.

Jepson sat forward and switched to English. 'I know that you've been slowly building a life for yourself here. In fact, I know a great deal about you, Lisette. You work at the Lyons Corner House and you volunteer one evening a week at the French Canteen. Why?'

'I get a very good free meal at the end of it,' she said. 'A proper French meal.'

'No doubt you can practise your French too. That's smart. Your father was German, wounded in action, and moved to France in 1918, where he met and married your half French, half English mother when they were both twenty. They settled in Lille, where you were born two years after the end of the Great War. Your family name is Foerstner but your parents adopted Forestier for convenience – being German wasn't terribly popular in 1918.'

She was sorry that he'd noticed her eyes mist.

'Forgive me. I don't mean to upset you.'

'It's all right. My father always said he felt more French than German.'

'Did he hate his own people?'

She looked up, stung. 'He was not a coward, Captain Jepson.'

'I didn't say he was; but I gather others did.'

'My father was an academic, a wise, gentle man. He hated that Germany started a war that killed so many of its fine young men. He was fourteen when it began, and he was injured at seventeen on the first day of his active service. He lost a hand – but I'm sure you know that too.'

Jepson nodded.

'He regretted that he could never pick me up easily as a newborn, could never hold my mother's face with two hands. He had to learn to write again, left-handed. But because he was sent home so early, he was called a coward. He began to hate Germany for that, and for killing his friends. His three best friends all died in the trenches.' She hadn't realised a tear had escaped, and she quickly wiped it away.

Jepson continued. 'Your parents moved with you to Strasbourg when you were three, after your mother became depressed over the death of your infant brother to the Spanish Flu pandemic after the war. Your father took a position at the university. I'm glad to note that your mother's health improved, although she had no further children and you became the adored only child.'

Lisette listened to him rattle off her life, not sure whether she was angry or shocked by how easily her history could be pared down to facts. She could feel her heart thumping at her chest in protest – like a child drumming its fists uselessly. She was digging her nails into her palms, wishing it would stop, and yet knowing he wasn't deliberately punishing her. She forced herself to relax and listen.

'Your paternal grandmother was German and your paternal grandfather French?'

She nodded, astonished at his wealth of information.

'Your mother worked as a private secretary to a banker in Strasbourg, Monsieur Eichel, who was a great friend and helped you to organise their affairs upon their death. Your maternal grandparents – your only surviving relatives – are living in Hampshire – Farnborough, to be exact – and your grandmother is French while your grandfather is British. No wonder language is your thing.' He smiled kindly at her stricken expression. 'It's our job to know these things. Your parents were nervous about what was happening in Europe and decided to come to Britain in 1937. While they finalised the purchase of a house in Sussex, you were packed off to England early and deposited at Roedean to finish off your schooling.'

She looked down again, not wanting him to say it, but knowing he would.

'Your mother and father died in a car crash the night before they were due to move permanently to England. That must have been very hard for you, although I note that you aced your final exams nonetheless.'

'I was eighteen,' she said. 'I couldn't give up, so I learned how to get on.'

Jepson sat back and regarded her. 'You've got money. Why do you live so frugally?'

She flashed him an angry glance. 'I don't want my parents' money. I'm happy to make my own way.'

'You want to be a normal twenty-three-year-old?'

'I suppose,' she said, glad her voice was steady. He'd reopened a wound she'd worked so hard to heal. 'There would be nothing normal about someone my age living in a big, draughty old house with nothing to do behind blacked-out windows.'

'Do you find London dangerous?'

'Yes.'

'I gather Harriet Lonsdale was killed in one of the air raids.'

Lisette took a deep breath. *Please don't ask me more*, she begged inside. *Everyone I love dies young. I'm a curse.* 'Yes.'

'You were close to her?'

Jepson had no intention of leaving any aspect of her life untouched. But she wanted this role he was offering – whatever it was – more than she could believe. It would change her life, give her reason to – Lisette wasn't sure what the word was that she searched for – breathe, perhaps. Right now it felt as though she was moving through life stifled. Captain Jepson was waiting. 'I was close to Harriet. She befriended me when I first came to London – she was kind, very funny, full of . . .' She shook her head, remembering first Harriet's gust of a laugh that was so indicative of the generous personality behind it. She preferred to remember Harriet with gleaming blonde hair and those blue eyes full of life and mischief, rather than how she last saw her. 'Full of dreams,' she finished.

'I know this may be painful for you to recall, but you missed being killed by that same event by moments, didn't you?'

Lisette permitted the banished memory back into her conscious thought. It was the last day she remembered ever being happy. The war then, when Harriet was alive, had seemed like something that was happening to others. Meanwhile they were full of plans for the future; Harriet wanted to make use of Lisette's languages, desperate to move away from her boring desk job as a typist in the city, and had suggested they set up a travel company together. 'Guided tours of the Continent, Lissy,' she'd said, eyes shining at the thought of it. 'Imagine that! Travellers won't be able to resist.' Harriet had seen a little of Europe, and the trips to France and Switzerland had whet her appetite to see the rest of the world.

'We'll marry disgustingly wealthy Europeans. I'll marry a baron – I think Baroness Harriett has a nice ring to it – while you must marry a count because "Countess Lisette" just slips so easily off the tongue,' she'd said, laughing as Lisette rolled her eyes. Harriet was lying on a slab in the hospital morgue two days later. Lisette had been required to formally identify her. By then Harriet's body had been cleansed of all the blood and dirt, and her face, mercifully unharmed – save a tiny bruise near one eyebrow – looked peaceful. But no longer smiling.

Lisette cleared her throat. 'I was meeting Harriet after work. We planned to meet in the forecourt of the station. She arrived early, just as it was hit by a German bomber. I . . . She was alive when I found her.' It all came rushing back now. Even the tangy, metallic smell of Harriet's blood assaulted her. She refused to remember what it felt like to cradle Harriet's head in her lap. It had taken Lisette months to lock that memory away. She no longer suffered the constant nightmare of feeling useless as her friend slipped away from life. Instead, she'd taught herself to become a bystander; an observer of Harriet's death but not the grief-stricken friend whose hands were stained with her blood, whose tears mixed with the grime of the bombing, or the person who heard Harriet's last words.

'Tell Mum and Dad I'm sorry, Lissy.' Lisette could recall every word, every grimace, every nuance of those minutes before her friend fell slack in her arms. Harriet had said, 'They always liked me to be early for an appointment but for once in my life I shouldn't have been. Then I wouldn't be dying.'

Lisette had lied. 'You're not dying, Hat, you're injured, and we have to get you to the hospital at Whitechapel. Can you hear the ambulance? They're coming for you.'

'And for once all the noise and activity can be about me,' Harriet had said, reaching up a bloodied hand to stroke Lisette's chin.

It was not meant with any malice. As much as Lisette railed against the constant refrain that she was the pretty one, the intelligent one, the one who would go places and leave a mark on the world, her best friend wouldn't give up. It had made Lisette shrink even further in social situations, but men still sought her out, still asked her to dance before Harriet.

Harriet had turned her normally bright-blue gaze on Lisette then. 'You're a good liar – you always were.'

'Don't talk,' Lisette had said, anguished by the blood she could feel soaking into her dress. The ambulance was certainly not coming for Harriet.

'Take my mind from here, Lissy,' Harriet had begged. 'You're so good at storytelling.'

'All right. Let's imagine ourselves in a vineyard in France.'

'No, a lavender field. We made a promise we'd go see the lavender one summer, didn't we?'

'We did. Can you smell the lavender?'

'I'm trying to.'

'Think of it swaying around at knee height while you stand in the middle of it. What can you hear?'

'Birds,' Harriet answered. 'The drone of bees.'

'Good. I can too. Think now. What can you smell?'

'That fresh fragrance of lavender when I rub it between my fingers.'

'Go on.'

'Summer. I'm smelling dry earth.'

Lisette looked up as one of the ambulance men finally arrived. Bending over, he examined her friend. He shook his head sadly. 'Won't be long now,' he whispered, and that perhaps had been the worst moment of all – to have a kindly stranger confirm that Harriet was not long for this life.

Harriet was one more loved person Lisette couldn't protect, couldn't hang onto, and who would leave her grieving once more, painfully alone. When Harriet closed her eyes, Lisette motioned to the ambulance man to tend to the next victim. She didn't want him to share Harriet's death; didn't want to feel his comforting hand on her shoulder, didn't want to hear any soft words to ease her sorrows. Those gestures were all hollow and meaningless – she'd been through loss before, and nothing worked. Nothing! Only time healed.

'Miss Forester?' Jepson prompted.

'Sorry.'

'How do feel about what happened that day?'

She glared at him. How was she supposed to summarise that? 'I feel angry, Mr Jepson. I feel bitter. It was such a hopeless waste of innocent life. But then so was the loss of my parents. These are emotions I'm familiar with; I've had to learn to hide them, because no one else needs to share this pain. Everyone has their own burdens. Harriet was the only person who died at the scene of the bombing that day. Why?'

'You could send yourself mad thinking like that,' Jepson cautioned.

'Exactly. Which is precisely why I don't. I prefer to deny myself the opportunity to think about it.'

'I've heard similar sentiments from war veterans. It's the only way they've found to protect themselves from the relentless pain.'

He continued, 'Despite what you've seen and experienced, I'm surprised you still take the same route home, still meet people near Victoria Station . . .'

Lisette shrugged, grateful that he understood why she felt the way she did. 'Lightning never strikes twice.'

'Is the threat of potential death exciting for you?' he probed.

She'd never really considered this before. 'Not exciting, no.'

'But you clearly don't shy away from the possibility. Is that your way of coping with your parents' deaths, Harriet's senseless loss of life?'

'It's happening on both sides of the Channel, Captain Jepson. Germans, French, Poles, Russians . . . they're all dying, all young, all with lost dreams. It's not just the British.'

'Indeed,' he said softly.

'I'm not scared of death, if that's what you mean.'

'What are you scared of, Lisette?'

'Of being ordinary,' she answered.

'Oh, let me assure you that there is nothing ordinary about you.'

She looked down.

'You're not vain, but you have looks that most women would kill for. That makes you uncomfortable, but, Miss Forester, good looks are an asset. You simply have to know how and when to use them.'

'That sounds very cynical,' she said.

'Why? You have a gift for language and you also have the gift of being beautiful. Nothing to be embarrassed about. In wartime, they're both valuable. And yet you do plenty to disguise those looks.'

'These are not the times —'

'These are the very times for swagger. A bomb could drop at any time. Life is short. People are behaving recklessly, living and playing hard, because their days could be numbered. But not you. You, who have the capacity to live a wealthy life, instead work in tearooms serving people. You, with your looks and slim figure, wear loose-fitting, colourless clothes that deliberately draw little attention. And you, who could afford to live safely in a rural area, choose to live in the most dangerous place in the world at the moment . . . in London, at its very heart, where Hitler is directing his most ferocious wrath.'

'I don't want to be a coward.'

'No chance of that, I suspect.' Jepson gave a soft sigh. 'You possess all the qualities I'm looking for to be one of our special agents in France.'

Lisette stared back at him in choked disbelief. Back to France? The words were spinning in her head. Could she do it? Did she *want* to?

'I have no concerns about your fortitude.' Jepson said it so confidently that she believed him. 'Remember, we've been watching you. When the sirens go off, you're as cool as a cucumber. We've witnessed you herding others in, hurrying mothers along, picking up their children at risk to your life. You tend to the victims without batting an eyelid. And you're flirtatious when you want to be, Miss Forester.'

'Pardon me?'

'Oh, yes. Our people were around when you had no money in your purse and talked the bus conductor into letting you ride for a kiss. All the passengers clapped when you skipped off the bus a few stops later and simply blew him a kiss. Your behaviour is creative, spontaneous, impeccable and controlled. The teachers at Roedean remember you well as a plucky and demure young lady during a time of bereavement. You dealt with your burden, relying entirely on fortitude to carry you through. You think on your feet and you're a natural risk-taker. These are all admirable qualities.'

They certainly had done their homework on her.

'Tell me about Miss Atkins.'

'Pardon?'

'Tell me what you recall about the woman who showed you in today.'

Lisette looked down, frowning. 'Er, tallish. Very lovely hair – thick and dark. She wears it in a shape that complements her uniform's hat.'

'Go on.'

'Her features are angular. High cheekbones, chiselled nose and chin, quite thin lips, nicely shaped earlobes. Eyes slightly hooded but her gaze is direct, quite daunting. She has a beautiful complexion. She's brisk, a bit prickly, and gave nothing away, even though I found myself talking to fill the silence as we climbed the stairs to this room. I would trust her, though.'

He grinned. 'Your intuition serves you well – she's the most reliable person I know. Yes, that's all Vera to a tee. Well done. Now a harder one. Tell me about the woman behind the hotel counter.'

Lisette blinked, thinking hard. 'Rake-thin, but by choice, not necessity. I think she likes being very thin.'

'What makes you say that?'

'Her clothes. From what I could see, they were extremely well cut. Expensive.'

'What do you draw from this?'

'She can afford good-quality clothes, which means she can also afford good food, but her gaunt frame is what you see at first glance, rather than her beautiful grayish-green eyes.'

'Go on.'

'Er, dark hair, beginning to grey at the temples, but she wears her age elegantly and stylishly.'

'What age is she?'

'At first glance, her well-groomed appearance could fool. But she would be in her mid-forties, I suspect.'

'Jewellery?'

'Small pearl earrings, to match a string of pearls. No wedding band, as I recall, but a ring on her right hand, an emerald.' She thought she'd finished but then found herself adding, 'She had a curious attitude to me – somewhat condescending, but it didn't suit her. It felt contrived.'

'Bravo, Lisette. Bravo. All of that in a glance and far more than you noticed about Vera.'

Lisette breathed out, unsure of why she was being tested. 'I noticed more of Miss Atkins that I haven't mentioned, but I knew what you were looking for on my second attempt.'

'Well, you're good at it.'

'I'm glad I passed your test.'

'Flying colours. If you agree to this we will train you and equip you. We will ensure that you are not alone, even though it will feel as though you are. I cannot pretend that what we're proposing is not dangerous. In fact, your life will depend on the nerveless approach you take in your everyday dealings. You intimated anxiety at my proposal, Miss Forester, but I believe you are excited.'

'Surely a man would be better —'

'I know you don't believe that. Frankly, women are damn good at clandestine activity. They have a natural propensity for cunning. And I mean that with great respect. Women can juggle many tasks while remaining calm; they are generally very observant, less reckless, and their very womanliness removes a lot of immediate suspicion. What's more, Lisette, you have youth and beauty enough to distract anyone.' He held up a hand. 'Don't wince like that. These are gold, and you must use them to their full effect – just as you made use of them with your bus conductor. Your looks could save your life . . . or someone else's. They are part of your arsenal, as is your superb recall of information and your ability to gather it in a glance. Your loner qualities are another attribute, as is your preference for living dangerously. I could go on . . .'

'No need, Captain Jepson. So, I'm to become a spy in France?'

'Essentially, yes. What your actual role will be I cannot say, but that will be decided once you have completed your training.'

'All right.'

He held out his hand again. 'Is that a yes, Miss *Forestier*?' he asked in French.

Lisette smiled. '*Oui, monsieur. Absolument!*'

8

Lisette was told to return to her work while the Special Operations Executive of the War Office – or SOE, as it was known – arranged the eight weeks' leave of absence required for her training, after which they would decide whether she was made of the 'right stuff' to be sent to France as an agent.

And so the following morning she was back in her work clothes and hurrying off to her morning shift at the tearooms. Air-raid sirens at eight twenty-five in the morning sent her hurrying with dozens of others into the nearest tube station. It meant she arrived late for her shift, patrons were pushing through the door fifteen minutes later than usual and staff were dashing about still tying on aprons.

Miss Mappleton found her soon enough. 'Ah, there you are, Lisette. Did you keep your meeting with that gentleman, Mr Collins?'

'Yes, Miss Mappleton.'

'And?'

Lisette didn't think Captain Jepson would want her to share more than was absolutely necessary. 'Well, Mr Collins believes my linguistic skills might be put to better use than they are now. Of course, I told him that I liked my job at Lyons,' she said carefully.

'Mr Collins told me he was from the War Office, but he was rather evasive, I thought.'

Lisette said nothing despite the question in her superior's face.

Miss Mappleton's lips thinned. 'Am I to understand that you are leaving us?'

'From what I was told, I must undergo some training – it's probably to be a secretary, as they seem short of staff who speak other languages.' Lisette tried to sound daunted, although she felt neither.

'Well, Mr Collins did say he'd contact me again. Carry on,' Miss Mappleton said, waving a hand.

Lisette's first customer of the day was Jack, the handsome airman. He had worked out which tables she normally waited on and had seated himself directly in her path. He looked dashing in his uniform, hair still damp and combed. His wavy mop was the colour of the dark sand she'd seen once on the beach at Brighton, where the shingle ended and the waves fizzed and frothed at the shoreline. And his eyes, smiling at her, were the colour of the sea on a bright day. She could almost smell the salt, looking at that breezy smile of his, his gaze sparkling like the sun.

'Good morning, sir.'

'You do remember me, don't you, Lisette?' he asked, glancing at her name badge.

'How are you?'

'Excellent, thank you. I didn't get shot down last night, and here I am, looking at you. Does it get any more perfect?'

Lisette's smile widened. 'What can I get you today, sir?'

'Oh, call me Jack, would you? That French accent is gorgeous. I'd love to hear you say my name.'

'We are not permitted,' she said, glancing toward Miss Mappleton who had an in-built radar for waitresses flirting with customers.

'I understand. I have to follow rules in my life too. So, Lisette, I would like a pot of tea and a slice of whatever cake you recommend.'

She knew it was a ploy to keep her standing at his side but she was happy to play along. 'I think the Victoria sandwich was iced only a few hours ago. There is no cream available, but the strawberry jam and butter cream work deliciously. Perhaps one piece just won't be enough.'

He grinned. 'A slice of that, then, it shall be.'

'Is there anything else, sir?'

'Well, yes, there is actually.' He leaned forward. 'Will you let me take you out this evening?'

She straightened, casting a glance for Mappleton. 'I, er, no, I cannot do that, I'm sorry.'

'Are you seeing someone else?' he asked, crestfallen.

'No.'

'Then let me take you dancing. Please. I want to see that beautiful hair of yours falling around your shoulders. Do say yes. I'll be flying off again tomorrow evening.'

'You've asked me three times now. Don't you get tired of me turning you down?' It wasn't said unkindly.

'No,' he replied, laughing. 'Never, Lisette. I'll just keep asking the same question. I must be in love. Can't you tell?'

'But you don't know me.'

'Does it matter? We could all be dead tomorrow.' His expression became bleak. 'I'm sorry, I'm making you uncomfortable. Let me take you out. Make me a very happy pilot.' He looked over her shoulder. 'Ah, saved by the kettle. You'd better get that cup of tea, because here comes the boss.'

Lisette returned a few minutes later with his tea and his slice of cake, noticing his whole mood had changed. He looked glum, his shoulders slumped, and it was as if he was lost. He was right, she thought, as she approached with his order. What was there to lose, in these strange times they were living through?

'I'm assured the cake is delicious,' she said with a wide smile.

'Thank you,' he replied.

'I'm sorry if I appear rude,' she began.

'No . . . please don't apologise. I've been an ass. I promise not to trouble you further.'

'That's a pity. I was going to say that while I can't go out tonight, if you come by later this week, I promise you I'll say yes.'

He opened his mouth in surprise. 'Really?'

She laughed. 'Yes, *bien sûr*,' she said, ladling on the accent as thickly as she could.

He grinned. 'You've made my day. I'll see you Thursday?'

'*A bientôt*, Jack,' she said, and he put his hand on his heart as though the very words lifted his spirits. She was surprised by how light her own heart felt. How long had it been since she'd been kissed? Too long.

The following day Mr Collins paid a visit to Lyons Corner House, and afterwards Lisette was called into Miss Mappleton's office. She learned that her last day at Lyons would be Friday, after which she was joining SOE for eight weeks of training, beginning in Surrey. She was to pack lightly, and a staff member would pick her up from her flat at nine in the morning on Saturday.

The week dragged while her excitement level escalated, and this was equally spiced by the knowledge that she was going out dancing with her airman on Thursday evening. She'd packed a small tapestry holdall by Wednesday. It was ready by the door for Saturday. Meanwhile, work continued as it always had, despite the new life that was beckoning.

On Thursday morning Lisette arrived at work and changed into her uniform, carefully hanging up the good dress she'd worn in readiness for the evening. She'd thought about throwing in a pair of heeled shoes but it was a lot to carry, and clearly her pilot liked her in her plain garb. It seemed fitting that she would go out tonight with Jack, almost as a celebration, before embarking on her new life. She had no intention of failing her training and being deemed unsuitable as an agent.

She drifted out into the tearooms as the doors were being opened and a beautiful array of cakes were being placed behind the glass counter. London was mercifully quiet this morning, free of the dreaded noise of sirens.

Jack was not with the first flush of patrons, although the floor was busy enough that she didn't dwell on his absence. At just a few minutes past eleven, she saw a flash of blue uniform and smiled, only to realise it wasn't Jack but another man who was watching her intently. She dutifully approached his table.

'Hello,' she said. 'You're one of Jack's friends, aren't you? I recognise you.'

He nodded and gave her a tight smile that didn't quite achieve the warmth he'd obviously intended. 'Yes, that's right. I'm Flight Lieutenant Andrew Phelps,' he said, holding out a hand. 'Jack talked so much about you; I feel as though I know you.'

Lisette shook her head. 'He hardly knows me,' she hastily said, feeling a blush rise.

'He was in love with you,' Phelps said, then his expression clouded angrily. 'I'm sorry. Forgive me for saying that.'

Lisette didn't know what to say – the man looked so forlorn. 'Can I get you some tea?'

'Er, no, actually.' He licked his lips. 'I came simply to tell you something.'

She waited. 'About me meeting Jack, do you mean? It's all right if he can't —'

'Listen, there's no easy way to say it. Jack was shot down yesterday over Germany.'

Shot down. She had to repeat it to herself to be sure of what she'd just heard. She swallowed. 'Did he bail out?' Was that the right expression? She was already imagining him as a POW in Germany. It could be worse.

Phelps was shaking his head. 'It was a big raid, more than sixty bombers. Jack and I are Pathfinders. We fly slightly ahead of the Lancasters and light up the targets with flares. You've probably seen footage on the Pathé News.'

'Yes,' she agreed, her thoughts winging to that handsome young man with his sunny smile and eyes like the sea. 'You're all so brave,' she added softly.

'There was lots of flak. His Mosquito took a direct hit. I saw it explode into flames and fall out of the sky. There were no parachutes to be seen. Jack didn't have a chance.'

Lisette gave a small gasp. Her legs felt like jelly but they held. She could hear a buzzing sound in her ears. The sensations were familiar; she'd experienced this sort of news before.

'He was a good man . . . the best,' the flight lieutenant said, then he gave a small, sad smile. 'Very dangerous in these times to make friends with anyone.'

For some bizarre reason, Captain Jepson came to Lisette's mind and she remembered that SOE was interested not just in her linguistic skills but in her ability to stay calm, to think on her feet. She took a steadying breath. 'I'm so sorry for you.'

He nodded, then stood abruptly. 'I wanted you to know. He's been talking about tonight for days and he's been talking about you for weeks . . . I didn't want you thinking badly of him.'

'I wouldn't. Andrew, I didn't even know his full name.'

'Flight Lieutenant Jack Caddy. We'll all miss him.' He shrugged. 'Goodbye.'

'Thank you for coming to see me,' Lisette replied, regaining control of her breathing, feeling her legs steadier. 'Take care of yourself.' Such empty words; she hated herself for uttering them.

Lisette's heart seemed to harden and she added Jack to the list of her victims. Another person who loved her and had to die because of it. She left the floor, muttering that she wasn't feeling well. She took off her apron and uniform, hung it on the hook and changed back into her day clothes. Miss Mappleton would be looking for her, but she no longer cared.

She deeply regretted not saying yes to Jack earlier. Now he was dead, and a ripple of anger erupted deep inside her. Everyone she allowed into her life was taken from her. Well, she would harden her heart and embrace her new role. She would play her part in combatting the enemy who was stealing the lives of her generation.

Lisette Forester walked out of the back door of the Lyons Corner House and through Trafalgar Square, pigeons flapping around her; she caught sight of Phelps, sitting alone, a flock of birds almost settling on him as he fed them with a packet of crumbs. He would likely be back in the air tomorrow, flying another raid. With that in mind, she hurried on, hoping he hadn't spotted her.

She left the Lyons Corner House behind and knew she would never return. A new and even lonelier path beckoned, and she was all but running towards it.

9

Lisette's life was turned on its head. One day she was a waitress wearing a starched apron, the next she was commissioned into the Women's Auxiliary Air Force and smartly attired in black lace-up shoes, grey stockings, a blue-grey skirt, matching belted tunic and peaked cap. She'd been issued with an overcoat, set of underwear and the obligatory gas mask. She'd left behind Captain Jepson and had passed through a series of country houses where she had tackled her training with great verve. She had an impressive collection of bruises and a lightly sprained ankle to prove it.

Wanborough Manor near Guildford was where it began: a glorious, rambling old country house that dated back to Elizabethan times. Here the potential spies were put through their paces and assessed for the next stages of their training, which would qualify them as genuine agents to be deployed overseas. They ranged in age from late teens to middle age and hailed from a bewildering array of backgrounds, careers and skills, although most were civilians. SOE believed civilian status offered a small measure of protection if the spy were captured. Passing through these doors had been everyone from a bus owner to a barrister. There had even been an acrobat! Men and women trained side by side.

At Wanborough only French was spoken. It mattered little to Lisette, but she was impressed at how well the other people she trained with spoke her language. She could tell, however, which region their teachers had hailed from, and regularly helped to correct minor errors in colloquialism.

Discipline was not overly strict, with the emphasis on strong social interaction, and for good reason. Trainees were encouraged to relax, and were even offered alcohol to test their resolve. Women were employed to flirt with trainees over drinks to discover how much information they could extract from them. The more rigorous training was saved for later, once Special Ops knew which of the recruits had the ideal qualities. Even so, the aspiring agents were not entirely spared the physical workouts. Lisette was not the strongest performer, but she was hardly Wanborough's weakest. In fact, she surprised herself with her previously untapped stamina.

She would have liked to spend a month training at Wanborough but the war wouldn't wait. Within ten days she was on her way to the beautiful west coast of Scotland. The rugged country surrounding the region was the ideal location for commando-style instruction. She noticed that there were far fewer recruits for this part of the training, and was thrilled that she'd been considered tough enough for the hardest physical challenges. She learned how to scale cliffs, how to navigate for hours across impossible terrain until her legs were burning with fatigue, how to move through wooded areas silently, even how to kill game to eat. She didn't want to make friends, because she knew they would be scattered far and wide once the training was complete. However, as one of just five it was difficult to remain entirely separate. The camaraderie in their quintet was bright, and this helped considerably during the most arduous tests as they urged each other to carry on.

It was exhausting, physically and mentally, but it was all about survival. Time and again the trainers pushed the group to what Lisette felt was breaking point – and then past it. She endured it all, despite many occasions when collapsing and weeping felt very tempting.

The one thing Lisette really didn't enjoy learning was killing, fieldcraft and raid tactics. Her trainer – a relentless Scot who never broke a smile and liked nothing more than to yell at his recruits – never gave them his name. 'Call me Sir,' was his only suggestion. It was at this point that Lisette came unstuck. She had to prove that she could kill a Nazi sentry – in reality, another recruit – silently with her F-S double-edged fighting knife. Being slight in frame, she simply wasn't tall enough to effectively cut his throat.

'I can't reach!' she moaned when the sentry had swatted her off like a fly for the dozenth time.

'What do you think Jerry's going to do when you mince up and bleat like a lost lamb? He's the one who is going to be slitting your throat, Forester!' Sir made a slashing motion in the air as he said it. 'Worse, he'll just haul your scrawny self off to the Gestapo or perhaps those lovely fellows in the SS for some Nazi torture. Jerry gets very creative, you know. I've heard with women spies they like to —'

'Sir!' one of the others admonished. His name was Paul. Lisette hadn't had much to do with him but rumour had it he worked in a bank.

'What, Lucas?'

'You don't have to talk to her like that,' Paul said, wiping his glasses that had misted in the rain.

'I'll talk to her any way I please,' Sir said, stabbing a finger just millimetres from Paul's chest. Lisette noticed, though, that Sir never touched any of them, other than to haul them over the top of a cliff or reposition their arms when holding a gun or blade. Otherwise he relied on his tongue to do all the injury. It was a fine weapon.

'Paul!' Lisette said, cutting him an angry glare. 'Leave it.' She turned to her torturer. 'Sir, I can do this.'

'You'd want to, Forester, or you're not going anywhere. Now, are you going to kill this man or not?'

'I am, Sir.'

'Silently, Forester,' he warned, flicking a hand at her, and she moved back to the hiding spot behind the tree from where she was supposed to attack.

Sir had taught them a method to use that he said was near failsafe. But on this last try, Lisette decided she'd attempt a new approach. Instead of stealth, she ran at the sentry and leapt onto his back, covering his mouth, exposing his neck and opening his jugular. Of course it all had to be done in a couple of heartbeats and with such fluidity that the sentry barely registered her arrival. Sir actually laughed at the sentry, who was no longer grinning but rubbing his neck.

'All right, Forester. That was messy, but quick. I'll give you that.'

'You told us to get creative, Sir.'

'I did,' he replied, nodding.

'Do I pass?'

He said nothing, but Lisette earned a wink from each of the men in her group. Her fellow female trainee – a towering farmer – clapped her on the back and whispered, 'Well done.'

And so it went, hours and hours of training that were devoted simply to killing the enemy. By the end of the first week Lisette was privately unhappy that she now had command of myriad ways to kill, both with her bare hands and a variety of weapons, from the obvious to the makeshift. She performed surprisingly well in handling explosives, but admitted that she hoped she would not be faced with having to blow up things. Lisette could only imagine the black mark against her name for such a comment.

Over the space of a second week, while the sun shone, she was holed up indoors at Thame Park in Oxfordshire doing a crash course in signal training. It was really down to business now, and she was a sponge for all the information hurled at her in such huge quantities. It was a relief to take a break from the physical activity, but her greatest challenge was still ahead of her, as she confronted parachute training. Lisette was the first to do it, and was getting the distinct impression she was being rushed through it all. Did they have something in mind for her already?

She found herself at Dunham House in Cheshire for the parachute training. Here, all manner of equipment was available to toughen recruits and train them to make a safe exit from an aircraft at night and to land, silently, avoiding injury by falling and rolling correctly in all-weather conditions. An old fuselage was on hand to assist recruits; ropes and swings helped in training for correct technique. Lisette could sense that one of the wing commanders handling the training didn't think she had it in her. But that only goaded her into volunteering first in her group. It was her enthusiasm and determination to prove him wrong that led to her sprained ankle, but while she grimaced under the agony, she never let on just how much it hurt. Binding her leg tightly, she made three more jumps from the aircraft – never once baulking – and a final training jump – this from a balloon, at night.

In the darkness, falling like a stone from the sky and waiting for her parachute to open, Lisette fancied that she felt close to her parents. She could almost hear her father, speaking in German, encouraging her. His gentle, professorial ways, his adoration of her elfin and beautiful Parisian-born mother, and his love of art, history and language, meant that he didn't fit the stereotypical boisterous, outdoorsy, beer-swilling German at all.

And if Maximilian was all sensitivity, her mother, Sylvie, was all laughter. In fact, Lisette was sure that her father, who was quiet and studious, drew life from Sylvie's bright flame. It was Sylvie who had been behind the wheel of the car when they died. Lisette knew her parents had been out, perhaps a little tight on champagne as they bid farewell to their beloved France, but she was glad they had died together. Either would be useless without the other. Her parents had been in love – truly in love – and she regretted deeply that she was no longer able to watch them together as they laughed, teased and touched each other with those surreptitious signs of affection – a small smile across the room, a hand on a shoulder briefly, the way her father would hug her mother while Sylvie was cooking. Lisette missed burying herself in the cocoon of her parents' love.

Lisette was selected for additional training in night-landing grounds, while others went off to learn about radio messaging or couriering. The whirlwind of activity continued, and nowhere was the training more important than in personal security and clandestine living. She was given a week's training in how to live within a busy neighbourhood – a nosy one, too – and do her best to disappear. Everything from how she spoke to how she dressed or how often she did her grocery shopping was discussed and rehearsed. The idea was to integrate quickly and seamlessly by being ordinary in every way possible.

Lisette already had valuable experience in living frugally, quietly and alone. She'd left a sizeable chunk of her parents' money in France, and her lawyers in Britain had sold the family home and put everything into a trust account. The French monies had been transferred into a similar account in France in her birth name of Lisette Foerstner. She hadn't touched a centime of either.

And still, despite all these natural advantages to help her as a British agent in France, the day-to-day living would be challenging. It was one thing to be French, sound French, even act French; it was quite another to know how to live in France and not be picked as an impostor, especially in a country now riddled with informers, collaborators and generally fearful people. Lisette reminded herself that although it had only been seven years since she'd left France, those were important years through her teens, when she'd let go of being French in order to fit in. British boarding school was hard enough, but to be European, the most important favour one could do oneself was to conform, not complain, not mention the bland, stodgy food or the curiously prudish attitudes.

In the dining room at Dunham Hall Lisette looked at her breakfast plate and smiled at the two slices of toast, expertly spread with the thinnest of smears of black, gluey Marmite. When she had first been presented with the squat black jar with its bright red-and-yellow label, she hadn't known what to do with it. The other girls at her boarding school had clearly revelled in her bewilderment.

'It's delicious. Try it,' her closest friend had suggested.

Lisette knifed some onto a slice of toast as someone had yelled, 'Not so thick!'

It looked terrible and to Lisette it tasted worse. 'Ugh!' she said, wincing.

'You'll get used to it.'

And she had. Leaving behind her preference for sweet bread and jam for breakfast with a big bowl of coffee, she learned how to eat porridge that nearly made her sick, drink pots of tea, and she persisted with Marmite until she acquired the taste and could honestly say she enjoyed it.

Now she had to reverse that. In fact, she mustn't even think of Marmite or porridge again . . . and especially not tea. She had to think like a Frenchwoman again.

Lisette was finally ready to complete the most important aspect of her training – security – and was to be sent on a bogus mission that stringently tested her readiness to go into the field. Lisette's first task was to find her way across just under 240 kilometres from Lincoln to London without using public transport. Once in central London her second task was to plant a fake bomb at one of three designated railway stations that, if it were real, would have the potential to seriously disrupt transportation.

Getting to London wasn't hard. Lisette was able to cadge rides from drivers, including one lorry-load of soldiers on their way south for dispatch to the Front. She got as far as the outskirts of London with the men, where they dropped her off in Twickenham. Here she paid far more than she should have to buy a passing youth's bike; it carried her the fourteen kilometres into London with a small cloth bag tied to the back.

Lisette was required to rent a room in a hotel; she made sure it was not so cheap that she would stand out but not too glamorous that undue attention would be paid to her. She'd chosen Victoria Station as her target because she knew its layout well so the nearby Imperial guesthouse was precisely the right place for her stay. Travellers stayed at the Imperial if they were leaving on an early train or arriving on a late one. It saw a multitude of people, from all walks of life, pass through its revolving doors, and a single woman traveller would likely go unnoticed by the weary concierge.

Lisette would pose as Sarah Baudrier, a writer compiling interviews with everyday Londoners as the basis of a series of radio plays for the BBC. Harriet had worked at the BBC and Lisette still had her old BBC pass. With some clever adjustment she'd managed to make it look as though it were hers. She hoped it would gain her a bit more freedom around the security-conscious Victoria Station. It was only when she arrived at the station's forecourt, however, still bearing the scars of its bombing, that a whole new idea struck Lisette. She'd been standing near the telephone box – as though waiting for someone – using the time to examine her surroundings and consider the practical aspects of her plan, when she'd overheard one of the station's staff talking to a newspaper seller. Apparently there were going to be long delays to all trains in and out of the station.

'Falling leaves on track, eh?' the newspaper seller had said mischievously as he'd handed a newspaper over.

'If only,' the staff member replied. 'No, the whole bloody signalling system's down at Clapham Junction. Nothing gets in or out until that's fixed.'

And as the man in uniform turned away, tucked his newspaper under an arm and flicked his cigarette, her new plan had slammed into place. Why on earth was she dabbling with a single track? If she laid her bomb at Clapham Junction's signal box she could theoretically bring much of the rail network – heading into and out of the south coast, east and west – to a complete standstill. It would cause chaos.

The idea fizzed like champagne in her mind, making her feel dizzy with excitement. It was so obvious and yet she'd been too focused on the wording of the task – *choose one of three railway stations* – that she had restricted her thinking. Wasn't this what the trainers had tried to instill in her during explosives training? Think big! they'd stressed. Be creative! Look beyond the obvious!

The trainers had constantly reinforced to her that agents should seek ways to maximise the effect of their explosives. Make it count! Ensure it doesn't just disrupt, but paralyses! These were all the catchphrases drummed into her while she learned to use dynamite, set fuses and work with the new plastic explosives.

The plan began to shape. She could change her cover to someone from British Rail. She didn't have to be in uniform. She could be an external specialist. But what? Lisette bought herself a small cake from a nearby café and carried it into the station proper. She walked as far down one of the platforms as she could and found a bench while she thought out a new plan of attack. Pigeons cooed above her in the lacy iron fretwork of the roof, their anxious flapping reminding her that precious time was ticking away. They'd given her three days to complete her task. It was already day two, and after eleven a.m.

The first three tracks of the station were empty and sunlight suddenly filled the space as clouds parted. In spite of herself, she smiled; the sunshine made such a difference to the mood of the British. They had a preoccupation with the weather, always pining for summer, filling entire conversations with chat about an inclement day.

Her attention was caught by movement on the tracks. She watched as a rat, then another, hopped confidently up and down the tracks. Her interest was piqued. What if she posed as a consultant writing a report on the problems of rats chewing exposed electrical wiring, threatening the workings of the signals at Clapham Junction? She could say she was a representative of the Department of Health, or better still, of British Rail, just needing to see the signals room to assess the level of damage. If she could get that close, she could lay her fake bomb.

She'd heard of successful missions being achieved on far less. But time was her enemy. Once again she turned to poor Harriet. Her friend had had a special British Rail season ticket that allowed her free journeys, thanks to her father's job. All of Harriet's paperwork was still in the flat at Eccleston Bridge Road. If Lisette could play around with that ticket, she might just be able to pull it off.

She flung the rest of her cake towards the rats – they deserved it – and ran to the flat. Her heart hammering with terror as much as excited anticipation, she reminded herself that perhaps ninety per cent of a successful mission was confidence. Her hands shaking, she found what she was looking for, and rushed back to the hotel. She did what every good Britisher would do in times of extreme anxiety and prepared a pot of tea. There was something lovely about the routine activity of putting the kettle on, warming the pot, spooning in the tea leaves, hearing the gurgle of boiled water as she poured it into the pot, and then the solitude of three minutes while the leaves steeped. Then there was the amber liquid itself, straining it before adding sugar and milk, and stirring. This made the process at least ten minutes of quiet ritual. By the end of it, staring at her steaming cup of tea, with no intention of drinking it, Lisette was heartened to realise that her pulse had definitely slowed. She was still nervous but she felt she had wrestled back under her control any potential to panic. Lisette recalled the training mantra: act out your part. Believe fully in your role. Look people directly in the eye. Speak briskly and with the courage to challenge anyone with assurance and a steady voice. Commit to it and once you do, don't look back.

She could do it.

No. She *would* do it! Lisette walked out of the hotel with fresh purpose and searched for a bus that would get her to within striking range of Clapham Junction.

10

Maurice Buckmaster sat behind his desk at Baker Street and sighed softly as he regarded the file before him. He felt the full weight of his role as head of the Special Operation Executive's French Section settle uncomfortably on his shoulders. Staring out from the file was a photograph of a young woman whose serious expression did nothing to disguise her brunette beauty. Most of the recruits had at least given some semblance of a smile in their file photos, but not this one. Her gaze seemed to look too deeply, and he found her stare vaguely unnerving.

It was as though she was challenging him, daring him to say yes to a ridiculously dangerous mission – for anyone, let alone a slip of a girl . . . a former waitress. He reminded himself that all his female agents were formidable, regardless of their backgrounds. He had to take his hat off to Jepson. The man certainly had a knack for picking out women with extraordinary reserves of courage and creativity. Most managed to stay one step ahead of the Gestapo, informants, French militia, collaborators, hunger, injury, accidents, disease.

He drew a deep silent breath. Could he send this elfin creature into the loneliest, most audacious mission SOE had dreamed up thus far?

She'd carried out her trial mission with such dash and daring that he and Vera were still a little lost for words. They'd designed the test to ensure she moved around a city with ease using her wits and stamina. They had wanted her to disrupt railway security on one of the tracks, but Lisette Forester had tackled the entire signal station at Clapham Junction – far more audacious, but infinitely more effective. It had the potential to create widespread chaos across the whole southern rail network.

Lisette had performed her role brilliantly. She had smooth-talked the Clapham Junction station manager into allowing her onto the tracks, where she spent the best part of two hours going through the motions of checking wiring before moving closer to the signals box. By then, her minders had lost interest in her and she was able to lay her fake package. No damage was noted, she had assured the staff, and thanked them for their cooperation. She had left Battersea on foot, crossed the river and melted away into the hustle and bustle of Greater London without a hiccup. Her suitability as an agent could not be denied.

Her daring and fortitude made Buckmaster almost envious. There were so many times when he wished he could return to active service, but it was forbidden. Since the spring of 1941, after retreating with his unit to Dunkirk, he'd been posted back to Britain and absorbed into F-Section of SOE, charged with building an organisation that would carry out acts of sabotage, work closely with the growing French Resistance movement, and create a vital information network that would allow clandestine communication between London and France. His experience qualified him well, but nothing could have prepared him to send dozens of brave individuals to work essentially alone and undercover, knowing that half would likely never return.

And this year had been vicious for SOE. For every good piece of information collected, it felt as though there was even more bad news. They had been bleeding agents, with a devastating number of brave men and women sold out by double-crossers or simply discovered by Abwehr and Gestapo work. Those agents – his people, his responsibility – were rotting in prisons being tortured, starved or otherwise helped along to difficult deaths. And he thought of the German generals, taken prisoner, during the course of the war and living a luxurious life at Trent Park in England – everything provided: gracious surrounds, waiting staff, decent food . . . hot tea even. He glanced at the cup that Vera Atkins had placed nearby.

It was that same imprisoned group of generals that had brought about this meeting. He had to know more before he could commit to this mission. It was so vague, so dependent on so many others – if he signed off on this plan, the beautiful woman with the sorrowful gaze would have few supporters, if any, to count upon.

He sat back, regarding the other men in his office; Boddington must have sensed his unease because he noticed his deputy push his round glasses higher onto the bridge of his nose and clear his throat as he glanced at Captain Jepson.

'She's very young for such a mature task,' Boddington remarked.

It was everyone's unspoken thought.

'Most of the female operatives are young,' Jepson said. 'But you can't deny that she's hard to ignore. We're relying on this, and she has what it takes to charm, I can assure you. She would make a fine operative. Mentally she's one of the strongest recruits I've put forward, and the trainers attest to her invulnerability to strenuous activities and pain. But the mission you have in mind for her makes use of few of these new skills. What you need is what Lark brought to us from day one, and it's a whole new dimension to what most of our agents offer.'

'Her French nature,' Buckmaster finished.

'Yes, sir,' Jepson agreed. 'She spent the first seventeen years of her life in France. What can I say? She's French to her core, even though she does her best to hide it.'

Buckmaster nodded. 'And now you're going to tell me that it's actually her German nature that makes her more valuable than any other agent.' He didn't successfully mask his sarcasm.

Jepson gave a brief dry smile. 'No, Colonel. I'm going to tell you that it's her half-German parentage, her German birth certificate and her brilliant fluency with the language that makes this whole mad plan sound . . . well, frankly feasible.'

'We couldn't risk anyone else in such a situation,' Boddington concurred.

'She can rely wholly on a background of truth,' Jepson pressed. 'I'm not supporting the mission, sir. I'll leave that to Bourne-Patterson to work out.' He glanced over at the silent Head of Planning. 'But I think this is a unique opportunity. She has the potential to get right under the skin of our enemy.'

'Thank you, Captain Jepson. We'll take it from here.'

'Sir,' Jepson said, standing and nodding at Boddington and Bourne-Patterson. He looked to Buckmaster and hesitated, as though he wanted to add something, but then turned and left the room.

Buckmaster said nothing for a few moments, steepling his fingers and considering what he'd heard. Then he looked at Boddington. 'So, give me a summary of what we know.'

Boddington referred to his notes. 'The recordings from Trent Park make interesting listening – the German generals are surprisingly candid in their remarks. Clearly it hasn't occurred to them that we might be listening to their every word. A few weeks ago talk of this fellow Markus Kilian began. The details are sketchy, sir, but his father was a Prussian war hero. He comes from a wealthy, admired family in Bavaria. Kilian is a thoroughbred and a blue blood.'

'Age?' Buckmaster asked.

Boddington flicked over a page. 'Can't be sure, sir, but we think early forties – young for a colonel.'

'I don't understand why this fellow is important,' Buckmaster said. 'Bring me up to speed.'

'From what we can tell, Colonel Kilian is something of a success story in the Wehrmacht, having caught the attention of Hitler.'

'Probably because he represents everything Hitler isn't,' Buckmaster said wryly.

'Quite,' Boddington agreed. 'Kilian's early mentor was von Tresckow. He came from a similar background, and served under him – it's how Kilian came to the direct notice of Hitler. We've gathered that Kilian had deep misgivings about waging war, believing initially that Germany could never prevail, especially if the Americans were persuaded to join the Allies. We know now that von Choltitz went so far as to tip off the political resisters in Germany about the sweep into France, but what we didn't know until recently was that it was very likely Kilian who provided the link between von Choltitz and the underground. Kilian, despite his Establishment background, has a way about him, sir.'

'A way about him?'

'Yes, sir. An easy manner with the common man. His command showed great success, even when other units began to fail against the Red Army.'

'And so now you're going to tell me how this gallant, lofty war hero of the German Wehrmacht has fallen from grace?'

'Indeed, sir. He was one of the few who defied the Commissar Order from Hitler last year, which proclaimed that any government officials identified within the captured Red Army would be instantly shot. This, of course, defied POW protocol, but most followed because they didn't want accusations of treason levelled at them. A few, like von Tresckow and Kilian, refused.' Boddington looked up from his notes. 'It seems Kilian was defiant in other ways too. For instance, he point-blank refused to order his men to execute women and children in any context. He had heavyweight protection obviously, in the likes of von Tresckow, Canaris, even von Choltitz. However, that defiance earned him a call back to Germany and he was demoted to a desk position, working within the Abwehr. For an admired soldier like Kilian, it must have been a blow.'

Boddington sighed. 'Anyway, he's been working as part of the intelligence-gathering machine – damn good at it too, by all accounts – but seemingly rotting in an outpost far from Berlin and the action —'

'All right,' Buckmaster said, placing his hands either side of Lark's photograph. 'How is it that he comes to fall beneath the gaze of F-Section?'

'Well, sir,' Boddington said. "Kilian has been brought under the wing of Rear Admiral Canaris, who we now know is privately appalled by the Nazi regime and its tactics. Even our own division has benefitted from some of the information he has permitted to "let slip" into political networks that resist the German war machine.'

'So Kilian has found another kindred spirit, you're saying?'

'Well, there are many, of course, who privately believe that Hitler is marching Germany to a place that many, certainly many rational men, are not willing to go. While Kilian is not against Germany's war effort – he's a loyal soldier – we believe he is very much averse to the Nazi cause and might be one of those who would help to bring it down from within.'

Buckmaster remembered his eleven o'clock appointment. He had ten minutes up his sleeve. 'Canaris is taking Kilian out of exile in Germany and into Paris – we know this for sure?'

'Our agent, Prosper, in Paris has confirmed this, sir.'

Buckmaster turned to Bourne-Patterson, the architect of this bold plan. 'So we're going to throw this young woman into the path of Kilian . . . and what? See what happens?'

The head of planning blinked. 'It's audacious and certainly unlike our traditional undercover operations, but it has to be worth a try. This man, if all we understand is correct, will be bristling with resentment. Plus Paris is hardly a hotbed of combat, so he's going to have time on his hands. And he's single.' Bourne-Patterson shrugged with a smile. 'Perhaps an upfront yet *softer* approach will give us access to Canaris, von Tresckow . . .perhaps even into the Gestapo through the Abwehr. We may be able to assist with an assassination of Hitler if it comes to it. Lark's role will be to get close enough to the architects to keep us briefed, or if all goes exceptionally well, she may even act as a conduit between Berlin and London.'

'If, if, if . . .' Buckmaster said. No one replied. 'Boddington?'

'I agree with Captain Jepson. Lark is German but she is also French, and she has the best cover of all of our agents. All we can do is put her into a situation where she can learn.'

'Who is going to support her? Who on earth can stay close enough to get the information relayed? Please don't tell me we're now expecting her to smuggle in a wireless to the French headquarters of the German Reich!'

Bourne-Patterson gave a tight smile that bore no amusement. 'No, sir. But Roger's come up with a couple of ideas.'

Roger. Codename for Francis Cammaerts, one of their most successful agents, who had created a formidable circuit of resistance fighters in the south of France from Grenoble to Nice. Roger had set up a highly active network of resisters known as Jockey, and London listened when Roger offered ideas.

Buckmaster's gaze narrowed.

'The first plan is for Lark to make use of Prosper's wireless operator. It's risky but it could work. The second idea involves one of the maquisards we know as Faucille. He would escort Lark from the south, which gives her a better shot at quietly entering Paris and integrating.'

'Ah yes,' Buckmaster replied. Faucille – the Sickle. He'd heard only good things about the fearless French resister.

'He's a tough nut by all accounts,' Bourne-Patterson contin-ued, 'but he's brilliant at what he does. Very high risk-taker, yet he minimises potential repercussions. He would be the best choice for our girl. But will he agree? It would mean him leaving the south and heading north with her.'

Buckmaster looked doubtful. 'He's one of the best smugglers in the Resistance, so if anyone can get Lark from south to north, he can. Roger is best placed to make that all happen. Is he ready to meet Lark?' Already it sounded like the mission would go ahead.

'Yes, sir. Roger's in the Luberon area. It will have to be a spe-cial drop into Provence. She'll leave in three days. Calm weather is forecast and it's full moon, so the conditions are perfect. Roger will meet her the following evening and we anticipate Faucille will take her from there. She'll link up with Prosper near Paris. We then have to wait until she can work out a way to make contact with Kilian.'

'And even then it's in the lap of the gods,' Buckmaster finished. He took a breath, held it, looked around at his colleagues' expect-ant expressions, checked his watch and gave a sigh. 'I agree. We have to try. Our little Lark flies the nest at the end of the week. Make sure she has the opportunity to see her folks in Farnborough too,' he added. 'Insist on it.'

Lisette warmed her fingers around the porcelain cup filled with rich, sweetened milky coffee. Her grandmother – who insisted upon being called Granny – was chattering away: Lisette looked too thin, she shouldn't live alone, she wasn't dressed warmly enough for this miserable drizzly weather that England did so well.

Lisette smiled and kissed her cheek. 'But I have you to spoil me.'

'We're in Farnborough now, in case neither of you has noticed,' Grandad grumbled from the small kitchen table where he sat dunking a digestive biscuit into his tea. He'd married his sweetheart when they were both twenty, and she had been working in England as a French governess for a wealthy family. Granny had embraced the English way of life quickly. Now she was, at times, more British than her husband, Lisette often thought; she'd even grown to love tea.

'In English, please,' he admonished.

They were in the kitchen of her grandparents' small but picturesque cottage in Hampshire, and she felt the memories beginning to crowd in. It was in this room, leaning just as she was now against the sink, that the news of her parents' accident had been delivered. She'd been spending the weekend with Granny and Grandad and they'd all got up very early for a picnic at nearby Frencham Pond. They were sipping their hot beverages at the crack of dawn while her grandfather was telling one of the many amusing stories of his childhood. His humour was dry, and a lot of the time her grandmother missed the fun of the tale.

As a couple they nagged and harried each other constantly, but they were useless without each other. If her granny was absent for more than ten minutes, Grandad would go hunting for her, while her granny never made any decision without running it by him. They'd been married before either turned twenty-one. They were such opposites, from the way they dressed – Granny was still extremely stylish – to their taste in music and food. Her grandfather was still trying to teach his wife the rules of cricket and how to say sorry even if someone else trod on one's toe. They had been happily bickering for nearly sixty love-filled years.

Lying in her tiny attic bedroom Lisette would hear them talking quietly, often late into the night, and she would revel in the deep rumble of her grandfather's laughter and the sweet giggles of her granny. She was convinced their sparring was all for show, and wondered whether she'd ever find someone she could spend a lifetime with.

But there was no laughter the morning when the police arrived at the cottage. At nearly eighteen, Lisette had been old enough to hear the news rather than be shielded from it, as was her granny's natural instinct.

Her grandfather had answered the door, still in his pyjamas and dressing-gown, and invited the inspector and his uniformed offsider into the house, leading them through to the kitchen. Before the inspector had even opened his mouth, Lisette and her grandmother had reached for each other. Only bad news came at this time of the morning, when people were still rubbing the sleep from their eyes.

And it was the worst sort of news.

Even now, years on, looking at her grandmother smiling as she prepared their lunch, she could recall Granny's wail of disbelief at their tidings and the stream of despair in French. Lisette could even conjure the feeling of how her grandparents had put their arms around her, and the three of them had stood, locked in a forlorn embrace of disbelief, as the policemen had cleared their throats and haltingly explained the news of her parents' car crash.

Details were still incomplete, as it had only been hours since the accident, but none of them had wanted to know more. The questions and soul searching, the anger and despair . . . that all came later. Granny and Grandad had never quite been the same. Their only child was gone, Sylvie's precious existence winked out just as they were to be reunited as a family. Granny dipped into a melancholy that was close to madness for a few months; meanwhile her grandfather had used routine to keep his emotions anchored. He'd gardened and cooked, tidied and stepped out for a few provisions each day, avoiding others as best he could, and he had done his best to move on for his 'two girls', as he called them. Lisette had taken a month's compassionate leave from school and during this time her grandfather's hair had turned silver-white.

They'd all helped each other through those daunting weeks of black sorrow, and while Lisette realised none of them would ever be the same, they were now eight years on and a measure of jollity and acceptance had crept back into their lives. Now they could talk – even laugh – about her parents without tearing up.

And so it was with the deepest of regret that Lisette was now in the midst of bringing fresh pain to her grandparents.

'Why can't you tell us?' her grandfather demanded, sounding anguished.

'I'm working for the War Office. They're all crazy about secrecy. I've signed papers. They could toss me into prison if I break my agreement.'

He gave a fresh growl of disgust accompanied by a sneer. 'They think we might tell the Nazis, I suppose.'

She sighed. 'No, Grandad. No one speaks about their work. It's a general precaution that all undertake. It's not personal.'

'And you're going away, you say?' Granny said, her French accent more pronounced when she was upset.

'Scotland's not that far,' Lisette said, fashioning her lie.

'Why Scotland?' her grandad asked, draining his mug of tea.

'There's a lot of work that goes on in far-flung parts of Britain that most of us don't know about. Including me. I don't know what my role is to be yet, but they trained me in all sorts of activities. I think I'll be doing some wireless operation. I was good at that,' she said.

'John,' Granny admonished, although it sounded more like the French name Jean. 'Be happy she's out of London and away from the bombings.' She reached up and touched Lisette's cheek. 'I'm glad you're going away, my darling, and that you will be safe.'

Lisette smiled weakly. The coffee soured at the back of her throat. If only they knew the truth.

'I suppose that is a mercy,' he replied. 'Well, you can bring me back a lovely old malt Scotch when you get leave.'

Lisette nodded, hating herself. 'Of course. Write down the name and I'll hunt it out for you.'

Granny took her empty cup from her. 'Come, darling. I've found some of your mother's clothes and want you to help me go through them.'

Lisette frowned.

'Don't pull that face. You'll get wrinkles. Come on, your grandfather got an old trunk down from the loft. It's full of teenage diaries and old photos, some of Sylvie's dolls and childhood things. You'll enjoy them. I'd forgotten we had it all.'

Lisette glanced at her watch. 'I'm leaving on the 4.09.'

'Plenty of time,' Granny said.

The precious hours flew by and suddenly Lisette was back on the platform of Farnborough station, Grandad pushing a bar of chocolate into her hands. He also handed her an envelope. 'That's for the Scotch,' he said, with a soft shrug. 'If you can find it, of course.'

She took the envelope, hoping he didn't see her shame.

'Many stops to Waterloo on this one?' he asked.

Lisette knew he was making conversation, deliberately trying to distract them from the farewell. 'No, I think it's just Woking and Clapham Junction. I should be back in London at quarter-past five or thereabouts.'

'And do you leave for Scotland immediately?' Granny asked.

'Tomorrow,' Lisette replied, the thoughts of her night parachute-drop into France at the forefront of her mind.

'Can you not tell us where in Scotland?' her grandfather pressed. 'What if we need to reach you?'

'I can't. I'll have someone call you so you know where to ring and they can contact me if you do need me,' she said. She could hear the train coming now, would see the steam soon. Lisette kept talking. She had to fill these last few moments to prevent her tears – but especially to prevent theirs. 'I think I'll have to go through some more training. I'm really such an amateur.'

'It's good to be useful,' Grandad said, and there was longing in his voice.

'We must all do our bit,' Granny echoed. 'We're proud of you, darling. And when this is over, come and have a proper holiday with us. We can have that picnic at Frencham Pond we never got to enjoy.'

Lisette wished her granny hadn't mentioned it, and if the train hadn't suddenly whistled, its wheels screeching as it drew level, she was sure they'd have all been a bit of a mess.

'Here's the train,' she said, far too brightly.

'Farewell, my beautiful girl,' Granny said, reaching for her. It took every ounce of Lisette's willpower not to cry. She hugged her grandmother a little longer and just a bit harder than she meant to, but it was her grandad who noticed it.

'You can give me one of those big hugs too,' he said, and his look told her he knew that she was keeping something from them. 'Come here,' he added, and wrapped long arms around her. She smelled coal tar soap as he pulled her close. 'Now you keep yourself safe, do you hear?' His voice shook slightly. 'Come home to us soon.'

She couldn't reply for the lump in her throat. And he seemed to understand that they would keep whatever secret was passing between them. She squeezed his hand silently and hard, sure her knuckles turned white.

'Look after each other,' she urged, busying herself in her bag for her ticket, even though she knew it was in her pocket. The train wheezed to a stop and her grandfather opened one of the big doors.

She all but leapt inside. She'd been lucky enough to be given a first-class ticket by SOE, and relished the thought of a quiet, private space. She took the opportunity to wipe her eyes surreptitiously, take a deep breath, fling her coat down at a window seat and return to hang out of the window facing the platform, feeling more in control of her emotions.

'I love you,' she called to her grandparents as doors began to slam up and down the platform and a whistle drowned out their responses.

The train jerked and its wheels squealed. She leaned out further and they both grasped her hand. She felt her insides twist as the train lurched forward and wrenched her hand from theirs.

'*Au revoir!*' her Granny called.

'*Au revoir,*' she said, blowing them both kisses and wondering whether she would ever see them again.

Later, when she opened her grandfather's note, it said nothing about whisky, and contained no money. Instead he had written that he would come to France and find her himself if she didn't stay safe. And she believed it.

II

After dropping by her London flat, Lisette returned to training with a small suitcase of clothes still in their French wrapping. She had never worn the clothes – they had been sent by her mother just a few days before her parents' accident. The clothing was stylish, tailored and had original labels, including a pair of low heels by Charles Jourdain. Her trainers were delighted. Meticulous care was taken with the clothing agents were provided with. Styling was replicated precisely, down to buttons being sewn on in 'the French way'. No one would be wearing new styles, and the trainers were pleased her clothes would look more authentic because the style was dated. She had to scuff the shoes and wash the blouses to let their colour fade.

With her training complete, Lisette met with Jepson at Whitehall. It felt exciting to finally be in the War Office.

'You've lost weight,' he remarked.

'I haven't, actually, sir. I've just gained muscle.'

He smiled. 'Feeling positive?'

'I'm ready, sir. I've taken the name of Angeline for the field.'

'Yes. It suits you. As does your code name.'

'Lark?' Her mouth twitched into a smile. 'They told our group to choose bird names. It has resonance. Lark hunting was banned in Germany and the Leipzig bakers, once known for their lark dishes, invented one of my favourite pastries as a result. I also thought Great Tit would be inappropriate, sir.'

The normally reserved Jepson laughed out loud.

'I'm pleased to say that my cover story is going to closely follow my own.'

'Your background is too authentic to ignore. It could keep you safer than most.'

'We've just had to manufacture some details about my schooling in Lille, some early work, and I'm near enough watertight.'

'Have they said anything about your mission?'

'Not yet, sir.'

'Where have they got you?'

'A flat in Knightsbridge. Very posh. I'm sharing it with another agent. We're both awaiting orders, sir. For now we've been told to relax.'

'Not too relaxed. You're about to join a tough network, with lots of hardened French guerilla fighters.'

'Absolutely, sir.' Lisette could sound very English when she wanted to.

'Right, well. I know you're going to make all of us proud, Lisette.'

'Thank you, sir. I hope to.'

'Come and visit when next you're back.'

They both knew that the chances of her returning were slim.

They shook hands and then she was gone, out into the watery sunlight of Baker Street to await her instructions.

They were not long coming.

While other girls waited weeks, sometimes months, for their call up, Lisette received a telephone call that evening. She was to report to the new Wimpole Street headquarters with a view to leaving the following night.

It took her breath away to be called up so soon, with barely a chance to enjoy her new address, but once the initial surprise was past she was glad of it. There was nothing to pack. The clothes, even the wristwatch she wore, would be left behind at Wimpole Street. Everything else would be ready and waiting for her in a small French holdall, in a large ground-floor room at the same address. The room held dozens of pigeonholes, each for a different agent, large enough to carry the specially assembled items that each had prepared in readiness for this moment of departure.

Lisette arrived at Wimpole Street and found her pigeon-hole – the number chalked above it keeping her appropriately anonymous – and collected her leaving outfit. She could feel the butterflies in her belly but she was already a different woman to the one who had first met Jepson. She had become Lisette Forestier again, field name Angeline, code name Lark, and the fluttery feeling inside was pure excitement.

Eight weeks was not very long to be trained as a special agent, but Lisette knew she'd become physically tougher and could now cope with genuine pain. She was also mentally stronger, having with-stood the psychological tests that trainers had put her though. She could keep her wits when thrown into strange and fearful situations; she could force herself to remain steady and think clearly when every-thing around was designed to confuse; she could depend on herself to remain calm when others were shouting just an inch from her face. When threatened, she betrayed no fear in her voice or her demeanour.

And so it was something of a relief when Lisette finally took off in the Halifax, bemused when the pilot asked her to empty her pockets before she pulled on her parachute.

'Why?' she asked, turning them inside out.

'Orders, miss. We have to make sure you don't accidentally take anything incriminating from home. Even a sweet wrapper could jeopardise your cover. And what are they thinking, sending a gorgeous wee thing like you into danger?'

She grinned. 'Careful, lieutenant. I'm trained to kill with my hands.'

'Aye, I can believe it,' he said.

If only you knew, she thought to herself.

'Looks like you're good to go. Been to France before?'

'Born there. Haven't seen it for a while, though.'

He looked impressed. 'We normally don't drop this far south but apparently you're special.' He winked. 'Buckle in, then.'

The time seemed to pass in a blink, and suddenly Lisette was freefalling through the sky over the country of her birth. It was exhilarating but dangerous, lit up by the moon. Lisette counted and then on cue pulled the ripcord. The chute opened, she heard the whoosh of the silk streaming out above her, felt the welcome and familiar drag that hauled her ruthlessly back against the harsh pull of gravity, and then came the floating sensation. It didn't last long; within a few heartbeats she was rolling on the ground, putting into practice all those drills for a safe landing.

The smell of the field and its surrounding orchards on this cool November night transported her instantly back to Lille, at three years old. It wasn't the same France she'd left, but she could almost have fooled herself it was.

'All right?' someone whispered in French, pulling her to her feet.

The line she'd been rehearsing on the flight – from a poem by Baudelaire – came to her in her native tongue: 'A breath of wind,' she said.

'From the wings of madness,' the man replied, glancing up at the sound of the plane, roaring away.

'I'm Angeline,' she said, quickly beginning to gather her chute.

'Welcome to Provence.'

She smiled in the dark. 'What's your name?'

'Frelon,' he replied. *Hornet*. 'Forgive the codename. Faucille prefers it that way.'

Faucille. *Sickle*. She'd heard him talked about at HQ – he would be her *passeur* from south to north. But first her mission was to link up with the Jockey circuit's leader, codename Roger, with an enviable reputation in southern France. Beyond that she would connect with Physician, the biggest clandestine network in all of France, based around Paris, with a contact named Prosper. All these codenames would have baffled her a few months ago. Now she took them for granted.

'I'm to meet Roger.'

'Yes. At the next village.'

'Do you know him?'

'Very well,' Frelon said, helping her to unhook her parachute.

'And Faucille?' she asked, clambering out of the jumpsuit and kicking off the rubber boots. It must look odd to suddenly be dressed in a wool coat and leather pumps, having just plummeted from the sky.

He pulled her deeper into the shadows of an orchard. 'Yes, you will meet him too.'

She looked up, could only just hear the haunting drone of the Halifax from 161 squadron that was already on its way back to Tempsford Airfield; her last connection with England.

'We must hurry, *mademoiselle*,' her companion urged.

She hadn't realised she'd stopped moving. Lisette told herself she was French again now; she had to think in French, be French in all her mannerisms. She knew how. She would not let herself down.

'*Allez, monsieur*. I'm right behind you.'

They found a good spot to bury the parachute and boots. Frelon made short work of it. Satisfied that there was no evidence of her arrival, she walked with him for what must have been fifteen minutes uphill until she realised they were on the fringe of a village.

'This is Saignon,' he said softly. 'Tonight you will have a few hours to sleep in the house of Madame Pascal. Her husband was killed by the Germans two years ago. She sympathises with the Maquis and helps us in any way she can.'

She nodded. 'And you?'

'I'll be fine. I'll collect you before dawn.'

Lisette looked up. The moon had re-emerged and she could hear voices from the village square.

'We'll go around the square,' Frelon said. 'Tonight it is one of the oldest villagers' birthdays. Everyone is involved in the celebrations.' He checked his watch.

'What are we waiting for?'

'They will begin the singing at exactly nine-thirty. Another minute maybe.'

Almost immediately a rousing chorus struck up.

'Now,' Frelon urged and grabbed her hand.

'How do you know we're safe?'

'No one in the village would dare not attend Madame Bernard's celebration. Madame Pascal has claimed a headache.'

At the opening of a small lane she glimpsed the village folk before Frelon was opening a side gate and pushing her through.

'Hurry,' he whispered, then pointed to the back door where she could make out a figure waiting. 'Madame Pascal.'

Lisette was led into the parlour, lit only by a single candle.

'Thank you,' she said to her host. 'I am very grateful for the risk you're taking.'

And it surprised her to feel her heart swell when the small, unassuming woman gave a familiar shrug.

'What else can we do?' Madame Pascal replied in a soft voice.

'I will be back at five, Angeline,' Frelon said.

'I'll be ready.'

He grinned in the low light; they were of similar age, she guessed.

The door was closed and she turned to face her host, who

stood by a long cherrywood table that held only a simple jug of flowers. Beneath her she felt the uneven red tiles rubbed smooth over years of wear, and a pot was simmering gently on a wood stove.

'Thank you. Do you have children?' Lisette asked.

Madame Pascal nodded. 'Our eldest son was killed in the fighting. His brother is doing his STO in Germany. Eight months to go and we hope he will return safely.'

Le Service du travail obligatoire, or the despised STO as it was becoming known, had been introduced earlier that year, replacing the notion of voluntary work in Germany with forced labour. The STO had been responsible for hundreds of Frenchmen being sent to work in Germany each week, labouring on behalf of the Reich. They had no choice.

'We have a daughter,' continued Madame Pascal. 'She is living in Marseille. Her husband is also on STO. She raises our granddaughter alone. I keep telling her to come home.' She sighed. 'May I offer you something? Some coffee, perhaps? Are you hungry?'

'I'm not hungry, thank you, but if you're having a coffee, I will share some with you.' Lisette was mindful that people in France were harshly rationed.

'Please, sit,' her host said. 'I baked a small cake earlier this week. I'm sure you could force down a little piece, eh?' She began to busy herself making the coffee, cutting a slice of the fruit cake.

It was lovely to hear French being spoken, albeit in the Provençale dialect.

'This clandestine work you do – are you not afraid of being discovered?'

Madame Pascal gave a snort. 'So they shoot me,' and gave Lisette a weary grin. 'I am very careful and I know you will be, so we will all live to fight another day. And his friend is the best in the region,' she said, nodding at the door.

'The one they call Faucille?'

'Yes. I have not met him; I have not met anyone who has met him, other than Frelon and Roger. But he's good. He will get you to wherever you need to go.'

Madame Pascal set down a small cup with black liquid in it that smelled nothing like coffee. 'Follow his ways. Tell no one anything, Mademoiselle Angeline. Then no one can harm you,' she said.

The drink was hot and strong. It would help to keep Lisette alert. She sipped gratefully, warming her fingers around the cup. Whatever it was tasted vile.

Madame Pascal smiled and in the low light looked somehow sadder for the gesture. 'Forgive me . . . we have no coffee any more in the south. We have to use roasted barley.'

'It is fine,' Lisette lied.

'Sometimes we can exchange coffee for our rabbits and a chicken or two from Marseille if anyone is passing through, but I think even the far south has run out of coffee. I taste it in my dreams sometimes.'

'Rationing is hard,' Lisette agreed.

'The Germans take everything; our *milice* is just as bad. But they can't take our spirit, eh?'

Lisette raised her cup. '*Santé!*'

They drank in comfortable silence for a minute.

'There is an old sofa in our salon,' said Madame Pascal. 'I have put a blanket there for you – please forgive that I haven't lit a fire. If anything happens, there is another small door leading off that room. It's a trapdoor, hidden behind the sofa. It will take you out into a shed. Do not leave the shed through the entrance. Go up the ladder into the loft and climb out onto the rooftops. Head to your right towards open country. Frelon will find you.'

'I hope it will not come to that.'

'We have to be ready for any event. Faucille's orders. The *milice* raid at all hours and they would probably like to take us by surprise on Madame Bernard's special evening.'

'I'm sorry you missed it for my benefit.'

'It has been a pleasure, *mademoiselle*. I am Gaullist. It is my duty to do what I can, however small.' Then she added softly with her hand in a fist, '*France libre!*'

Lisette was kissing Madame Pascal on each cheek at a minute to five the following morning, and emerging into a cold, crisp and silent Saignon. Her hostess made sure that Lisette had a hot cup of barley coffee, and she'd packed some bread and goat's cheese into a napkin. She pushed an apple and a pear into each of Lisette's coat pockets. Frelon was waiting.

'It is nothing,' she whispered at Lisette's profound thanks.

Lisette hugged her hard before heading off into the darkness once again.

'We're going over the hills this way,' Frelon pointed. 'On the outskirts of the next village I have a horse and cart waiting for us.'

'What's down below?' Lisette said, looking into the distance where a sprawl of lights were winking at her.

'That's Apt. Not a good place right now. Crawling with Germans. Let's go. Faucille is waiting and I don't want us seen here.'

They left the pretty village of Saignon and began the long climb up.

Out in the open, Frelon relaxed. 'Did you manage to sleep, *mademoiselle*?'

'Please, call me Angeline. I dozed for a couple of hours.'

'Good. It will be a bit milder today. I'm glad we got going early. Here, let me take the bag for you.'

'No, please.'

'I was raised to be polite, Angeline. Besides, the path's about to get much harder, and you'll be grateful to use me as your goat.'

'If you insist.'

As she handed him her small holdall, a scent of lavender drifted over her and she gave a small gasp. 'Oh, how beautiful that fragrance is.'

Frelon nodded. 'It will be even more beautiful when the sun warms the fields. Best in the evening, though.'

'I come from a big city, where you never smell such things.'

'So you're from the city. We try not to ask too much, but it's horrible to walk in silence.'

She agreed. 'Are you from around here?'

'Yes. I know the region well. These lavender fields belonged to a family from this village.'

'Not any more?' She frowned.

He shook his head sadly. 'They were Jewish. Taken away last year. It was dreadful. They were a good family; had lived here all their lives. They were probably sent to the prison camps.'

'I'm so sorry. We have not been told of this in London.'

'Your government chooses not to tell its people perhaps.'

She shook her head, shocked. 'I'm sorry.'

'We heard through our circuits that more than ten thousand Jewish people – whole families, including newborns – were rounded up by the *milice* obeying Nazi demands. They were held at the Winter Velodrome.'

'I know that place,' she admitted, her tone full of sorrow.

He nodded. 'That building became a prison last year.'

'I remember a glass roof. It was magnificent.'

'They've painted it over so it doesn't attract the Allied bombers.'

Lisette suddenly wished she'd never mentioned the lavender. 'Well, Frelon, I do hope the Jewish family from around here can return to their lavender fields one day,' she said.

He shot her a dark look. 'I don't think so. If the rumours are right, no one is ever coming back from those camps.'

Lisette didn't want to talk about it any more. 'Are you married?' she asked, for want of anything else to say.

'There was someone but these are not the right days to be thinking too far ahead. Perhaps I should ask you to marry me when it is over. After all, you are the first of our visitors who seems genuinely French.'

Lisette grinned. 'Are you sure we're safe to talk like this?' She looked around, surprised at how high they suddenly were, now that the sky had lightened.

Saignon was a long way down and she could no longer make out Apt; all the effort in clambering almost vertically – or so it felt – had been worth it to climb such a great distance so quickly. In fact, they were about to crest a ridge, along whose natural line various settlements seemed to link up.

'We are safe. We are now in Maquis territory. Over there is Bonnieux. Down there is Lourmarin.' Frelon rattled off a few other names that sounded like places she'd like to see one day. 'But we're going to follow this track. Are you hungry?'

She lied. 'I'm fine.'

'Good, then you can wait until we're travelling to Bonnieux.'

The transport Frelon had promised was waiting with a man who regarded her from hooded eyes.

'Most of our horses have been requisitioned by the Germans,' Frelon explained as she settled herself next to him in the cart. 'Thank you,' he called to the man.

Without saying a word the man nodded and left.

'Forgive his manners. He is fiercely Gaullist. Without people like him the Maquis couldn't survive.'

As soon as they were on their way, Lisette began digging in her bag for Madam Pascal's food.

'They are very courageous these farmers, you know,' Frelon continued. 'We hide, we run around in the dark, we do everything in secret, using codenames in whispers. People like him or Madame Pascal have to live in the open, face the *milice* or the Germans if they bang on their doors, and keep a straight face when they lie, knowing it could cost them their lives.'

'Their lives?'

'Why, yes. Only a week ago, in a nearby hamlet, a man was shot in front of his family because it was suspected that he had helped some Resisters escape.'

'Summary executions?'

'We have heard all sorts of incredible stories. The Germans take reprisals on whole villages if someone from that village offends. It's why men like me run away from our families, keep ourselves secret, so that our loved ones and neighbours don't pay the price for our patriotism.'

Suddenly all the dangers that SOE had trained her for felt horribly close. Lisette had plenty to think about as Frelon fell quiet; only the sounds of the pony's efforts punctuated the silence.

12

Lisette could finally see the soaring church tower of Bonnieux. The village spilled gently down the hillside to the plain. Her heart told her she was home . . . even though she had never been south of Paris. This was the rural France of stories and paintings; tumbling stone buildings that looked as though they were carved from the rock, vivid colours, stony hillsides, pinewoods and chequered plains. From this distance life looked peaceful and picturesque, but Frelon told her a different story.

'We're on foot from here,' he warned, 'and we must be alert. We can trust no one.'

'What about the pony?'

He leapt down from the cart. 'Someone will pick up our four-legged friend. We must cross the hillside rather than use this track.'

'Are there Germans here?'

'No. Sometimes I'm not sure what's worse. German soldiers or *milice*. They both want every maquisard dead. But we don't know who might be friend or foe within the village.'

'Then why come here?'

'The decision was made by Roger.'

'How long will we stay?'

'Just one night. Roger will be here too. He never stays longer than a night anywhere if he can help it. But he's never refused a bed.'

'Really?'

Frelon winked. 'I'm sure you'll understand why soon.'

She laughed, surprised by his implication.

'Roger is truly admired by the Maquis. You will like him. If we're stopped, we are brother and sister. My name is Alain and you are Angeline. I am twenty-five. You are . . .?'

'Twenty-four.'

'I come from Apt but you have been studying up north.'

'In Lille,' she said immediately.

'You know it?'

She nodded.

'What have you been doing in Lille?'

'I studied at the university and worked in Strasbourg. I'm here in the south for a brief visit before going to Paris to start a new job but with the same company as in Strasbourg.'

'You have all the paperwork? A permit to enter the free zone, all your identity papers . . .?'

'Yes.'

'Good. Let's go.'

They skirted the village for an hour before Frelon brought them alongside the low wall that rimmed a stone cottage. Lisette could smell something baking. The aroma drew them through the sprawling, meadowy garden, crammed with herbs outside the back door. Frelon knocked.

'Who is it?'

'It is Alain, *madame*. We are here at last.'

He sounded entirely unrehearsed and casual. A small, round woman answered the door. 'Ah, Alain. Welcome, welcome. And this is your sister. Hello, I've heard so much about you.' She ushered them in and as soon as the door was closed, all pretence was dropped. 'No problems?'

'None,' Frelon replied.

'I'm Angeline,' said Lisette. 'It is very kind of you to have me here.'

Their compact host danced lightly on her feet. 'Anything to defy them,' she said. 'I'm Madame Marchand. You are so young, my dear, and thin.' She pinched the top of Lisette's arm. 'Oh! But strong, eh? It's good then that I baked, although I made biscuits because it keeps nosy neighbours from wondering . . .'

'They smell delicious,' Lisette admitted.

'Come,' the woman said, leading them into her scullery. 'Sit, please,' she offered, immediately putting water on to heat. 'How are you, young man? Are you staying?'

'I am well, as you can see.' Frelon smiled. 'But I cannot stay. Take care of Angeline.'

'With all my heart,' Madame Marchand replied.

Late into the evening, dozing in an armchair, Lisette heard the sound of a motorbike. She glanced at her wristwatch – her mother's. It was French-made and enhanced her cover. It was a few minutes before the ten o'clock curfew. She yawned, stretched and shook the dull feeling from her mind. She wished she could brush her teeth and wake up instantly but she hadn't been allowed to bring any toiletries. Madame Marchand was at the back door welcoming new visitors in hushed whispers. All lights had been turned off in favour of a couple of candles, which flickered as a cold draught stirred the room's peace.

Lisette stood as two men entered the kitchen; both were tall and bent to kiss Madame Marchand once, twice, three times. The tallest of the strangers regarded Lisette with a grin. Even in this low light he possessed the dashingly good looks of a film star; there were strong echoes of Ronald Colman about him. This must be Roger.

'Angeline?'

'Yes,' she replied, unsure whether to shake hands. She was relieved when he took the lead.

'Let's keep it French,' he said amiably and kissed her in the same manner as he had Madame Marchand. 'I'm Roger.' He had to be six-foot four at least, she thought, as he bent low to greet her. She felt his moustache graze gently against her cheek.

'Welcome to Provence,' Roger said. 'This is the Luberon, a mountain that runs from east to west and is cleft in two. The region is flanked by two valleys and their rivers. I'm telling you this for two reasons – firstly, we are relatively safe up here, and secondly, so that you understand it will be a challenging journey ahead. I hope you're up to walking rough terrain.' He smiled kindly. 'Paris is a long way from here.'

'You learned your French in Belgium, Roger?' Lisette asked.

He grinned. 'My grandfather is Belgian, although I spent a lot of time in France. You'll have to tell me what gave me away. Now, let me introduce you to my friend. He prefers simply to be known as Faucille.'

Sickle, Lisette repeated in her mind. Appropriate, given the dark look he cut her. '*Monsieur*,' she said. 'Angeline.'

He did not kiss her but simply nodded from where he seemed to brood in the shadows. 'Angeline,' he repeated.

His voice was low but far smoother than Lisette expected, given his glare. As he pushed away from the sink and turned to face her square on, she realised with a jolt how handsome he was. His yellow-blonde hair and penetrating, light gaze was uncommon in this part of the world.

'I hope you have some other clothes,' he added.

'Blunt as ever,' Roger said.

The smile she'd given Faucille faltered. His French was perfect, southern, perhaps, although she heard none of the singsong giveaway of the south. His accent could pass for Parisian. 'My clothes?'

'They're not appropriate,' he said to Roger, ignoring her.

'But they're French,' she argued, dismayed.

He looked back at her, unmoved. Lisette was irritated now, but couldn't help herself from noticing his strong build and the two small lines either side of his mouth that hinted at laughter in his life. 'They are too expensive,' he said dismissively. 'You can risk your life, *mademoiselle*, but not mine.'

This was the man Madame Pascal had spoken so highly of? A brute. 'They're years old,' she pressed.

He shook his head, his gaze narrowing. 'They look new and too chic for this part of France. No doubt you might get away with them in Paris, but here they will win you the wrong sort of attention. Besides, we're going across the mountains. They will not do, especially those heels. You will not pass for a country girl, and unless you want to freeze, they are not warm enough.'

His arrogance! 'I appreciate your concern for my wellbeing, Faucille, but —'

'It is not your wellbeing I am concerned about. I do not wish to carry you across the mountains because you have frostbite. And I do not want a bullet in the back of my head because your clothes gave us away.' He gave a shrug. 'Change them or find a new *passeur*.'

She looked open-mouthed at Roger, who returned her glance with a wry laugh. 'He's so much fun, isn't he?' he said.

Lisette watched Madame Marchand touch Roger's arm gently. 'Roger, you are welcome for as many nights as you like. You know that.'

'I know, *Madame*, but one night is more than enough.'

Madame Marchand glanced at Lisette. 'We call him big feet – he hangs over the ends of our beds.'

Lisette found a smile for this kind woman who took such risk, but she was still seething inside about Faucille; the man she knew she would have to spend time with from tomorrow. She refused to look at him, but every one of her senses was attuned to him. The smell of lavender he had brought in with him, the way the candle-light lit the light growth of his beard, his voice. Even now, without looking at him directly, she was aware of how he stood relaxed, large hands plunged into his pockets, staring openly at her. Her cheeks were burning and she was very glad of the low light.

'You must be exhausted, Roger,' said Madame Marchand. 'Come, let me feed you, men. Sit down, sit down.' She poked Faucille on the chest. 'Sit!'

'No, *madame*. You are taking too much risk, I fear, with so many.'

She made a harsh tutting sound. 'I'm old enough to be your mother. Don't tell me what I can or can't do.'

Lisette saw Faucille steal a glance at her again but she looked away.

'Come, Angeline,' Madame Marchard said. 'I insist you eat something.'

A cold supper was laid out and while Lisette went through the motions, she tasted little of it, struck instead by the presence of these two men who were now in control of her future.

Roger was every bit as charismatic as his looks hinted at, but she also recognised a fierce intelligence. After sharing stories of training in Scotland, Lisette noticed the circuit leader effortlessly shift the conversation. Roger never once asked her about her personal life, her mission, or indeed any of the details of her cover. And she understood that he did not expect to be questioned either.

'We live in the moment, Angeline,' he said, quietly. 'And my job is to ensure that you get away safely and can head north.'

Their hostess was pouring out slugs of alcohol, likely made with potato skins, to go with the barley coffee that was brewing.

'I understand.'

'And you must promise me that you will put your faith in Faucille here. He knows this region like the back of his hand, and he will keep you safe.'

Lisette glanced at her compatriot. If he would only lose his scowl, she could imagine him breaking hearts all over Provence; there was something utterly compelling about him. She decided that it was his silence that made him interesting – he had refused to reveal anything at all about himself. It was more than the necessary secrecy – he simply remained remote. She'd caught him looking at her on a couple of occasions and each time, there was a flash of something in those blue eyes. But she noted that he paid infinite respect to Madame Marchand, and she wondered if behind that gruff façade lived a man of gentle heart.

'If Faucille says you are to take a certain route, don't question it. Just do it,' Roger said.

'Of course. And Faucille will take me as far as . . .where?'

'You may ask me directly if you wish,' Faucille suddenly piped up.

Lisette had provoked a reaction. Good. So he did have emotions. His accent was Marseillaise, definitely, but there were overtones of other influences. And it was only now, really looking at him, that she realised what had been nagging at her from his arrival. He had the type of honeyed complexion that darkened easily beneath the sun, his eyes were a bright blue, and his hair was clearly golden. Surely he had some Saxon blood in him.

'*Haben sie Deutscher blut?*' she asked suddenly, softly.

A distinct chill descended in the room. Roger and Madame Marchand sat back and shared a glance of concern.

'Yes, I am German,' Faucille replied in French, holding her gaze without so much as blinking.

'Forgive me, *monsieur*,' Lisette said.

Roger laid a hand on her arm. 'You have nothing to fear from Faucille. Actions speak louder than words, and he has proven himself to be a French patriot.'

'How well do you speak German?' Faucille asked and she detected a trace of fascination in his tone.

'Fluently.'

'That could be helpful,' he said softly to himself. He took up the conversation. It seemed she'd finally thawed him. 'Initially London asked me to take you through to Paris. I can do that, *mademoiselle*, but things are heating up in the south; the Gestapo is suddenly a lot more active and I may be an encumbrance once you are on that train headed north. You may travel with greater security alone, but we shall make that decision when the time comes.'

'Right,' Roger said. 'I shall leave you in Faucille's care, Angeline. And I wish you every success. Be safe. I'll be heading off before first light.'

'We will too,' Faucille said.

The conversation shifted to the journey. Lisette suddenly felt tired; she wasn't relishing long days ahead spent in the company of the prickly maquisard, with his secrets and scowls and few words.

'Through Gordes?' she heard Roger ask in response to Faucille.

'At the abbey we can find a sympathetic ear.'

The low drone of the men's voices and the physical toll of the last couple of days began to show. Lisette shook her head free of the blurriness that was taking over and forced herself to stand and begin removing dishes. Madame Marchand fussed but Lisette preferred to be busy. She cleared the table, leaning across Faucille once to take his glass. He barely moved to allow her access. As she wiped down the crumbs, the men stood. Faucille kissed his host, and began making excuses.

Roger said to Lisette, 'He has an errand to run.'

'Oh,' Lisette said. 'I thought we were all here this evening.'

'We were, *mademoiselle*, until I saw your clothes,' said Faucille. 'I know someone who can lend me some for you.'

Feeling stung for the second time, Lisette couldn't help but retaliate. 'Perhaps you could stay there?' she said.

He regarded her with a sardonic smile but the scorn passing between them was unmistakable. She had barely been on French soil for just over twenty-four hours and here she was, ruffling the feathers of the one person who could now keep her safe.

'Thanks, Faucille,' Roger said, slapping him on the back. 'If I don't see you tomorrow, good luck. Be safe.'

Faucille nodded at Roger. 'Our paths will cross again soon. You too, stay safe. Don't go too fast on that motorbike down the hill, eh?'

They both grinned. Lisette realised in that instant that each time they said farewell it could so easily be the last time.

'*Bonne nuit, mademoiselle*,' Faucille said to her without any handshakes or kisses. 'I will return before first light. Thank you for the food, Madame Marchand,' and with a final nod at Roger, the man of Provence disappeared silently into the night.

Roger watched him leave before turning his handsome face to regard Lisette sombrely. 'I'd put my life in his hands any day. Please remember that when you're travelling with him. It doesn't achieve anything to come here with a superior attitude towards people who are risking their lives, their families, to keep us safe.'

She hung her head, feeling the well-deserved sting of his words. 'Does he have family?'

'His family was killed by the authorities. He has good reason for being Maquis.'

She looked up, frowning. 'Why kill a French family?'

'I'll let him tell you, if he chooses. His war is personal. You've got to keep yours detached and as impersonal as possible.'

She nodded. He shifted to practicalities. 'Remember, if you're on a bicycle – it's how most of us get around – don't break any road rules. If you give the Germans an excuse to check your ID and they find it's a number that doesn't exist, it's over. Get some rest, Angeline.'

'I will, sir,' she whispered in English.

He grinned. 'Haven't been called that since I was teaching,' he admitted. 'Goodnight. Do us proud.'

13

Lisette was woken in darkness by Madame Marchand. She realised she hadn't stirred from the position she'd fallen asleep in. She sat up too quickly, disoriented for a moment, then gathered her wits. 'Is Faucille here?'

'He is. He brought you these. You'd better try them.'

Lisette stared at the small bundle of clothes in her host's hands. 'Thank you.'

'There's water in the bowl – even a little soap. And I've left a brush. Be watchful for other villagers when you go outside to use the toilet.'

She nodded. 'Is Roger awake?'

Madame Marchand turned from the doorway and smiled. 'He left two hours ago. He never stays long.'

She felt strangely alone. 'I didn't hear his motorbike.'

'He pushed it out of the village. He asked me to wish you well. Remember that you wouldn't be here if people didn't think you were made of the right stuff.' She squeezed Lisette's shoulder affectionately. 'He said for you to trust your instincts. Intuition has saved him a bullet more than once.'

Lisette smiled as the kindly woman left. She stared at the jumble of clothes that had been donated and, with a sigh, changed into them. The no-nonsense dress fitted her well enough and was austere in its cut and shape, belted at the waist with three-quarter sleeves that looked slightly threadbare. It was warm, though, and Faucille had brought her a cardigan of pale blue, darned at the elbow. She now had lace up brown brogues, but older, thick stockings replaced her new ones. She couldn't work out why, looking at herself in the cheval mirror, those stockings made her feel more ugly than the entire battered ensemble.

She shook her head. Vanity had never been a problem for her, but then again, as Harriet had suggested, she'd never had to wonder whether men would find her attractive.

By the time she arrived in the kitchen, Faucille was at the table helping himself to some breakfast. She wanted to start afresh with him – *needed* to.

'Thank you for the clothes,' she said, closing the door.

He glanced up. 'Now you look like you're from Provence, which means you'll hardly be noticed.'

'Should I pack mine or . . .'

He bit into some bread, then eyed her. 'No need. I've dealt with them.'

Lisette poured some coffee from the pot. She was already getting used to the barley brew. 'What does that mean?'

'They'll go to a good home. A fair exchange.'

Her mother had sent her those clothes. The last gift from Sylvie before . . . Oh, she couldn't think like this.

'Is there a problem?' he asked.

'No. I hope your friend gets good use out of them.'

Faucille regarded her. He had a gaze that looked too deeply for her comfort.

'In public I can hardly refer to you as Faucille,' she said. 'Is there a name I should use?'

'We should use one you won't forget. How about your father's name.'

She smiled. 'His name was Max. Maximilian.'

'Not very French.'

'He was German,' she said.

'That explains it, then,' he said, his gaze even more intense.

'My mother was French. They're both dead, though.'

'We could use the name of your first boyfriend?'

She hadn't the heart to say Jack. She thought about the first boy who kissed her. 'Olivier,' she answered.

'Then I am Olivier.'

'But your papers?'

'Ah, that's different,' he said, almost playfully. 'In fact, I want to talk to you about a cover story as we walk. It's time to go. Are you ready?'

She'd barely put food on her plate. 'Almost.'

'Hurry, please, *mademoiselle*. We must leave before first light and be far away from the village.'

It was the most courteous he'd been since she'd met him.

———

They'd walked fifteen kilometres, by Lisette's calculation. She was weary because it had been uphill but she was not going to admit fatigue to Faucille, of all people. As if he had dropped in on her thoughts, he turned to her.

'You should rest.'

'Only if you —' she began, trying not to sound out of breath.

'This is one of my favourite views,' he interrupted. 'Look, down there is Bonnieux. Lacoste to the right.'

'And in the distance?' she asked, catching her breath. It was certainly a very beautiful landscape, despite the rockiness underfoot. When she looked out across the valley, the autumn colours became hazy and softened the ridges and crags of the hillsides.

'Right over there, if you squint, that's Avignon,' he said, pointing further than she could see.

'I'll trust you,' she said and felt pleased to see him crack a smile. The gesture deepened the attractive creases at the edge of his cheeks. And his eyes . . . they were not just blue but a startling aquamarine, the sort that made people look twice. His voice, now that he was more relaxed, had softened further – it made her feel comforted . . . safe, even. He held his lithe, muscular body with great control, moving easily over the terrain while she often overbalanced or stumbled. His contained manner gave off an aura of confidence that was undeniably attractive.

'Where are we going?'

'To a place called Gordes; tomorrow to Cavaillon. A train north from there.'

She nodded. It was all meaningless to her anyway; he alone knew the way over the mountains.

'Eat the fruit you brought and perhaps that dress will fit you better.'

'Trousers might have been more sensible.'

'Perhaps. But then you'd be picked out by a German patrol – or worse, the *milice* – because then you'd look like a maquisard.' He gestured for her to sit next to him as he perched on a rock. 'We can stop for a few minutes.'

Clearly he was more comfortable outdoors. He seemed more open, relaxed.

'Tell me about your life as a maquisard,' Lisette asked tentatively, careful not to pry into his days before the war.

He shrugged. 'There is not much to say. We live rough, we sabotage everything we can to make life more difficult for the Boches, and we die . . . regularly.'

'So do you aim to kill?'

'Oh, yes. We kill when we can but it's rare,' he said, and his matter-of-factness sent a chill through her. 'Mainly we aim to disrupt – we cut telephone lines, we blow up rail tracks, destroy bridges and roads, block access points, stop mail getting through, divert deliveries, cut transmissions. We are like a hive of bees, stinging as often as we can. We can't deliver the death blow but we can certainly weaken the monster.'

'How do you feed yourselves, if you have to stay hidden all the time?'

'There are sympathisers everywhere who are proud of what we're doing. The village folk send food up the hills, carried by children in their toy carts covered by teddy bears and dolls. No one ever suspects the children.'

'Do the children see the Maquis?'

'Never. We follow a creed of secrecy, so much so that I couldn't even tell you if one man of the village is Maquis or a collaborator.'

'Really?'

'This way I cannot compromise another and he cannot compromise me.'

'What a way to live.'

'It is the only way of the Maquis. We move in twos, threes at most.'

'You and Frelon?'

'And another. You will meet him up there, in Gordes.'

'Do they grow lavender there?'

'Why do you ask?' He looked almost melancholy.

'I smelled lavender on you when you arrived.'

He nodded but didn't elaborate. She didn't press. 'It was beautiful in Saignon with all the lavender.'

He nodded sadly. 'I am from around there.'

She felt her throat catch at the sorrow in his voice. She remembered what Roger had confided about Faucille's family.

'I shouldn't have told you that,' he said. 'Of course now I shall have to kill you.' He smiled – a proper smile – and for a few heartbeats his entire demeanour changed, as though the November sun had peeked out from behind the overcast skies to warm them. Lisette found herself acutely aware of him at every moment. When their hands had accidentally touched or their bodies had lightly bumped as any walkers might, she'd been quick to apologise. She'd noticed him start from her in a similar way. She wondered whether she might ever learn his real name.

'Not until after my mission, please,' replied Lisette, smiling back.

'Given the strange route you're taking to Paris and the arrangements we've had to put in place for you, Angeline, I have to presume you are important to the British . . . and your mission extremely dangerous.'

The mission. She had tried not to think too hard about it. It was a fluid concept relying on her intuition and own decision-making in terms of how she was to approach it. At this point she didn't know whether she would simply seduce her target and learn from him, or whether she'd attempt to turn him. She was being cast into the lion's den, and asked to tame the lion.

'Yes, it is. I hope I don't let them down.'

'How old are you?'

'Twenty-four.'

'Do you have any family?'

'Just grandparents. Since we're being so frank, what about you?'

He sucked in a breath. 'I think we should go.' He stood, bursting the fragile bubble of civility that had formed.

She leapt up, stung. 'I didn't mean to pry.'

He turned back. 'Family is difficult to talk about. Maybe . . .'

'It's all right. Talk to me about Gordes. Where is it?'

'Up there.'

How could she have missed it? The last few kilometres she'd fallen into a rhythm of staring at the ground, planting her feet precisely where his larger feet had trod. And she had allowed her mind to wander. It helped pass the silent hours, the hunger, the loneliness. And yet rearing up above her was an incredible village built into the base of the cliffs, almost classical-looking, bathed in gold light. The sun was already past its peak; they'd been walking for seven hours.

'A main settlement from Roman times, a fortification ever since, and now a stronghold of the Resistance,' Faucille said, grinning at her gaping stare.

'It's breathtaking,' she murmured.

'Yes, but the *milice* know we use it. We have to be very careful. They can't patrol it as we do but they have been raiding ever since the Germans took over the so-called Free France.'

'Why risk coming here?'

'It's still safer than overnighting in Cavaillon. Shall we pick up our pace? We still have to get to the abbey before dark.'

They walked for another three-quarters of an hour and finally reached Gordes proper but Lisette's sense of awe and delight was short-lived. Within moments of entering the twisting alleys of the town her pleasure had turned to a liquid fear, rushing through her veins, pounding at her ears. The unmistakable sounds of troops marching and vehicles approaching came from the square – only Germans had those boots or petrol.

'I should have warned you,' Faucille said, sensing her disquiet.

'I have to get used to it.'

'Yes, you do. Paris will be worse.'

'What do all these posters mean?' she asked, noticing them stuck up on many of the walls.

'These are new,' Faucille remarked.

Des Libérateurs, the heading screamed, and below were printed nearly a dozen grainy photos of men. They were described as being part of the Army of Crime. It was the duty of all villagers across the region to speak up if they'd seen or heard anything of these men.

And unmistakably, Frelon's face smirked out at Lisette. She froze, scanning the poster for Faucille. He was not among them. Even so, he appeared shaken.

'We can't stay here,' he said, grabbing her hand. It was the first time he had touched her and his hand was large and dry; a farmer's hand, she thought to herself, reassured at the warmth it brought. 'Walk with me as if we are more than friends,' he urged. She took a breath and pushed herself closer to him, so he could wrap an arm around her in a casual embrace. Lisette leaned into him so they didn't appear stiff. It wasn't a moment too soon. Soldiers turned into the alley, terrifying her. And yet all she could think about was the fragrance of lavender that enveloped her.

'Talk to me,' she whispered pleadingly. 'Anything.'

He didn't miss a beat. 'And so I told him to get lost,' Faucille waved an arm expansively. 'He thinks he is so clever, but I tell you, my flowers are far superior. I leave mine just a little later so the bees can —' She couldn't believe it when he deliberately knocked the arm of one of the soldiers pushing past them. 'Ah, pardon, *monsieur*,' he said politely.

The soldier grimaced, his gaze sliding to Lisette, whom Faucille now held in a close hug by his side.

'Papers!' the young soldier demanded. 'Do you live here?' he asked in terrible French. He was younger than either of them, with rosy cheeks and hair that was so short it was almost shaved. They both began digging into pockets for their papers. Lisette couldn't imagine she could ever be more terrified than she was now, meeting the enemy at such close range.

Surprisingly, Faucille was neither tense nor nervous. 'No, I'm visiting an old flame,' he replied easily, switching into German.

'You speak German?' the young soldier exclaimed, his demeanour instantly friendlier.

'I *am* German!' Faucille replied, still fumbling in a pocket. 'I am a resident of France, though. Forgive my blundering way. I'm excited to see her again, eh?'

'Don't worry about that,' the soldier said, grinning now and dismissing the search for papers. He waved to his compatriots. 'We're off for the evening, in search of beer.'

'Try Monsieur Grigon's bar,' Faucille said, conspiratorially. 'He keeps some German beer. Beneath the bar. Insist!' Faucille gave a mischievous grin. 'Tell him Lukas sent you. But don't tell the rest of your unit, eh?'

'You live around here?' the soldier asked.

Faucille gave a short jut of his chin. 'North, in Sault.'

'No STO?'

'I'm a farmer,' Faucille admitted.

'A German farmer in France?'

The smile on Faucille's face broadened but not a hint of warmth touched his eyes. 'Sounds mad, doesn't it? I was born in Bavaria, my mother ended up in southern France with me. To the authorities I'm regarded as a French national.' He touched his heart. 'But I'm German here.'

The young soldier grinned. 'Be careful you aren't called up.'

'I would gladly go, but they need my crops. I'm not allowed to leave the farm.'

'Lucky you.' The soldier's gaze slid to Lisette. 'Got a sister?'

Faucille spoke before she could. 'No, but I can fix you up with her friend.' He winked. 'Hey, these Maquis dogs,' he said, pointing jauntily at the poster. 'Caught any yet?'

'Four so far. That one,' he said, pointing to Frelon, 'is about to fall into our trap, I gather. Make sure you're there to watch the executions tonight.' He grinned.

'See you then,' Faucille replied in a brightly feigned tone.

The soldier moved on and Faucille clutched Lisette tightly by the waist but didn't increase his pace. 'We have to get out of here.'

'I gathered. Was that all rubbish back there about the bar?'

'Mostly. Monsieur Grignon is going to get a surprise.'

'Will he turn you in?'

' He won't even know who sent them. I know he's a collaborator. But he pretends otherwise.'

'Where are we going?'

'Senanque Abbey. I have to get a message to Laurent.'

'Laurent?'

'Frelon. Forget you heard the name. If anything, it's a burden to know.'

'I'll take my chances. Are you going to tell me your name?'

But he didn't respond, instead looking fretful as he cast a gaze up and down the road that led to the town square.

Soon Lisette and Faucille were in a cart heading to the monastery, with a taciturn monk at the reins.

'This monk is stone deaf,' Faucille assured her. 'He's given me a ride before. We can talk freely and we must plan a cover story. That poster changes our plan. If they know about Laurent, then they will soon know about me.'

'What do you mean?'

'It means I won't necessarily be putting you on a train to Paris alone.'

'You're coming with me?'

'I'm not sure. It may be too difficult to remain in the south – at least for a while. I can work with the Resistance elsewhere.'

Like so many pilgrims before her, Lisette couldn't help but marvel at the narrow wooded valley they were passing through.

The elegantly spare stone Cistercian monastery lay ahead, at the foot of a steep incline.

'I'm sure Prosper would welcome you,' Lisette said, secretly glad that she might not be travelling alone.

'We shall see.' Faucille paused, a look of consternation crossing his face. 'But now I must break my own rules, Angeline. Tell me about yourself – I need to build my story around yours, in case we are stopped for any reason. You can call me Luc, but my real name is Lukas.'

The name suited him, she thought. But Luc's plans made a mockery of her training dogma about the importance of secrecy. She knew he was breaking his own code of silence too. SOE had impressed upon her that in the field, the only thing she could really count on was her herself and her instincts. Luc was her only hope to get out of the south. Under torture, could he keep her secrets? She couldn't be sure of that even for herself. She took a deep breath and began.

'My name is Lisette. I was born in Lille to a German father, Maximilian Foerstner; he was wounded in the Great War – lost the use of one arm – and became entirely disillusioned with the country of his birth. When he married my mother, a Frenchwoman called Sylvie, he settled in France with her and they lived under the French surname of Forestier.'

'Wait,' Luc said. 'Is this a cover?'

'The truth . . . it is my best cover because it can all be proven.'

He looked worried. 'Go on.'

'We moved to Strasbourg when I was born, and according to my cover story I've been living in the east of France until now; I'm going to Paris to work in a German bank for a friend of the family.'

She felt the weight of his gaze as he considered what she'd just told him.

'And the real Lisette?'

She hesitated. But this intimate moment seemed to transcend the rules they were meant to live by. She wanted to tell him. She wanted to share the truth with this man whom she sensed was as damaged by the loss of his family as she had been by the loss of hers. That counted for something . . . that bound them. Before she could think, she began to talk, and it felt like a key had been turned in a lock. It was a release to speak of her life.

'I was seventeen and my parents were becoming nervous about the rise of the Nazis in Germany. I was sent to live in Britain, but before my parents could join me they were killed in a motor vehicle accident.' She reeled this off matter-of-factly; she did not want him to ask any hard questions. 'But according to my cover story I moved to live with family friends in Dunkerque when I left school in Strasbourg.'

'No records because of the bombings. Clever.'

'Certainly much too hard to trace.'

'No other family members left in France?'

She shook her head. 'Father's parents dead. Mother's parents both dead, according to my papers, but my maternal grandparents live in England.'

'So, according to your cover, what have you been doing since then?'

'I remained in Dunkerque until the outbreak of the war and returned to Strasbourg. I worked there for a banker – an old family friend,' she said. 'He exists. I'm lucky he cares for me and has agreed to support this version of events, although he knows nothing of my work for SOE, only that I am desperate to return to France.'

'Where is he?'

'Walter? He's in Paris now.'

'And your papers reflect all of this,' he pressed.

Lisette nodded. 'I have been taking a break down south

because of health reasons. I'm going to work in the Paris branch of Walter's bank, where he has relocated. So now, what about you?'

He hesitated, she noticed, his face darkening. This was hard for him. She couldn't blame him. The Maquis lived under such secrecy that telling anything, even a fabricated life, could mean death.

'My name is Lukas Ravensburg. I was born in Germany . . . in Bavaria. My father, Dieter, was killed the day before the Armistice. My mother, heartbroken and pregnant, somehow found her way into Strasbourg, where she was discovered by Wolfgang Eichel, who was a professor at the university, and his wife. My mother died soon after I was born in their home. But the Eichels, like your father, wanted to move far away from Germany. Wolf's wife died suddenly, and Wolf brought me to Provence. We have been close my whole life.' Here Luc paused and looked out into the distance. He said nothing for a long time.

'Is something wrong?'

He sighed deeply. 'Yes, something is very wrong. I was brought up by a loving family who raised me as their own. They knew my story but kept me in the dark. I only learned the truth last year.'

Lisette stared at him, hardly daring to say anything. His story sounded even more pitiful than hers.

'Why are you angry?' she risked.

'I'm angry that my family, who are Jewish, have been taken away to what we suspect are death camps. My grandmother didn't even survive the belting that the *milice* gave her as she was dragged from our family home. I kissed her dead face while the screams of my beautiful sisters rang in my ears.'

Lisette could hear the pain in his voice.

'Everyone has lost someone, and my tale is echoed all over France. But I would rather take a bullet in the head than go to work for the German war effort.'

'Where is your friend Wolf?'

'I have no idea. I saw him the day my family was taken. After that I fled into the hills with the Maquis. It was months before I returned to the region, although I have never returned to my village.' He gave a shrug. 'By then nobody knew where Wolf had gone.'

He continued, 'Let's keep it as close to the truth as I dare. I am Lukas Ravensberg. I was orphaned, raised by a family in the south. I am a lavender grower in the mountain region of Sault, which is far enough away from my real village to avoid suspicion.'

'Why do you have such strong German?' Lisette challenged.

'I am proud of my German heritage. I have taught myself.'

'Be sure to make mistakes, then, if you're stopped.'

'Don't fret on my account. I've told Roger that I will get you successfully on the train to Paris. Whatever happens beyond that is irrelevant.'

'Please don't say that.'

'We are all expendable, Lisette,' he said, looking away.

There was no more time to talk. They'd arrived, the cart rolling slowly onto the gravel of the monastery's approach. They waved their thanks to the driver, who leapt down nimbly and helped Lisette alight. The sun was lowering and it had become colder the deeper they'd sunk into the valley; it was positively cool now, and the monastery looked a lot more imposing in shadow.

'Visitors are permitted?' Lisette found herself whispering.

'Not encouraged, but never turned away. Père Auguste is a monk here I can trust. Wait here for me? I won't be long but I need to be sure we are safe first.'

As Luc and the monk walked away Lisette inhaled the smell of the forest, enjoying the silence. She turned from the monastery and looked down the valley, imagining it carpeted by lavender. No doubt Faucille – no, Luc – would enjoy telling her about how it would grow here.

She heard sudden footsteps approaching. Without warning, Luc appeared out of the shadows. 'Up,' he said, 'into the cart. Hurry!'

'What?'

'No questions. No time. Do as I say.'

She leapt back into the cart as he untied the reins. 'Luc?' she implored, but his teeth were gritted. They left the way they had come, and although she had not seen another person, she was sure that eyes were watching them as they clattered away back up the hill.

When the horse hit a steady clip Luc turned and she saw a wildness in his expression.

'What?' she urged.

'They've caught Laurent. He's going to be executed.'

14

They'd leapt from the cart about a quarter of a mile from the town and had run the rest of the way. Luc could hear Lisette sucking in air as silently as she could as he forced them to a walk.

Luc reminded himself that his job was to get her onto that northbound train – and everything else was secondary. Except it wasn't. Père Auguste's news had rattled his normally clear thinking. According to the monk, Laurent had made it to the monastery; the plan had been for him to travel alone ahead of Lisette and Luc to organise paperwork and safe houses for them in Gordes. What no one could have known was that the *milice* would choose this day to stage a raid. Laurent had wisely followed the back-up plan and got to the monastery in time to leave the paperwork with the sympathetic Père Auguste. But the *milice* had paid a visit, and one of the monks had inadvertently betrayed Laurent.

'You have to forgive old Claude. He's slipping into dementia and doesn't really grasp what the Maquis does. He was trying to help the authorities,' Père Auguste had tried to explain. Worst of all was that someone in Gordes had confirmed Laurent as being the man they sought. He did not know who had given Laurent up.

All the Maquis accepted that death's cold embrace could encircle them at any turn, on any day, but Luc and Laurent's youth perhaps permitted them to believe they would see this war out. They had felt certain they would dance on the graves of their pursuers and they would, one day, raise a glass to the loved ones they had lost. Together they would tell their sons of their fathers' adventures. He couldn't just let Laurent go. Luc wasn't ready to accept Père Auguste's advice to leave Gordes well alone.

With a creamy white Cistercian's robe adding some semblance of disguise, Luc led Lisette up one of the cobbled alleys until they were level with the main square of Gordes.

'Are you mad?' Lisette asked in a hiss.

'I have to be there.' He saw her swallow; knew there was a struggle being waged inside her but she had no rank to pull, no way of leaving him.

'You are *crazy*; there is no more dangerous place for you right now. Luc, we can't risk the mission – and I won't watch an execution.'

'We won't risk the mission, I promise,' he said and held her gaze. 'And you can't avoid being present – where will you hide? It's safer in the square with everyone else.'

She nodded, as though accepting the situation, but shook her arm free. He hadn't even realised he was squeezing it. 'Let me go. You're a monk, remember!'

The *milice* were herding people into the square, aided by German soldiers. The situation was becoming more dangerous. Lisette was unhappily swept up with the tide of people but it was best she stand in the square or risk notice. She knew how to blend in. Her clothes were perfect, her language too. If not for her beauty, no one would look twice. Luc noticed she was sensibly reaching for the woollen cap he'd added to her pocket at the last minute.

Luc twisted into a doorway, leaping into the shadows beneath a flight of stairs, and ripped off the cassock. It was too obvious – what had he been thinking? It was prayer time and no monk from Senanque would be in the square at Vespers. He emerged, allowed himself to be hurried along and made sure he was at the back of the crowd, bending his knees and almost crouching against the castle wall to detract from his height. He could see Lisette, immersed in a group of women.

Luc's attention was caught by the first prisoner being led out. He'd seen it before – the victims needed no shackles. They walked bravely to their place of death, usually defiant, never anything but proudly French.

Luc's eyes widened. It was not Laurent, but Fougasse! The man wore a placard around his neck proclaiming him a traitor, a criminal, a murderer. His hands were bleeding and Luc saw that several of his fingers were missing. But the baker of Saignon wore a brave smirk with such triumph that Luc felt his heart pound with pride. And impossibly, Fougasse glimpsed him in the crowd. Their eyes connected for a second, then Fougasse seemed to stumble; Luc was sure it was deliberate.

Proceedings were to be supervised by the Germans, not the *milice*; Luc recognised the hated grey uniform of the Gestapo as two of its officers strolled out into the fading light of the afternoon. But Luc despised the *milice* more; Frenchmen, for whatever reason – work, pay, rations, vengeance – had donned the blue coat, brown shirt and dark-blue beret that proclaimed them one of Petain's special force. They acted above the law, with a creed to crush all forms of resistance.

Luc's moment of anger passed swiftly, replaced by despair as his dear old friend, Laurent, suddenly appeared from behind three *milice*. He had been beaten so badly that both eyes were closed and his face was bruised and bleeding. His shirt was stained with blood; Luc could barely breathe for the impotent rage he felt. His mind desperately sought a reason to create a disturbance. But they were Maquis. If any of them were caught, their pact forbade others from risking their lives to rescue them.

And yet, faced with reality, the temptation was overwhelming.

Luc didn't bother to read the sign hanging from Laurent's neck. He saw Fougasse whisper something to his younger compatriot that earned the older man a pistol butt smashed viciously into his face. A collective gasp from the crowd followed. Fougasse dropped but made no sound; his wrists were tied behind him so he couldn't reach for his face as blood poured down it. Luc's fists balled with fresh fury as he squinted at the pistol bearer, not quite believing it. Yes, it was Pierre Landry, dishing out the violence – no longer in the uniform of a gendarme but now a strutting Vichy *milicien*.

Seeing Landry again brought back all the old emotion, surging from the place where Luc had kept it locked. The blood pounded in his head as rage filled him. He knew it – he was going to do something very unwise.

Be still! the voice of reason urged. It was like Fougasse and Roger yelling at him at once. If Luc survived, escaped and carried on, he could make his friends' deaths count for something. He blinked and his gaze shot over to Lisette; she looked pale. Looking at her now was a timely reminder of the task that Roger had expressly charged him with.

'Little things,' that's what Roger often told him. 'It's the little things we all do, every day, that can change the course of this war.' Lisette could be one of those little things, the rational half of his mind argued. He would do nothing, which is just how Fougasse would want it.

While the four-man firing squad was lining up, Luc's notice was caught by a head of reddish hair glowing in the dying afternoon. A familiar woman was standing not far from where the SS officers loitered, laughing quietly, talking to some of the *milice* who'd gathered.

It couldn't be. He held his breath. *Catherine?* He hadn't seen her since that terrible day when his family had been ripped away from Saignon. He hadn't asked after her, and Laurent had never mentioned her again. Luc stared coldly as the realisation began to sink in: this woman was not only a collaborator, but had likely tipped off Landry to Laurent and Fougasse.

And if she was handing over Laurent, then she surely was keeping her eyes peeled for Luc. Luc ducked as she turned in his direction, her red-painted lips still smiling, looking like a gash of blood.

He slid down the wall, pressing the heel of his palm to his eyes. *Think!* He could hear the accusations levelled at his friends as they resisted under torture. He could smell his own sorrow – not for himself, but for Laurent. Laurent, who still talked about the good days and who believed they'd come again, when both of them would have their lavender fields and honey back.

Luc heard the *milice* cock their rifles. They took aim. Just a second or two now. He couldn't bear to watch; let his memory of Laurent be of the ever-optimistic, smiling young man by his side for as long as he could remember.

'You can kill me, but you can't kill us all!' he heard Laurent yell.

Landry gave the order to fire with a bored air of detachment.

A burst of gunfire sounded. A woman shrieked nearby, stifling herself with her hand; men ground their jaws, threw down cigarettes and stubbed them out in disgust. As he heard the thump of bodies crumpling to the ground, Luc straightened, forced himself to be sure.

Landry was standing over Laurent, who groaned. Luc refused to close his eyes as the brute collaborator delivered the *coup de grâce* with a bullet into the back of Laurent's head. His friend's body jerked once and lay as still as Fougasse's. Landry gave loud orders for the corpses to be strung up in the town.

People began to disperse, but Luc couldn't move. He wanted to run and tear Landry's black heart out. Instead he watched the *milice* drag away his friends by their feet. Their brutal deaths demanded that Luc avenge them in the only way any resister would. He simply had to hurt the Germans and those who supported them.

He looked over to find Lisette and saw that she was drifting away with the crowd. When he caught up with her, she glanced at him, her eyes still wet with tears. 'We have to get out of here,' she warned.

'Not yet,' he said and grabbed her arm, pulling her back to the wall.

'What?'

'Go down this cobbled alley to the café. You've got a book?'

She nodded dumbly.

'Order a coffee. Wait for me.'

'People will —'

'They won't! I won't be long.'

'What are you doing?'

'What I must. Wait for me. One hour.'

She ripped her elbow from his grip and stomped away down the alley. Luc melted into the people moving like a river away from the square . . . and went in search of his prey.

15

Catherine was easy to follow. She suspected nothing, cocooned in safety by her alliance with Landry and his cronies.

Luc knew Gordes. He was sure she didn't. Before last year Catherine had barely travelled beyond the boundaries of Apt, but her life had clearly changed drastically.

He was certain now that Catherine had fingered Laurent and Fougasse. No doubt she had told them about him too. He racked his mind. Would she have a photo? No, or it would have been published by now. After Luc's family had been taken away, Fougasse had stolen back into the Bonet family home to collect every photo he could find of Luc. Burn them, he'd advised. They can incriminate you. Luc had refused. They were all he had left of his family. Instead he'd buried them in the mountains.

Luc blinked as he watched Catherine walking so carefree and confidently in her nice new coat – where did she get the money for it? He hated her with such intensity it shocked him; he had never contemplated killing a woman. But Catherine was no different to any other collaborator. In fact, she was worse, for she had no reason to support the Germans – no children to protect, no STO, and she lived in a quiet village off the German radar. If she had kept her red head down, she could have very likely got through the war without suffering. And yet here she was, working with the enemy, promoting the death of loyal French people; people she knew and had shared laughter and conversation with.

She deserved no mercy. This was war. She'd chosen her side. Once upon a time she had plaited his little sister's hair – and yet she had watched that same child being thrown into a truck, screaming for mercy without saying a word. Catherine must have known Laurent had always loved her; callously handing him over to Landry made her treachery seem even more evil. This woman had no heart . . . and a soul that feared no god.

From a safe distance Luc watched her enter a bar and settle at a large table, her curls bouncing. She gave the waiter her order, then moved deeper into the bar, towards what was surely the bathroom at the back. She climbed a small flight of stairs. This was it. His chance. He checked the time. Lisette had been waiting nearly fifteen minutes.

Before Luc could make a move, Landry arrived to divert his focus. Luc sucked in a breath and moved into the shadows of a doorway. The waiter welcomed Landry and pointed him to Catherine's table. Luc watched her emerge from the bathroom, and then place three kisses on his fat cheek. She slid into the seat next to him and giggled when he touched her.

Luc looked down, feeling sick. Catherine wasn't just a collaborator; she was Landry's woman. And it seemed the *milicien* was in a hurry – he knocked back his Pernod in two gulps. Her drink was largely untouched when Landry stood. She smiled and followed him. So did Luc, all the way to a guesthouse on the rim of town. It was quiet here, overlooking the valley. The couple walked in, oblivious to his presence, and he waited, checking his watch; twenty-seven minutes gone.

Should he do this? Was it wise? Roger would say no on both counts. His common sense echoed the same. But his heart – that most unreliable of judges – contradicted wisdom. He couldn't live with himself if he didn't try.

Luc sidled around the property, arriving at the backyard. He had no plan. There was an oldish woman bringing in linens from the line. It was late for her to be out, but he should have been more cautious. Now he'd been seen.

'What do you want?' she asked. 'We have no spare food.'

'Pardon, *madame*,' he said, and pulled his jacket collar up to shield his face as though against the cold. He turned to leave as fast as he could.

'Come back later,' she offered. 'After we've fed the guests; there may be some bread left, perhaps some soup.'

'Thank you,' he said. 'Many staying?'

She regarded him with hard eyes, then shook her head as she folded a pillow slip. 'Just the *milicien* pig and his whore,' she said and spat at her feet.

His luck was holding. 'Which room, *madame*?' he asked softly, moving back into the shadows.

Now she fixed him with a baleful stare, regarding him for so long that his pounding heart nearly made him take flight and run. 'Four,' she finally replied, even more softly than he. 'First floor. Wait until they finish. He's drunk, no more than five minutes.' She looked up to the laundry roof, and then further up to a window from where the faintest light bled. Then she turned away as though he wasn't there.

He waited ten minutes before stealing quietly from the laundry roof through the open window and onto the narrow landing within. He waited, listened. Nothing. He tiptoed down the hall and stood outside room four. He thought he could hear a tap; had imagined he'd encounter laughter, perhaps the springs of a bed.

Against all his better judgement he touched the flick knife in his pocket, hard, unyielding . . . and sharp. This was madness. Then he fingered the pouch of lavender strung around his neck and he remembered his grandmother; how Landry had viciously assaulted her. The screams of his little sister pierced the tense silence of his mind. He thought of Catherine's red smile, Laurent's head exploding from Landry's bullet . . . the two smears of blood on the ground where his friends had lain after their execution.

And he turned the knob on the door. He fully expected it to be locked. Perhaps he even hoped it would be, but the door opened silently. Inside it was dark and he could hear snoring: Landry's. From behind another door he could hear a tap running; Catherine was drawing a bath.

He crouched by the side of the bed and studied the face of the man he hated more than any. He could smell his fetid breath – a mixture of garlic and fish with aniseed from the Pernod. Luc grimaced, wondering what Catherine could see in this repulsive man. *This is for you, Saba*, he said to himself. *For you, Fougasse . . . and for you, Laurent.*

Landry's eyes flew open with pain but Luc already had a hand clamped over the meaty flesh of his mouth. Landry fought briefly but Luc was too strong.

'Listen to me, Landry,' Luc whispered, as the *milicien*'s eyes grew wider with panic. 'It's no use struggling. I've already punctured your heart . . . you have only seconds. The Bonets and the Martins and Fougasse of Saignon wish you *adieu* . . . all the way to hell.' With a savage satisfaction Luc watched the light die in Landry's eyes.

It was not the first time he had seen death close at hand. Of course he had seen a number of Nazi soldiers killed as a result of the Maquis bombs. Lighting a fuse or watching one of his fellow rebels pressing a detonator somehow removed him from the responsibility of slaughter. But once he'd been required to kill at close range – an older German soldier, fatally wounded but determined to take a French resister with him. He had felt sick after shooting the soldier, and Fougasse had sensed his disquiet. 'You're blooded now; the next will be easier.'

And it had been. Killing Landry hadn't just been easy, it had been satisfying. What had Luc become? A man who relished the death of another. Could he blame the war? This was about survival. Even here in Provence, removed from the blood and terror of battle, every day was still about surviving the next twenty-four hours without losing someone you knew, or loved . . . or losing your own life. It made you angry, defensive, territorial, suspicious, secretive . . . and above all, vengeful. Even the most generous soul could learn how to hate during wartime. Even the most peace-loving could kill if it meant making a choice between their own or the enemy.

And Catherine had chosen the side of the enemy.

With the smell of blood fresh in his nostrils, moving as though in a trance, Luc opened the bathroom door. There was a small lamp on. Catherine lay in the bath, her hair pulled up into a towel to keep it dry. She'd laid a damp flannel across her eyes. Steam rose from the water, scented with lavender. It was the lavender that caught him off guard. It made him remember how they'd lain together in the fields. He looked at her creamy skin and recalled those freckles on her shoulders. He'd kissed them often enough.

And with that thought erupted a squirm of panic. He couldn't do it. As much as he loathed the air Catherine breathed, he knew he could not kill her. No. He would let God punish her as he saw fit. Luc knew he had to get away fast – now. He was done for if she took off that flannel and saw him.

But she didn't. Instead Catherine smiled lazily. 'You were done so very quickly I didn't think you'd want more, especially with your Gestapo friends expecting you downstairs.'

Gestapo!

Luc took a deep breath. With his instincts screaming at him, he stepped back into the bedroom and closed the bathroom door softly. He didn't even look back at Landry's corpse but dimly registered the traitor's blood splattered darkly on his shirt. Landry's shirt lay discarded nearby, and Luc grabbed it and quickly undressed. The blood on his own shirt would make him a target. Suddenly he heard the bathroom door open. Catherine had come to see why her lover had not replied. For a second or so, naked in the bathroom doorway, she stared in disbelief at Luc.

The spell of silence was broken when her gaze shot to the bed, and in the couple of heartbeats it took for realisation to sink in, Luc was upon her. In two rapid strides he was across the room, and as she took a breath to scream, his hand whipped through the air brutally to backhand her. It was the first time he'd ever hit a woman; he hoped it was the last. The scream died in her throat.

And then it all seemed to happen so fast. In shock and in sudden pain, Catherine staggered backwards. Her arms flailed as she slipped on the wet floor and fell awkwardly, banging her head with an almighty crack on the edge of the iron tub.

She lay still, eyes closed, legs splayed, her fiery hair spread out around her like a halo. Luc was frozen in the doorway, listening for any sound that indicated they'd been heard. He took a breath and calmed himself, running a hand through his hair and buttoning up the shirt. Outside a car pulled up and he tiptoed over to the window. Gestapo. Catherine hadn't moved; he wanted to see if she was breathing but didn't dare waste another second. Instead he made sure he had his knife and the key to the room.

He emerged from the room silently and locked the door before climbing back through the window at the end of the hall. He crept across the roof and was already running sure-footed down the hillside before the first knock at the room. It would be several more minutes before a spare key was found and the alarm raised, by which time Luc had already made his circuitous route back into the town.

Luc was sure he would return to Lisette within the hour, taking only a couple of minutes to hide the key in a crevice, which he covered with rocks. His only nagging worry was whether Catherine would recover sufficiently to name him. He should have killed her. In her unconscious state it would have been easy to let her drown. Luc could see Fougasse in his mind's eye, shaking his head at leaving such a dangerous loose end.

Speed would protect Luc. If he could get them into Cavaillon and Lisette onto a train before the authorities began looking beyond Gordes, then he had a fighting chance of dispersing into the Luberon, where they would never find him.

Lisette had read the same line of her book six or seven times already. All she could hear was the sound of the gun shots as Laurent was killed. Even now, nearly an hour since, she was still trembling. The execution had been so vicious; no amount of training could have prepared her for the horror of the premeditated, deliberate and cold murder she'd witnessed today.

Lisette reached for her drink, begging her fingers not to shake. She couldn't sip the *pastis* but it helped to grip the glass to steady herself. She had to go through the motions and deflect even the casual observer's interest.

What had stunned her the most was the stoic resolve of the people around her; presumably they'd seen this sort of horror before. Few wept or cried out, no one said much at all. They bore witness, as their enemies insisted, but perhaps also out of a strange sort of respect.

She tried to banish the memory by closing her book and taking a proper sip of the throat-burning, milky licorice drink. Lisette had resisted checking her watch; but she estimated fifty minutes had passed since Luc had shoved her towards the café. He'd said one hour. Then what? He hadn't given her an alternative.

She would give Luc the ten minutes he was due, after which she would leave and somehow make her own way to Cavaillon. But just as she had resolved to do so, she saw Luc finally arrive. Her heart leapt with relief as he rushed up to her and kissed her on the lips. She knew it was for show but she couldn't help but tremble all the more. As he held her hands, gazed into her eyes, she could see a fierce energy burning behind them.

'Ready to go?' he murmured close to her ear.

She giggled, keeping up the pretence. 'Shouldn't you order something?'

'We have to go,' he said casually, throwing some coins onto the table before guiding her out of the café.

'You've changed your shirt,' she said as he began to run.

'Well spotted. We have to get to Cavaillon on the last bus. We've got nine minutes. I hope you're up to a run.'

The bus had already started its engine when Luc rushed up and banged on the door. The driver had let them in and sighed as he accepted their fare.

Luc led Lisette to the back of the bus and deliberately took a seat nearest the window. There were few passengers on board and they were left to themselves to catch their breath. The bumpy bus ride took them down into the Durance Valley, at the foot of the hill Saint-Jacques. Cavaillon, their destination, was an important trading post of Marseilles in its heyday and had since become a lively market town famous for the best melons in France.

Luc yawned. 'Wake me if there are any Gestapo raids,' he warned.

Lisette dug him in the ribs. He knew what was coming – Lisette was no fool. He stared now into her grave face, her large dark eyes looking far too deeply.

'What did you do?'

He regarded her blankly.

'Tell me.'

'Leave it,' he said.

'You killed him?' she asked, her voice a deathly whisper. 'That man who shot Laurent?'

He took a deep, silent breath and closed his eyes, thinking about just how close he'd come to killing Catherine too. Visions of his father's disappointed face, his elder sisters staring at him in disbelief. Was he becoming as bad as the very men he despised?

'Yes,' he answered. 'He was a truly evil man, Lisette. Laurent took his chances, knew what the price might be, but Landry has murdered so many innocents.'

Her eyes flashed in anger. 'And you are his judge?'

'He has been responsible for the death of too many good people.' Luc wished she wouldn't hold his gaze like that, and he wished even more that he could turn away at this moment. He felt so vulnerable, so impaled by her stare. 'He kills children – babies and infants – as easily as you watched him kill Laurent.'

'Will the *milice* take reprisals on the people of Gordes?'

That fear had been nagging at him too.

'Probably.'

'And so you're helping him to kill more children,' she replied, her words like ice. 'Does that sit comfortably on your conscience?'

'No,' he squirmed, stung.

'And you've jeopardised my life for your vendetta. What is his name?'

'What does it matter?' His discomfort deepened. '*Milicien* Pierre Landry, for all that might mean to you.'

'Did *Milicien* Landry kill your family?'

He inhaled; knew his expression gave her the answer. 'You ask too many questions. You should know better.'

'I want to know what I'm dealing with. Your actions might compromise my situation.'

'You let me worry about that.'

'No. You might be my guide but I'm in control of my own mission. I will make my own decisions – and I will make my own way to Paris without your help.'

'That wasn't Roger's plan,' he said.

'Neither was murdering someone, but that didn't stop you,' Lisette hissed. 'No, Luc. Now you've become a liability and you're risking my mission. I will go on alone from Cavaillon.'

He ground his jaw. She was right, of course.

She grabbed the front of his shirt in her fist. 'Will this incriminate you if we're stopped?' Then she blinked. 'What's that?' she said, looking at his chest.

'Nothing,' he said and slowly removed her fingers from the shirt.

'What is this?' Lisette asked once more, reaching inside and pulling out a pouch, warmed by his chest.

He didn't stop her. As she held the pouch he moved to touch it too; he ended up simply covering her hand with his. Neither moved.

'Just some lavender seeds,' he said, with a slightly embarrassed shrug. 'And a few flowerheads.'

In that moment her expression changed. The anger dissolved, and while he hated the pity that he thought he saw, there was compassion there too.

'Tell me about this lavender, and about Landry.'

And before he knew it, Luc was talking. Talk was dangerous; he knew that. And he hadn't spoken of his former life, not with anyone. Even with Laurent, they'd never spoken about Saignon or their families. Did Laurent know it was Catherine who'd sold him out? Perhaps it was Laurent's death that made him want to talk, to spill his memories to this pretty English agent with her beautiful French voice and beguiling smile. He told her his story. She didn't ask any questions; she just listened. He watched tears glisten in her eyes, and knew his own were misting as he spoke. 'They keep me safe. I'll plant them one day.'

When he finished, her eyes were soft with understanding. 'You are brave to have shared so much with me. I feel as though I know you better than anyone I've called a friend before.' She shook her head. 'I had to watch someone I loved die not so long ago. I understand your pain better than you think. You can trust me, Luc. I will never betray you. And when this is all over, then I will help you sow your lavender seeds again. You'll have your perfumed lavender fields, once more, I promise.' Lisette gave a small smile.

'I don't think that your hard demeanour is the true you at all,' she continued. 'One day I hope I'll see you throw back your head and laugh loudly. I want to hear that laugh. Thank you for taking care of me and . . .' Her eyes grew teary again. 'I'm sorry that you lost your friends while looking after me. Perhaps if not for me, Laurent might . . .'

'No! This was not your fault.' There was something in the earnest manner she had spoken that touched his heart in a way that no one else ever had. He squeezed her hand beneath his, and without any warning leaned across the few inches that separated them and kissed her softly. He didn't mean for it to last, but Lisette did not pull away; in fact, she deepened it.

It was the bus lurching to a stop that separated them. Suddenly Lisette looked embarrassed.

'Do up your shirt,' she murmured, reaching below her seat for her small holdall. 'How long before the train leaves?'

Luc cleared his throat. 'You have about forty minutes to wait.' He felt a strange awakening, an unfamiliar sensation, as though his heart was racing.

'Good. Perhaps we can get something to eat.'

Lisette stood and walked down the aisle of the bus without looking back. Her breathing felt ragged. What was she doing? She let Luc kiss her, and the truth was she had been helpless beneath his lips. And his kiss – so tender, so needy. She'd sensed all of his vulnerability and sorrow in that sensual touch. *Stop it!* Her pulse quickened again at the memory. Lisette knew if she so much as turned to glance back at him, she would be lost in him again. And she couldn't afford to – not with her mission at hand.

As he had told his sorrowful tale, she had been absently watching the way his large hands pushed back his blonde hair. And when he had been looking down, unaware of her observation, she'd returned her gaze again and again to the long lashes that framed his eyes. His voice fascinated her most of all; for a big man he spoke surprisingly softly, and there was a mellowness to his tone that spoke of poetry.

Perhaps, when this ugly war was done, and if they were both alive to see that happy day, they might . . . What was she thinking? *Walk, Lisette*, she told herself, *and don't turn around.*

16

In the Place Gambetta, Luc pointed towards l'Avenue Garibaldi. 'There's the railway bridge we drove beneath,' he said. 'Over there is the station.'

Lisette could see the station was probably three hundred or so metres away.

Quickly they agreed upon a cover story: they had been in Gordes today, but not after four p.m. They would say that they'd taken a lift from the Senanque Abbey with Père François, who was making a delivery of honey.

'Just follow my lead if we're asked,' Luc assured her as they made their way into the main street. 'We don't want to wait around the station. It's too inviting for *milice* to check our papers, so let's just keep walking to kill some time. We'll find somewhere to eat. And maybe we could talk too? It looks more natural for a couple to talk,' he added dryly.

The kiss was haunting Lisette's thoughts, and she hadn't realised how awkwardly silent she'd become. 'Where do the Germans stay here?' she asked.

'They've taken over the two schools in the town. All their meals are prepared daily at the hospital and a patrol fetches them.'

'Is the Maquis ever tempted to poison the food?'

'All the time, but frankly we can achieve far more by sabotaging an electric transformer or blowing up the cylinders of trains. It sets the Boches back badly, buys the Allies more time. Besides, it's quicker, takes two men at most and is generally less dangerous to our people.'

'I suppose the reprisals on a town for something like a poisoning would be savage too.'

'Unthinkable. And really for little gain.'

They strolled down Boulevard Gambetta, one of two main boulevards; it was typically wide, lined with huge plane trees that were naked for winter, their bare branches clawing at the cold air. Lisette imagined they would be beautiful and shady in summer. The smell of food wafting from the cafés made her belly grind.

Luc led her past the Café Riche in the main street and another, Café de l'Orient. Both looked welcoming but also appeared crowded, especially with German soldiers, so they moved closer to the station where they ate in silence at a tiny terminus café that smelt of old bouillabaisse and tobacco. The woman serving them added the sour note of old sweat.

Lisette didn't feel at all like eating – the cook's grubby apron alone put her off – but she knew she must. The long walks uphill, the constant activity and the small amounts of food she'd consumed in recent days all added up to weight loss. She'd always been slim but had never considered herself scrawny. Food rationing and intensive training had stripped her already lean body to nothing but muscle. And now she could feel her ribs a little too keenly through her borrowed clothes, and the coat Luc had got for her was not keeping out the cold. Her teeth were beginning to chatter.

She ordered an omelette of mushrooms and courgettes and quietly moved her fork around her plate, pleading silently that Luc would not say another word other than goodbye. An hour earlier he had been a stranger. Now she felt closer to him than she had to any other human being. She could barely look at him, unsure of her feelings, frightened to admit that their brief intimacy had weakened her when she most needed to be strong. Her head was still spinning from his kiss, his touch, so tender, and bringing with it the sorrow of his life and the brightness of his fields of lavender before war had come to France.

For that reason alone, it was a relief to know they'd part company here. She had already bought her ticket and there was not long to wait now. She carefully crossed her fork over her knife on the plate. The omelette was tasteless but she'd forced it down.

Luc touched her hand briefly. 'Lisette . . . I'm sorry. It was wrong.'

She nodded, not looking at him. 'Killing a man in such cold blood can never be —'

'No. I meant kissing you.'

Her traitorous eyes flashed helplessly up to meet his. 'They say times like these make us reckless,' she replied.

'Do they?'

She didn't know what to say; didn't have enough experience with men to know how to handle this. 'How much longer before the train leaves?'

He sighed. 'We can start walking to the platform now.' He dug in his pocket for money but she was too quick for him and tumbled out some coins from her purse.

'Where will you go now?' she asked, deliberately avoiding eye contact, fiddling with her things.

'I'm not sure. I'll have to lay very low for a while. I'll stick to the mountains.'

She found her courage and looked at him with a brief smile. 'Through winter?'

Now he had her, his eyes gazing into hers. His had become the colour of a stormy sky over the Brighton promenade. She wondered if this man of sorrows would ever reflect sun in his eyes again.

'Winter is our safekeeper,' he replied.

She nodded. Then stood. There was nothing more to say. They drifted out into the crisp night air and almost walked into a handful of German soldiers.

'*Pardon, messieurs,*' Luc said amiably and put his arm around Lisette casually.

There seemed to be a lot of soldiers out on the street despite the cold, sitting outside the cafés, chatting up shivering girls. Lisette gave Luc a brief questioning look.

'We're barely eight kilometres from Avignon,' Luc explained. 'It's the headquarters for the south. Plenty of soldiers around . . . even a Gestapo base at l'Hôtel Splendid.'

Lisette felt sick, and wished he'd never mentioned it. Now she wanted to run into the station, a rather lovely old two-storey build-ing with huge shuttered windows, tall arched double doors and a clock in the roof. But with Luc's solid arm to hang onto, she man-aged to hold her nerve and walk calmly. She couldn't talk but he kept up a stream of chatter, pointing out buildings of significance, including the cathedral, and telling her of the remains of the once triumphant Roman arch that she'd seen soldiers leaning against.

They walked onto the platform; the train was waiting but the porters were busy and not yet allowing passengers to board.

She turned to him. 'Thank you for getting me here.'

He regarded her deeply. Just when she thought the silence could last no longer, he cleared his throat. 'Stay safe, Lisette.'

She nodded, hesitated, looked around to be sure there was no one close. 'I lost my closest friend not so long ago in a bombing raid. It's one of the reasons I'm doing this, but I hope my anger won't make me do something reckless. I hope the same for you. Please take care of yourself.' She touched his chest and felt the slim pouch of seeds against his hard body. 'Or who is going to plant the lavender fields again?'

His smile was brief but soft, reaching his eyes. He bent

forward and kissed each of her cheeks gently. 'Don't forget your promise,' he replied. 'One day we will plant the lavender fields together.'

There was such tenderness and vulnerability in his look that she had to turn away. He helped her onto the train and carried her holdall. Once she was settled, Luc stepped off the train and she came to the door to wave goodbye. It was important to keep up appearances. It would just be a few minutes now.

'I'll wait until you go,' he said.

Neither of them was aware of the soldiers until one of them cleared his throat behind Lisette.

'Excuse me, please?'

The man was Gestapo. He smiled, pushing past Lisette politely and stepping off the train, followed by his henchman. 'May I see your papers please, *mademoiselle*? Yours too, *monsieur*, if you please.'

Stay calm! Lisette repeated in her mind. 'Is something wrong?' she said in German, relieved to hear her voice sounded steady.

The man gave her a look that said he was impressed and blew out his lips in a casual gesture of insouciance. 'Routine checks, although we have reason to believe that someone fitting your description, *Monsieur* . . . er . . . ?'

'Ravensburg,' Luc finished for him.

'Ravensburg?' The officer grinned, clearly bemused by the German name. 'Indeed, as I was saying, someone of your description might be wanted in connection with the criminals who call themselves Maquis.'

Luc gave a snort. 'With a name like mine, I doubt I could get within shouting distance of a resister, Herr . . . ?'

'Kriminalsekretar von Schleigel.'

'Nor, may I add, would I want to,' Luc continued in flawless German. 'I would fight for my country if I were allowed.'

Lisette noticed how Luc stood very straight; he was making a very good show of it. She mustn't falter, she told herself, realising she was committed to this man in more ways than she had anticipated.

She took a slow, silent breath and began to perform as she had been trained.

17

Luc's papers were a brilliant forgery, but he was far more concerned that Lisette's papers wouldn't hold up to scrutiny.

'You are German?' The Gestapo man stared at the paperwork. 'But living in France?' He was speaking in French and Luc was sure he was showing off.

'I am,' Luc replied, knowing he must try to sound almost bored with the explanation. 'I'm from Sault, sir.'

'Ah, it is very beautiful there . . . the mountains, the snow, the deer locking antlers in the frost-covered fields. Very picturesque. So, where are you going?' The man reached for Lisette's papers.

'I am not going anywhere, sir. I have come to Cavaillon to see my friend, Mademoiselle Forestier, off to Paris. She has been visiting Provence.'

'Paris, *mademoiselle*?' he said. 'Ah, but I see you are of German background too. How interesting.'

'Yes, sir,' Lisette replied in German. 'But I know it's going to be freezing up north. I wish I could stay here just a bit longer.'

He gave her a charmless grin. 'Are you romantically involved?'

Luc didn't wait for Lisette to reply. 'We hope to be engaged. But not yet, Herr von Schleigel. You know how it is, what with war . . .'

'I do, Herr Ravensburg. You live in Paris, Fraulein Foerstner?' he asked.

Luc watched her face light up. 'I will from tomorrow,' she said. 'I'm moving to the capital.'

'For work?'

Luc scrutinised the man and decided they would have to tread extremely carefully. The officer was probably in his early forties; small, slim, viciously neat in the cold way that Gestapo officers prided themselves on. He wore the grey uniform with evident conceit and wore a monocle that he squeezed in front of his right eye to read their papers in the low light. Luc could hear the man's boots creaking as he rocked on his heels, and his matching black leather gloves looked soft and warm. Kriminalsekretar. It was a lowly enough position. Luc wondered if he'd been overlooked, perhaps, or had made enemies. Either way, he was a zealot; it was written all over him.

But what mattered right now was the cunning spark in the man's eyes. He was toying with them. Lisette was answering all the man's questions without hesitation or any stumblings. She didn't sound frightened, though. And she was flirting slightly; he'd begun to see how this girl had been chosen for her role. When not her cool, somewhat prickly self, she could present as a confident, bright young woman.

The stationmaster gave the signal for departure and Luc heard the porters beginning to slam doors down the platform.

Von Schleigel could hear the unspoken question. 'Pardon me, Mademoiselle Forestier,' he said, 'please, you are free to go,' he said, giving a curt bow of his head. 'My apologies for detaining you – it is merely routine. Monsieur Ravensburg, I will have to ask you to accompany us,' he said. 'I just have a few more questions for you.'

'Lukas?' Lisette queried.

'Do not worry yourself,' von Schleigel said. 'Mere protocol, *mademoiselle. Bon voyage.*'

The porter arrived to close her door as a whistle shrieked. Luc turned and kissed Lisette again on both cheeks as he took her hands. He squeezed them. 'My best to Walter and good luck with your new job. Think of me often,' he said, and touched the lavender beneath his shirt. 'Off you go,' he said with a grin. He closed the door on her himself, glaring at the look of concern she was showing. *Nothing silly, Lisette*, he pleaded inwardly. He stepped back, closer to von Schleigel, giving her a final wave. She was on the train. One more blow of the whistle and she would be out of the station and beginning the journey north. His job would be done. Another blow struck for French loyalists against the Germans.

'Wait!' Lisette called.

He couldn't believe it. She was opening the door, flinging out her holdall. A third whistle sounded.

'What are you doing, my darling?' he asked, just short of yelling.

'Mademoiselle Forestier? Is something wrong?' von Schleigel asked.

'Forgive me, but I can't leave my beloved alone like this. What sort of fiancée would I be to leave my intended to be questioned by police?' She gave a soft sigh. 'There is always a train tomorrow. If we can help with your enquiries, then as dutiful Germans we will.'

Luc's spirits plummeted as fast as his heart rate accelerated. What did she think she was doing! Rescuing him? He was so angry he couldn't even look at her.

'Well, that's very thoughtful of you. I'm sure we shan't need to keep you very long.' Von Schleigel gestured the way off the platform. 'These days we cannot be too careful – I'm sure you understand – and we are checking all the trains headed out of the south.'

'Why?' Luc asked, shaking off Lisette's arm when she tried to link it with his.

'New orders. There's been an ugly event in Gordes today and we can't be too careful.'

'Do you mean the executions?' Luc asked.

'You know about them?'

'We heard in one of the cafés,' Lisette said.

'Those men were criminals; we had to make an example of them to deter others,' von Schleigel said, showing them to a big black car.

Luc paused. They couldn't be onto him . . . Why weren't they going to the l'Hôtel Splendide? 'May I ask where we're being taken? We've had nothing to do with the event in Gordes,' he risked.

'No, Monsieur Ravensburg, forgive me. Our interest in you is separate to that. Please,' von Schleigel said, achingly polite. 'Just a few questions.'

They drove in a tense silence from Cavaillon; von Schleigel sat in front with the driver, while Luc and Lisette were watched by a granite-faced *milicien*.

'Ever been to l'Isle sur la Sorgue?' von Schleigel asked.

Lisette shook her head wordlessly. Luc noticed even her feigned bubbliness had burst. He could feel her leaning into his body, away from the *milicien*. As much as she had infuriated him, he wanted to touch her reassuringly. But under the stony-faced gaze of the man with them, he refrained.

'I've been there,' he remarked.

'Such a delightful spot. You French – er, may I call you that? You have it so good down here in the south. Who would know a war was on? You can stroll around the wide streets with the water-wheels and that splendid river curling around the town. And, oh, Fontaine de Vaucluse. Well, I've never been so glad of such a place this summer . . .'

Von Schleigel was up to something. Why the friendly banter? And why l'Isle sur la Sorgue?

Luc stared glumly out of the window of the car. It reminded him of the one his father had once driven in Paris. He blinked, trying not to think of anything connected with the past. The only thing that now mattered was getting both of them away from the oily von Schleigel.

Rows of grapes stretched into the darkness as they fringed the outlying vineyard region that the Popes of Avignon had planted in the eleventh and twelfth centuries.

'Ha! Those Popes knew about having a good time, eh, Ravensburg. I must admit, I too have enjoyed a bottle or two from Chateauneuf du Papes. I had not tasted burgundy until I came here.'

Luc pasted a smile on his face. 'Us farmers wouldn't know, Herr von Schleigel, although I was once fortunate to taste a riesling of the Rhine,' he lied, 'and I can't imagine any wine could be more exquisite.'

'Ah, now you're talking about what we call a dessert wine, Ravensburg. Noble rot!' the Gestapo said, with a flourish. 'Who would have given you such a thing growing up in France?'

Another mistake. Why did he embellish? He was breaking his own rules, while Lisette kept her lips wisely sealed.

Luc gave an expansive shrug. 'I was a child. I can't remember anything about it, other than its sweetness.'

'Hmm, interesting,' von Schleigel replied, although Luc couldn't imagine what he referred to.

Mercifully, perhaps, they rolled into l'Isle sur la Sorgue. The oldest part of the town, which Jacob Bonet had once told his son could likely be traced back to a fishing village in Roman times, became a haven for the Jewish people in the fourteenth century when they were expelled from most of France and fled to the papal territories. Luc blinked at the horrible irony of this thought. The traditionally bustling market square – these days operating mainly for the benefit of two German garrisons – was hugged by the two arms of the River Sorgue, with its great church – Notre Dame des Anges – held within that embrace.

Von Schleigel was waxing lyrical about the church. Luc nodded as though paying attention, but his mind was racing to where they were being taken. The black car drove by the old town and kept going. The place was eerily quiet; the locals moved around by foot, or bicycle if they had them. Curfew was approaching.

The car began turning left into a grand property. The two stone pillars that sat at the entrance were draped with Nazi flags, which in Luc's frame of mind looked almost like blood was dripping from the pillars. Soldiers guarded the gate, and as von Schleigel announced his arrival, Luc saw Lisette steal a glance at him.

Her eyes, looking even bigger in the dark of the car, were expressive, and they conveyed only apology. He gave her the small reassuring nod he'd wanted to all the way here.

'Ah, here we are,' von Schleigel was saying. 'Headquarters.'

The *milicien* gestured for Luc and Lisette to get out of the car. Luc emerged first and took Lisette's hand.

'Don't worry, my dearest,' he said, but then whispered, 'No heroics. Get yourself out.'

Lisette walked close to him, allowing him to take her arm, somehow achieving a mix of fearfulness and awe at being permitted into the sanctum of the German command in this part of Provence.

Von Schleigel was met by two men. One was so young he still had pimples.

'Now, Mademoiselle Forestier, if you please, I will ask you to go with our assistant,' von Schleigel said. 'He will make sure you are comfortable and perhaps we can offer you a coffee – a real one?'

She nodded blankly, looked towards Luc. 'And —'

'Oh, please don't worry your pretty head for your Lukas. We just want to have a chat with him. You'll be reunited before you know it.'

Luc gave her a push. 'Go ahead, Lisette; I'm keen to help.' And then he grinned. 'Real coffee . . . have one for me too.'

She smiled faintly and allowed herself to be escorted away.

Von Schleigel turned to Luc. 'Come this way.'

Luc didn't move. He frowned as he stood there.

Von Schleigel made a show of turning. 'Well, come on,' he said in German.

'What do you want with me?'

'Just a few questions about a man we're hunting. But let's wait until we're somewhere more private, *monsieur*.'

18

Luc shook his head. 'You have me mistaken, sir.'

'Perhaps. Come.'

Luc felt he had no choice. He couldn't make a break for it. A bullet would find his back in seconds; he was sure von Schleigel was just itching for an excuse.

He allowed himself to be shown into a room, very tastefully furnished and with the lingering smell of leather and tobacco. He was led through to another room – much smaller, windowless, with just a little table with two metal chairs on either side. It looked to be an old storage room. Now it would serve as his interrogation room, Luc realised. For a brief moment he wondered whether he should have carried the cynanide pill that Fougasse had shown him. The suicide pills – or 'poppers', for the sound they made when bitten down on – had been made by a female Jewish resister who had since been arrested, tortured and executed in primitive fashion.

His mind was wandering. *Block out everything.* Only the cover story mattered, he silently admonished.

'Please?' von Schleigel said, waving at the chair on the far side.

Luc sat down and met the man's cold stare. 'Whoever this person is you are hunting, it is not me.'

'Ah, I like a man who cuts straight to the point, although I never did say that it *was* you.' Von Schleigel carefully plucked at the fingers of his leather gloves and laid them on the table next to a manila folder. 'German or French?' the man offered.

Luc shrugged. 'As you wish. I'm sure you'll find it easier in German.'

'Tell me again about your life.'

Luc didn't sigh, didn't raise his eyes, didn't sound frustrated by having to repeat what had already been said. In deliberately flawed German he told von Schleigel everything he'd already told him at the station and a whole lot more that stuck very closely to the truth.

'Your German is really rather admirable, considering you grew up in southern France.'

Luc was glad his subtle errors had been noticed. 'I was determined to learn my mother tongue. I hope to return to Germany and refine my language.'

'So you grow your lavender in Sault?'

'From wild stock. It is the premium *Lavendula angustifolia*. My essential oil forms the base of most of the perfumes that the German officers will give to their wives and their mistresses this Christmas,' he remarked, as lightheartedly as he dared. 'But naturally I must devote some fields purely for antiseptic. That's what's in demand right now.'

'And what of the lavender fields around Apt?'

'Where?' Luc asked, playing for time. He knew what was coming.

'Saignon, for instance,' von Schleigel said, pronouncing it wrong.

'What of it? The Saignon fields provide only the more astringent oil,' he lied. 'Soap, antiseptic.'

'But you don't grow much lavender for antiseptic?'

'I do, sir. Men are dying at the Front and if my fields can help save lives, then that is what I'm doing. Is this about me not being at the Front? Because —'

'No. Let me tell you what this is about.' Von Schleigel smiled.

To Luc it was the same smile that Landry had worn when he'd punched his grandmother and ordered his family to be thrown into a truck; the smile of the devil. 'I have been asked to supervise the crackdown on guerilla activities in and around the Vaucluse region. These are little more than criminals – murderers among them. This whole region believes itself a stronghold for the cowardly partisans who, I'm sorry to say, find some sympathy with disgruntled locals. However, we've had some success.' The leather of his boots creaked as he sat back. 'The executions today at Gordes took out a particularly nasty pair. My men tell me it will be a very good deterrent. We shall leave them swinging from the gibbet through the rest of winter.' He smiled his little ratlike smile. 'I'm hoping they freeze and remain a monument to cowardice for the entire season.'

Luc kept his expression slightly baffled. 'So what has this got to do with me, Herr von Schleigel?'

There was a knock at the door and an aide returned, whispered something to his superior and left quietly.

Von Schleigel nodded thoughtfully. 'I've made some enquiries about you, Ravensburg.'

Luc showed a dash of indignity. 'And?'

'It seems you are indeed German. I gather your father died at the end of the Great War.'

'On the very day the Armistice was declared.'

'A man fitting your description is rumoured to be friends with the two executed maquisards.'

'And that's a crime?'

Von Schleigel's eyes remained glacial. 'We think he too is a maquisard.'

'And you think I am that man?' Luc asked incredulously.

Von Schleigel gave a bemused shrug. 'The description is similar. I'm not quite sure yet how a German-born man, raised in France, can quite come to terms with the occupation of his adopted country, with his friends sent away, and his life so disrupted. I have to wonder whether he would feel French or German.'

'And yet here we are, speaking German. What's more, my German fiancée is in a nearby room, my crops are growing for the German soldiers. I'm not sure how much more proof you would want, Herr von Schleigel. And let's not ignore the fact that no resisters are going to let a German near them.'

The Gestapo officer held up a finger. 'Very good points. This is the conundrum I face, Ravensburg. Are you German or are you French? Are you working against Germany or for it? Are you telling me the truth, or are you a very accomplished liar?'

'I am a lavender grower from Sault. Until a few years ago I knew nothing about war other than that it was responsible for the death of my parents. I know only how to extract the essential oil from my flowers. I think like a Frenchman, but in my heart I'm German. Are you asking me about my politics, Herr von Schleigel? I don't have any. I am someone who straddles two nations. Right now, I feel more German than I ever have; I don't want anyone to die – German or French. I have ambition to extend the farming operation, a woman I want to marry . . .' He opened his palms. 'Why would I want to jeopardise that?'

Von Schleigel nodded. 'You were in Gordes today?'

Luc didn't dare lie here. 'Yes.'

'You saw the executions?'

He had to risk it. 'No. We'd already left for the abbey. I wanted to show Lisette the beautiful valley and where lavender grows in summer. We heard about the executions in a café when we got back.' Luc felt confident that Père Auguste would substantiate his story. 'I don't see where this is leading.'

Von Schleigel's eyes glittered with malice. 'I'm accusing you of being a maquisard who slit the throat of Milicien Landry earlier today as retribution for the death of the two partisans.' His tone was even.

Luc looked at him with shock and disbelief. He stood up angrily, scraping his chair. 'With all due respect, Herr von Schleigel, this is an outrageous accusation.'

'Sit down, please,' the Gestapo man said, annoyingly calm. 'Don't make me insist.'

Luc ran a hand through his hair and sat down.

'There is a man from Saignon who fits your description. His name is Bonet.'

Luc's heart, already pounding so hard he was sure von Schleigel could hear it, felt as though it had suddenly stopped.

'Mean anything to you?'

'I know of Saignon. I have only passed through it once, though. Bonet?' He shrugged. 'Never heard of him.'

'Information is thin. We think he may have been a farmer. Fruit, perhaps.'

Luc felt relief loosening his twisted insides. 'Is that the connection? Both of us farmers in Provence!'

'He is tall and his hair is not dark, we're told.' Von Schleigel gave a small laugh, glancing up at Luc's hair that glowed golden beneath the single bulb.

'I don't know what you want me to say. That could be a score or more different farmers of the Luberon. Does he speak German?'

'I don't know . . . Does he?'

'Herr von Schleigel, how can I be this man Bonet? My name is Lukas Ravensburg. There are many of my height and weight. You have checked out my details, you say. Why doesn't that convince you?'

Von Schleigel shifted again. It was his turn to stand. He clasped his hands neatly behind his back. 'Your German is too good for you to be anything but what you say. I agree your papers are exactly in order.'

'I am Lukas Ravensburg of Sault, originally of Bavaria,' Luc pressed, lacing his tone with frustration. 'Have the people of Saignon pointed you to me?'

'No, not at all. I have been following the trail of all maquisards from the region. This fellow Bonet is a suspect; not confirmed. The gendarmes of Apt believe that when his family was taken away Bonet left the region, and is probably dead. He was never seen beyond that day.'

'His family was taken away?'

'Vermin,' von Schleigel said tightly. 'An old Jew and his slut women.'

'Is this a joke?' Luc said, hotly, feeling his cheeks burn with rage. 'Look at me, sir. Do I look Jewish?'

'Absolutely not. In fact, you embody precisely what a true Aryan should. But there is some question that this Bonet fellow may not have been a blood relative member of the family. Too many coincidences?'

'You could look at it that way, or you could say that anyone could willfully misinterpret information to suit their own ends. Who is giving you this information?'

Von Schleigel gave a sigh. 'Milicien Landry was murdered today. Did you know him?'

'No,' Luc replied firmly.

'Well, Landry's fiancée was a young woman from a hamlet nearby.'

Fiancée! It was pointless saying anything further or trying to deny any more. Catherine had talked. Luc would not give von Schleigel the satisfaction of watching him squirm. Let him make his accusations. He looked expressionlessly at the German, waiting for the sword to fall.

'This woman, Catherine Girard, was also killed.'

He felt instantly sick. Catherine dead? Practice taught him to betray nothing.

'Convenient, don't you think?'

'I have no idea.'

'Perhaps she caught the killer in the act.'

'What does this *milicien* and his fiancée have to do with me?'

Von Schleigel threw up his hands in mock despair. 'Precisely. But this Girard woman tipped us off about Bonet. Until yesterday we thought she was an unreliable source, but when she delivered two known maquisards, I must admit I became very interested in her knowledge. I sent a car to pick her up. But here we have feminine wiles at work, Ravensburg. She told Landry that if the *milice* caught anyone fitting Bonet's description, she wanted to confirm it herself. Such a shame she's dead. You see, Ravensburg, I would have found all the information I needed from Mademoiselle Girard. Instead I have no real description of the man she wanted to give us, not even his full name. She just called him Bonet.'

Luc was stunned. Catherine had wanted to hurt him – but not just that, she wanted to be there for the final blow. She had wanted to look into his eyes when she pointed the finger.

'And then I have you, arriving into Cavaillon from Gordes, fitting my description on the very day that Landry and his fiancée are murdered.' Von Schleigel smiled, blinking behind his monocle.

'And that's precisely what a coincidence is, Herr von Schleigel . . . unbelievable timing.'

Von Schleigel gave a dry laugh that sounded more like a cough. 'Wait here please, Ravensburg.'

As Luc's confidence rose, he took another chance. 'And where are you going? To rustle up another witness who can unequivocally tell you I'm not Lukas Ravensburg?'

'No, *monsieur*. I am going to have a little chat with Mademoiselle Forestier. Make yourself comfortable.'

Luc slumped in his seat but his hand absently reached for his precious pouch of seeds.

19

Lisette waited in a small, comfortable room but despite the opulent armchairs and warm lighting she felt every inch the prisoner of the Gestapo. She'd practised this very event during training: how to look untroubled, bored even, while you knew you were being watched.

She sighed, made a show of walking around the small room, glancing at the few token books on a shelf, and then staring out of the window. Her face was impatient and she escalated her indignity for every fifteen minutes that passed.

After about an hour, the door opened and von Schleigel stepped into the room.

'Ah, please forgive the long wait, Mademoiselle Forestier. I hope you've been comfortable?'

She followed her instincts and went on the offensive. 'In truth, Herr von Schleigel, as a German, I'm most uncomfortable to find myself as some sort of detainee of the Gestapo.' She summoned one of her iciest looks.

He tutted. 'We must do our job, *mademoiselle*.'

Lisette could see in his crafty, intelligent eyes that he loved the challenge of baiting.

'Is the Gestapo above the law, Kriminalsekretar?'

He hadn't expected that question. His smile faltered slightly. 'No, but we are charged to uncover those who work against the regime.'

'And what have you uncovered about my fiancé?'

'There is something about him that raises my suspicions. Instincts urge me to dig deep.'

She gave a slow, measured sigh and decided to play the ace she held. It was not a card she could play again easily. 'Herr von Schleigel, have you heard of Walter Eichel?'

He blinked behind his monocle. 'Which German hasn't?'

'When I told you I was going to work for a prominent German company I failed to mention that it is for Walter Eichel's bank . . . and what's more, I will be working directly for Walter himself. He is a personal friend of my family and he is the gentleman you are keeping waiting by holding me here for no solid reason. He knows Lukas very well. Herr Eichel can and will vouch for Lukas Ravensburg, but even so, I can't imagine he's going to be very happy when he hears that his goddaughter and her fiancé have been detained by the Gestapo in a sleepy town in Provence on little more than a personal whim.' She warmed to her act. 'We have proven who we are and we have co-operated with your wishes and your questions.

'Now, sir, I'm sure your people have checked our details. I'm certain that Herr Eichel, when he picks up the phone to his various government connections in Berlin, will rightly remind them that my father lost an arm fighting for Germany and that Lukas's father made the ultimate sacrifice. And here you stand, casting aspersions on us, their children, good, loyal German citizens! What exactly do you suspect Lukas of, Herr von Schleigel? Is he perhaps an Allied spy, or one of those French partisan peasants, little more than thugs and murderers? Does he look like one, talk like one, act like one of them? He may live the life of a *lavandier* for now, but he has been well educated, and the only reason he's probably not an officer in the Wehrmacht is because he's providing our army with essential antiseptic.' Her voice had risen in volume as much as intensity and she was breathing hard now. She glared at the horrible little man before her as she gave a final twist to the noose. 'Herr von Schleigel, I am no longer tolerant of your small-minded behaviour. And while you made a big show of giving me my leave, we both know that I would never have left Lukas. You have worn my patience, and I expect to be allowed to telephone Herr Eichel. Perhaps you would personally like to explain to him the reasons for my detention, my tardiness of arrival into Paris, and my thoroughly bad humour this evening.'

'That will not be necessary,' von Schleigel replied, his voice brittle.

'No?' she queried innocently.

'No. You are both free to leave, with my apologies for any inconvenience.'

Lisette beamed at him with a brief, bright smile. 'Well, I thank you, Herr von Schleigel. Then there is nothing more for us to discuss.'

'Perhaps you will pass on my best wishes to Herr Eichel?' he asked.

She wasn't sure whether to be more impressed by his audacity or her own.

'If you can help make arrangements to get me to Lyon where I might pick up that train I missed, I'm sure Uncle Walter will be grateful to you, Herr von Schleigel.'

The man dipped his head and she smiled inwardly at how hard it must be for him to show her that respect.

'Where is Lukas?'

'Follow me please, *mademoiselle*,' he said, gesturing towards the door.

Luc was both amazed and amused, though he betrayed neither when von Schleigel returned with Lisette in tow. She made a good show of running to him and putting her arms around him.

'Oh, my darling. Everything is sorted, as I knew it would be.' She gave him a bright smile. 'Come on, we can leave now. Herr von Schleigel has even offered to help me get to Lyon so I can meet up with the Paris train during the early hours.' Lisette gave him a fierce hug. 'Uncle Walter is going to be so pleased – and grateful to Herr von Schleigel – that I wasn't delayed. You know, darling, you should just come with me. He'll want to see you. Sault will be snowed in soon enough. Come for that visit you promised.'

Eichel's name presumably meant a lot more to von Schleigel than it did to Luc. Suddenly they were herded from the room and out into the main part of the house, where he could see the large doors beckoning towards him, and escape.

Lisette had pulled off something extraordinary. He could hear von Schleigel muttering about them being driven to Lyon. It was laughable. One minute prisoners under interrogation, and now a chauffeured car. Luc moved in a daze, carried along on Lisette's arm and by her breathy chatter.

Von Schleigel was holding out his hand. 'No hard feelings, Ravensburg, eh? I hope you understand that I must do my job to keep all Germans safe.' He gave Luc his tight, forced smile, the monocle firmly in place, his gloved hand squeezing Luc's naked one.

'Of course,' Luc said, trying to sound mollified.

'The driver is ready for you, but can we offer you anything before you leave? A good French cognac perhaps, on this cold night?'

'Thank you, but no,' Lisette said with disarmingly good cheer. She took Luc's hand. 'Are you ready, Lukas?'

He nodded, not quite trusting himself to say anything. He even found a smile for her, but as they walked towards the front door, just a few steps from where he could see a car and a man in a dark suit awaiting them, some movement caught his attention.

He looked across the large reception hall of the house and he saw an old man stumble between the clutches of a pair of SS uniformed men. The old man had his back to them and was on his knees. They hauled him to his feet.

Luc felt his heart give. Was he seeing things, or was there something ominously familiar about the manner of the old man, the way he limped, the tilt of his head, the set of his shoulders? Luc begged it not to be . . . Surely, it couldn't be.

'Herr Ravensburg, is something wrong?' von Schleigel asked, looking back at Luc.

Luc felt as though he was swallowing glass shards.

'Lukas, come on,' Lisette said, stepping back through the doorway. 'The driver is waiting.'

Luc could see Lisette glowering at him, silently pleading with him to move. He could see von Schleigel take a glance back at the old man and then return his gaze to Luc, cocking his head to one side like a dog picking up a scent. He fixed Luc with a stare. Luc's heart began to pound all over again.

Walk! He could hear Fougasse, Laurent and even Roger yelling at him. *Ne fais pas ça!* It was his father, Jakob, talking in his mind as clearly as if he were standing right beside him. *Do not do it!*

He seemed to lurch forward and the spell was momentarily broken; Lisette looked relieved and turned.

'Herr von Schleigel?' Luc cleared his throat and with it all those voices in his head.

'Herr Ravensburg?' the man said amiably, looking like the cat that had just got the cream.

'Who is that man?'

Von Schleigel blinked rapidly. 'Why, that old fellow is called Dressler.'

Luc became very still. 'What do you want with him?'

Lisette stood in the doorway silent, angry; he didn't need to look at her to know it.

'Who is Dressler to you, Ravensburg?'

Luc noted that all the squirming politeness had gone. 'He is no one special. He used to live in the region. I recall meeting him once in passing,' he replied.

'So he's not a stranger?'

Luc ignored the question. 'Why is he being treated like this? He is German.'

'Indeed he is. But he's also a Jew-lover. He's been helping Jews in the south to get passage to Spain; helping young men to join up in the Armée Juive. We have proof that earlier this year he smuggled money from Switzerland into France to help Jewish partisans to fight back. For a German he is not terribly patriotic.'

Luc frowned. 'He is German, Herr von Schleigel, and he is old; he deserves respect.'

'Well, perhaps you'd like to talk to him?' von Schleigel offered. His tone was innocent but Luc saw only smugness in his expression.

'Wait in the car, Lisette.'

'Lukas —'

'Please,' Luc growled. 'I will not be long.'

Just as she had left him a few hours earlier in Gordes, fuming with despair, he watched her now seething afresh as she spun on her heel. 'Good evening, Herr von Schleigel,' she managed to say, before she climbed into the car without a backward glance.

'This way,' the Gestapo man indicated.

Luc followed him back into the lion's den on the trail of a frail old man who had held him before his mother had, and who had protected the secret of his nationality. *Wolf.*

Von Schleigel looked sideways at Luc. 'I am intrigued, Ravensburg, by your interest.' At his signal, two of his henchmen fell in behind them, cutting off any thoughts Luc might have harboured about changing his mind. No, it was too late now. He hoped Lisette had the presence of mind to give the driver instruction to leave for

Lyon immediately. Luc began to doubt he would emerge from the grounds of this stately home alive.

———————

This time there was no pretence, not even the disguise of an ante-room; just an outhouse of sorts. Everyone knew why they were here. It was being used for storage; everything from paint to paper supplies. There was a single light bulb eerily swinging from a draught through a broken window. It was freezing, but old Wolf had been stripped to his underwear and sat shivering on an iron chair, staring at the ground. He had been beaten. Livid bruises had erupted over his body, and the toes of his twisted, bleeding feet had been broken. It was Luc's beloved Wolf; his teacher, his second father.

Luc's chest was so constricted that he didn't dare speak. The sight of Wolf, far more than Fougasse or Laurent, threatened to undo him completely. For here was a man of peace. Wolf would help a German as quickly as he would a Jew.

'*Salauds!*' Luc whispered. *Bastards*.

'Ravensburg, is that shock I see? Do I sense that you care about this old swine?' von Schleigel asked with a smile.

'Care? I wouldn't treat a dog like this.'

'He's lower than a dog, Ravensburg. This man is not worthy of licking the dirt from my boots.'

Luc's head began to pound. It was as though he was seeing this scene through a misty curtain of shining light. He was in what his grandmother had once termed 'white wrath'. Now he finally understood what she had meant. And as hard as his temple throbbed, a strange calmness descended at the thought of his grandmother. He reached to his chest and touched the lavender; the sparkling mist cleared, as did his mind.

'I thought you wished to speak with this man,' von Schleigel remarked. 'You'd better hurry.'

'Where was he arrested?' Luc asked. He'd tried to contact Wolf this last year but after the Bonets had been taken by the *milice*, Wolf had disappeared.

'He has been living in Marseille. But he was picked up in Lourmarin three weeks ago using the hill villages for cover while he moved some Jewish orphans into safe houses. I'm glad to say the children have already been shipped off to Drancy.' The repulsive satisfaction in von Schleigel's expression sickened Luc. 'But Dressler is now my problem. Or perhaps yours?'

Luc knew he was clutching at straws The kind professor's life was as lost to the Gestapo as the Bonets were lost to the lethal Polish camps.

He turned to face von Schleigel. 'This man is old enough to have fought for the Fatherland in the Great War. Does it not disturb and humiliate you that this German war veteran fought just so you could all strut around in your fancy uniforms and act important? How much active service have you seen, von Schleigel?'

The man's features twisted into a sneer. 'I would caution you, Ravensburg, to be careful with how you speak. The Gestapo is not answerable to you, the German people, the Wehrmacht or the armed services . . . to anyone but Reichsführer Himmler and our Fuhrer.' He took a step closer to Luc, secure in the knowledge of his position. 'And it is only because of Herr Eichel that I refrain from arresting you.'

'Re-arresting me,' Luc corrected in a snide tone.

'No, Ravensburg. I did not arrest you at the railway station; I simply asked you to help me with some inquiries. If I were to arrest you, that pretty young woman you hope to marry might have to wait a very long time to get your ring on her finger.'

The threat was thinly veiled. They both understood that von Schleigel had the power to have Luc held indefinitely.

And now the lunacy of his challenge became clear. Luc didn't believe, even in the most hopeful part of his mind, that Wolf would survive his wounds. The old man was dying painfully already. And there was Lisette waiting for him outside; a British agent with her cover still intact, in a position to wreak damage on the regime that was killing everyone he had ever loved. Keeping himself alive to help her had to be his first option.

It was unthinkable that he might leave Wolf to these animals, though. He thought of his father, and how he'd begged him to use his German background to save himself; was he going to throw that away now and let the Bonet name, its very memory, be lost? The last time Luc had seen Wolf, the professor had implored him to heed his father's words and do whatever was necessary, no matter how hard, how unpalatable.

Luc rubbed his face, not needing to feign fatigue, and in that moment found the contrition he required. 'Forgive me, von Schleigel. This has been a long and trying day.' He watched his enemy's face relax slightly. 'It horrifies me that Germany is reduced to this,' he said, pointing. 'Beating up old men . . . our own kind.'

'No!' von Schleigel yelled. It was the first time he'd raised his voice. 'This man is *not* our kind. He does *not* deserve to call himself German. I should do him a favour and send him on the trains with his Jewish friends.'

Wolf now began to speak. The grating guttural words sounded harsh and laboured; few would have understood the sentences spoken in Old Norse.

'What did you hope to discover from him?' Luc asked, his heart feeling fractured.

'We believe he knew the Bonet family. He would have known the Bonet we are searching for . . . the Jewish cockroach that has escaped our net. I insisted he give him to me.'

So they really had no idea who Luc Bonet was, what he looked like, that he could speak German. Luc realised he was inadvertently touching the hidden lavender pouch. He dropped his hand casually. 'Clearly he doesn't know this Bonet fellow.'

'Oh, but I'm sure he does. He lived in the next village. But you hear that rubbish he's talking? That's all we can get out of him.'

'Why this obsession with Bonet?'

'It's not an obsession, Ravensburg. I'm chasing all the resisters we know of just as keenly as those who fall into our traps.' He shrugged. 'I can't help it if I enjoy my work. Go ahead. Talk to Dressler,' von Schleigel added slyly.

Luc realised he had trapped himself. All it would take now was for Wolf to recognise him. It would be more than enough proof for von Schleigel.

'Say goodbye to the old man for me.'

Luc stared the cold blue eyes of the man he now loathed even more than Landry.

In truth, did he really care about himself any longer? No. He did care about Lisette, however. Somehow during their brief time together she had slipped beneath his hardened exterior and found her way into his heart. She was more than a duty now, more than an obligation. He felt heart-bound to help her . . . but she could carry on without him if it came to it. Paris and her mission were within her grasp. Apart from Lisette, there was only one other person in the world that was left for him to care about . . . and that person was sitting here, broken and dying.

Wolf clearly had accepted this was his end. Reciting prayers in the mysterious, almost forgotten language he loved was indication enough that he had found a safe place from which to farewell the world, no matter what they did to him.

'Wolf,' Luc whispered. 'I'm Lukas Ravensburg.'

He forgot about von Schleigel and his henchmen. He ignored the war and the terrible sorrows it had inflicted; he set aside the woman waiting for him and the greater good that the Maquis demanded he fight for. And for a few brief, bright heartbeats he was Luc Bonet with his dear, much-loved friend and teacher.

He fought back tears when Wolf lifted his sunken head slowly and opened bloodshot eyes that hadn't fully lost their genial intelligence. Luc alone saw the spark of recognition in Wolf's eyes. Lukas Ravensburg was his son too, for he had loved him on sight, and there was love in those eyes now.

'The *kráka* must fly. Stay *útlagi*,' Wolf said in the forgotten language, a vacant smile on his ravaged face. *Remain an outlaw?* Luc translated. He was telling Luc to flee and stay safe, keep his identity secret. 'My time to die,' he whispered.

'What is he saying?' von Schleigel demanded.

'I don't even know what language he's speaking. Part German, part nonsense.'

'Well, there's enough of him left for us to try once more.'

Luc turned slowly from where he crouched. 'What does that mean?'

'It means, Ravensburg, that it's time you went. We have work to do here with Herr Dressler.'

'What are you going to do to him?'

'What is it to you? When I'm satisfied that no amount of *persuasion* will loosen his tongue, I shall put the old Jew-loving goat out of his misery.'

'If he hasn't told you anything after this heinous beating, he's not worth torturing further.'

'You think so?' Von Schleigel sighed. 'There's almost always more you can learn. It's obvious he doesn't recognise you.'

'Did you hope he would?'

'Yes,' he laughed. 'Actually I hoped just that.'

'Let him be. Let him die peacefully. He's German, damn it!'

'In the comfort of a warm bed, perhaps?' Von Schleigel shared a laugh with his henchmen. Then his face grew serious. 'I think not,

Ravensburg. But how about this?' He unfastened his pistol from its holster and offered it to Luc. 'If you want to put Dressler out of his misery, then go right ahead. I presume you know how to use a gun? Shoot this man dead, if it will ease your conscience as a good German.'

Not even in his nightmares could Luc have imagined something so vile, so terrible as the situation he now found himself faced with.

'*No!*'

Von Schleigel tutted. 'And yet you claim to be a patriotic German, ready to fight for your country.'

'I *am* patriotric. I am fighting for my country,' Luc said, speaking more honestly than von Schleigel could ever know.

'Then shoot this dissident. He works against the Nazi regime and all that we stand for.'

'The Fuhrer wants to get rid of the Jews. Dressler's helping you achieve that.'

The Gestapo man smiled. 'We want them dead, not hiding like sewer rats in Spain or Denmark, waiting to re-emerge. As a good German I'd imagine you'd want that too.'

'I won't kill a civilian in cold blood,' Luc said, his voice brittle.

'As you wish.' Von Schleigel glanced sideways to one of his men. 'See Herr Ravensburg out.' He turned back and regarded Luc expectantly. 'Your friend must be very cold in the car now.'

'This is barbaric!' Luc spat. His ears were beginning to ring with alarm.

Von Schleigel shrugged, unmoved. Once again he held out the pistol. 'Save him the pain, Ravensburg. Deliver him. You can walk away knowing that you did a good deed for Germany this evening.'

Luc glared at him. The unspoken message was clear: any question of Luc's identity would be erased by this single act. He didn't think he was capable of speaking. They stood in silence, neither blinking. The atmosphere felt heavy and cloying, their breath rising in the freezing air. Time seemed to move achingly slowly.

Von Schleigel blinked first. 'Prove yourself.'

Luc felt the cold weight of the service pistol land in his hand. He had fired a Walther P38 during his training in the mountains; it had been stolen from a dead German soldier. He dropped his gaze from von Schleigel and stared at the weapon. He had no choice. They would kill Wolf anyway, painfully. How would he live with himself, whichever choice he made?

And then he heard Wolf's familiar, gravelly voice cutting through the trauma. He spoke words that Luc had heard many times previously, reciting Psalm 23. It was a text that was as precious to the Jewish faith as it was to Christians. The Bonet family had shared this psalm every Saturday, and then on Sundays Wolf would read it to them. This was Wolf's signal, telling Luc that it was all right to do this.

'Yea, though I walk through the valley of the shadow of death, I will fear no evil,' Wolf murmured in Old Norse.

'Shut him up, for heaven's sake, Ravensburg,' von Schleigel said in exasperation.

Luc ignored the Gestapo, bending to tenderly kiss the old man on each cheek. 'Fly away, *kráka*.'

The old man nodded and bent his head. Luc took aim, closed his eyes and, holding his breath, he pulled the trigger.

The pistol clicked on an empty chamber. Everyone laughed, especially von Schleigel, who seemed deliriously amused by the trick. Luc wanted to vomit.

'You did it, Ravensburg,' von Schleigel congratulated, slapping Luc on the back. 'I didn't think you had it in you.'

Luc turned around and something in his expression clearly startled von Schleigel. The Gestapo officer took a step back. 'So now,' he said, straightening his jacket, 'let's do it properly.' He carefully inserted a single live round into the weapon and smacked it back into Luc's hand. 'One bullet. Send the old man on his way.' He grinned maliciously. 'I'll wait outside, but these soldiers will have their pistols trained on you,' he warned.

This time the gun fired a bullet, and the last of Luc's connections to his family was severed. His ferocious glare stopped von Schleigel's henchmen from stepping forward as Luc shifted Wolf's body to lie flat. He gently placed Wolf's hands on top of each other on his chest. Despite the cold, he draped his coat around Wolf, and without looking back, he stalked from the shed. Now more than ever it was important to stay impassive, although his heart was in turmoil.

Von Schleigel escorted him to the car, where Luc saw Lisette, pale and worried in the back. She leapt out. 'What's going on?'

'We're leaving now,' Luc growled. He was barely hanging on. His eyes pleaded with her and she understood.

'All right. Good evening, Herr von Schleigel,' she said and eased herself back into the car.

'*Mademoiselle*,' von Schleigel replied. 'Farewell, Ravensburg. I doubt our paths will cross again.'

Luc turned to face the despised soldier once more. 'There will be a reckoning for this, von Schleigel. There is a code in war, especially for a man in uniform.'

'Is that a threat?'

'No. But perhaps you'd better hope our paths don't cross again.'

'You do not frighten me, Ravensburg. You are best off in your lavender fields, making your oil. Men like you should leave war to men like me.'

'Is that why you're here in this sleepy outpost away from all the action?'

Von Schleigel laughed. 'As a matter of fact, I've been promoted. I'm going to a prison camp called Auschwitz. Heard of it?'

Luc shook his head numbly.

'It's probably where the Bonet family was sent. Berlin obviously thinks I'm well suited to the disposal of Jews.' He grinned maliciously.

Luc was glad no one could see his whitened knuckles. Without another word he slid into the car alongside Lisette.

'*Auf wiedersehen.*' Von Schleigel waved through the window as the driver gunned the engine and the big car rolled out of the drive.

They drove in silence through the main street of l'Isle sur la Sorgue. The streets were deserted except for Germans in uniform, who could be heard singing from the bars.

Luc knew Lisette was watching him surreptitiously but he had nothing to say. He felt numbed. He knew his hands were trembling. His whole body was as he sat forward, tense, shivering.

He felt Lisette's tentative hand on his back. His mind was filled with the deafening sound of a gunshot, of blood, of an old man's resolve and a younger man's hate. But while salty tears ran silently down his cheeks, he was aware of her arms reaching around him; holding him tight. She knew not to ask any more questions, not to talk even; she just held him. Through her touch he understood that there was one person left in this world to care about. Her mission, her survival, was all that mattered. He let his head lean against her shoulder and she responded by softly kissing his temple.

'Whatever this is about, I'm so sorry,' she finally whispered.

And her gentle voice and touch gave him comfort. Love still existed in the world, despite all the ugliness. He thought he heard his grandmother sigh, but it was just Lisette reaching to touch the pouch of lavender against his chest. The vaguest breath of its scent wafted up and enveloped them for a heartbeat.

PART THREE

PART THREE

20

Paris, 3 May 1944

Markus Kilian sighed. The young woman admitted she'd forgotten some papers and stammered her apology in halting German as she left the room. As a highly effective colonel, he wondered again at the vacuous role he had recently been appointed to. On the other hand, he knew he should be grateful to be in his favourite city and not trapped in a backwater in Germany. He could work at convincing himself that Hitler's wrath had cooled, although it was obvious that the Führer had not yet finished with his punishment.

Until the autumn of 1942, Kilian had been the rising star of the German generals. He came from a proud and wealthy Prussian background; his father was a hero in the famous Bavarian Jäger Battalion during the Great War and the son had proved that the apple did not fall far from the tree. Kilian had won praise from his superiors for his daring leadership in the push into Russia.

The problem was that while Kilian was a ferociously patriotic German, he was not pro-Nazi and certainly not pro-Hitler. But after the crushing humiliation of 1918, he had felt obliged to support anyone with the leadership skills to rebuild the Fatherland. He had survived the bloodiest of all battles at Ypres during the Great War and swore at just twenty-five that he would commit his career to changing the prevailing German approach to war.

He kept this promise. By the time Germany went to war again on a grand scale, Kilian's belief in small, fast, mobile units had paid dividends. In the Russian offensive he'd led his men from one success to the next in what would prove itself to be the most ferocious of military campaigns ever fought. His skill had come to the notice of senior officers in the Wehrmacht; here was a charismatic and fearless commander who could surely motivate his men to follow him into Hell if he were asked to. The Führer especially was impressed.

Kilian had the tall, wide-shouldered and finely featured looks of his Nordic ancestry; a perfect Aryan specimen. And even though he ran a tight fighting unit, he was popular with his men. This stemmed from his readiness to lead by example. Unlike most of his counterparts, Kilian trained with his men, slept rough and shunned the traditional comforts afforded senior officers. It was a common sight to see Markus Kilian sharing a cigarette with unranked soldiers. He was increasingly noted for his lack of disciplinary actions; while his counterparts might punish men for not raising their arms fast enough for salutes, he saw that as nothing more than the oversight of hungry, bone-weary men.

Kilian had been privately angered by Germany entering into another war. If Hitler had known of his treachery, Kilian might never have survived beyond the spring of 1940, when, following the lead of Ludwig Beck, chief of the German general staff, Kilian had actively helped to leak information to Carl Goerdeler, then working for the German civilian resistance. Goerdeler was in contact with London and Britain's then prime minister, Neville Chamberlain. But despite their efforts, the invasion of France went ahead.

If committing Germany to war in western Europe was the action of a man inflated by his own sense of power, then to Kilian, taking on Russia was lunacy; few others openly agreed.

The sycophants in Berlin went along with Hitler's vision that the Russian campaign should be a war of annihilation, destroying particular peoples, places and their history as a priority. Meanwhile, Kilian had looked ahead to what a Russian winter might do to German troops a long way from home, without reliable support lines, and his sense of foreboding had deepened. The size of Russia alone should have been warning enough – resources would be stretched far too thinly. Insufficient firepower meant not enough support for infantry units, which would bear the real brunt of this disastrous decision to take on the Red Army.

Kilian refused for his men to be used as fodder in the Führer's twisted vision of empire. But with his men committed to fight in the summer of 1942 in the loathsome Operation Barbarossa Offensive, Kilian had little choice but to lead as he knew best. And in typical style he had shown great dash, leading his units across the border into Soviet lands, winning ground and taking plenty of Red Army prisoners along the way.

But it was those very Soviet prisoners who had catapulted him off his meteoric trajectory. The Führer's heinous Commissar Order had been Kilian's undoing. He wasn't the only senior officer to criticise it, but it was Kilian who openly defied it. The Commissar Order asked all German officers to root out Communist officials within the ranks of the Red Army prisoners of war. They were then to be summarily executed. Kilian argued that this order would serve only to boost the morale of the Soviets. The executed men, he had said, could well become martyrs. He went so far as to demand that the order be revoked. Kilian was duly informed that 'the war against Russia cannot be fought in knightly fashion', and promised pardons for the soldiers who fired the bullets and for the commanders who ordered it.

It had outraged the professional soldier in Kilian, who had grown up believing in the Prussian ideals of war and the protocols they adhered to. He had told his officers to follow their consciences, but went so far as to forbid anyone under his command to shoot

Russian prisoners. To the men he trusted most he admitted that he feared Nazi daydreamers in Berlin were committing a generation of Germans to watering Russian soil with its blood.

It wasn't his own death that troubled Kilian. He believed it was heroic to die fighting for one's country. What mattered was that the Russian campaign was pointless; it was a war they could never win. Nevertheless, trapped by duty, he led his men, claiming small victories in the Russian hamlets. Finally came the moment when Kilian openly breached the edict that came direct from Nazi headquarters. He had noticed a prisoner wearing the giveaway red star on his sleeve, denoting he was a Soviet commissar. Following orders, he had taken the man alone from the raft of hungry, hollow-eyed Red Army prisoners into the surrounding forest.

They'd talked during this brief journey. He was a farmer; he didn't believe wholly in collectives, but he did believe that the collective farm – at the root of Communist ideology – made practical sense. The commissar had a family – a wife, three young children.

Kilian had found himself telling the man about the time not long before when he had teetered on the brink of engagement. Ilse Vogel had followed a career in science and had almost forgotten about marriage until the softly spoken, intelligent Markus Kilian had sat down next to her one evening at a dinner party in spring 1936. While the rest of the guests had talked about the Olympic Games, Markus and Ilse had eyes only for each other. They had become lovers – great friends as well – over the next couple of years, but the brewing war clouds had made Kilian nervous to commit.

'You should have married her,' the commissar had said in Russian.

Kilian smiled and offered the man a cigarette, replying in his language. 'Yes, I think you're right. We were a good match.'

They had shared a smoke peacefully in the quiet of the forest. Finally, they both stood.

'Let's get this over with,' the Russian had said. 'But face me when you do it. Don't shoot me in the back like I'm scum. I am a soldier. I've fought for my country. I'll die for it now. Don't take away my dignity.'

The man had offered a hand and Kilian had been moved by the simple gesture; they'd shaken. The Russian had then walked to a tree before turning stoically to face his executioner.

'Make it quick,' he said. 'Head or heart.' Then he'd grinned. 'Surprise me.'

Kilian had shaken his head, resolved. 'Go. Go back to your family. Kiss your wife, hug your children,' he said. He waved a hand, gesturing that he was dismissed. And then he saluted.

The man had stared back at him in disbelief but hadn't moved. So Kilian had sheathed his pistol, to show he had no intention of spending a bullet.

The soldier had frowned, then a bemused half-grin had twitched on one side of his mouth. Raising a hand to his heart as thanks, he'd turned and melted away through the forest.

That simple act of mercy had been witnessed by a visiting officer. It didn't take long for Kilian's recall to Berlin, where he had received a gut-twisting dressing-down from his superiors, although it could have been worse. A few months later the Commissar Order had been revoked but it was too late for Kilian. He was already cooling his heels in a dead-end desk job. It was two years of penance in the backwaters of Germany before he was given an opportunity to claw his way back, initially to the Bendlerblock in Berlin. It was not what he wanted, but those superiors who'd protected him and shared similar feelings towards the Nazi ideology reiterated their advice to keep his head down and do what was asked of him.

Although his sense of honour prevented Kilian from outright rebellion, he had long ago decided that Hitler was a monster. He had seen too much that hurt his soul in the Ukraine, and even though he had not made it easy for Himmler's death squads to carry out their devil-inspired duties, he felt the cloying stain of their work clinging to his uniform and all that he held dear.

Little did Hitler know that Kilian had maintained contact with the Underground and had known of two attempted assassinations on the Führer's life. Under the protection of others within the Party who shared his feelings, Kilian had been transferred to Paris quietly in December 1943, slipping into a city that couldn't fully hide her beauty beneath red flags and bold German street signs. On his first day his anger had been flamed by two thuggish *milice* mercilessly beating an old man with a yellow star wrongly pinned on his coat.

However, he'd come to realise that for most Parisians – unless they were Jewish or Roma – life went on smoothly enough. In the more elite circles families went without little. In fact, well-heeled Parisians led what could only be described as a jolly existence. There was no lack of private parties, nightclubbing and drinking, and all the usual excesses of the *bourgeoisie* were still to be found, despite the curfew. Nevertheless, Paris was quieter than he remembered – probably because it was now a city of bicycles. The only people with access to petrol were the Germans and wealthy French.

Kilian liked the French; he admired their pluck and especially those who, in the face of stringent reprisals, still defied their occupiers. A trip to the cinema proved comical. As soon as the propaganda reels flickered on, the French audience would whistle and stamp. The only way the police could monitor the audience was by leaving the lights on, negating the effects of the propaganda that no one could now view.

Kilian was particularly fond of the way idealistic teenagers rode up to German cars on their bicycles and stuck signs on them, urging the people not to trust the Vichy government or obey the 'Boches'. But his fellow Germans lacked all sense of humour and he'd had to step in once, pulling rank on soldiers beating up a youth who'd been caught.

He sympathised especially with the hungry, knowing a lot of the Parisian population spent most of their waking hours worrying about how to make it to the next meal or keep a roof over their heads. And as Europe moved into the depths of winter, even growing food in window boxes became impossible. How many times had he watched Parisians searching the public squares for chestnuts, twigs, dead leaves, anything vaguely flammable that they could burn to stay warm? He'd observed sadly as men and women alike had sold their jewellery, even wedding rings, just to feed their children, stay alive, survive another month. Lentils that he loathed were normally a few francs, but by 1944 could sell on the black market for seven or eight times the official price. He grew to detest the smell of Swedish turnip – rutabaga – that emanated from Parisian households, seemingly the staple of life for the less fortunate.

Unless Kilian was officially required to dine out, he was content to munch on bread and cheese, with the odd slice of cold meat for his evening meal. He couldn't stomach fine dining when there was so much conspicuous poverty. As a result he had become even leaner, but his gaunt appearance gave him a curiously roguish look. His slightly sunken cheeks made him look younger and accentuated his strong jaw. He was clean-shaven, usually tanned – although paler these days – and kept his blonde hair trimmed around his ears. His eyes could appear anything from a flinty grey to a glacial blue, and his gaze was intense. But Kilian liked to smile, as the lines around his eyes testified. Everything about him was tidy and spare – save his thoughts, but he rarely shared those.

There were more than enough of his fellow officers who would help to fill the packed restaurants around the city, from the hugely popular Maxim's on the Rue Royale to the Café de l'Opéra near the Grands Boulevards, and happily tuck into rich food bought on the black market at up to four times the official price, before spilling into the cafés, cabarets and concert halls. While its greater population was trying to cope with just staying alive, Paris had never been so effervescent as it seemed now with the cash-flushed German military and its visitors. Art, music, literature were flourishing. Fashion clung on – no matter what hardships were pressed upon the French women, they still managed to look elegant and fashionable. From staining their legs to appear as though wearing stockings, to crafting new hats from old tulle and feathers, their ingenuity was admirable. Clothes were constantly remade into new garments. Even high heels were maintained using old wood or cork.

Paris was still Paris if Kilian squinted his eyes a little and ignored the jackboots and the daunting red flags they marched beneath. And if he was to be in exile, he preferred to be here than any other place. He liked to stroll through the Jardin des Tuileries with its structured and orderly pathways and gardens that had once held beautiful beds of flowers – now replaced by vegetables. He made an effort to enjoy the brass band of the Wehrmacht on a Sunday and avoided the Hotel Crillon as best he could, where the German High Command resided, or Rue de Saussaies, where the loathed Gestapo had set up its French HQ.

There were times when all he wanted to do was get back to the Front, although the Russian campaign was going so badly that every German military strategist could surely see the end result. The Battle of Stalingrad, sprawling over five months, was catastrophic, with nearly 100 000 German soldiers in custody. They were all that was left of upwards of 330 000 men.

Kilian's secretary returned after a lengthy departure, full of apologies. She dragged him from his bleak thoughts, nervously handing him some papers. Sandrine was French, but too uncertain working at this level, and her German was halting at best. Someone at dinner the previous night had heard Kilian bemoaning his help and had quipped that the girls were probably all too in love with him to take the job seriously.

He'd had to grit his teeth. Didn't these people take war seriously? He was not looking for romance in Paris. How could his colleagues be so flippant when whole platoons of fine young men were being destroyed? Frankly, he wished he'd perished in the frozen wasteland rather than dying of guilt here in this office, a gracious chamber of the Palais Bourbon, where hot chocolate was served in exquisitely painted Limoges porcelain jugs and men smoked cigars and drank cognac.

'Leave them there, Sandrine,' Kilian said in French. 'I'll sign them later, thank you. You know, it's a nice spring day out there despite the cold. Why don't you take the afternoon off?'

The young woman stared at him. 'But . . .'

'Go on. Take the afternoon off,' he said and stood.

'Are you sacking me, Colonel Kilian?' She looked terrified.

'No. But I think this position makes you unhappy; you are constantly nervous and perhaps a bit lonely working here with me. I know you were drafted from the secretarial pool. Would you like to return to it? Would that make it easier for you?'

'Well . . .' she hesitated.

'Let me arrange it. No change in wage. Will that be satisfactory for you?'

She glowed. 'Oh, yes, thank you, sir.'

He nodded and smiled. Now he was without any support, but he didn't care. He would have to find someone new with flawless German and French. Anything to make his department more efficient and his efforts noticeable. If he could not return to the Front, he needed to manoeuvre into a position to aid those men fighting on the lines.

He spent the next few hours working diligently, immersed in all the nonsense paperwork that seemed to flow in a relentless torrent across his desk. Berlin was pedantic about copies of all letters, and the records it kept of every decision by every small bureaucrat seemed beyond paranoia, but he followed the routine, clenching his jaw.

When he next looked up to glance out of the picture windows it was past four-thirty and already dark. He could suddenly feel the chill from outside biting through the vague warmth of his large office. He smirked at himself for noticing; in Russia his men were freezing to death, literally. Many a soldier had been found frozen solid at his post.

He consulted his diary, hoping the appointment that he knew was there might have miraculously disappeared over the last few hours. Instead it stared back at him in bold black ink: a social meeting with one of the German bankers of Paris at seven p.m. Could he get out of it? Absolutely not. The man had solid connections with Berlin. It was only a drink, after all. The man could prove a handy contact.

So while a hot bath and an early night sounded inviting on this cool spring evening, he would not dash back to the Hotel Raphaël. Instead, he would freshen up at the office and set out on foot towards stylish St Germain to Les Deux Magots. He checked the time again; yes, he could probably even give himself the pleasure of a skirt around the Jardin du Luxembourg before cutting past Saint Sulpice up towards the café. The evening sounded instantly more bearable: perhaps he could even hear the Saint Sulpice choir or the church's grand organ.

Markus Kilian stood. He needed some sustenance, hot food – and he might even sip a warming cognac tonight as he charmed his new acquaintance in the hope of good words fed back down the line to Berlin.

Lisette could barely believe it had been seven months since she had arrived in Paris. She'd successfully met up with the local resistance circuit and found herself a top-floor flat in a quiet back street on the Right Bank. The eighteenth arondissement was well known for its famous cabarets and nightlife and was often crawling with German soldiers. Lisette knew she probably should have moved, but didn't wish to chance her luck more than she already was.

Many of the German servicemen liked to holiday in Paris, and they flocked to the Pigalle district for their entertainment. Theatres such as the Grand Guignol were never empty. The Moulin Rouge thrived, as did a great many brasseries and brothels. By night the area was a hotbed of restless eroticism and by day it seemed to sleep within its own hangover. It was to the bohemian, arty Montmartre that Lisette was drawn. The hilly, sleepy streets nestling beneath the Sacré Coeur, where she now lived, had nourished artists such as Monet, Lautrec and Van Gogh. The basilica was set on the highest point in Paris, and several times a week Lisette would climb its travertine stairs to sit in the forecourt of the bright white church and look out over Paris. After the French Revolution many nuns had been guillotined at this spot, and Lisette shared a curious sense of sisterhood with the forgotten women.

Unlike most of SOE's operatives, Lisette didn't have to report back to London regularly. As a result she was safer than many of her colleagues operating in France. She was free to live the life of a Parisian – in fact she'd been encouraged to immerse herself in the city's routines – without the stresses of having to hide a wireless and move flat constantly. When the time was right she would get in touch with a young man from London living in Paris, codenamed Playboy, who had audaciously set up a number of wireless sets in safe houses. He was posing as a student, studying hard but all the while tapping out messages to London.

It was a lonely life. She never fully relaxed – every time she left her bedsit she rehearsed her cover in case she was questioned. She slept lightly, sometimes fretfully, in the small room she'd rented, but it had lofty ceilings and tall windows that let in a great deal of light and air, which she found calming. The tiny, rickety cherrywood table was left by the previous occupant and sat over mismatched chairs. Along with her bed, the sink and a very small wood stove, it was the only piece of furniture.

Lisette warmed herself as best she could from a flowerpot brazier she had constructed using paper waste from the bank. It would burn long enough to thaw frozen fingers before she hugged herself into bed from the early evening. She was planning to grow some food in pots on the balcony in summer, and she even entertained the hollow daydream of a parachute drop that might contain some soap or shampoo. Nevertheless, despite the mean facilities, the solitude and the constant sense of danger, she was curiously content.

She was fortunate in many ways: not only did she have regular work at the bank but the folk of the neighbourhood had taken her under their wing. She found herself giving salutations and stopping in the street to chat about the ridiculous price of potatoes or offering to run errands on her way into work. The greatest danger was complacency; this was a luxury she could ill afford. Lisette had to treat every day as though it were the day she would be discovered. Never let down the guard! This had been drummed into her during training, even though that felt like a lifetime ago. So much had happened since the day she'd met Captain Jepson.

Not least Lukas Ravensburg. If she considered everything from the past year of her life, it was Luc who burned in her memory, and the evening he had wept in her arms. She knew it should be the execution of Laurent and the man known as Fougasse that kept her awake at night; or perhaps the knowledge that Luc had killed the *milicien*. But no – it was the man she barely knew who seemed to stalk her in her quiet moments. Watching him crumble, witnessing those tightly held defences crash down was more heartbreaking than anything she'd ever experienced. And his tender kiss had made him impossible to forget. He was like no other man she'd met. Luc was such an enigma, and like herself, a person full of private pain. She held the fanciful hope that they were two halves who could make a whole, if given a chance. A day hadn't gone by since that terrible evening in Provence that she didn't think about Luc and didn't yearn for his kiss, to share his pain and soothe his hurts.

Where was he? Was he safe? He had left her in Lyon. She desperately wanted to ask the network for information, but she knew making contact with him would risk her own cover and might compromise his.

'Just knowing other Resistance members might get you thrown in prison or executed,' Playboy had told her. She knew he was right. Prosper, who was to have been her original contact in Paris, had been arrested the year before. His cover had been blown – something to do with his ID papers and the wrong rivets used. London's forging error was disastrous. Around five hundred *résistants* had been arrested, most packed off to Germany for interrogation, imprisonment, and probably execution. Playboy had assured her the best and only defence was to remain independent.

Her first task had been to establish a place where she and

Playboy could exchange messages without having to meet. It was known as the 'dead drop' – all agents had one.

A café on the Rue Pergolèse was chosen, ironically in the heart of the German business district, just off the Champs Elysées. Playboy had explained that using an establishment favoured by Gestapo added a curious sense of safety. The best hiding place was in plain sight.

The café owner was a cunning black marketeer and a passive resister who despised the Germans. He would place a green tea towel over his shoulder to signal to Lisette if Playboy had a message for her. If she sent one to Playboy, she would write it on cigarette papers at home and stick the tiny note with its handy glue strip to the inside page of a newspaper that she would leave behind the counter for Playboy. They'd take turns calling into the café every other day to check for messages. So far she had sent only one message to SOE, months before: *Accommodated and employed in Paris. Lark.*

All in all, it had been a dream immersion into her new Parisian world. In fact, Lisette would almost consider herself happy if she only knew of Luc's whereabouts. She was cross with herself for caring so much.

Luc had refused to explain what had occurred between him and von Schleigel that night, or what had happened to the old man who had caught Luc's attention. He'd all but dragged her onto the platform at Lyon, bundled her on the carriage and closed the door. When she'd opened the window to say farewell he had simply shaken his head.

'Say nothing more, please. Be safe, Lisette. Forgive me the dangers I put you through.'

There had been so much she wanted to say, but his expression and the way he took both of her hands and kissed them had choked her. His eyes could not hide the truth of pain. Something truly terrible had happened with von Schleigel.

As the train lurched forward he'd let go of her hands – let go of her – and Lisette had felt as though something was tearing inside her. Even leaving France all those years before to board in England had been easier than this. Looking at Luc as the train pulled away, Lisette suddenly couldn't bear to be parted from him. Would she be safe again without him? He regarded her sadly as he raised a hand in farewell. She'd clutched at the rim of the open window, and had uncharacteristically begun to cry as she watched him standing there forlorn, his gaze riveted on her.

Lisette had felt instantly empty when she could no longer see him. She'd got used to the lilt of his voice, the way he spoke in French low and quietly, like he was telling secrets, and in German like a poet. She'd become familiar with his repressed energy and the bristling anger.

Their link was severed on that platform in Lyon, but the memory of him travelled with her. He would likely take a German bullet fleeing from some place of sabotage. But she had made a promise to him, and if she survived this war, she would find Lukas Ravensburg again.

———————

Today was Lisette's day off. Spring had arrived but it had been a cool morning – one of those crisp, sunny Parisian winter days that could almost trick you into believing life really wasn't that bad. She was aware that daily British bombing raids over Germany were intensive, and the Wehrmacht was dying on its feet in the frozen fields of Russia. Yesterday the aero-engine factory at Limoges had been bombed. Lisette's instincts sensed a change in the war. The previous year had been disastrous for the Allies and she hoped she wasn't imagining that the tide might be turning. And now her tiny part in the fightback was finally becoming a reality.

She felt a little guilty about Walter Eichel. He played an

unwitting role in her cover story, and if she were discovered, Walter would suffer. He had warmly welcomed her into his plush office near the Champs Elysées. His office had the sweet smell of old cigars and Armagnac, the comforting sound of leather that creaked and a mantelpiece clock ticking sombrely over a fireplace that no longer had fuel.

Her godfather lived well; she could see that from his paunch. Even so, his bearing was straight and his skin was not liver-spotted, his complexion healthy. He was not as tall as she recalled, but his genial grin was intact and his voice was thick and throaty, with that measured way of speaking that she had always liked. His hair was now fully silver but still lustrous, slicked back neatly. He was really very old-fashioned in his ways, but she found it all deeply reminiscent of childhood, when he would visit the family home.

She had told him she was back in Paris because she couldn't bear to be away from France, and he had accepted her story without further interrogation. He was happy to offer her a job, happy to make introductions, but she sensed that beneath the surface Walter did not entirely believe her reasons for returning to France.

'When did you arrive?' he'd asked.

'Oh, I've been back in France for a while; I hated living in Britain,' she lied. 'As soon as I left school I came back to the Continent, travelling as a nanny with an English family. When war broke out they rushed back to England and I made my way to Lille. Then I took ill. I was sick for almost a year, Walter, but you may remember my family's friends in Dunquerque?'

He frowned. 'I don't recall.'

She wasn't surprised – they didn't exist. 'The Pernots took care of me. When I felt well enough to travel, I headed south for some warmth. I needed to get my strength back. I lived quietly and reasonably well with the family of one of my friends from school. I helped out in a local school. Last year I couldn't face another alpine winter so I decided I'd come to Paris. That's when I wrote to you.'

'Well, I was very pleased to hear from you,' he remarked. He didn't ask anything else. He had loved her father and was determined to help her, but that was where their relationship ended. Lisette knew she could never take Walter into her trust. Nobody should have to choose between friend and country.

He did warn her that she was never to mention her time in Britain. As far as he was concerned, she had come direct from Strasbourg via Provence.

Since that meeting she'd been working at the bank, acting as an intermediary when required to bridge the gap between German and French. Walter and she had shared a couple of evening meals together, where he had regaled her with happy stories of her parents. If she were honest, she admitted that she had never enjoyed an evening in recent memory as much as she had with Walter – he was jovial company. He had insisted on paying her first few weeks' rent until she was settled and earning, and impressed that she refused any further favours from him. He had, however, been determined to buy her some fashionable Parisian clothes.

'I have no daughter of my own, Lisette. Let me do this for you. We can't have you walking around looking like a peasant. It reflects badly upon me.'

And so she'd agreed to go shopping, under the eagle eye of his German personal assistant who favoured austere, dark clothes. Without a need for ration coupons, Lisette had been kitted out in a series of winter outfits suitable for the bank, including two skirts, a dark suit, three blouses, two cardigans, a plain but elegant dress for evenings, an overcoat she cherished, leather gloves, two scarves, and two pairs of shoes – one for work, heels for evenings – as well as sundry underwear and a single pair of silk stockings. When given to her, she felt as though someone had just handed her a bar of gold bullion. Silk stockings were currency on the black market. She could probably get enough real soap in exchange to last the war. Or feed a family for weeks.

Nevertheless, she needed those lovely clothes, now more than ever. From her first day in Paris, she had been trying to ingratiate herself with Colonel Markus Kilian. It had consumed her every waking thought. And this evening she hoped to finally meet him.

She'd had a striking piece of luck from the outset: on the first day she'd met Walter, she'd learnt that he was an acquaintance of Colonel Kilian's. If Walter knew her target, surely she could contrive a reason to be introduced.

She took things slowly and patiently, stealing glances at his diary when she could. She had to find the perfect occasion before she made her play. She'd been working at the bank for several months without success but had held her nerve – and it had paid off. Two days ago she'd felt a pulse of excitement to see the entry in Walter's diary for this Wednesday at seven p.m.: *Les Deux Magots. Markus Kilian.*

Lisette's fingers trembled as she buttoned up her square-shouldered, oyster-coloured silk blouse, teamed with the charcoal skirt that hugged her hips and showed off her slim, neat figure.

She checked the time. It was nearing five, darkening outside, and the temperature was dropping. She would need to set off very soon if she was going to walk to St Germain. It would have been easy to take the Métro, but Lisette adored the cityscape, and there was far less likelihood of being stopped on foot.

She checked herself in the small mirror, pinched her cheeks and made sure her eyebrows were perfectly groomed. In these days of sobriety, she had to make the most of her features without make-up. One of the older ladies in Montmartre village had given her some dried rose petals, suggesting she crush them and mix them with a little glycerine to make a sort of lipstick. Lisette now dabbed a little of the pink paste onto her lips with a handkerchief. She looked at herself critically, touching the bounce of a gleaming curl, washed as best as she could with a homemade soap. She cast a prayer of thanks to her parents for her high cheekbones, heart-shaped face, clear complexion. She'd never studied herself so critically before. Tonight, however, it was her looks as much as her language skills and ability to charm that would count.

Finally satisfied, she pulled on her heavy coat, ensured her ID papers were in her handbag, dabbed on some lavender scent and reached for her gloves.

Lisette Forester, now Forestier, with her sights firmly set on a ritzy café in St Germain, set out with purpose and the faint scent of lavender perfuming her thoughts.

22

Kilian smiled broadly. 'Herr Eichel, it's good to see you again.' He extended a hand as the banker stood to greet him. 'Have I kept you?' He hated to be late.

'Not at all,' the older man said, shaking Kilian's hand before gesturing to the seat opposite. 'My driver made much better time than I'd imagined she would.' A friendly grin stretched across his features. 'Call me Walter, by the way. I'm glad we've had this chance to meet again.'

Kilian pulled off his gloves and coat. It was stuffy inside the large café after the brisk night air. 'As am I. It's cool but a magnificent evening isn't it? Perfect for walking.' He looked around at the crowded space that was known for its scholarly and artistic patrons.

'You walked here? I'm impressed. I thought all of you uniformed men liked your drivers and cars.'

Kilian sighed. 'I must admit that being behind a desk is a most unhappy place for me.'

Eichel smiled. 'What will you have?' The waiter had appeared.

'Cognac. Bring some food too. Something to graze on, or the cognac will go straight to my head.'

'Of course, Colonel,' the waiter said, recognising Kilian's uniform. 'And for you, sir?'

'I'll have the same,' Walter replied.

Kilian watched the waiter disappear into the crowd. 'It's certainly a busy watering hole.'

'Been here before?'

He shook his head. 'I've been meaning to. I'm told it's one of the places to be seen.'

Walter shrugged, casting a glance around the thriving establishment. On a street corner in the elegant sixth arondissement, it was said to be the best café in Paris. 'It is, but I suspect that's the very reason you've probably stayed away.'

Kilian gave him a wry look; it seemed Eichel already had his measure.

'You should come in the morning,' Eichel continued. 'It's peaceful, just a few writers debating philosophy or working off hangovers, and even the wintry sun smiles here nice and early.' He waved a hand at the nearby church. 'And St Germain des Prés looks lovely in the morning light. It dates back to the sixth century, you know.'

'Les Deux Magots? What does this name mean?' Kilian wondered as the waiter returned with balloon glasses of cognac.

Walter turned and pointed. 'Those two statues on the central pillar are traditional Chinese merchants. *Deux Magots* – it came from a play of the same name last century when this place was a drapery, I gather. Now it's the haunt of academics, philosophers, artists and particularly writers,' he said, 'a place where us Germans can feel intellectual . . . pretend we haven't been imbecilic enough to wage war on the rest of the world.'

Kilian gave a burst of laughter. He raised his glass. 'What are we drinking to?'

'How about to the survival of artists through these dark times?' Walter replied. 'Ever seen the work of the Spaniard, Picasso? Curious and haunting, always provocative. He's here all the time. Likes that table over there.'

Kilian clinked glasses with him. 'To art and all things beautiful.'

The food arrived and so began some small talk about the progress of the war, of business in troubled times, and ultimately of Hitler's disastrous decision to take Germany into Russia, where men were dying daily in the tens of thousands.

'The Russians don't need bullets,' Kilian was saying, 'the weather and starvation is doing the work for the Soviets. Besides, the real threat is not the east – it's in the south. The Americans already have North Africa. If they take Italy, it will open a new front and the British and the Americans can strike us right where we're exposed.' He shook his head. 'I'm not the only one who thinks this, of course.' He couldn't say more without crossing an invisible line. 'I feel so pointless in the scheme of things.'

'One can only wonder whose toes you stepped on to land yourself such a curious desk job.' If anything, Walter sounded impressed.

'Highest possible, I'm afraid,' Kilian admitted. They shared a comfortable chuckle and sat back to sip their cognacs. The café had become even more crowded but Kilian liked its atmosphere. He glanced beyond the windows to the terrace, where lesser mortals braved the cool evening to enjoy their drinks on the pavement. His attention was caught by a young woman standing near the door, peering in as though searching for someone. He watched her absently, admiring her sweet heart-shaped face, pinches of colour at her cheeks from the cold; he was surprised when her gaze fell on their table and she reacted as if she knew Walter.

'Walter, are you expecting company?'

'No. Why do you ask?'

Kilian blinked. 'Well, a vision has just glided in and seems to be looking your way.' He stared over Walter's shoulder at the approaching woman, who became more beautiful the closer she came.

Eichel swung around, frowning. 'I can't imagine . . . Oh,

wait – yes, it's Lisette, my goddaughter.' He waved her over. 'Her parents and I were very good friends; they are both sadly deceased. She's been doing some work for me these last couple of months while she settles herself in Paris.'

Kilian watched the young woman pull off her headscarf to reveal glossy, shoulder-length raven hair; she shook it carelessly as she weaved her way through the crowd. She had a dazzling smile, with dimples, no less, and what eyes! Now that Kilian could see them clearly he realised they were an incredible blue, like that child actress he'd seen on posters for a film about a dog called Lassie. He couldn't think of a more beautiful colouring. He was even more enchanted when, ignoring him and full of gushing excuses and kisses, she allowed Eichel to help her off with her coat. Kilian couldn't help but notice how her silk blouse tightened across her breasts – just for a moment – as she stretched to shrug off the heavy garment. He was staring, lost in a bubble of pure eroticism before he realised Walter was making introductions.

He immediately stood to his full height, towering over the newcomer as she offered her hand. '*Enchanté, mademoiselle.*' He kissed her hand.

Her smile was as warming as his cognac. 'Forgive me for interrupting you, Colonel,' she offered in flawless German. 'I thought I saw Walter sitting here and had to say hello.'

'Indeed,' Walter said, pulling out what must have been the one spare chair in the whole café. 'Were you passing?'

'No, I'm supposed to be meeting a friend, but . . .' She shrugged. 'He doesn't appear to be here.'

'Then you must let us claim you for ourselves,' Kilian offered. 'At least until your friend arrives.'

'I don't think I should interrupt —'

'Please,' Kilian insisted. 'It would be a delight. Walter, we had nothing specific to discuss, did we?'

'Not at all.' He turned to Lisette. 'The colonel is quite new to Paris so I thought I should make him feel welcome. This is purely social.'

'Mademoiselle Forestier, can we offer you an aperitif?' Kilian asked.

He noticed how she glanced at her benefactor, almost as though seeking his permission. He found her deference charming. Walter gave a small nod. Bravo! The evening had brightened considerably; he was tired of talking about Hitler, the price of gold, the winter in Russia.

'May I suggest a calvados?' he offered.

Her eyes widened. 'Do you know, I've always wanted to try one.'

'And you never have?'

She gave a slightly embarrassed shrug. 'I'm not very worldly, Colonel Kilian.'

'Well, we must work on that,' he replied. 'I personally believe that very few French drinks, including your heralded champagne, can match the singular joy of a fresh calvados in the summer served over ice. Except perhaps the dark beauty of a calvados aged maybe four, even six years, in a barrel, served at room temperature on a frosty evening in Paris.' He had held her gaze intimately, and it was worth it to see her break into a dazzling laugh.

'Colonel Kilian, you make a drink sound like poetry.'

'Calvados is art,' he said, raising his forefinger for the waiter.

'A glass of Boulard for the *mademoiselle*.' He spoke in German.

'*Merci*,' Lisette said to the waiter with a polite smile, then turned to him with a much wider one. 'Thank you. What a treat,' she continued in German.

'Walter, how is that you have a flawlessly bilingual girl working for you and I can't find anyone who knows her German even vaguely as well as her French?'

Walter shrugged amiably. He was leaning back watching, enjoying his cognac.

'Mademoiselle Forestier, how about coming and working for me?' Kilian quipped. 'I shall pay you double whatever your god-father does.'

'Oh, but I am very expensive, sir,' she remarked in the same light-hearted tone.

Kilian wondered whether this bright young thing was flirting with him. He did hope so. Her drink arrived.

'Swirl it around the bowl,' he advised.

While she watched the amber, syrupy apple brandy move like liquid gold around the glass, Kilian regarded her. Eichel's god-daughter was gorgeous; he imagined she must be mid-twenties, almost half his age. She was lean and angular, just how he liked a woman, so her clothes hung off her shoulders like a mannequin.

'*Santé*,' she said, seemingly unaware of his appraisal as she lifted her glass to each of her companions. 'Thank you for keeping me company.'

'It doesn't look as if your friend is coming,' Walter remarked. It's nearly seven-thirty. What time were you supposed to meet?'

'Seven,' Lisette said. 'And I was late.'

'Then it is his loss,' Kilian said. 'If he arrives now, I would feel obliged to punch him on the nose.'

This amused Lisette. Her response made Kilian realise that it had been too long since he'd enjoyed a woman's happy laughter.

They picked at snacks and talked about the opera, about Montmartre, about rationing and about life in Strasbourg before the war. Kilian told them a little about his family and made them laugh at his 'near misses', as he termed the times he'd almost married. He was impressed at how Lisette remained quietly captivated. By nine p.m. promises had been made between the men to go to a musical recital together, more than a couple of cognacs had been consumed, and Walter had begun to look at his watch.

'Well, I must get home. My housekeeper will have left some

food and I dare not miss it in these days of rationing. Do you need a lift, Lisette?' Eichel said, after draining the last of his glass.

'That's very kind of you, but I think I'll walk. I've been inside all day.'

He shook his head. 'Curfew – you'll never make it by eleven.'

'I walk fast. It will clear my head of the effects of my delicious calvados . . . Thank you both so much once again for your kindness.'

Eichel didn't look convinced by Lisette's explanation. Kilian took his chance.

'Walter, with your permission, I don't mind seeing Mademoiselle Forestier back to Montmartre. No one will dare question her; at least with me she is safe.'

He'd meant it sincerely but the innuendo was there. Walter laughed and Lisette had the grace to blush.

Kilian turned to Lisette. 'May I walk you back to your flat?'

'That would be lovely, thank you.'

'Well,' Walter began, hauling his bulk into a standing position. 'This has been most enjoyable. Good night, my dear,' he said, kissing Lisette lightly on both cheeks. 'I'm sure I'll see you at the bank tomorrow. Kilian, good to see you again.' The two men shook hands.

'Please, I shall see to the bill,' Kilian said, pulling out some notes. When Eichel began to protest, he made a tutting sound. Walker thanked him again and made his way out.

'Well, Mademoiselle Forestier, shall we take some night air?'

She smiled, and allowed him to help her with her coat. He gazed approvingly at her slim shoulders, and when he unintentionally brushed her skin with his hand, he felt a thrill pulse through him. He was as giddy as a teenager. He shook his head behind Lisette as he watched her tuck the last strands of hair into her scarf, and wondered if his self-imposed solitary lifestyle for the past few years had begun to work against him.

She turned and he was nearly caught staring wistfully at her. He smiled just in time and was able to offer an arm to lead her through the café, whose population had drastically thinned out as everyone made tracks to beat the curfew. Only men in uniform were in no rush.

The fresh air hit him like a slap and he was glad of the glow of cognac in his belly. He yawned. 'Forgive me, *mademoiselle*.'

'A big day?' she asked.

'Yes, lots of paper shuffling around my desk and no navigator. I am a man of action, not one who likes signing his name.'

'You should get your secretary to forge it, then,' she said with a giggle before shivering visibly in the cold.

He hesitated. 'Let me call for my driver.'

She gave a soft, utterly delightful noise of protest. 'No, Colonel, please. I'm fine, and truly, I do prefer to walk. After the winter we've had, this is nothing. Besides, Paris is beautiful at night, especially when it's so quiet like this.'

He smiled. 'I suppose you've never had the opportunity to walk Paris when it's truly deserted.'

She shook her head.

'I do it all the time. I pretend the city is mine.'

'What a dream.'

'Then, let us walk slowly and very soon there will be no one on the streets but you and I.'

'Oh, how romantic!' she murmured to herself, and once again he was charmed by this breath of fresh air that had breezed into his life.

'Please, call me Markus,' he instructed warmly and held out an arm, which she readily linked hers through. 'Do you have a favourite route?'

'Through the gardens, via the Louvre, up past Madeleine, Galeries Lafayette and up the hill to Montmartre. And please do call me Lisette.'

'Quite a long way around, then, Lisette.'

'If Paris is mine tonight, I want to take my time to enjoy her.'

'Indeed,' he said, and led her towards the river. He sighed inwardly, imagining they must look like a pair of lovers heading deeper into the mist. If only it were true.

Lisette hadn't been prepared to enjoy Markus Kilian; in fact, for all of the preparation since she'd first been briefed about her curious mission, she'd hated him in her mind. It was the only way. She'd already known he was well bred, but she'd been disarmed by his charm and handsome looks. She'd anticipated a more stereotypical heel-clicking, tightly wound officer, lacking in humour; someone who bragged of his soldiering achievements. Instead, here was a charismatic man who enjoyed music, talking about favourite films with the glee of a teenager, and yet described brandy in the lofty tones of an art critic. He liked women – of that she had no doubt – so London's mission was spot on; Kilian had been aware of her for every second of her presence. She'd seen him notice her through the café windows and he'd barely taken his eyes off her until she'd promised to join them. She'd made sure she'd shown off her attributes to their best effect and it had worked. Kilian had fallen for all her carefully orchestrated flirtations.

Now she had to quickly ingratiate herself into his life. He'd given her the opening. It was her intention to make that offer of a job a reality in the near future.

'I enjoyed my calvados, thank you,' she said. 'It was a lovely evening.' Lisette was careful to keep her distance even though they walked arm in arm.

'I like Walter,' he said. 'Too many of us are caught up in Hitler's madness, believing ourselves invincible. Walter isn't one of them. But I think I am the one who should be thanking you for a delight-ful evening.'

'Not at all,' she said. 'I'm just very glad that Pierre never turned up.'

He turned. 'Really?' The question was loaded with meaning.

She hesitated slightly. 'Yes, Colonel, I am.'

'Call me Markus, would you? It's been a long time since a beautiful woman said my name.'

His gaze was so intent she faltered momentarily. Even in her dreams the mission hadn't proceeded as quickly as this. The reality was unnerving.

He watched her struggle with the compliment and stopped walking. They'd reached the gate at the end of the Tuileries. 'Don't be frightened of me, Lisette. And don't worry about your godfather.'

She tried to shrug and genuinely had to look away from his eyes, which seemed to turn her into a statue like those in the gardens behind her. 'I feel it would be disrespectful not to use your title.'

He gently gripped her arms. 'I understand. In fact, your reluctance is charming. But you have my permission. And if you're referring to our age difference . . .' He shrugged. 'It is not my fault you were born fifteen years too late.'

Her laughter was genuine and spontaneous. They continued walking.

'Ah, I enjoy amusing you. How old are you, anyway?'

'Twenty-four,' she replied. 'I'll be twenty-five in a few days, actually. My birthday is on the eighth.' She'd almost forgotten.

'On Monday, really? Have you something planned?'

'No. I'm on rations, remember.'

'What about Walter? Your friends?'

'I don't think Walter would recall. And Pierre is my only friend.'

'Is he your lover?'

She smirked. 'No. But he's been a good companion to me since I arrived.'

'Where did you meet?'

'On the platform at Gare de l'Est. He tripped over my bag and knocked me down. We became instant friends as he helped me up.'

'It sounds romantic.'

'It wasn't. My elbow was bleeding,' she said, embellishing her fabricated tale as she went.

'I would have kissed it better.'

This was the moment, she felt it; he was vulnerable now. 'Unfortunately you weren't there, Markus . . . or I'm sure I would have let you.' Even though she couldn't see well in the darkness, she felt the full intensity of Kilian's ice-blue eyes fall on her.

'I would never stand you up. Along with being clumsy, this Pierre is an idiot. I would never let another man be alone with you as we are now.'

Lisette swallowed. 'That sounds very possessive.'

'When something *is* mine I protect it . . . with my life, if necessary.'

'Your men must love you, Markus.'

It proved the right sentiment to express. She watched him drop his gaze. By deflecting his advances, she showed that she was not hunting for romance. Lisette knew she had to make Markus Kilian want her, and to do that meant giving little ground. She needed to arouse his ardour, his jealousy, his anxiety. Right now he was fully in control, toying with her. She had to reverse that role . . . but she found him alarmingly sensual. It was a struggle not to fall under his spell.

He sighed. 'And I love my men.' He gave a growl of frustration. 'I feel so helpless here in Paris. We know the Allies are preparing a final push to take place in the summer. Berlin should have all of its best men in place.'

She remained silent. It was a shock to hear him speak so casually and yet so confidently of the Allies' intentions. London must be warned.

'Well, you can't change anything tonight, but perhaps tomorrow will bring the news you want to hear,' she said placatingly.

They paused to stare absently into a shop window.

He turned to her. 'Forgive me, Lisette. I don't want to discuss strategy with you. It is wrong of me.'

'Don't apologise. My father was a soldier in the Great War. I grew up listening to war stories.'

He began to walk again, groaning. 'I hope I don't remind you of your father?'

'Not at all, I just find men in uniform undeniably attractive.'

He gave her a sidelong grin and something unspoken passed between them.

'Come. Let's get you home before you catch a chill.'

They walked briskly, Lisette mostly listening, as he gave her a guided tour of the famous places of Paris. She was genuinely interested in his commentary; he was knowledgeable and clearly loved the city, unable to contain his joy at its beauty. And he was right – walking the streets this late gave Paris a haunted quality; its beauty, even in shadow, managed to shine through.

The most direct route would have taken them an hour but Lisette's more scenic path meant it took another twenty-five minutes. They finally arrived, sighing softly and laughing as they emerged into the main street of Montmartre. There were still a couple of cafés open, with the clink of glasses and men's laughter echoing from them. The lights inside had been dimmed and would be turned off by midnight.

'What do you actually do?' Lisette asked, guiding Kilian towards her building.

He gave a groan. 'I'm a facilitator for discussion between the Church in France, Paris mainly, and the German regime of the Occupation.'

'But you're a colonel of the Wehrmacht,' she observed.

'It is a punishment, Lisette, for my defiance of the Führer.'

'Really? You don't believe in the regime?'

'I believe in Germany. I believe that it can rise from the ashes of the Great War, be a world power again. But no, my political views do not embrace the vision of our Führer. And now I shall have to kill you for hearing me utter that. Where is that pistol of mine?' he asked casually, reaching towards his belt.

She felt a thrill of fear pass through her.

'Oh, my dear Lisette. That was just a jest. I frightened you,' Kilian said, stopping to take her hand. 'Forgive me. We Germans aren't known for our humour.' He kissed her hand. 'I do apologise. I think I shall be the one killed before you.'

'Don't say that.'

He looked down. 'I shouldn't be so bleak. But you know, years ago, when I was a youngster, perhaps fourteen, I went to our local fair. My mother didn't approve but I sneaked out of my bedroom window and went with my friends late at night. There was a clairvoyant.'

'And?' They were nearly at her apartment.

'And she told me that I'd die on foreign soil. I'm a soldier – I shouldn't be surprised.'

Lisette felt genuinely sad. 'Markus, set no store by fairground foretellings. You didn't die in Russia. And the closest you'll get in Paris might be dying of boredom in some cleric's rooms?'

He laughed. 'Yes, and you're right – if the fortune-teller had been worth her salt, she'd have mentioned that I'd meet a beautiful young woman in Paris who would enchant me one spring evening.'

Lisette shrugged awkwardly, desperately not wanting to appear coy or girlish. She already sensed coquettishness would not work with Kilian. He was far too dry and direct.

'Now I've embarrassed you.'

She met his gaze firmly. 'No. I'm just not sure how to respond. We hardly know each other.'

'All right. It's your birthday on the eighth, you said?'

She nodded.

'Be dressed gorgeously for dinner. A car will pick you up at seven p.m.'

Lisette was stunned. Her silence clearly amused him.

'You will have dinner with me, won't you?'

'I had in mind a piece of cheese with the mice that plague my bedsit.'

He grinned. 'You sound like Cinderella. Instead, enjoy a birthday dinner as my guest.'

'No, Markus. Like Cinderella, I have absolutely nothing *gorgeous* to wear. Please, you don't have to do this.'

'I know I don't. It's a purely selfish decision; I wish to see you again and I don't want to be in a crowded café or walking the streets. Besides, I must continue your education in calvados. And where I shall take you serves the finest. It will be my gift to you. A balloon of calvados at the Hotel Ritz.'

'The Hotel Ritz,' she repeated in a shocked squeak. The heartland of the German government in Paris! SOE would be thrilled.

'I can't tell if you're shivering from anticipation or the cold, but we must get you home,' he said kindly.

'We're here,' Lisette said, looking up at the whitewashed three-storey building they stood beside. 'I'm on the top floor.' She pointed. 'That's my balcony.'

'You must have a splendid view over Paris.'

'The hill can be challenging some evenings but it's always worth it once I'm inside. Thank you for walking me home. Will you be all right?'

He laughed aloud. 'I am a soldier who survived Russia. I think I can manage to get back to my comfortable hotel in Paris.'

'Yes, I'm sorry. You make me nervous.'

He grinned. 'So, let me watch you go safely inside, Mademoiselle

Lisette. Thank you for tonight, and don't worry about next Monday. I shall take care of everything. Just agree to come.'

'All right.'

He leant forward and gently kissed each cheek; she felt the evening shadow of his chin. It surprised her how seductive that fleeting graze of skin on skin felt. He wanted to kiss her properly, that much was obvious – but she needed to keep hesitating, holding him at bay.

'*Gute nacht*, Markus.'

'*Bonne nuit*, Lisette.'

She felt his gaze follow her up the small pathway to her building's entrance. She turned at the doorway and gave him a wave, then dashed up the two flights to her door, fighting with the keys to open it. She ran to her window and looked down. He was still there. She watched the flare of a match and then the tip of a cigarette glow; it burned brightly as he inhaled and his handsome, angular face lit momentarily.

Then Colonel Markus Kilian turned and disappeared into the darkness of the night's curfew. Lisette trembled as she wrote out her message on the cigarette paper immediately. She would drop it in tomorrow; London would know that Lark's mission was finally in play.

23

Walter Eichel didn't seem surprised to hear of Lisette's birthday date with the colonel. 'I think he was captivated from the moment you arrived.'

Lisette blushed. 'I can't say I regret running into you, but I wanted to be sure that you didn't disapprove in any way.'

'No, my dear. I'm surprised and rather delighted. Kilian may be in some sort of disgrace but privately, I admire him. Rumour has it that he's taking the rap in the wilderness for a lot of others who defied the same orders.'

She frowned in consternation. 'I have nothing to wear to the Ritz.'

He smiled. 'You could walk in wearing a hessian sack and still every woman would envy you. Take a day off as my gift to you.'

She kissed her godfather. 'Thank you, Walter.'

On the afternoon of her birthday, she was in the process of getting ready when she heard a knock at the door. She froze while holding up her one dress against herself, looking at her reflection in the mirror.

There was nowhere to hide but also nothing to hide, she was sure of it. She looked wildly around her tiny bedsit for anything incriminating. The morning after meeting Kilian, she'd been in such a hurry to deliver her information that she was among the first patrons to walk into the café in Rue Pergolèse as it opened up. Once there she'd stuck her cryptic message into the newspaper. *Lark has made her nest.* It was then up to Playboy to pick up the message and transmit it to London.

By now SOE would know that her mission was in play. The knock at the door came again. Few knew where she lived, so she couldn't imagine who could be calling at three in the afternoon. Maybe Walter had sent something for her birthday?

Lisette opened the door and instantly felt cold tendrils of fear reaching down from her chest and squeezing themselves around her gut. But she betrayed nothing other than an enquiring smile. Snapping to attention before her was a man in the familiar green uniform of the Wehrmacht. He was young, his boots polished, his freckled face rosy and scrubbed to a gleam.

'Yes?' She cleared her throat. 'Can I help you?'

'I'm Corporal Otto Freyberg from the ministry. I work for Colonel Kilian.'

'Markus,' she whispered in a gust of relief.

He blinked at her use of his superior's first name. 'Are you Mademoiselle Lisette Forestier?'

'I am. Is something wrong?'

'The colonel asked me to deliver this to you, *mademoiselle*,' he replied.

It was only then she noticed the box in his hands and the bag beneath it.

'Oh . . . What's this?'

'I am simply the courier,' he replied with a grave expression.

She nodded, bemused. 'Thank you, Corporal Freyberg.'

Lisette could hear his boots clomping all the way down to the front door. Her neighbour below stepped out and looked up the narrow staircase. 'Are you all right, Lisette?'

'Yes, Sylvie. Sorry to disturb you.' She assumed her new neighbour must work shifts; she'd once mentioned going for an interview at the telephone exchange. She was beautiful with a wide mouth that gave generous smiles, while her dark eyes held a hint of mystery. They were on cordial terms, but Lisette had found Sylvie to be a little too curious for her liking.

'It's lucky you did,' Sylvie said with a yawn. 'I had to get up anyway.'

Lisette waved her farewell and eagerly carried her parcels inside. Something clunked heavily in the bag and she couldn't resist checking it first. She gasped softly. It was the unmistakable white box of Chanel No. 5 perfume. In fact, there were two Chanel boxes. She dared not touch either but just stood, staring at the gift that prompted a score of thoughts at once and a dozen sensations, ranging from terror at the expense of this gift, to joy at understanding they were for her.

Finally, she lifted the boxes out of the plain brown bag as though carrying treasure. The first contained the square bottle of perfume, reminiscent of a whisky decanter that she remembered from her childhood. Once, while in a perfumery together, her mother had pointed out the Chanel brand and told her daughter it was the one to look forward to when she grew up; even dabbed some on her tiny wrist. As if in a dream, Lisette opened the black lid and inhaled the amber liquid. The fragrance instantly transported her back to childhood, to happier, more plentiful times, when her mother's infectious laugh rang through the house.

The *extrait* was intoxicating. A helpless grin claimed her. The second box contained something even harder to believe. Soap! Not just the real thing but waxy white and exquisitely perfumed to give her a moment of pure rapture. She couldn't imagine what Kilian had paid for it, and dared not try.

Her gaze drifted treacherously to the plain white box. She could guess what it contained. It took her a full five minutes of internal battle to find the courage to lift the lid. Finally she decided that if Kilian was choosing to shower her with gifts . . . so be it. London wanted her to become his companion, and to do so meant to accept his favours, no matter how corrupt it was when people in Paris were starving.

It was no ordinary dress, of course – it was a gown. And it was so beautiful to behold that she backed away from it initially, too overcome to touch it straightaway. But she did eventually reach for the fabric, a black silk chiffon, and lifted the dress from the confines of the box. The silk lining rustled deliciously as the gown loosened from its billowy folds. She stared at the gorgeously unfussy design – even Coco Chanel would have approved: a thick halter neck to flatter her shoulders, slightly ruched around the bust but with a fitted bodice that would hold her in figure-hugging style. Achingly simple, black as night, exquisitely stylish and undoubtedly breathtakingly expensive. Lisette realised it would also reveal plenty of skin. It was the sort of dress that movie stars would wear with a fur coat to a premiere. She barely spared a glance for the sheer stole that accompanied the dress and which had probably cost another small fortune.

Kilian wanted her to wear it for him, she kept telling herself. Even so, her mind was in turmoil. She laid the dress down on her bed and sat beside it, feeling numb. What was she to do? What would Buckmaster say? What would Vera say? She nodded, already knowing. She was playing a role now. People were counting on her to give the performance of her life because maybe something she did could help to save lives.

So she would wear Kilian's dress, and she would wear his perfume – neither was a hardship – and she would permit him to become her lover, because that was what was required of her. Others risked their lives daily to tap out Morse messages or pick up arms and fight with the Maquis – and some, like her, were required to use other attributes.

Lisette picked up her soap with a fresh resolve and walked into the cubby that served as her bathroom.

Kilian had been unsettled through Monday; he knew why but was determined not to acknowledge it; seven p.m. would come soon enough. In the meantime he had a meeting with senior clerics about their ceremonies for Pentecost. He tried not to dwell on the frustrating pointlessness of his role. He'd brought it on himself, after all. Perhaps within the priesthood he might find some answers to his own doubts about the war.

He knew that among the clergy were many troubled men whose consciences kept them awake at night. Like him, they searched for ways to wage their own private war against the atrocities foisted on innocents. But for every man who resisted, there were nine others who acquiesced to the regime, and a surprising number who privately supported the extermination of the Jewish people, the Roma, homosexuals, the disabled and the mentally ill.

He shook his head clear of his burdens and reached for a piece of writing paper. Without thinking, he began to pen a letter to Ilse, the woman he'd left behind in Germany almost six years ago. They had communicated only once in that time, during the first year of the war. Her letter had been hesitant, and revealed little. All the same, he had been glad to hear from her. He sensed an undercurrent of sadness in her words as she wished him only safety; she had quietly suggested that when he finally returned after the war, he might look her up.

It felt cathartic to write to Ilse; he told her everything that weighed heavily on his mind, and in doing so wondered whether it would ever reach her, certain that mail was read and confiscated. He thought it would be a short letter but it turned into one that was several pages long in his neat, small handwriting. He wasn't surprised when Lisette Forestier crept into the letter; he told Ilse that he thought he had found the perfect translator and hoped that with her arrival in his life he could communicate far better and with greater subtlety with the French. By the end he realised he was simply pouring out his stream of consciousness, and wondered whether he'd ever send it. Nevertheless, he addressed the envelope and put the letter inside his pocket with the resolve to add more to it and send it some time. His mind wandered again to the young woman who had blown into his life two evenings earlier.

It might have been Lisette's youth. Or the fact that she was strangely aloof. She hadn't latched onto him as so many other women had, trying too hard to win his attention. Lisette had paid far more attention to her godfather.

He'd not slept well that night, nor last, thinking about the cool young woman with the dark hair and secretive dark-blue eyes. He could see certain traits that reflected her German heritage, in her slightly reticent manner, but these were softened by what were more classically French traits – a certain tendency to romance and flirtation. He was intrigued by her. It had been too long since Markus Kilian had kissed a woman or felt the security of a genuine embrace – one without an ulterior motive.

Now that his gifts had been dispatched, he began to wonder whether his spontaneity was premature. Would it scare her off? Offend? Had he misread her taste . . . or was he imposing his own too soon? Agitated, he moved through his day speaking to as few people as possible, eating nothing, sipping from a tumbler of water. He remembered little of his meeting with the clerics; but then something both alarming and exciting occurred that shook him from his stupor. Waiting for him on his return from the meeting was a lieutenant colonel, who said he was passing through Paris and brought news from the Front. Kilian decided the impromptu visit meant the man must have presumed he'd be missing the action and his men.

'I'm sorry. Have I kept you waiting?' Kilian asked. Without an assistant he had no way of knowing.

'Not at all, Colonel. I arrived unannounced; I'm pleased I caught you,' the man called Meister said amiably.

'And you are on von Tresckow's staff?'

'Yes, indeed. Have you met him?'

'Twice. He seemed a good sort.'

'He is a good man,' Meister replied.

'Are you on your way to Berlin?' Kilian asked. 'Or stopping a few days in Paris?'

'Actually, I've come from Berlin, on some business here for my superiors. I'm heading back east tomorrow.'

'I pity you,' Kilian said.

'And still you say those words with longing, Colonel Kilian. I'm sure you miss your men.'

'No doubt. Can I offer you something?' Kilian looked at his watch. Too early for a snifter. 'A coffee, perhaps?'

Meister smiled. 'Thank you. Perhaps we can walk out together, Colonel? It's a beautiful afternoon for a stroll.' Kilian frowned, curious about this visit from a man with no reason to be visiting. Perhaps Meister was a spy from Berlin, sent to assess whether Kilian should be given a more challenging role.

Meister stood. 'Shall we?'

Now Kilian was sure that Meister wanted to speak somewhere they could not be overheard, for nothing in their conversation thus far gave any reason for his presence. Once outside of the ministry building, Meister's demeanour changed.

'Forgive me, sir. I'm sure you realise that I wanted to speak privately.'

'Indeed.'

Meister pointed and Kilian followed him towards the Tuileries. It was another sparkling day. Kilian hoped its mildness would hold for this evening. Meister led him to an isolated bench, and after taking a surreptitious look around, he dropped his voice. 'I was sanctioned to pay this visit by General Friedrich Olbricht and Colonel von Tresckow in Berlin.'

Of a hundred different explanations that Meister could have given, this would have not have made the list in Kilian's mind. His shock showed.

'I think you should laugh as though I just made a joke, sir. Gestapo are everywhere.'

Kilian feigned a chuckle and sat back, trying to adopt a natural pose.

Meister smiled. 'Here, Colonel.' He put the newspaper down that he held under his arm. 'Inside this is proof that what I have to say is the truth. It is written by General Olbricht. He said you would know his signature.' Kilian took the newspaper casually and opened it. Meister pointed, so that to anyone watching it would appear they were talking about an article, but Kilian quickly scanned the hand-written note inside. Meister smiled and took the newspaper back, folding it quickly and neatly. He took a breath. 'Forgive me, but we can't be too careful. You have highly placed supporters, sir, and we are assured you are a kindred spirit, wanting change.'

Kilian gave a mirthless grin.

'Was that a yes, Colonel?'

'It was.' Kilian took out a packet of cigarettes. He didn't smoke much, did it more to keep his men company, or whenever he felt rattled. He offered one and Meister took it. Kilian lit both.

'The general has asked you to trust me. I have come directly from him in Berlin.'

'Go on,' Kilian said, taking his first joyless puff. He listened with a mixed feeling of dread and elation as Meister briefly outlined a plan to assassinate Hitler. Once Meister was done, Kilian stared at him, trying to hide his shock. 'You're serious about this?'

'We are well advanced in the plan.'

It was as daring as it was dangerous. Kilian almost wished he was the one planting the bomb in the wolf's lair.

'Why am I being told? I'm not in a position to do anything helpful,' he said.

'Because we know you, like us, believe the Führer's actions to be immoral, illegal, abhorrent.' Meister dropped his voice still further, and hid his mouth behind an open-handed drag on his cigarette.

Kilian nodded, saying nothing.

'To arrest him is not enough; he must be assassinated for any change to occur, for any truce to be negotiated with the Allies.'

A thrill passed through Kilian but he kept his features even. 'And?'

'Are you with us, Colonel?'

'You wouldn't be having this conversation with me if you didn't already know it.'

It was Meister's turn to nod. 'We know what you have given up.'

'But with me stuck in Paris, what use am I to the generals?'

'When it is done, we will need all loyalists to be in place. Soldiers will rally to you and we need a man who understands the language of the Wehrmacht. We need Paris secured.'

Kilian nodded, excitement turning somersaults in his chest. 'Who else can I count on?'

'You will find out soon enough. For now all I need is your agreement.'

'You have it . . . in blood if necessary.'

'I hope it will not come to that,' Meister said and stood.

They shook hands like two old friends saying farewell. 'When?'

'Soon. Summer probably, after attempts last winter failed. Word will be sent to you. Trust only those I have mentioned. No one else.' Meister laughed as though Kilian had said something amusing. 'Next time perhaps, Colonel Kilian, I would be delighted to have that drink in celebration,' he said, turning to leave.

'Good luck, Meister,' Kilian replied, and then walked with a far lighter step back to the Hotel Raphaël to bath and shave for his dinner appointment at the Ritz.

24

The car was embarrassingly large and Lisette couldn't wait for it to be out of her neighbourhood. It was hardly inconspicuous and plenty of her fellow Montmartre villagers, including a frowning Sylvie, saw her climbing into the big black car with its ugly swastika flag flying at the front. She was grateful she wore her everyday coat in the dash to the car to cover up the beautiful dress.

This is not a date. This is a mission, she repeated in her mind, her cheeks on fire as the car rolled down the hill to the first arrondissement in the very centre of the city. Here sat the Louvre with its gardens, the Tuileries, in a neat line that led the eye up the Champs Elysées towards the Arc de Triomphe. Lisette's destination, the famed Ritz Hotel, was in the city's largest, most magnificent square – the grandly historic Place Vendôme.

It was a minute past seven when the car drew up quietly outside number fifteen, and the driver stepped out of his door to open Lisette's.

'Here we go,' she whispered as the door swept open and Lisette emerged, stepping out carefully in her new black heels from Walter. She pulled the sheer stole around her shoulders as she approached the hotel's doors, the concierge already swinging them back for her.

'Your coat, *mademoiselle*?' the driver enquired.

She turned. 'May I leave it in the car?'

'Of course. It may be a different driver but the car will be the same.'

'Thank you,' she breathed, reminding herself not to get used to such treatment. She did her best to glide into the palatial foyer, where awaiting her was Markus Kilian, standing on a plush rug of royal blue. Furniture around him, which she took in with a glance, was heavily gilded. Lamps cast light that glittered off massive mirrors, and huge vases were filled with striking greenery in the absence of flowers. It was warm inside, but the colonel's smile radiated a heat all of its own.

She took in a breath. If he had looked handsome in Les Deux Magots, tonight he was taller, broader somehow, with an even more determined chin, even more sparkling eyes. There was no other way to describe him than golden and dashing. In a few heartbeats she took in everything, from the soft grey-green of his dress uniform to the huge gilt clock on the mantelpiece behind him. His eyes seemed to have changed from the pale blue she remembered to be a steel grey, reflecting his outfit.

He was still smiling. Too handsome, she thought. And he looked flushed, excited. Was this because of her? No, she was convinced he was used to sweeping women off their feet. This would be second nature to him. Something else was pleasing him.

'Lisette . . .' He didn't finish.

'Good evening, Markus.' His hesitation unnerved her and her bright expression faltered. 'Is something wrong?'

'Wrong? No, pardon me, please.' His smile broadened. 'You are dazzling.'

She gave him a demure half-smile and there was nothing contrived about it. Her heart was beating hard. Everything about tonight mattered. If this evening went as she hoped it might, then she had achieved arguably the most important stage of her mission.

'I feel honoured that you wore the dress; I bought it on such a whim.' He looked her up and down, clearly impressed.

'I have never owned anything so beautiful. I don't know how to thank you. How could I not wear it?'

'You more than do it justice. Come, I hope you are hungry?' he asked, offering her an arm.

'Am I hungry?' she whispered. 'The whole of Paris, except perhaps those here, is famished.'

He broke into a gust of embarrassed laughter. 'I'm sorry. That was a foolish remark. I thought you'd prefer to go straight to our table?'

'As you wish.'

'What I wish is to have you all to myself and not share you with other officers already ogling you.' He swept a glance around the foyer. 'The tongues will be wagging all over the city tomorrow.'

'Then let's give them something to wag about,' she said, throwing him a dangerous smile.

The restaurant L'Espadon was filled with German officers, mainly Luftwaffe, and military personnel, dignitaries and political figures, the fashionable elite of Paris and a single SOE agent, who was reassuring herself that she could hold her own in such company. Lisette could feel other women's eyes on her but she fought the inclination to catch them in the act of staring. Instead she chatted amiably and animatedly to her companion. They had spoken of their childhoods, of their parents, of their different upbringings in different eras.

She was amazed by the lilac tree that was the focal point of the room. Its colour must be gorgeous in summer, its fragrance exquisite and potent enough to scent the whole restaurant. Booths had been built around the twisted trunk of the old tree. Opulence was the word that came to her mind.

Several people had interrupted them during their dinner and

Kilian had been polite, duly introducing her as Walter Eichel's god-daughter. Lisette realised she was being assessed in a new light. Walter's name counted for something among these people, and she hoped her mission would never tarnish his reputation. Several women had also stopped by their table and lingered to chat to her host, to kiss him hello and then steal another kiss goodbye. Were they making a point? She didn't care.

The one person she wasn't introduced to had been ushered to their table by the maitre d' with soft apologies.

'Colonel Kilian?' the man in uniform asked, respectfully bowing his head.

'Yes.' He looked surprised to be interrupted.

'Please forgive me for interrupting your dinner. I took the liberty of making a few calls to find you, sir. I have a message from General Stülpnagel.' The man opened a small leather satchel and withdrew an envelope. 'I am his adjutant.'

General Stülpnagel! Lisette couldn't imagine how the military commander of Paris could be connected with Kilian's office, other than in the most cursory way. But as she thought about it, she realised they were both ex-field officers who had resigned or been removed from their critical roles in Russia to be given administrative positions far from Berlin. Both men had noble Prussian backgrounds with proud military heritages. Perhaps they were family friends? She schooled her features to remain blank as the men spoke, but she tried to take in every nuance of their conversation, of Kilian's body language.

'Could this not have been sent to my office? I shall be there first thing in the morning.'

'The general regrets the inconvenience, sir. I gather his communication is in connection with Church holy days. He has been very busy, but has an opening tomorrow morning that he hopes you can take advantage of; it's why he sent me at such an hour.'

Lisette couldn't tell whether the man was lying, although he might well be. Kilian appeared mystified by the special delivery . . . perhaps even suspicious.

'I'll read it later. Thank you,' he said.

The adjutant nodded, closed his satchel. 'The general will expect you in the morning, sir.' He gave a salute and Kilian flicked a lazy one back, already turning away.

Lisette watched the man walk out of the restaurant. It seemed normal enough; this was wartime, after all, but she wasn't experienced enough to know just how unusual it was to disturb the colonel at a social occasion. Something about Kilian's hesitancy suggested it was odd . . . perhaps it was an unexpected contact?

Kilian shook his head. 'I'm sorry about yet another disruption.'

'Well, that one sounded important,' she said.

'To be honest, I have no idea. I'm sure I'll discover soon enough.' He slipped the note into his pocket but she sensed the lie.

'How well do you know General Stülpnagel?' she asked casually.

'Why on earth should that interest you? Dear Lisette, you don't have to feign curiosity in my work.'

'I'm not feigning anything,' she said smoothly. 'Forgive me. He's an important man in Paris. Everything you say is interesting. You have to understand, I'm not used to socialising at this level.'

He smiled. 'Your bashfulness is charming, but I suspect, Lisette, that you would be adept at any level.'

'I hope that's a compliment,' she said, sipping from her wine glass.

'Be assured of it. You would grace anyone's table. And to answer your question, I don't know the general in any other capacity than to salute him at a formal occasion.'

It was clear Kilian did not want to discuss Stülpnagel and yet here was the highest authority in Paris looming into her view. 'How does the work you do cross over into his?'

'No doubt I shall find out tomorrow morning.'

Kilian was bored and shutting her down. Lisette smiled, took a different approach. 'I think Walter knows him. He described him once as a man of sound morals.'

'I hope we all are.'

'Surely morals come into question in wartime,' she said, interested to see what she could provoke.

His eyes widened. 'Are we to discuss philosophy over dinner?'

Her ploy hadn't worked. He was clearly not about to give anything away.

'Later perhaps. I agree it's very dull. Now I think we should discuss your immense popularity. That was the sixth visitor to your table already . . . and four were women.'

He laughed delightedly. 'You counted?' He shook his head. 'I suspect they're all just curious. The men want to know who you are and the women are insanely jealous of you.'

'For being in your company?'

'You miss my point. And I think that's because you have absolutely no idea of the effect you have.' He covered her hand with his. She had to stop herself from snatching it away. Not because she didn't want it there; to the contrary, she found herself drawn to him far too strongly. On paper he'd sounded old and cold; a prized and heartless colonel on his way up the ranks. It was a surprise that she found his company so easy.

'How many romantic liaisons have you enjoyed, Lisette?' he said, while they waited for their main course, clinking together their wine glasses.

'That's a rather personal question. How would you feel if I asked you the same?' she teased.

'You already know of the few that mattered.'

'What about the ones that didn't matter?'

'Dozens, scores,' he said mischievously.

'I can't match that,' she said, hungrily watching her food arrive and admiring it with equal measure of awe and guilt. She didn't think anything could top the rabbit of the first course, but this was an exquisite pale-fleshed fish, cooked in butter. It smelled divine.

'Well, I'd be shocked if you did.'

'Because only men are allowed to be with many lovers?'

'No, because you're nearly half my age.'

She laughed prettily.

'So answer me,' he said, resetting his napkin and picking up his fork and fish knife. 'How many?'

'That mattered, or in general?'

'That mattered,' he replied. '*Bon appétit.*'

'Then my answer is only one.'

'Ah, the lost love.'

'Yes, you could say that.'

'What did he do?'

'He was a farmer.'

Kilian looked surprised. 'You seem too refined, altogether too French, to be interested in a farmer.'

'Mother taught me never to be predictable. I have lots of surprises.'

He grinned. 'I can believe that. Tell me about your farmer.'

'Why?'

'Because I'm jealous of him. You loved him?'

She shook her head. This was dangerous and surprisingly painful. 'I don't know.'

'Why not?'

'We didn't have enough time.'

'If he walked in here now, right this moment, how would you feel?'

'Markus . . .' She gave him an admonishing look.

'Come, Lisette, life is too short for the mundane. I want provocative conversation. I want to know what ticks behind that controlled façade you present.'

She admired his energy. 'I don't know what I'd say to him but yes, I'd probably feel in love,' she admitted truthfully. She needed to stay focused on her mission, but Kilian was far too charming. Luc, whom she thought about daily, whose memory was as vivid and painful as the day she'd left him, had never felt further away.

'And what would you then say to me, sitting here watching you?'

She laughed. 'All right. Now you're just teasing me.'

'I am. What did he farm?'

She hesitated. Glide near the truth, SOE taught her. 'Lavender . . . er, amongst other crops.'

'Lavender? In Strasbourg?'

Her first mistake. 'No, of course not. It was a summer romance before the war. I was sixteen, in Provence with my parents. I met him briefly and then had to leave.'

'How long were you together?'

She was about to say the summer but something inside forced her to be honest. 'Just a day or two.'

Kilian looked surprised. 'That was fast.'

'I believe that if you fall in love with someone, it happens from the outset.'

He swallowed his mouthful. 'Eat. Don't let this fish go cold. So you don't believe love can develop between two people?'

'I do believe love can grow, and I'm sure it does in many marriages. But the sort of love I want has bells jangling and fireworks in my mind, and that's how it felt the first time he kissed me.' She pushed food around her plate, suddenly self-conscious. 'I felt lost in his kiss . . . I felt . . .'

'What?' he pushed, staring intently.

'Lost and yet found,' she replied, emerging from the memory.

'I hate him,' Kilian said. 'Actually, I envy him.' Then he took on a more devilish tone. 'He's French, of course?'

'Of course. They make the very best lovers, don't you know?'

'Give me his name. I shall have him hunted down and shot!'

She laughed nervously. 'I must protect his name to my dying breath, then.'

'Is that why you went back to the south?'

Lisette looked puzzled.

'You said you'd come to Paris from the south after a sabbatical.'

'Oh, yes, but I didn't go back to look for him. That was a long time ago.'

'But perhaps why you were drawn there, no?'

Let him think that if it made him jealous. 'You're probably right.' It was time to change the subject. She put her fork and knife together carefully in the French way and sat back. 'I am not used to this rich food, Markus.' *Markus*. The familiarity rolled so effortlessly off her tongue.

'Neither am I, to tell the truth.' He told her of his habit of eating very little normally.

'That's admirable.'

'I don't do it for admiration. I just . . . Well, it's out of respect for all – not just Germans – who go hungry. Look at this,' he said, waving his hand at the ostentatious surrounds, rich fabric hanging in great swathes from the ceiling. 'Maybe a hundred young German soldiers have died in the time we've eaten two courses, and an equal number of Russians.'

'Oh, that's bleak.'

'It's your birthday. I'm sorry.'

'No, don't be. I should be reminded of it. We all need to be. It makes the hunger pangs easier to ignore, the cold easier to bear.

We're alive to feel those sensations. Too many young men no longer are.'

He cupped his chin in his hand, leaning an elbow on the table to gaze at her. 'Do you see yourself as French or German?'

'Neither. I am a woman of the world, that's all. And I think if women ran the world, we would not be at war.'

'You could well be right.'

She smiled ruefully. 'How about you? Are you a good Nazi, Markus?'

He obviously wasn't expecting such a question. His expression clouded, and after glancing around he stared at the white starched tablecloth, teased at a stray crumb on the table. 'Let's not talk politics.'

She swallowed. Tonight . . . her dress . . . her perfume . . . his attention . . . all the flirting – it had to amount to something worthwhile, or the guilt would smother her.

'Why not?' she pressed. When he looked up, she gave him a soft smile. 'I'm not a girl who has to be protected. We're in a devastating, seemingly endless war. To sit here and sip six-year-old calvados in my gorgeous dress and eat rich food, drink real coffee . . .' Her voice reflected the awe she still felt. 'It's . . .'

'What?' he frowned.

'Obscene,' she finished, her expression instantly apologetic the moment she'd uttered the word.

'I'm sorry,' he replied, now looking wounded.

Lisette instinctively moved to reach for his hand. It was a large, warm hand, the nails blunt and well kept with neat half moons. Her touch was gentle, affectionate. Surprised, perhaps, but obviously also delighted, Kilian returned it with a gentle squeeze. In that moment there was a heartbeat of intense connection.

'Forgive me. That came out wrong.' Their hands had been noticed by others and he seemed to understand when she gently withdrew hers. 'I think what I was trying to say, and badly, was that I don't want us to pretend.'

His gaze met hers again and in that instant Lisette could no longer fool herself. She was no cool professional playing her role in this piece of theatre. She could not force the way her cheeks burned, or deny that her heart was pounding, or ignore the rare and exquisite tingling coursing through her body. Markus Kilian. German. Wehrmacht colonel. Her enemy. But nonetheless a devastatingly attractive man, and not just in looks – in fact, in spite of them. There was something inherently decent and fine about him as a person, and everything about him appealed to her – from the timbre of his voice to the sorrow that seemed to walk alongside him.

'Pretend?' he echoed.

This was the moment to strike . . . to win him. No more innuendo. She would be direct.

'We shouldn't pretend that nothing is happening between us. I'm young, not stupid. We both know what is going on.'

Again she'd caught him unawares; she could see it in the set of his mouth, the flare of surprise in his eyes. Kilian fixed her with a gaze she couldn't fully read and she held her breath. Had she really just uttered those words? Did she really know what sort of precipice she was now standing upon?

'So what *is* going on, Lisette?'

She didn't have the luxury of time to tease him. Taut silence stretched between them as they regarded one another. For a second or two she wasn't sure what to say.

'Colonel Kilian, I'm sorry to interrupt you, sir.'

The tension snapped and they both blinked, drew a breath.

'Yes?' Kilian said, cutting his gaze away from her to the maitre d' looming at their table.

'My apologies,' he said in perfect German. 'Your driver is here. You asked him to return at nine.'

'I did. Tell him to wait,' Kilian said curtly, only just refraining from snapping.

'Yes, Colonel.'

'*Merci*,' Lisette said. Be friendly with everyone, she had been taught. You never knew when it might be useful. And it didn't hurt to demonstrate good manners. 'Dinner was exquisite. The hay-smoked rabbit was the way I remember my grandmother cooking it,' she lied.

The man paused to regard her. 'Thank you, *mademoiselle*. I will pass on your remarks to our kitchen.'

He nodded and beneath the polite smile she saw the glow of pleasure ghost across his face. When she looked back at Kilian, his gaze had softened.

'The way you swap languages so effortlessly is wonderful to witness. It's another reason why I need you in my life, Lisette. You speak the right languages at the right time.'

'Another reason? What is the first?'

'I'll leave you to ponder that. But I do want you to consider working with me.'

'You barely know me.'

'I know I can trust you.'

She swallowed. 'And not others?'

He smiled sadly. 'I've explained that I'm not Berlin's favourite officer.'

'But you are a loyal German.'

'And therein lies Berlin's problem with me.' He dropped his voice to a murmur. 'I am indeed a loyal German, Lisette, but I'm far from being a loyal Nazi.'

She decided to play dumb. 'Are they not one and the same?'

He gave a choked laugh and shook his head. 'No. They're worlds apart. There are many good German officers who don't share the ideology of our Führer.'

'So why —'

'Why follow his orders? Because so many of the people who are now in power are good men. They never had a chance under the Weimar Republic. Hitler promoted them, has given them status and opportunity. It's a double-edged sword. The right men, in the right places . . .'

'Under the wrong leader?' she asked softly.

His forehead furrowed, full of burden. 'I would die for my country – and probably will – and I hope history will show that the Wehrmacht was led in the main by honourable officers following orders. Those of us who disobey those orders do so with a respect for human life.' He sounded desperately sad suddenly.

'Markus . . .' she whispered.

He raised his eyes, glittering pale in the candlelight, and shook his head. 'Don't. The excellent food, wine, the good listener has loosened my lips. I've said too much. Come,' he said, standing. 'This is no conversation for a beautiful dinner guest on her birthday. Can I offer you anything else?'

She shook her head and smiled but was disappointed the moment was lost. He might never speak so candidly again, and she was sure he'd had more to say. Markus could be ripe to be turned . . . and she could become his go-between instead of spying on him. Should she allude to it? No! Report back first; let the decision come from London. Her thoughts tumbled over each other as he spoke.

'I've kept you out long enough. I don't want to excite Walter's wrath.'

She stood and let him wrap the stole around her shoulders.

'Tell the driver to turn the heater on in the car please, for *mademoiselle*,' he instructed the maitre d', who had returned silently.

'Very good, Colonel.'

Kilian escorted her out of the fabulously ornate chamber with its *trompe l'oeil* ceiling of dusky pinks and soft golds.

'Will you be accompanying me home?' Lisette asked, suddenly unsure.

'I don't think it will be good for you to be seen too often with a German officer in your neighbourhood.'

'And you think your car slipped out of Montmartre unnoticed earlier today? Or how about Corporal Freyburg delivering your gifts in broad daylight?'

He paused in the hotel lobby.

'You're right, of course. We shall have to think that through better next time.'

Next time.

'I'll tell you what,' he said, grinning. 'How about you ride with me to my hotel and then go on with the car? It means a little longer together.'

'That sounds nice,' she replied. Had she lost control of this situation? She had hoped he would ask her to spend the night. For a woman like her it was not the done thing to say yes, but she did not have the luxury of propriety. There was no time to worry about what others might think. But now he seemed reticent, almost apologetic. She had to press him. 'But, please don't feel you have to do anything more for me. You have ensured I've had the most glorious birthday in years – in fact since I turned five and my father gave me my own pony,' she said. She had never ridden a horse in her life. 'I will treasure tonight always, Markus.'

He stepped around to face her. 'You sound as if you are not wishing me goodnight but goodbye, Lisette.'

'No . . . I . . .' Damn her hesitation. And now he was laughing at her. 'Don't grin like that at me.'

'I rather like to see you flustered. It's endearing.'

She straightened and found a smile. 'Thank you for a lovely evening, Markus.'

He grinned more widely. That was plain infuriating. She

turned to leave but felt him take her arm, and then he was pulling her around the corner, away from the main lobby to where a small telephone cubby was. He pulled her inside it and closed the door. He stared at her in the soft gloom of their compartment. The air was close and warm between them.

'All night long I've wanted to do this,' he said as he bent to kiss her.

It was the reaction she'd intended to provoke – certainly what London needed her to achieve – but nothing could have prepared her for her feverish response. He pulled her so close that she could feel almost every inch of his body. And while one hand held her in the small of her back, his other hand pushed away her stole so he could kiss her shoulders, her neck.

He groaned, returning to kiss her lips.

'Markus, stop.'

Kilian pulled away, breathing hard. 'I'm sorry. Forgive me. That was wrong of me, I . . .'

'Take me back to your hotel,' she urged softly.

'What?' Again she'd surprised him. He stared at her, his breathing slowing. 'You're sure?'

She nodded. 'I want to be with you.'

'You're young, beautiful Lisette. And I should know better.' He shook his head, looking irritated with himself. 'I have already behaved badly and it would not be fair to —'

'I'm *not* a child. This is my decision. Please.' Her gaze slid over his body. 'Let me help take your mind off things.'

He grinned in surprise. 'I adore you, you know.' He held her face between his hands and gazed at her for several seconds before kissing her tenderly.

'Let's go before we're seen,' she begged, but he took his time wrapping his heavy military coat around her shoulders.

'There. Now Walter can't entirely blame me if you catch a cold.'

The doorman opened the car door for them. It was warm inside and she relaxed as the heat enveloped her. Kilian put an arm around her. 'What would your mother think of you?'

'She'd remind me that history repeats itself. She was French and fell in love with a German.'

He smiled softly, cradling her hand in his lap. 'Hotel Raphaël,' he called.

The driver stared ahead and simply nodded. Lisette barely spared him a glance as Kilian leaned forward to close the glass partition. The drive was a blur. She was aware of moving through streets she recognised, but beyond that her attention was fully focused on Kilian. He was certainly paying no attention to the cityscape that was rolling by.

He pulled her closer and first kissed her hair. 'You smell unbelievably good,' he said, gently nipping at her earlobes and grazing her neck with soft lips.

'It's your fault,' she whispered, surprised at how aroused she felt.

She closed her eyes, sure that the driver was watching them in his rear-view mirror . . . but she didn't care.

Kilian kissed her deeply. She couldn't help herself; her treacherous arms snaked around his neck and she could feel the small curls of hair at his collar under her fingers. Just for that minute, nothing else seemed to matter – not that he was German, that he was wearing a Nazi uniform, that he had probably killed dozens in the war. For this tiny window of time he was her lover . . . and, she hoped, one of the courageous few who might bring down the Nazi regime from within.

The car lurched to a stop, a little violently, but Kilian didn't seem to notice. He reached forward to open the partition and speak with the driver. 'Wait until you are sent for. Later I will need you to take *Mademoiselle* to an address in Montmartre. You are to park outside her doorway and watch that she goes inside safely. Better still, escort her up. Understood?'

She saw the man's head nod.

'Lisette.' Kilian sighed. 'You can still change your mind, you know. I will not be offended. I did not anticipate this, but now that it has happened I feel as if I've been given a glimpse into heaven. I'm not sure I deserve it.'

'You really are a romantic, aren't you?'

He shrugged bashfully, not meeting her gaze.

'Take me upstairs.'

Once again she moved in a daze. She didn't register leaving the car when the doorman rushed to open their door, or entering the hotel, or arriving at Kilian's room. She was vaguely aware of the plush interior of the lobby – not as grand as the Ritz with its huge mirrors and crystal chandeliers, but full of rich ornamentation and plenty of German uniforms. Kilian spoke to a couple of men and she was sure she was introduced, but although she went through the motions of politeness, she felt disconnected.

And then they were truly alone and he was pulling off his coat from around her, sliding his fingers tenderly over her bare shoulders.

'Lisette? Are you all right?'

She blinked and came out of her curious stupor. It had been filled with the smell of lavender and of blood, and of another German she barely knew – one whose memory was tugging unfairly at her heart when she least wanted it. Kilian was staring anxiously at her. The room was still dark, although moonlight had seeped in to illuminate the bed.

'If this is too fast for you —'

'Hush,' she whispered as she reached up on tiptoe to give him a teasing, lingering kiss. She began to unbutton his tunic.

'Champagne?' he murmured.

'Just you,' she breathed as the zipper on her beautiful new dress was expertly undone and the silk chiffon slipped away from her body.

He stared at her in the soft, ghostly light and sighed. Lisette couldn't believe this was her, standing near-naked, allowing a man to hungrily watch her as she carefully unrolled her precious stockings. Finally she was brazenly naked; an alter ego had emerged and a new Lisette was carrying her through this evening.

Markus ripped off his tunic, flinging it carelessly towards a chair. She was sure he would tear buttons on his shirt but finally that too fell away and she caught her breath. Silvery scars on his muscled body traced memories of wounds and battles she knew nothing of, but reminded her that this was a soldier . . . the enemy.

Looking at him standing there, vulnerable and filled with the same helpless lust that she was experiencing, she didn't see his nationality or his age. It made her smile inwardly to hear an echo of her grandmother's voice: 'Choose an older man for your first lover. He'll worship you, like no young man ever would.' Markus would not be her first lover, but he would be her first older man. Lisette was bewildered, suddenly unsure whether she was doing this for King and Country or for herself. It would be a lie if she said she didn't want him to be her lover in this moment.

To Markus she whispered, 'Hold me.'

Suddenly they were locked together in a slow and sensuous kiss, sinking them deeper and deeper, lasting long enough for Lisette to lose sense of time. As he lifted her onto the bed, she wasn't sure she was ready. But once there she gave herself entirely over to the laughter and the loving that Colonel Markus Kilian lavished upon her.

25

Lisette stirred first. Her wristwatch, the only adornment she still wore, told her through sleepy eyes that it was a few minutes to four. Not even a bird was awake with her. The silence was comforting, and although the realities of life were now crowding into her thoughts, she managed to hold them at bay – for just a while longer – to enjoy this private aftermath of her birthday celebration.

They'd made love for hours, it seemed; Markus claimed that he was determined not to sleep as long as she was in his arms, but of course he'd lost the fight. She'd made sure he knew that of all his rivals on and off the battlefield, he had been her conqueror. He'd drifted asleep still smiling.

The memory of the last few hours would always be sweet. The colonel had been tender, generous and above all funny. They'd laughed together as much as they'd loved together.

She had thought when they moved to the bed that it would be a fierce, rushed affair; she had been so eager to feel him on her, in her, that in fact it was Lisette who had been the more hurried. She sighed softly, recalling his gentle, rhythmic lovemaking and the tender way that he'd paused to stare at her until she began to feel shy.

Although her British school had been all but Victorian in its straitlaced attitude to men, Lisette was far from prudish. Nonetheless, there was something about the intensity of Kilian's gaze that had caused her to blush.

She watched his face in repose, lit softly by the moonlight that had seeped into the room. As he slept she admired his strong jaw, furred by a shadow that he would shave in a few hours. His face was symmetrical and perfectly balanced; even the slight graying of the hair near each ear was identical, as though a mirror reflection. She carefully reached to touch the tiny wisp of hair that curled on the pillow at his neck. Golden and soft. An Adonis, she thought, imagining all the hearts that trailed broken in his wake.

And so it was time to go; she must leave him wanting. She instinctively knew they would never have a night like this again. She leaned forward and brushed his lips with hers. His eyelids flew open and she saw alarm flare before he blinked and smiled.

'Is it morning?'

'No, but I have to go.'

He sighed, tried to reach for her, but she had already slipped away from his grasp and tiptoed to the bathroom, gathering up clothes as she went. Not much later in the gloom of the lobby, lights out for the curfew, and with barely even skeleton staff in the early hours, he asked if he could see her again at nightfall.

She shook her head. 'I've got some work to catch up on.'

'Change your plans.'

'I can't.'

'Don't hold back on me, Lisette.'

She took a risk. 'You held back on me last night. You wouldn't tell me about your work, about Stülpnagel.' She tried to make it appear airy but worried it sounded far too specific.

Luckily he wasn't paying close attention. 'You don't need my burdens. None of my secrets are relevant to the joy that is you. Happy birthday, beautiful Lisette,' he said, escorting her to the car. Once she was inside, he leaned in and kissed her once at length. 'Time will drag until I see you,' he said, when he finally pulled away.

'Markus.'

He leant back in and pulled the connecting glass closed so the driver couldn't hear them. 'Yes?'

'Are you . . .' she hesitated. This was too fast. But she needed to give London something.

He grinned. 'Am I in love with you? Ask me again tonight.'

She blinked with consternation, covered it with a cautious smile. 'Don't tease me.'

'I thought you were the one who believed in love at first sight.'

Lisette had no answer for that. 'I was going to ask something else, actually.'

'Don't be shy.'

'Are you in some sort of trouble?'

He looked at her intently. 'No. But trouble does seem to find me,' he replied cryptically.

She covered his hand with hers. 'There were moments last night when you sounded wistful, as though you wished you could change things.'

'Most soldiers do. Few of us would choose war. And those of us who can effect change should . . . or we would regret our cowardice.'

She could see he'd said far more than he'd intended; she couldn't push him any further at present. So she smiled. 'I can think of no man further from cowardice,' she whispered and blew him a kiss. Kilian stared at her longingly as he reluctantly closed the door. The driver eased the vehicle from the kerb and set off into the darkness of Paris. Lisette twisted in the deep leather to watch Kilian, noting that he was walking away from the hotel, not turning back inside. For a few seconds he cut the loneliest of figures, a solitary man on Avenue Kléber, and then he was gone, lost to the darkness as the car gained speed.

Something was on his mind. He'd alluded a few times to his regrets, and the contact from Stülpnagel had clearly surprised him.

The meeting sounded plausible and yet her instincts judged that Kilian had not bought it. Why did the military commander of Paris, who with a single order could mobilise all soldiers in the city – in all of France if it came to it – need to discuss security arrangements with the liaison officer for the Church in Paris? Credible, perhaps . . . but only just. Stülpnagel had minions to do that sort of job. He would not call a sudden face-to-face meeting with Kilian, she was sure of it. She frowned, wondering whether she was just desperately trying to read more into it than there was.

The truth was she was feeling suddenly protective of Colonel Kilian. Damn him for being so likeable! And damn him for making her body react as it had to his touch. It wasn't meant to be like this. She was the spy, the cold user of others . . . so why were her cheeks hot and her supposedly hardened heart pounding?

She felt self-conscious that she was alone with the driver, who had presumably witnessed their languid affections earlier. She was shocked when the driver reached behind his head to push the partition down. It was as though he had eavesdropped on her thoughts. He slowed the car to a halt.

She blinked, frowning in confusion and the beginnings of fear.

'Yes, driver?' she asked, nervously smoothing her hair.

'*Bonsoir*, Lisette,' he said, turning. Even in the dark she knew that voice, and even in shadow she knew the face of Lukas Ravensburg.

26

Luc had no idea how Lisette felt about him now after the previous
autumn when he'd stolen a kiss in the back of a bus winding its
bumpy way down from Gordes into Cavaillon. Seven months since
that night in the Gestapo car, after a day filled with rage and blood,
murder and despair, it was Lisette's lips, Lisette's arms, Lisette's
presence that he'd clung to like a raft in stormy seas.

How he had let her go he would never know. No woman had
ever affected him as Lisette had, but then no woman had shared
such trauma with him, or seen him so raw. Watching her train draw
out from the platform in Lyon had been an agony, but he had been
so anxious for her safety that the train was all that mattered in his
fractured mind, which was still spinning with the memory of Wolf's
death. The chilling *coup de grâce* he had delivered under the gleeful
orders of von Schleigel still haunted him most nights.

Over the weeks that had followed Wolf's death, Luc's grief had
hardened. He hated how cold he'd become. Where was that man
who had made carefree love in the fields? The man who could
appreciate the sight of sunlight turning a single lavender stalk into a
thing of luminescent blue beauty? Or who had seen the moonlight
silvering a curious, magical-looking wild patch of white alpine lavender, whose seeds he carried with him, along with the blue?

Amid his grief, Luc could not stop thinking of Lisette. Neither
of them had been looking for love, he was sure of that. And yet two

wilful people had been thrown together and their sorrows had connected. It was her resistance to him, her ability to confront him and provoke him, that had broken through the barriers he'd put in place around his heart. And now she owned that heart. He knew all he needed to about Lisette – that he loved her. Ever since that realisation, he had committed himself to keeping her safe, as best he could.

At the start of the war his father had made him bury a box with money, among other items, in one of the family's lavender fields away from Saignon. Luc had laughed at the time but Jacob had tapped his nose.

'Trust me, son. That money could save your life one day.'

And save his life it had. He'd made his way back to Mont Ventoux, dug up the box and used some of the money to find his way to Paris. Once there he'd made contact with the Resistance network and discreetly discovered Lisette's whereabouts. And it was then that he began to follow her. He told himself it was to keep her safe, but knew in his heart that it was to keep her close.

Luc had learned to keep his distance, trailing Lisette daily from her flat to the bank, shadowing her infrequent visits to the café off the Champs Elysées, even watching her at weekends when she strolled through the markets or wandered around the gardens. At night he would follow her home and then shiver in the cold until the light in her flat went out. Then he would hunch his shoulders, push his gloved hands deeper into his pockets and wander away, back to his grubby bedsit or whichever late-night job the resistance network had allocated him for.

There had been one occasion when Luc had almost revealed himself. He remembered how he'd taken a circuitous route to his destination one weekend afternoon through Montmartre, in the hope of seeing Lisette. Just as he had given up hope, he recognised her from behind in the street – how she moved, the sway of her hair and he even recalled how it felt between his fingers. He'd eased his way closer, hoping to feel her presence in his lonely life.

Lisette had stopped to cross the road and he'd seen her profile. It had sent a wave of desire and pain through him. And as she'd waited, sharing a few words with her neighbour, he'd got close enough to hear her voice, touch her even, but he'd had to keep walking. She'd crossed, and then something had happened to cause her to turn back. He'd had to instantly duck down to retie his shoe-lace in case she saw him. Shaken, he'd disappeared down a side street. Since then he'd refused himself any opportunity to openly see or be seen by her – until now.

With his German heritage and Aryan looks, Luc had managed to get a job as a driver for the German command some months earlier. It was a useful position for a member of the Resistance, but as of a week ago, it had become more than useful. Everything had changed on 1 May. London had begun broadcasting a stream of *messages personnels* at a rate and volume never experienced before, and the flurry of coded messages caused great excitement. It was the signal!

In homes and farmhouses up and down the country people had become accustomed to clandestinely tuning into the BBC for the daily coded messages. *There are no bananas, Yvette has ten fingers, the Trojan war will not happen.* These codes alerted SOE agents and their fellow French resisters that a plane was arriving in their region with a new agent, or that a cache of weapons would be dropped by parachute, or that new wireless equipment was being sent. Most listened in vain, some waiting months, even years, for regional communications.

But not on 1 May 1944. That night clutches of resisters gathered by their hidden radios were bombarded by a torrent of messages that galvanised every SOE agent throughout the country into immediate action. It was time to prepare for the Second Front that could be expected within weeks. Courageous men and women who'd been working independently in their own small knots of Resistance were instantly bound into a single, cohesive push to disrupt, delay and destroy the German military in France from reaching the country's northern beaches in a last heroic attempt after nearly five years of despair.

Luc knew he had to get Lisette away from Kilian and out of Paris if he could. If there was something to learn or an advantage to be gained he could understand her role, but given the overarching new instructions, her mission was redundant. Nothing she did here was of any use, and to stay was to endanger her life recklessly.

He had waited for the right moment to reveal himself to Lisette and urge her to escape. Being Kilian's driver provided the perfect opportunity, although seeing her with Kilian was a cruel penance. Keeping his cool while the colonel touched the woman he loved had felt impossible . . . but he would not have to watch it again. He had to get her out before she got in too deep. It had to be tonight.

Lisette sat in a stunned silence in the dark of the car. She'd gone to sleep thinking about Luc every night since they'd parted, promising herself he would not be the first person she thought about when she woke up. She had broken her promise daily – except for today. And now here he was.

'Where have you been?' she finally whispered.

'In and around Paris.'

Her tense silence spoke plenty.

'I couldn't stay in the south,' he said, becoming defensive. 'When we last spoke —'

'When we last saw each other, I was the one talking. You had nothing to say. Nothing!'

He hesitated. 'What happened was too terrible to speak of.'

'But abandoning me wasn't too hard for you.'

'I never abandoned you,' he said, and his voice was so hurt it tore at her heart. 'I have watched over you most days. Often I've been close enough to reach out and touch you. And when I couldn't watch you, I've made sure someone else had you in their sights.'

Her mouth gaped.

'Remember that time you tripped and dropped your shopping.' She blinked. 'Your baguette broke.'

'And a precious egg I'd saved for. A young man helped me.'

Luc nodded. 'His name is Jacques.'

She stared at him, speechless.

'On another occasion someone warned you that the Germans were checking ID papers on the Métro.'

'Yes. A young woman with very short dark hair.'

'Her name is Isabelle. And your new neighbour —'

'Sylvie,' she said for him, shaking her head with disbelief. 'No!'

He looked down. 'She agreed to keep an eye on you for me.'

'Why?'

'Because she's a friend.'

'Why are you doing this?'

He shrugged slightly. 'I have to make sure you are safe. Don't walk to Saint-Germain in the dark again as you did a few days ago. It is not safe.'

'You've been in Paris the whole time?'

His voice was thick with emotion, overlaid with contrition. 'Not all the time. That's when I depend on the others. But yes, I have stayed close to Paris . . . close to you.'

'Why couldn't you —'

He turned around to face the steering wheel. 'Lisette, I understand your mission. I know what you're doing with Markus Kilian.'

'How do you know?'

'I am no fool. You're not spending time with him for pleasure.'

'No, I'm not,' she agreed, her voice barely above a whisper.

Luc restarted the car. 'That is why I couldn't reveal myself. I couldn't risk compromising your mission. Until now.'

They drove back to Montmartre in silence. When the car finally purred to a stop he dutifully opened the door for her. 'I will walk you up to your door. Once we are inside the building we can speak more freely.'

He wouldn't look at her yet, and she was glad – her emotions were ragged and looped into knots. She might have pined for Luc, but she wasn't prepared for him to walk back into her life just as she'd succeeded in seducing Kilian. Markus had asked her last night how she'd feel if her farmer were to suddenly reappear. She felt dizzied by how close to reality his question had been. Luc had been in the car, had driven them back to the hotel; had known where they were headed and how long they'd spent together. The carefully built walls of her façade were crumbling.

Was Luc still here because he loved her or simply because he was a hunted man in the south? And if he did love her, then how could he bear to be near her under these circumstances? She had to be equally strong and composed. Nevertheless, his presence was a complication.

'You looked very beautiful tonight,' Luc remarked as she moved past him. 'You smell very expensive. Chanel, if my experience in perfumery serves me well.'

'Don't,' she pleaded.

'And you're very convincing in your affections for the colonel.'

'Luc . . .'

He skipped ahead to hold open the door of the apartment block.

Lisette glowered at him but stepped through the doorway.

'I'm impressed at your speedy work, but I'm not surprised. After all, I fell for your charm just as quickly and as hard as the poor colonel.'

She rounded on him. 'How dare you!' she snapped in a whisper.

'After you, Mademoiselle Forestier,' he said in a hard voice, gesturing at the stairwell.

'I don't need your help.'

'Oh, yes you do.'

Lisette had a mind to stomp up the stairs but she didn't want to wake others. She hurried instead, all but running up the flights. Luc took his time, striding two steps at a time, and was just behind her when she arrived at her floor.

She was aware of her deep breathing. The shock of his presence was smothering her.

'Are . . . are you all right?' She gestured at his leg. 'The limp.'

'A cover, or I would be fighting. I have to keep it up constantly, or risk forgetting.'

'Why are you here?'

He held his silence.

Lisette turned to open her door but she dropped the key. Furious with herself, she bent to retrieve it but he was quicker. Her hand searching in the dark found only his. Her instinct was to pull away but he held her hand fast and placed it against his heart.

'I've thought about you every day since that train took you away,' he whispered hoarsely.

It all came flooding back, all the emotion she'd wrestled under control: the despair of Laurent's death, the knowledge that Luc had likely killed at least one person that night but perhaps more, the helplessness of not being able to comfort him as he grieved and then that cold, wordless farewell at the station. She was back in Provence again, infuriated by him, wanting him more than anyone. But now Kilian stood between them.

'Oh, Luc, come inside, please.'

He shook his head and stood, helping her up. 'Too risky with the car outside. I must go. But we need to talk, and soon.'

'Then come back later. I won't go to work today. Any time that you can.'

He nodded and opened the door for her, handed back the key. He left without touching her again, without another word. She listened to his departing footsteps, almost frightened to let him go, and heard him pause on the landing below as a door opened. Lisette strained to hear. It had to be Sylvie – was she spying on them? She didn't know whether to hate her now or like her all the more.

Lisette kicked off her shoes and tiptoed back out onto her landing. She risked peeping over the banister to see Sylvie grasping Luc's coat, whispering at him urgently. It was obvious he was trying to leave. He shook his head and gently pulled Sylvie's hand away. She had no need to hear their words to know what was being said.

Lisette stepped back inside her room and rushed to the window. Soon enough Luc emerged, and within a few heartbeats he and his car had disappeared. But he'd promised to come back. And she knew she probably only had a few hours to get her shattered thoughts and mood together . . . as well as head to the café to send her missive to London.

_____

Lisette could not sleep. She filled a small tub with hot water, peeled off her beautiful dress and slowly bathed herself. Her pale skin flushed under the warm flannel as her mind wandered through her memories of Markus Kilian. She needed to 'compartmentalise' – that was the word they used in training. She had enjoyed Markus; to admit anything else was a lie. A couple of months ago she had no one in her life. Now she had two men to consider. How was she to separate them? And especially when one now worked for the other! Luc was playing a most risky game. *But he's doing it for you*, a small voice reminded her. *To be close to you, to keep you safe.*

Lisette put the flannel over her face and took a deep breath. This was no time for her emotions to dictate her actions. She had to think with her head, not heart. London was expecting more of her, especially since she'd ingratiated herself so swiftly with Kilian. She didn't need London to tell her that the Soviets were making great inroads in the Ukraine and that the German army was likely in retreat. It had become even more crucial to know of potential German countermoves. Berlin was on the back foot, with the Americans adding new credibility to the Allied push, but nothing was more unpredictable than a wounded animal.

She hurriedly dried off and dressed, and left her apartment before eight a.m. Sylvie was ready for her, opening her door as she passed. Lisette did not speak.

'You know?' the Frenchwoman said.

Her gaze narrowed. 'That you are spying on me?'

'I have been watching over you . . . for a friend.'

Lisette looked at her neighbour. She was attractive, and somewhere in Lisette's mind this knowledge rankled. 'It would have been easier to just tell me.'

Sylvie shook her head. 'I would have compromised your situation. I, better than most, understand your need to operate alone.'

'Then why is it different now?' Lisette wasn't successfully keeping the sharpness from her tone.

'Because Luc has shown himself to you. He has his reasons – and for telling you about me.'

Lisette swallowed. Was there a warning there? And what right did she have to be feeling proprietorial?

'Lisette . . .'

'I have to go. I'm running late for work.' She skipped down the stairs and forced herself to put Luc – and the company he kept – from her mind.

She would walk to the Champs Elysées and work off her

jealousy and frustration. It took longer than she'd anticipated, and she'd been stopped as she'd entered the first arrondissement.

'Papers,' a German soldier demanded in a bored tone.

'Yes, of course,' she said in flawless German.

He blinked. 'Where are you headed?'

'For a treat at my usual café.'

'Where do you work?'

She told him the name of the bank. 'I work with its president, Walter Eichel.' It worked. He barely looked at her ID card. But he didn't hand it back.

'We don't meet many German girls.'

She smiled. 'I hope you get home soon,' she replied kindly, reaching for the card.

He pulled it out of her reach. 'How about meeting me this evening?'

'I can't,' she said, feigning disappointment. 'I'm meeting Colonel Kilian – perhaps you know him?'

The soldier looked astonished. 'Colonel Kilian,' he repeated, not quite stammering.

She grinned. 'Walter Eichel is my godfather. Colonel Kilian is a very good friend of his.'

'Forgive me.'

She looked at him, quizzical. 'Nothing to forgive. I'm flattered.'

Whatever confidence his uniform gave him had suddenly fled and now he just looked shy and awkward.

She beamed him another bright smile and took her ID back, feeling relieved that he hadn't studied it. '*Danke. Guten Morgen.*' She had always felt confident of her papers, but even so didn't want any soldiers checking them too closely.

Lisette hurried up the famous boulevard to the café, quickly catching the attention of the café owner. She ordered and added casually, 'Is there a spare newspaper behind the counter?' She noticed he was wearing a green tea towel over his shoulder.

'*Oui, mademoiselle*,' he replied, without even glancing at her as he dried a cup. He put the paper on the counter and turned away to talk to another customer.

The café wasn't crowded this morning, but then it was still very early. Most people were standing at the bar and drinking a quick *café* to start their day. There was only one German patron, marked by his uniform, and he had his back to her, but even so, Lisette was cautious. The Gestapo were certainly no strangers here. She settled herself at the back of the room and started reading the front page, until her drink was delivered.

Lisette sipped, and although her eyes were on the paper, she was surreptitiously gauging who might be watching her. No one seemed interested. She rummaged in her bag and pulled out a spectacles case. The glasses were a helpful prop as she could carry the cigarette paper in the case. She didn't need to re-read her note; she knew it by heart, alerting London to her suspicion of conspiracy and her desire to see if Kilian could be turned.

Placing the note on a page, she checked it was stuck fast and turned the page to continue reading, looking for the note from Playboy. She found it on page five: *Contact Spiritualist urgently.*

What was happening? It couldn't be from London, or Playboy would have specified. And if it wasn't a specific order for her, then it would have to wait a bit longer; she was at too delicate a stage of her mission, too deep undercover, to risk contact with the Resistance group. After another five minutes she looked at her watch and made a show of packing up her things, retying her scarf, checking her hair in a small compact.

'*Merci, monsieur*,' she called to the café owner as she handed back the newspaper and sauntered out. She took a different, circuitous route to avoid the ID checks at either end of the boulevard and deliberately avoided the Hotel Raphaël, whose proximity she was all too aware of.

She then went to the bank and left a handwritten message at reception, excusing herself from work due to sickness. She feigned weakness as she handed it over and then rushed to the bathroom. She was out of the building within minutes, and finally arrived back at her apartment. She hoped Sylvie had left for the day. And it was surely still too early for Luc to have returned.

Once inside she couldn't sleep. She was unsure what to do with herself, feeling unsettled – nervous, even – so she killed time putting away her frock, folding up the stole, hiding all the Chanel boxes and any reminders of her evening. She set to with some menial tasks; sewing on a button, tidying her few cupboards. Realising that she had nothing to offer a guest, she gathered up her ration coupons and hurried to the grocer's to buy a little wedge of cheese and a stick of bread. She knew she could rustle up a mug of hideous pretend coffee but wasn't sure Luc would drink it, and she had no honey to sweeten it. At the last moment she ducked into a café and grabbed a half-bottle of wine. Only a few hours ago she had been sipping a calvados whose single-shot price could have provided a slap-up meal for her tonight.

She ran back to the apartment, clutching her few provisions, and found Luc waiting at her door.

'Luc,' she said, nervously. 'Have you been here long?' It was uncanny how much like Kilian he looked, now that she faced him in daylight. His straw-coloured hair was longer than she remembered but the colour was almost identical to Markus's. Luc had a fuller jawline, but she wondered if that was because he was younger. They were of similar height, Luc undoubtedly broader, more muscled, but it was in the eyes where the real difference was. Luc's eyes were luminescent when the sun lit them, like cornflowers . . . no, like the lapis lazuli gemstone Lisette's grandmother wore set in a beautiful brooch. There was a fire glinting within the blue – just like the gemstone – and it warmed her. But Markus's eyes were the opposite. His were every bit as haunting, but they were pale, his gaze sharp enough to cut through her. She was yet to see them by day but she suspected they would sparkle in their glacial way.

Luc shook his head in response to her question. 'You said any time was fine.'

'I did.' Again she found herself fumbling for her key. 'Here, come in.'

'Let me help you.' He reached for her groceries.

She went inside first. 'You can put those down over there,' she suggested, pointing at her tiny table.

'This is a nice place,' he said as he walked over to the window, then turned. His gaze swept over the meagre furniture, the tiny sink, the equally tiny stove. He seemed to avoid looking at her bed, despite its bright bedspread of patchwork.

'No different to Sylvie's, I suspect,' Lisette said, her tone tart. Then she felt embarrassed. 'I mean, they share the same layout.'

Either he hadn't noticed or he chose to ignore the barb. 'But you have so much light coming in here,' he said, turning back to the tall double windows. 'It's good for the soul.'

She nodded, feeling suddenly overwhelmed. He hadn't lost that dreamer quality. 'I suppose it is.' She could sense the underlying pain he carried with him still, as though permanently bruised. 'How are you?'

'As you see,' he replied, irritatingly calm.

What she saw was the man who'd stolen her heart and her peace of mind. She could almost hate him for it.

Lisette cleared her throat. 'Well, you're safe and in one piece, and I'm glad to see you.' She turned to the table to put away the items she'd bought.

'Are you?'

Lisette picked up her bottle of cheap wine. 'It's very early for wine, I know, but I have coffee substitute to offer you.'

'I'll bet there was real coffee last night,' Luc remarked quietly.

She turned. 'Stop it,' she warned, and was surprised to see only injury in his expression. 'I didn't choose my mission.'

'Are you enjoying it?' His eyes glittered with sorrow. He said nothing further but took the corkscrew from her and reached for the bottle, and she moved to stand by the window.

She was angry, hated not being in control of herself. 'Colonel Kilian is a surprise,' she admitted, glad that her voice was steady.

'As a Nazi or as your lover?'

She shook her head and closed her eyes with resignation. 'Simply as a man, Luc. How well do you know him?'

'Not as well as you,' he retorted, putting down the wine and corkscrew.

Her first realisation that she'd slapped him was the terrible echo, sharp and angry as it bounced off the walls, followed by the sting of her hand. His head had snapped to the side but he made no sound, and didn't reach for his cheek but simply turned to regard her, his face ablaze with rage. Or was it triumph?

What happened next shocked her even more. Luc grabbed her by her shoulders. She thought in a heartbeat of panic that he was going to fling her across the room. Instead he pulled her angrily towards him; she was like a trapped bird, small and fragile in the strong cage of his arms. Luc kissed her. It was nothing at all like the first time. Now his lips were hungry, urgent, and his arms wrapped even more tightly around her, until she was no longer sure whether she was breathless from his lust or his strength. And she responded, helplessly, furiously.

He suddenly twisted away, wiping the back of his hand against his mouth. He was breathing hard as he leaned against the table. She saw the storm in his expression.

'Luc . . .' she stammered. This shouldn't happen – not now. He knew it too.

He raised a hand to stop her talking, poured a slug of the wine and swallowed it in two gulps. He filled both tumblers again and handed her one. They both drank silently, Lisette sinking into one of the two chairs she owned and Luc leaning an arm against the wall and staring out of the window.

They stayed like that, both silent, both angry with themselves and each other, and both very aware how dangerous their situation had just become.

———————

Before he arrived, Luc had promised himself that he wouldn't touch Lisette. He just had to get her out of Kilian's clutches and to safety. But all he could envisage was Kilian kissing her neck in the back of the car, chuckling softly with her hair draped across his face while he whispered in her ear. And now he'd failed spectacularly in his promise. If he were truthful, he'd admit that to be in love was to be in pain. In ordinary circumstances that pain would be exquisite and welcome. But in wartime it became something dark and fearful. To love someone so wholly, and to know you could lose them in a blink, was akin to a sort of madness.

Did she have any idea what seeing her with Kilian was doing to him? Keeping his rage silent while he watched Kilian touch her, knowing what the filthy Boches had been doing with her in his hotel, had been torturous. Why did he ever leave her? Why had he deserted her when least he could afford to?

'The fault is mine,' he said. His cheek stung but it was the emotion driving her slap that hurt far more. 'I should go.'

'No, Luc. Wait!' she whispered. 'Tell me how you come to be here. Talk to me.'

She was right. If his intention was to keep her safe, then she deserved the explanation. They needed to work out how best to proceed, now that the Allies were coming. He watched her shoulders drop with relief when he turned and leaned back against the wall and finally raised his gaze.

'Here.' She stood nervously to hand him his refreshed glass. '*Santé*,' she added softly. 'Let's begin again with me saying that I'm so relieved you're safe.'

'*Santé*. I'm alive, not safe. Neither are you.'

Lisette gave a rueful smile. 'That's because I don't have a pouch of magical seeds around my neck.'

He gave her a sad smile back.

'I've thought about you every day,' she admitted. 'You're my first thought as I wake, and my last thought as I sleep.' Her eyes glistened; she was holding back tears.

Before he allowed himself to think it through, he'd reached for her again; she didn't resist. At first it was an embrace, close and heartfelt. They simply held one another. Instinctively he lifted her higher and she responded by pulling him closer still. It was all the encouragement he needed; within a blink he had lifted her body to him, her legs wrapped around him and they'd lost themselves in the kiss he had been dreaming of sharing.

How he loved her. On first sight he'd known he was in trouble. He hadn't been prepared to meet anyone . . . not with this war raging and life so fragile. His saba had once counselled that love chose you – you could never control it, never harness it, never hope to outwit it or imprison it. 'It is a free spirit, my boy,' she'd warned. 'With sharp teeth.'

Luc had found it difficult to envisage love with fangs, but he'd grown to understand what his grandmother had been teaching. His love for Lisette had not been kind and gentle; it had hounded him by day and growled at him by night.

He deepened his kiss, pulled her even closer and blotted out visions of Markus Kilian doing the same. But she suddenly pulled away; strands of her hair had come loose from the combs that held them back, her eyes were full of longing, but while her dishevellment spoke of ardour, her voice was filled with remorse.

'I'm sorry,' she whispered.

'For what?' He nibbled her already soft, swollen lips.

'For my mission.' She groaned softly as he moved his attention to her neck. 'Can you ignore it?'

It hurt to even have this discussion. 'You're here with me now, in my arms, not his. That's all that matters.'

'But you know I have to go back to him.'

'I don't want to talk about him now.'

'But it was only —'

Luc gently bit her earlobe and she groaned again to feel his warm breath on her. 'Lisette,' he mumbled into her neck, his lips barely losing contact with her skin as he spoke. 'This is real. When you're with Kilian I'll remind myself that you are acting. And just know this: I have never felt this way about anyone before.'

She stared at him with a gentle, almost fearful expression.

'I love you. And no war, no politicians, no scheming network, no distance, no English spymaker, and certainly no German colonel will ever change that. I love you. I have never said that to another woman.' He frowned at her. 'I doubt I ever will.'

Lisette's expression became serious as her gaze intensified. 'I have wanted you from that evening you brashly sauntered into Madame Marchand's and gave me your first sneer. I hated you, and yet I couldn't get enough of you. And then . . .'

'Then what?' he whispered, kissing her face and neck until she was sighing and squirming in his arms.

'And then Gordes. All I wanted to do was put my arms around you . . . and love you; never let you go.'

Luc buried his face in her neck. 'Don't let me go,' he urged. 'Ever.'

'Close the shutters, Luc, and then undress me,' she whispered.
'I thought you'd never ask,' he replied.

_____

Luc was in no hurry. He undressed her achingly slowly, kissing every inch of her back that he revealed as he undid each button. The subdued light and silent apartment only heightened the sweet tension. When he finally reached the last button, he undid her brassiere and it followed her dress to the floor. For a fleeting moment she registered his expertise at this undressing, but the thought fled with a gasp as Luc kissed the arch of her lower back. He kneeled to help her step out of all of her clothes until at last she stood naked. Last night she was brazen in her nudity, but today she felt meek . . . humbled by his tenderness and her desire to consummate the passion that had fired with a single kiss.

He stood, still clothed, and looked at her in the low light that glimmered through the shutter slats. 'You are beautiful. I hate him for having you.'

'Don't,' she pleaded, stroking his face. 'It's just us. Don't think about him.'

It was her turn to undress him. She savoured each moment, hungering to lie with him, to feel all of him so she could remember him. She'd never again have to imagine how it felt to be with Luc.

Lisette reached for the lavender seeds around his neck. 'May I? I don't want to spill a single one,' she said. He lowered his head so she could remove it and place it by the bed. She wondered what his other lovers might have thought of it, for there had surely been others.

'Do you think we'll ever plant the seeds?' she said, tracing a finger over his chest. His body was more sculpted than Kilian's, she noted, and instantly hated herself for comparing her lovers. Lisette was confused by warring emotions. Just hours earlier she'd been in the arms of Kilian – and now she had melted into the embrace of Luc without a moment's hesitation.

'I do,' he answered, pulling her to him. As their bodies finally touched, thoughts of Kilian were banished and for the next few hours, Lisette knew the loving of only one man.

27

Kilian had woken even more enchanted by Lisette Forestier than he'd been the previous evening. Once she'd left, he couldn't face his empty room. Instead he'd gone for a walk in the dark to give some thought to his meeting with Meister and the coincidence of Stülpnagel's summons. If yesterday he had felt dispassionate, today he felt excited about the fresh potential for love and the thrilling terror of being part of a conspiracy to assassinate Germany's supreme commander.

Finally he returned to the Hotel Raphaël – it wasn't quite six-thirty a.m. – and with Lisette's perfume still lingering in his room, he bathed before re-reading the note from Stülpnagel. Kilian had naturally run into the military commander of Paris at official occasions, but there was no other reason to cross the general's path. The typed letter was politely formal, noting that it was time for him make his office's services available for Church events in coming months. Stülpnagel finished by suggesting that they meet in the Jardin du Luxembourg at nine to take advantage of the brighter days, after a long and tedious winter.

There was absolutely no reason for this communication – certainly not hand-delivered at a social dinner. Stülpnagel's sudden request to meet outdoors at such an odd time must surely be connected with Meister's visit.

Kilian checked his watch. It was just past seven and the sky had brightened; in the corridor he could discern movement, and distantly he could hear the clank of cutlery on china. A new day in Paris had begun, but for him a new era was unfolding.

He couldn't bear to stay trapped in the hotel room any longer and so went out into the streets, walking aimlessly, circling closer to the gardens until at the appointed time he strode to the famous fountain of Marie de Médicis in the Jardin du Luxembourg. Arriving at almost the same moment was the familiar granite-chiselled Carl-Heinrich von Stülpnagel.

'General, it's very good to see you again, and looking so well.'

'Likewise, Colonel Kilian. I'm glad you could make it. I'm sorry it's so early. No café is open yet. These French, pah!'

Kilian smiled. 'I'm happy to walk if you are, General.'

'I am. I'm glad to be free of stuffy offices and sniffling staff. Let's hope spring ushers in a healthier time.'

'I doubt it, sir. It will take more than the warmer season to bring change for Germany.'

Stülpnagel cut Kilian a sharp look, cleared his throat and gestured to move on. He needn't have worried. There was no one else around. 'I've been advised by our mutual friends that you already have a history of defying orders.'

'It pains me to admit it, sir. I come from a line of proud military men and I fear my behaviour dishonours them. If I may qualify, I have certainly defied our leader, but my reasons are for the good of all Germans.'

Stülpnagel sighed. 'We are damned, Colonel, for I too spoke the same oath as you must have to him.' The general nodded at the Palais du Luxembourg at the heart of the gardens as they strolled to face it. 'Beneath the noses of the Luftwaffe we plot.'

They walked in silence for a few moments before Kilian felt compelled to speak. 'I admit to feeling redundant in Paris.'

'We will all have our part to play, Kilian. Right now our

colleagues are waiting for the right opportunity, which we all agree will occur in the summer at Rastenburg.'

'Why Poland? Why not strike in Berlin?'

'Hitler is rarely in Berlin these days. If not at the Wolfsschanze in Prussia, then at the Berghof in Bavaria. But Berlin is the prize. If we take Berlin, we take Europe. And that's when people like us in Paris become critical. Be ready to act.'

'When, General?'

'June perhaps, probably July. It will be all about mobilising fast enough to smother Himmler's squads.'

'They should kill him too, while they're about it,' Kilian growled.

'If we achieve our aim, then the second most-hated German must die too.'

'But who will form government?'

'Colonel, I say this with respect: don't concern yourself with administrative logistics. We are the soldiers in this fight. Rest assured the right people are masterminding this.'

'Yes, General.'

'You can put your trust in Lieutenant Colonel von Hofacker but no one else in Paris – apart from myself. Come, walk me to the gates.' They walked in silence a moment before Stülpnagel continued in a lower voice. 'You will receive the call from either myself or von Hofacker once we've heard through Berlin that Valkyrie has been activated.'

'Valkyrie?'

'Hitler's contingency in an emergency to mobilise the territorial guard.' He noticed Kilian was frowning. 'It's to counter any breakdown in civil law following bombings or uprisings and maintain the chain of command. Our collaborators plan to use Valkyrie to seize control of Berlin by rounding up Himmler's henchmen, thus negating the SS as well as arresting the Nazi hierarchy.' His voice was little more than a murmur now. 'By the time it's invoked, Hitler's body will already be cooling and we will have the power to appoint our own chancellor. The new government will negotiate an immediate truce.' He stopped walking as they reached the gates. 'Your role is to take control of the soldiers at ground level in Paris and set up the chain of command through France. There are SS and Gestapo as well as the *milice* to nullify; I'll be counting on you for that.'

They shook hands. Nothing more needed to be said. Kilian walked back to the office with a smile on his face.

———

It was around lunchtime when the switchboard put through a call from a Kriminaldirektar von Schleigel, Gestapo. Kilian held his breath. It felt like an omen.

'Are you there, Colonel Kilian?'

'Yes. What can I do for you, von Schleigel?'

'Perhaps it's what I can do for you.'

'Given my role with the Church, I see no reason to have need of the Gestapo.'

'This has nothing to do with your work, Colonel.'

Kilian paused. He could hear the blood pounding at his temple.

'Colonel? I am on my way to Auschwitz, one of the work camps in Poland, but some information has come to my attention that I thought would interest you.'

'Work camps?' Kilian gave a laugh that contained no warmth. He felt sickened to be reminded of them; he'd discovered their true purpose the previous year and it kept him awake at night. It was another reason to want Hitler dead. 'There is nothing of interest for me in the work camps,' he said carefully. 'You said you might be able to do something for me?'

'In connection with the company you keep.'

Kilian could hear the slyness in his tone. He despised the man. 'Spell it out, man. I don't have time for dancing around the daisies.'

He could all but see the man's smile across the phone line. 'Her name is Lisette Forestier.'

Kilian opened his mouth but no words came out.

'I'll take your silence to mean you know precisely to whom I refer. After a chat with Herr Eichel I learnt you'd been socialising with her.'

Kilian took a breath to steady his voice. 'I barely know her.'

'Precisely. Therein lies the danger, Colonel,' von Schleigel replied snidely.

'Herr von Schleigel, if you have something to tell me about Mademoiselle Forestier, I'd be grateful if you would do so. I have a meeting to attend.'

'There is nothing specific, Colonel. This is simply a friendly call from one loyal German to another. I ran across Mademoiselle Forestier in November last year and had no reason to hold her . . . but she keeps odd company down south.'

'You arrested her?'

'No, not really,' the Gestapo officer replied lazily. 'I think "detained briefly" might be a more accurate description.'

'Who was she with?'

'A man by the name of Lukas Ravensburg. Ever heard of him?'

'Should I have?'

'Not necessarily. But if you do, I would recommend you keep an eye on him.'

'Who is he?'

'Her fiancé,' von Schleigel said, and made a tutting sound while surprise shot through Kilian like a bullet parting flesh. 'You *did* know she is engaged?'

Kilian closed his eyes, and the pencil in his hand snapped. 'Why should that interest me?' he asked evenly in spite of himself.

'I mention it simply in passing, Colonel.'

'Why did you detain Mademoiselle Forestier and her fiancé?'

'Ravensburg matched the description of a man whom we believe is a dangerous maquisard.'

'So you are not watching her?'

'Not formally.'

'And informally?'

'It is out of my jurisdiction now, Colonel. I leave Paris tomorrow for a break in Switzerland before I head to Krakow.'

'Enjoy your holiday, Herr von Schleigel,' Kilian said, doing his best to give nothing away in his voice.

'And should I run into Frau Vogel, I'm sure you'd like me to give her your best.'

Kilian felt as though his blood had turned to ice. He reached to his breast pocket and felt the reassuring crinkle of the envelope he hadn't yet posted.

'I don't know why you'd be interested in an old flame of mine.'

'Oh, we're interested in everyone's connections, Colonel.'

So, Gestapo knew who his friends were. But he suspected von Schleigel was needling him, letting him know that he could be put under observation in a blink. Kilian wouldn't post the letter yet.

'I haven't seen Ilse in nearly six years, but do give her my regards,' he said, summoning all his courtesy.

'Indeed I will. Good day to you, Colonel. *Heil Hitler*.'

Kilian refused to say it. He put the receiver back in its cradle, cutting the connection, but the taint of von Schleigel's innuendo lingered.

It had to be nearly midday, Luc realised, when he and Lisette awoke. They lay in silence a while before he finally spoke.

'I don't want to let you go,' he admitted.

'Do you have to leave already?' Lisette whispered, stroking his shoulder. 'I rather like waking up in a tangle of you.'

He smiled. 'I wish I could stay, but it's dangerous for both of us. And I have a shift to keep. But next time I come back here, I need you packed and ready to leave.'

She sighed. She'd anticipated something along these lines: why else had he made himself known?

'How did you come to be Kilian's driver?'

'I'm a loyal but injured German, helping the Reich any way I can. My name as far as any of his staff are concerned is Christian Loewe.'

'I won't even ask how you managed to get that close to him, but what did you hope to achieve?'

'Listen, Lisette,' he said gently, turning to face her. 'Until now it's been all about watching over you, just making sure you're safe.' He shook his head. 'But London's mission for you is no longer relevant. Kilian no longer matters in the scheme of things.'

She stared at him. 'You're just —'

'Jealous?'

'I was going to say upset with me.'

'I'm not explaining this properly,' he said, shifting to swing his legs out of the bed. 'You've been so isolated that you aren't up to date. We've all received new plans. Every resource is going into the invasion in the north.'

She shrugged. 'That's been promised for years.'

'Well, it's happening. Every resistance fighter in the country is readying for D-day. Spying on people like Kilian is no longer necessary.'

'I take my orders from London.'

She could see him forcing himself to keep his voice even. 'There are nearly a million Americans readying across the Channel. Your missives from Paris about a single man are now pointless.'

She turned away, feeling angry. 'Luc, you can keep saying it, but until I'm given orders to the contrary, I have my mission.'

He stood to dress. 'Everything has changed now. Nothing you send London is going to alter the fact that the big push to crush German defences will occur in the next few weeks. The messages have been clogging the radiowaves,' he said, pulling on his trousers and doing up the buttons. 'The Allies are mobilising all of us.' He sat down on the bed and took her by the shoulders. 'But you could be caught in the crossfire. Heads will roll. If Kilian discovers your treachery, there's no saying what might happen. I will die before I let you be placed into the hands of the Gestapo.' He gave a lopsided grin. 'Do you want that on your conscience?'

'He will not hand me over to the Gestapo.'

Luc frowned. 'Don't be naive. Do you think he'd put you before his duty, before his country?' He searched her face with astonishment. 'You do, don't you?'

Lisette twisted free. 'I don't know what to think,' she groaned. 'I don't even understand why you're here.'

'I'm here to get you out,' he said earnestly.

'I'm trying to understand how you knew about my mission,' she suddenly demanded.

Both their faces showed the strain of talking in such low voices, fearful of being overheard.

'It didn't take a genius to work out that you were marking someone in particular. There were other clues too, like the fact you didn't bring a wireless. But it finally came together when I spoke to the head of your circuit; he trusted me, and told me you had once mentioned Kilian in more than passing. I knew immediately that Kilian had to be your mark. I spent weeks angling to get myself hired as a driver in the team that serviced his section. They're struggling to find Germans with good French – frankly, they're struggling to find any men.' He was aware of her hard stare, and ignored it.

'And there's another reason to get you away: if I can work out your mission, so can your enemies.'

'Do you honestly think that on your word I'm going to desert this mission?'

'Yes, I do. And it's not on my word. It's on Churchill's and de Gaulle's. Your life is in jeopardy.'

'And you think I don't know that?'

'You're missing the point. Please trust me when I say that the entire Allied focus is now on Pas de Calais. We have to slow up the German lines of communication to buy time for the final preparations. Every telephone line we can cut we will, every rail transport we can will be disrupted or even stopped, every movement of soldiers will be hampered at every turn, all weapons and ammunition stores will be destroyed as best we can. Rail, road, ships, air . . . you name it, our people up and down the country are going to put their lives on the line to destroy the routes north. There's a whole operation in motion just to ensure that the Germans have to use radio, not telephone, so your people can listen in. This is it! Believe me, Lisette, absolutely nothing you do as Colonel Kilian's lover can help; Kilian is not involved in the chain of command.'

He could see the anger flash again in her eyes.

'And what if he's part of a plot that aims to bring down the German administration from within?'

Luc hadn't expected that. 'What?'

She ran a hand through her black hair, distracted. 'Something big could be going on between Kilian and Stülpnagel.'

Luc looked at her quizzically while she told him everything she knew. He listened but wasn't convinced. 'Are you sure you're not just painting him in a sympathetic way?'

'Very sure. And I don't think every German national who walks this earth should be tarred with the same brush as Hitler.

I have German blood too – does that make me guilty? You have German parentage, Luc – are you part of the atrocities? What about that beaten up old man in l'Isle sur la Sorgue? He didn't look like he sympathised too much with the Nazi regime.'

He sagged, as if punched.

It had been cruel to say it, but Lisette couldn't stop herself now. 'And I am not one of your fellow Maquis to do as you say,' she finished.

He was not to be deterred. 'There is time to get away, and no one need be hurt. We can —'

'Luc, I appreciate your loyalty.'

'My loyalty?' he repeated, sounding injured.

'But I have to find out what's going on between Kilian and Stülpnagel. I'm not going to just do as you ask. I must follow my orders – and my own heart.'

He stared at her for a moment with deep sorrow. 'Well, pity me for following mine.'

She looked at him, bewildered, as he dragged on his shirt and jacket, but when she finally reached for him, he was already walking out of her door. He leapt down the stairs, two and three at a time, angrily ignoring her calls from above.

Lisette took the Métro to the bank and within an hour was behind her desk. Even though it was nearly two p.m., she was happy to get out of the apartment; she'd be busy enough at work so that neither Luc nor Markus could invade her thoughts. She couldn't explain her attraction to Luc in the same way that she couldn't explain her angry opposition to him. They could make such tender love and a few minutes later be at loggerheads. And now she was without him once again, left with that bereft, hollow sense of loss. Her mind reeled with the knowledge that Luc had watched her with Markus.

How hard would that have been for him? She couldn't juggle them both if her mission was to succeed.

Lisette opened a note that had been left by Walter, asking her to come to his office as soon as she arrived. She headed to the director's office immediately.

Walter stood when she arrived and surprised her by coming around his grand desk. She thought he was coming to kiss her but he reached for his hat and coat, and threw a scarf around his neck.

'I'd been told you were unwell.'

'I felt better as the day wore on.'

He forced a smile. 'That's good. I'm glad you're in. I thought we might go out for a coffee.'

Walter was stiff, awkward. And he would never suggest going out when his PA could serve him the best of any drink he felt like.

'Is something wrong?'

'Fetch your coat, Lisette. I'll see you in the lobby in a couple of minutes.'

He shooed her out of the office and Lisette had no choice but to do as she'd been asked.

Outside he pointed down the road. 'There's a café here called Trois Moineaux.' Then he shifted to German. 'Three sparrows. Where do they get these names?'

Spring had definitely arrived, but the walls she had carefully built through the long Parisian winter were crumbling, threatening to choke her. By the time they were seated, the tension had escalated. Walter was past seventy – Lisette was sure he would far prefer to sit inside but he'd insisted on the terrace. He all but dismissed the waiter with a snapped request in German for two coffees.

'Are you upset with me for calling in sick?'

He glared at her and she shrank. 'An officer from the Gestapo paid me a visit yesterday.'

Alarm bells began to shrill. 'Oh? Why?'

'To talk about you,' he said.

'Me?' Her surprise was genuine.

'Yes, a detestable fellow by the name of von Schleigel. Ah, I see his name is meaningful to you. Do you mind telling me why, Lisette?'

'What did he want?'

'You don't deny you know him. I didn't think he'd have any reason to lie, even though I found it difficult to come to terms with mentioning you in the same breath as the secret police.'

He discreetly held up a finger for her to remain quiet while the waiter placed their coffees on the table.

'What did he say, Walter?' she asked firmly, then reined in her tone. 'Forgive me, but the man's loathsome politeness is just a front for his cunning.'

'What were you doing in l'Isle sur la Sorgue when you told me you'd come from Lyon?'

She made sure she looked both angry and wounded. 'I also told you that I'd travelled into Provence.'

'Marseille, you said.'

Lisette gave a sigh of exasperation. 'All the southern trains route through Lyon. Why do I feel like you're accusing me of something?'

'Should I be?'

She refused to answer. Her chicory coffee was strong and bitter, suiting her mood. She glared out into the street.

They sat in uncomfortable silence for a few more moments. 'Why didn't you tell me about Lukas Ravensburg?'

Her insides felt as though they'd flipped a somersault. There was no point in lying if he knew the name. 'Walter, you've been very kind, very generous to me since I arrived, and I remain grateful for your support. But you never asked me much about my life, and I took it to mean that you didn't want to know.' She shook her head as he opened his mouth to interrupt. 'I wasn't offended at all. Why should you care about the personal details of an employee? I know that you are admired and respected by the French as much as the Germans. I'm sure you walk a fine line sometimes between the two – I understand your need to protect your position.'

'To protect the bank,' he corrected, eyeing her angrily.

'Do you think I would jeopardise it?'

'You tell me.'

The truth could and would hurt him. And by now he most likely *did* suspect her of having ulterior motives for returning to France. 'Listen . . . Walter. Lukas Ravensburg is a friend of mine.'

'Friend?'

She gave an embarrassed nod. 'More than a friend.'

'Your lover?'

'I wouldn't call him that.'

'Really? Von Schleigel tells me this Ravensburg fellow is your fiancé!'

'He's not. He's German. Has lived in France. Both parents dead. His father was a war hero.' She hoped all of this would appeal to Walter, and as he finally began to sip from his cooling coffee, she could see he was calmer. 'We had mutual friends in France, became sort of penpals, and decided to meet when I headed into Provence. He's from the south. I do like him very much, but as you can imagine, these are not times to be getting involved. We had a few days together . . . just friends, just fun.'

'Are you in love with him?'

She smiled sadly. 'There was no time to fall in love. I had to get to Paris.'

'How does von Schleigel fit in?'

'An unlucky ID check. Lukas was seeing me off on a train platform after a day's sightseeing in Gordes. We had a very unhappy day, actually – two maquisards had been executed publicly while we were there.' Lisette's eyes watered conveniently. 'It was horrible, Walter. They shot two men just a few yards from me, one in the head. I'll never be able to erase that ghastly image from my mind.'

Walter covered her hand with his, his voice sounding genuinely concerned. 'I'm sorry, Lisette.'

'We couldn't wait to get away. Lukas put me on the train to Lyon and suddenly von Schleigel appeared out of nowhere, checking our papers before making accusations and arresting us.'

'He prefers to say "detained".'

'Whatever he calls it, we felt like prisoners. He interrogated Lukas. I was in another room, so I can't tell you much more. I gather von Schleigel mistook Lukas for a resister. The Gestapo had nothing on Lukas – nothing. It was a case of mistaken identity.'

'How did von Schleigel get my name?'

Lisette looked contrite. 'I am sorry about that. I did have to use your name to get us out of there.'

'It worked, I gather.'

She nodded. 'Like magic. I had to do something.'

'And where is Ravensburg now?'

'I don't know,' she said, holding his gaze and her nerve. 'We said farewell in Gordes. It was under difficult circumstances, as you can imagine. We were both a bit shocked. He knew where I'd be working.'

'And you haven't heard from him?'

'No. What did von Schleigel want?'

'I'm not quite sure. Perhaps he was concerned that you might have said something to me, and that I might create problems for him with his superiors. He was likely just feeling me out. He made no accusation.'

'Nor would he want to. On what basis did he visit you?'

'Making sure I knew what you'd been up to in the south.'

'I'd done nothing.'

'As you say, he's a cunning fellow. The Gestapo officers invariably are. I don't know anyone, German or otherwise, who has a single good word to say for any of them. But I have lied for you, Lisette. I told von Schleigel you worked at the bank in Strasbourg.'

She nodded gratefully. 'I know we can't reveal I spent any time in Britain.'

'If anyone knew that, you'd not be trusted, no matter what I said. You understand I had to make sure.'

'Of course. And I'm sorry for disappointing you. You know I would never do anything to hurt you, Walter.'

He waved a hand as if it was of no concern. 'I do. Which is why I told him I knew of Ravensburg.'

Her eyes flashed at him. 'You did?'

'How else was I to rid you of that toad?'

She looked down, played with the handle of her cup.

'Once I'd confirmed that I knew your young man, von Schleigel left with his tail between his legs. But what I'd like to know is why you told the Gestapo you were to be married.'

She took a breath. 'For the same reason you lied for me. I told him that because I was terrified. I truly thought he would kill Lukas, and if I said I – Walter Eichel's goddaughter – was to marry him, I hoped it would protect him.'

'I see. Do you feel close to this Lukas?'

'I . . . Yes and no. When I was with him it was wonderful, but as I said, war is no time to be thinking too far ahead.'

'And now there's Markus Kilian in your life.'

She hesitated and knew he saw it. 'Yes.'

'Are you playing with Markus?'

'I hardly know him.'

'Because I suspect that would be dangerous. I don't want you getting into a situation beyond your control.'

'What situation?'

'Being the lover of a high-ranking German Wehrmacht officer.'

She stared at him.

'I know you spent the night at his hotel.' He looked away, embarrassed.

She felt ill. 'Are you spying on me?'

'I'm looking out for you, Lisette. I am your godfather.'

'I have no reason to lie to you, Walter.'

'No, but you may have reason to try to protect me.'

'From what?'

'From whatever it is that Lukas Ravensburg and von Schleigel have between them.'

'You're seeing something that isn't there.'

'I hope so. I hope I'm wrong. But if I'm not, then I'm obliged to warn you that where the Gestapo is concerned, my influence is minimal. You might be able to impress a lowlife like von Schleigel with my name, but I can assure you, if Berlin or even Gestapo headquarters in Paris starts to take an interest in you, I am no shield. Himmler is ruthless, and what's more, he's paranoid. It's a terrible combination for someone who is chief of the secret service *and* the paramilitary.'

She nodded.

'You're fortunate that von Schleigel is on his way east to Poland, to work in the camps. Frankly, I hope he freezes and dies there!' Walter said, his voice full of disgust. 'But people like him never do. Anyway, I sent him on his way believing that I know and like Ravensburg. I trust that my lie will not come back to bite me.'

'Thank you, Walter,' she said softly.

'Before you start thanking me, you need to know one more thing.'

Their eyes met.

'Von Schleigel asked many questions about you before he asked about your so-called engagement.'

She frowned. 'And?'

'I mentioned Colonel Kilian.'

Her mouth became instantly dry. 'Is that relevant?'

'Von Schleigel was certainly interested.'

'Why did you mention Kilian?'

'He asked if you were romantically involved with anyone. I wasn't going to risk a second lie.'

'Does Markus know about your conversation?'

'With von Schleigel?'

She nodded.

'Not to my knowledge.'

'Well, hopefully the toad hasn't stirred up any trouble with the colonel.'

'Have you told Markus about Ravensburg?'

'No. Markus is . . .'

'A fling?'

She gave a helpless gesture with her hand. 'I was going to say an irresistible force.'

'Apart from the Führer and his henchmen, I don't know anyone who doesn't admire him.'

'The perfect man?'

He shook his head. 'The perfect soldier. But he is a man, Lisette, with all the usual foibles, and he has fallen for your charms. Be careful. He is proud. If you plan to pursue his affections, I suggest you cut ties with Ravensburg . . . or you tell Markus of the southerner and bring this budding romance – or whatever it is – to a halt.'

She nodded. If only he knew that she could do neither.

'I've said enough. Shall we go?' Walter stood and rummaged in his pockets for some money. 'When do you see Markus next?' he asked, dropping coins into the saucer.

'Perhaps tomorrow.'

'Think on what I said. Can you find your own way back? I have some errands to run.'

She kissed him goodbye.

'Be careful, child,' he said softly, returning her embrace. 'I don't want you hurt.'

Lisette smiled gently and turned to walk away, deeply troubled but showing none of her concern, knowing he watched her. She was not ready to tell London her cover had been compromised, especially so hot on the heels of her last few notes that she hoped would have impressed London. She decided to say nothing, and risk that von Schleigel had been simply 'fishing'. If Buckmaster wanted her to continue, then she would persist with Markus at all costs. But what if Luc was right and they no longer cared about anything other than the promised D-day? Then she needed to hear that from SOE.

London would decide her next move.

28

Kilian moved through his work on Tuesday distractedly; none of it was important anyway. He ranged in mood from excitement to despair; he was proud to be part of a plot that could destroy Hitler's evil hold over Germany but the call from the Gestapo had been unsettling.

Was he to believe von Schleigel? If not, what reason had the man of the Gestapo to lie? Where there was smoke, there was usually fire.

Most importantly of all, why would Lisette lie? If she was unhappy enough with her fiancé to gladly accept Markus as her lover, then why did she not tell him? It was that last thought that roamed around his mind. *She must have something to hide, or she would have told you about Ravensburg.*

But what could she be hiding? A girl in her mid-twenties. German background and German sympathiser, French national. Beautiful, young, intelligent.

Kilian went for a walk, hoping to shake off his unsettled mood by strolling along the Seine. Right now he was peering out mournfully from Pont Neuf on the western edge of the Isle de la Cité. He loved knowing that he stood on a bridge whose first stone was laid in the late Middle Ages by Henry lll, favourite son of the great Catherine de Medici. But not even his favourite bridge in Paris could lift the gloom that had settled on his shoulders.

Until this moment he had remained open – to ideas, to women, to the future. How could he fail to be taken in by Lisette? The momentarily heart-stopping response slammed into his mind – what if he was *meant to*?

Was Lisette a spy?

Why? What could he possibly have to offer a spy? He was simply an officer, and in disgrace as much as exile. Surely that would make him . . . the perfect candidate. Unhappy, resentful, disgruntled and vulnerable. Did the Allies think they could turn him with a beautiful, young, clever agent?

He swallowed hard. Was Lisette with him to find out information? But he had no information!

There was a flap of wings and he saw a small troupe of sparrows see off a crow, its black shape incongruous among the tiny birds, all seemingly identical, all following some instinctive order to chase away the intruder. He blinked as the scene resonated in his heart like an omen. He was the black-hearted figure among the otherwise uniform brown of the military. Everyone followed orders – few drew attention to themselves.

Had he come to the attention of the Allies? And then a dramatic realisation hit. Could Lisette be working for the Gestapo? Had the embryonic plan to kill Hitler been compromised? No! The men involved had been so careful. Besides, he knew none of the detail.

Kilian let out a groan. Even though he knew he was grasping at ideas, he had to speak with Stülpnagel. He could not be the one who destroyed this last roll of the die for Germany.

He all but ran back to his car, whose driver leapt to open the door. The driver was not Wehrmacht – not even military.

'Back to the offices, Colonel?'

'No. Take me to General Stülpnagel.'

'Yes, sir. Are you all right, Colonel?'

323

'Why do you ask?'

'Forgive me. You looked worried, sir.' The car pulled away from the kerb and eased forward.

'I'm fine,' Kilian assured the driver. 'What's your name?'

'Loewe, Colonel. Christian Loewe.'

'You're the one who took Mademoiselle Forestier home last night, did you not?'

He watched the man's eyes glance in the rear-view mirror. 'Yes, sir. I saw her up to her apartment.'

'Does she live alone?'

'I couldn't tell you, sir. I've never met her before.'

'I know that, Loewe. Don't be dim. Were there any signs of another person or other people living with her?'

'No, sir. Not that I could say.'

They fell silent again. But soon Kilian spoke again. 'Have you ever been in love, Loewe?'

The man blinked. 'Yes, Colonel.'

'Reduces men to pulp, don't you think?'

He smiled. 'It's dangerous in wartime.'

'My thoughts exactly. Do you still love her?'

'I do, Colonel. I'm not sure that she loves me, however.'

'Someone else?'

'Yes. He's older, more powerful.'

Kilian gave a wave of his hand. 'Is she fickle?'

'I don't think so. Confused, perhaps. The war has made us all do things we regret.'

'Indeed,' Kilian sighed. He could see they were to be held up by an obstruction in the street.

'I'm sorry about this, Colonel. I can't reverse easily to —'

'It is not your fault.' He sighed again and his attention was caught by a Jewish couple outside on the street, the yellow star of David sewn onto their coats. They were perhaps in their early forties, neatly dressed, and they held the hands of a boy who skipped between them. Kilian wondered how this family had escaped being rounded up so far; what sort of protection they had. How much longer would their luck hold? He wished that he could save this trio and in doing so, somehow save his own soul.

'Tell me about the woman you love,' he continued.

He didn't see his driver glance again into the mirror or the way his jaw tightened. 'What would you like to know, sir?'

'How long have you known her?'

'Only since last year.'

Kilian shot him a glance. 'That's not very long.'

'No.'

'But you know you love her.'

'Yes, sir.'

'How do you know?'

'Because I have been with many women, and none have affected me as she has.'

'In what way?'

'I argue with her a lot. She can make me so furious!' Loewe chuckled.

Kilian gave a brief laugh. 'A good sign, then, that she's got under your skin. Is she pretty?'

'She's beautiful, dark-haired, although there's not much of her.'

Again Kilian smiled. Loewe could be describing Lisette. 'Do you trust her any more?'

'I don't know how to answer that. She has fallen for someone else. I feel betrayed, but at the same time you can't plan to fall in love.'

'Did she lie to you?'

'No.'

'Don't give up on her, Loewe. She'll leave the older man, come to her senses.'

'We're here, Colonel.'

Kilian looked out, surprised to see that they had arrived at the Hotel Meurice on the rue de Rivoli, opposite the Tuileries. He sighed.

'Would you like me to wait for you, Colonel?'

'No. It's a short walk back to the office from here. I'm sure you can be more use elsewhere.'

'Very good.'

Kilian frowned. 'Tell me something, Loewe.'

'Sir?'

'You're German?'

'Yes.'

'Why aren't you fighting?'

'I was wounded early in war, sir. I have an injured leg. Not much use to the Wehrmacht.' He gave an expressive shrug. 'I was assigned to your department in February, Colonel.'

'And you've been discreet. I appreciate that.'

'We all have secrets, Colonel.'

Any other senior officer might have reprimanded the man for such familiarity but Kilian smiled. 'And what is your secret, Loewe?'

'That I'm a much better lover than I am a driver or a soldier, Colonel.'

Kilian smiled more broadly. 'Thank you, Loewe.' He gave the man a conspiratorial nod as he emerged from the car, reminded of how much he missed the camaraderie of ordinary men – men with no hidden agendas.

Stülpnagel didn't keep him waiting as long as he'd anticipated. 'Colonel Kilian,' the general said, overly warm as he approached through the long sweep of the main lobby, his heels clicking on the marble floors of the grand and gilt-laden Hotel Meurice. 'Thank you for coming personally. I hear I left my file with you yesterday.'

Kilian blinked and caught on. 'Yes, I was passing and thought I'd check you got it. I sent it immediately it was discovered,' he said.

'Yes, thank you again. I was just about to take some air. Would you care to accompany me? A coffee, perhaps?'

'Why not?'

Stülpnagel walked him out to the Tuileries and Kilian soon found himself engaged in small talk as he was steered towards Café Renard. There were a lot more people than usual strolling through the gardens and sitting around the fountain but only Germans were taking their refreshment at the café. They looked to be soldiers on leave, wooing young women. Most snapped to attention, their backs stiffening at the sight of the general and a colonel.

Stülpnagel accepted their salutes and found a table at the rear of the café, turning his back to the fountain and the patrons.

The general finally dropped the pretence. 'Why are we here?'

Kilian took a breath. 'I can't be sure, but I'm obliged to tell you that I may have been compromised.'

Stülpnagel gave a soft sigh. 'How?'

In the lowest of voices Kilian told the general what he knew.

'So no accusation was levelled at you?' the general confirmed.

'No. Nonetheless I see it as a warning.'

'Yes. The timing of this woman's arrival in your life is rather coincidental.'

Kilian agreed. 'Why me, though? I have no connection to the sort of information the Allies would be after. Surely everyone knows that I'm in exile here?'

Stülpnagel pulled at his lip. 'I have to agree it makes no sense. Could it be nothing more than a coincidence?'

'I hope so. She is goddaughter to Walter Eichel. He introduced me to her. I find it hard to see Eichel involved in something sinister.'

'And you say you only met her a short time ago?'

'By chance last week. On Monday I met her again for dinner.

But two things give me pause. Firstly, the timing is wrong; how could the Allies or the Gestapo know of your intention to involve me in the plot before I knew it myself? Any spy with that information would have made contact with me after our meeting yesterday, not before. More importantly, I don't see how any spy network could have known that all these seemingly unrelated elements might work in concert: meeting Lisette, the plot, this Lukas person and his connection with the Gestapo.'

'It's impossible,' Stülpnagel agreed. 'As you say, von Schleigel was simply confirming Eichel's story – and stirring up trouble with a Wehrmacht officer. You know the Gestapo as well as I do, Colonel – its people are always looking to seed doubt.'

'You believe he's lying then?'

'No, Kilian. He has no reason to lie about Mademoiselle Forestier but he's reaching for invisible connections.'

Kilian looked pensive. 'He struck me as little more than a cruel thug with an axe to grind. And I suspect he privately detests men like myself who have led a more . . . well, shall I say, privileged existence? But the mere fact that the Gestapo has even looked at me is potentially dangerous. I don't want anything to trip up our cause. And if I'm the potential obstacle, then I should be removed from the picture.'

The general nodded. 'Yes. But there is no one else I can risk trusting in Paris. I need someone with your experience on the ground.'

'So what do you want me to do?' Kilian asked.

'Nothing,' the general said, draining his cup. 'As you say, this fellow has gone.'

'What about Lisette Forestier?'

'You like this woman?'

Kilian nodded, not ready to admit how much.

'She comes from a good family. I'll look into her. Maintain your relationship, but you could arrange to have her followed, perhaps. There's enough at stake. Make sure you use someone with no vested interest . . . obviously someone you trust, but definitely not from inside the ministry. A civilian is the best option.'

'I can do that.'

'And perhaps you have some business out of Paris you could attend to for a week or two? Give yourself some breathing space. Just make sure you maintain regular contact with my office; we may need you to return at a moment's notice.'

Kilian looked thoughtful. 'There is a trip I've been putting off . . . Thank you, General.'

'I think all is well, Colonel Kilian. But I appreciate your prompt action. Let me know if anything further strikes you as odd.'

Kilian stood. 'And you'll let me know if your sources uncover anything unusual about Lisette Forestier?'

'Of course.' Stülpnagel finally twisted in his chair to look across the western sweep of the gardens. 'I might enjoy some of this spring sun, Colonel . . . for a few more minutes.'

They shook hands.

'Perhaps you could introduce me to the bishop of Paris soon,' Stülpnagel said in a loud, jovial voice.

'Of course, General.'

'Excellent. Goodbye, Colonel Kilian. *Heil Hitler!*'

Kilian threaded his way through the people taking advantage of the beautiful spring day to warm frozen bones and chilled hearts. He felt none of the sun's joy touch him today.

After her meeting with Walter, Lisette had returned to her desk silent and worried. She wasn't concerned about the threat of meeting von Schleigel again. But she was worried the Gestapo officer might have met with Markus Kilian. If he had, then her mission was surely over; her life could be in the balance already.

Focusing on her tasks was the only way that Lisette managed to make it through the remaining working hours. Finally her colleagues began to pack up around her and even then she dawdled, determined not to think about Markus or Luc, or von Schleigel – or of what being tortured by his kind would entail. Perhaps they'd not bother with interrogation and simply declare her guilty, taking her out of the back of some unknown building and putting a bullet in her head. That was what had occurred in l'Isle sur la Sorgue, she was sure. In fact, she was convinced that Luc had been involved in the old man's death. She wished she'd had the courage to ask him about it. She wondered now whether she'd ever have the opportunity to talk to him again.

She needed to warn him about this turn of events. But how? She hardly noticed the remains of the warmish day, lost in her gloomy thoughts as she headed home quickly.

29

Kilian looked at his driver closely for the first time. He'd not real-ised how similar they were in height and looks. They could almost be brothers.

'Were your people from Prussia, Loewe?'

'Bavaria. But I don't know where either of my parents were originally from.'

'Hitler would want you for one of his posters.'

'Then that must be true for you, too, Colonel.'

'I'm a bit old for that.' He took the risk. 'And sadly, I'm not the type of model Nazi he might require.'

'Neither am I, sir,' the man before him said carefully, and Kilian found himself being studied.

Kilian nodded brusquely, aware that the conversation was heading into dangerous territory. 'Thank you for coming at short notice, Loewe.'

'I'm at your service, Colonel. What can I do for you, sir?'

'It's an unusual request,' Kilian began. 'Please, sit down.' They were away from his desk in the corner of his room, where comfy chairs and a low table gave the impression of a relaxed place for casual conversation. Kilian liked Loewe's pride; the man, though his inferior, did not cringe in his presence.

'You may recall we spoke earlier about your discretion . . . and that I was impressed with it.'

'Yes, sir.'

'I want to make use of that again.'

'You want me to pick up Mademoiselle Forestier?'

Kilian gave a tight smile. 'It's a little bit more complicated. I do want you to pick her up, yes; in fact, from now on I want you alone to be responsible for taking Mademoiselle Forestier to any of the destinations she requires.'

'I'll be glad to do that for you, Colonel, but —'

'Don't worry. I'll clear it with your supervisor.'

'All right. But there's nothing complex about driving Mademoiselle Forestier around, Colonel?'

'There is if I attach a different slant to that escort.'

He watched Loewe pause, then frown. 'I'm watching her?'

Kilian nodded.

'Why?'

'It's not really necessary to know, surely?'

'But what am I watching for, sir?'

'For wherever she goes, whomever she meets.'

'That's not just watching someone from the convenience of the driving seat, sir. You're asking me to follow Mademoiselle Forestier . . . is this right?'

'Yes. I want her followed as closely as her own shadow. And it must be kept entirely secret.'

'Does anyone else know about this?'

'No,' Kilian lied. 'I'm asking you to do this for me.'

'Why me?'

'You are a civilian, you are of her age and thus can move more freely in her circles. But mainly, Loewe, it's because I believe I can rely on you. Can I trust you?' Kilian asked, impaling the man with a hard stare. He was impressed that Loewe's gaze didn't flinch.

'Yes you can. But you speak of trust, and it cuts both ways. Can I equally trust that my work spying on a young woman is for a good cause?'

'You can. I must take due precaution.'

'Against what, Colonel?'

'I'm required by my rank to be careful. She has come into my life unexpectedly, and I am simply being cautious.' He shifted, feeling awkward about his lie. 'Any officer might take that precaution.'

'Has something happened, sir, to make you worried?'

'No. It is simply that there is a new order decreeing all new relationships with civilians must be monitored,' he lied again, feeling even more uncomfortable beneath the penetrating gaze of Loewe.

'That must be very cumbersome for the officers, Colonel.'

'Like much to do with this administration,' Kilian snapped. Loewe blinked and Kilian smiled wryly. 'Now they'll definitely have to rouse the firing squad for that.'

Loewe stood and smiled back. 'Your secret's safe with me, Colonel Kilian . . . and so is Mademoiselle Forestier.'

Luc was in a state of fear. How had they become suspicious of Lisette so quickly? Whether she liked it or not, she had to start easing herself out of the web being spun around her. For the time being she was safe – Kilian had no idea that his new civilian spy was in fact a real one. But Luc knew his cover could blow up at any moment.

Using the Métro, he made his way to Montmartre. He ran up the stairs to Lisette's apartment, looking at his watch anxiously. She should be home from work by now. There was no answer when he knocked on her door. He paced, knocked again, louder this time. Still no response. She wasn't home and no amount of willing would make her so.

'Luc?'

He swung around to see Sylvie leaning against the wall behind him. Despite her beauty, Sylvie was every inch a fearless warrior and Luc would happily stand by her side and face off against any enemy. She ran into danger as fast and angrily as he did, but she wrestled no personal demons. She simply wanted France for the French again.

Lonely and grief-stricken in Paris, Luc had fallen into a relationship with Sylvie. He was sorry for that, but he had never lied to her about his feelings. For him the relationship had always been one of companionship and convenience. Looking at her now, he was reminded of Catherine – of the nature of the relationship he had taken for granted. He had not lied to Catherine, either, but look where that had led. Honesty doesn't always win friends, his grandmother had once counselled.

'Hello, Sylvie,' he said, forcing himself to appear amiable. 'You're on nightshift?'

She nodded.

'I needed to speak with Lisette.'

'Obviously.'

'Look, Sylvie —'

'Not here, Luc. Talk to me downstairs.'

He sighed and followed her down and into her apartment.

'So,' she began. 'Can I get you anything?'

He shook his head.

'You'd normally enjoy some afternoon . . . comfort,' she said, choosing her words with care.

'Sylvie, please . . .'

'What? I'm not good enough for you now that you've finally shown yourself to her?' Her green eyes blazed with barely controlled jealousy.

He gave her a look of sorrow. 'I was honest with you at the beginning about Lisette. And I didn't plan on hurting you.'

She flicked her dark golden hair self-consciously. 'I know. But it does hurt. And don't remind me that you made no promises, because I know that too.'

He stared at her, lost for the best approach. Sylvie had been a rock for him, especially in the early days of his anguish at being so close and yet so far from Lisette. It was Sylvie who had talked him through the hardest times, forbidden him to make contact, diverted him when he felt most vulnerable, and, yes, comforted him in her practical, no-nonsense way. Never once had they discussed their physical attraction as something romantic.

He reached for her and she didn't protest. Luc held her close and, despite all that his senses were telling him, he returned to honesty. 'What do you want me to say, Sylvie?'

'What I want you to say I know you won't . . . or can't,' she murmured.

'I'm sorry,' he whispered.

'I am too,' she said, pulling away, and he saw the effort it cost her to smile.

'Sylvie —'

The knock at the door took them both by surprise and they parted as if burned.

'Who?' he mouthed silently.

She shook her head with a frown, waving him back behind the door. He nodded and tiptoed to lean back against the wall. Sylvie opened the door.

'Lisette! Hello.'

Luc froze.

'Er . . . hello, Sylvie,' he heard her say. 'Have you seen Luc today?'

His heart felt as though it stopped for a beat. She was looking for him. If she listened hard enough, she could probably hear his heart hammering against his chest.

'Today?' Sylvie replied. 'No, but I expect to.'

'I see,' Lisette replied, sounding embarrassed. 'Do you know how I can reach him?'

He watched Sylvie shake her head slowly. 'He comes and he goes. You know how it is. None of us tell each other more than we need to know. He stays with me when he's in Paris, and as I don't expect him to be warming my bed this evening, I imagine he's out of the city.'

'Well,' Lisette said, awkwardly, 'if you do hear from him, would you let him know there's something very important I have to tell him?'

Luc was about to pull back the door and take the consequences of being discovered in a lie. But he hesitated and the moment was lost; Sylvie closed the door. He heard Lisette running up the stairs.

'Don't look so fraught. She didn't suspect anything,' Sylvie said, amused.

'I'm not worried about that. I want to know what she has to say.'

'I suppose you want her to tell you that she loves you, and sleeping with her German is all for the good of the country.'

He moved to open the door angrily.

Sylvie grabbed his arm. 'Luc, wait! Don't do anything rash. Let's not muddle what has happened between us or between you and Lisette with our work. We cannot endanger ourselves and compromise the networks.'

'I'm not muddling anything, Sylvie. I'm very clear. I am in love with Lisette, that's the truth of it. Nothing's changed. You've been a wonderful friend to me. You are brave and beautiful, loyal and . . . you've given me strength when I most needed it. But I do not love you. I'm sorry.'

Her eyes glittered with the pain she was holding back. 'I'm sorry too,' she said, her voice hard again. Here was the Sylvie he trusted; the Sylvie who wore her cold approach as armour. She went looking for a cigarette. 'You'd better go to her, then.'

'Sylvie, I —'

'Don't worry. I'm always here for you if you need me. We still have a war to fight.'

She made sure her back was turned while she rummaged for a box of matches until he closed the door behind him. Only then did she let the tears break softly and silently, hardly noticing the unlit cigarette between her fingers.

———————

Evening was closing in when Luc knocked on Lisette's door. He thought she looked pale.

'Sylvie told you I wanted to see you?' He nodded. 'Thank you for coming. I . . . I wasn't sure you would.'

'Are you all right?'

'Yes. Can I offer you more of the cheap wine or a nasty coffee?'

He didn't care much for the coffee but chose it all the same. He watched her quietly as she busied herself with the brew.

'Lisette . . . about Sylvie —'

'I don't wish to talk about her, Luc. That's your business in the same way that Kilian is mine.'

'Well, I have something to tell you that makes Kilian my business,' he replied.

Her reaction was unexpected. She smiled sadly and seemed nonplussed.

'What's wrong, Lisette?'

'Tell me about your family, Luc,' she said, her tone almost dreamy. She was looking out of the window, and the neon signs from a bistro below cast a red glow onto her face, making her look ill.

'Why do you ask that?'

'I want to know about your family. I want to know what happened in l'Isle sur la Sorgue.' She turned. 'We could both be dead tomorrow.'

He frowned, concerned, and it was only then he noticed the envelope on the table, the Nazi crest emblazoned on its front. Luc took a breath before he nodded at it. 'Is that from Kilian?'

She turned and glanced at it, then returned her gaze to the window. 'Isn't it lovely that spring is here?' She gave a cheerless laugh. 'I could almost pretend we weren't at war.'

'Lisette!' he urged in a low voice.

'I'll tell you what's in the envelope when you tell me what I want to know . . . all those things you held back from me when we were in Provence.'

'We were barely together long enough for —'

'We spent hours walking. We had plenty of time. Tell me, what happened with von Schleigel at l'Isle sur la Sorgue?'

'It's not relevant . . . it's —'

'Humour me, Luc. Please.'

'I need it inside me, Lisette. You don't understand. If I tell you, I risk losing the rage,' he said, clapping a hand to his chest. 'And I refuse to do that. It's not just von Schleigel but . . . I can't let the anger out. It's mine.'

'So you can go after him?'

Luc gave a short bark of laughter. 'I don't have the luxury of making plans. We all live in the present. You know that. We can't think beyond today.'

She sighed. 'The note is from Kilian, as you suspect. He wants to meet me tomorrow afternoon after work.' He waited, sensing there was more. 'I fear it could be a trap.'

'What makes you say that?'

'I learned something today that may have damaged my cover.'

'Tell me,' he urged.

She slumped against the windowsill. 'Von Schleigel met with Walter Eichel,' she said, raising her eyes to meet his.

Luc turned away to take a breath as a thrill of fear snaked around his body. 'Von Schleigel? You're sure?' He turned to her. 'You know it's him?'

'There is no doubt. He told my godfather that I was detained by the Gestapo because of the man I was travelling with. My fiancé.'

Luc stared at her, shocked. 'This happened today?'

'Von Schleigel met with him yesterday.'

'And your godfather told you?'

'Yes. Of course he wanted to know about my fiancé. I told Walter that you were a friend and the only way we could escape the Gestapo was to claim we were engaged.'

'I understand now why von Schleigel let us go,' Luc said.

'But he never forgot us.'

'Never forgot me, Lisette. This has nothing to do with you. He never accused you of anything.'

'No, but he certainly followed up by calling in on Walter to make sure that I hadn't darkened his name. But what Walter really wanted to know was why the Gestapo thought he could vouch for my fiancé.'

'What?' Luc asked.

'I was desperate. I told von Schleigel that Walter knew you.'

Luc ran a hand through his hair. 'That was a huge risk.'

'I had to take it.'

'What did your godfather say when von Schleigel asked him about me?'

'He vouched for you, of course.'

Luc stared at her in fresh surprise. 'Why?'

'Because he took the same instant dislike to von Schleigel that I suspect most people do.'

'And what happened?'

'Von Schleigel left for Poland, apparently satisfied, for his new role at the prison camps there.'

Luc nodded grimly. 'If I survive this war, Lisette, I'm going to find him . . . and either spit upon his grave or put him in one.'

'He's not important, Luc.'

'Not to you, perhaps. But I owe him.' He watched her gaze narrow, but whatever she wanted to ask she decided to keep to herself.

Lisette continued, 'Unfortunately, Walter mentioned my link to Kilian to von Schleigel.'

'And what? You think von Schleigel confronted Kilian?'

'I guess I won't know until tomorrow. By which time it could be too late.'

Luc suddenly began to realise the true nature of his new duties with Kilian. 'I told you that I have something to tell you too; maybe it's connected.'

She looked at him dumbstruck as he told her of driving the colonel to Stülpnagel and then Kilian's orders. 'He's spying on me?'

'While you spy on him.' Luc gave a crooked smile. 'Lisette, we're lucky. I can tell him whatever you want until we work out how to get you safely away.'

'It's too late, Luc. I think he knows, or else why have my every move followed?'

'Listen to me. He said it's protocol: a new directive from Berlin.'

'And you believe that?'

'Well, if he thought you were a spy, wouldn't you already be in detention? Why didn't you hear jackboots at the bank coming to pick you up? Or Gestapo waiting for your arrival home?'

She blinked, unable to process the sense of his words with the fear of what had rattled her. 'I don't know.'

'I think he's taking precautions, which is wise of him.'

'But —'

'If what you say about him is true – that he is part of a plan to bring down the German hierarchy – then don't you think he would protect that above all else? If you were even a vague threat, he wouldn't hesitate to hand you over to authorities. He has to protect his secret more than his reputation. I think you should get out, but carefully.'

'No.'

'What?'

'Playboy was waiting for me outside the building when I came home today.'

'The wireless operator?'

She nodded. 'We never meet. I send messages via a dead-letter drop.'

'So what was different this time?'

'This,' she said, holding up a piece of paper. 'A response from London to my coded message. It was so urgent they made Playboy take the risk of personally delivering it.'

'So what does it say?' He held his breath.

'I am to continue with my mission and find out everything I can about whether a conspiracy exists, its timing and who the architects are.'

'They're mad. Kilian is too far away to be privy to such a plot.'

'Instructions come from the highest level, apparently; from Churchill himself. Playboy said my mission was prompted by information revealed by German generals imprisoned in England, suggesting a high level of anti-Hitler sentiment in the Wehrmacht. And what would Stülpnagel have to do with Kilian? It doesn't add up, given their roles.'

'Lisette, you're getting in too deep.'

'If when I see Markus Kilian again there are no repercussions from von Schleigel, then I'm staying with him and I'm going to learn everything I can about whether this plot exists. I have to.'

'I can't leave you alone, Lisette. We're bound, whether we like it or not. I have orders from Kilian.'

'Then do what you must.'

He stared at her, lost for words.

She took a breath. 'This invitation doesn't ask me to come to his office, not even to his hotel. It suggests a coffee by the river. I suppose it doesn't sound like a man who feels threatened. He may well be interested to hear my side of the tale.'

Luc began to pace. He knew better than to try to dissuade her in this mood, her mouth set like it was. On their walk up the mountain in the Luberon he had asked her what it felt like to live during the bombings over London and she had answered so casually. She wasn't afraid at all, it seemed to him. 'We're all dying a little more each day,' she'd said to him. They had recruited well when they chose her; alone, lonely, rudderless. Perfect. Add to that her obvious talent for espionage and her ability to blend in, as well as her intelligence and charm, and she was tailored for her role. She could be cold, so cold when she chose to be. But it was the serious, romantic girl that Luc loved; the girl who'd taken joy in lavender fields, who revelled in speaking French again, who'd admitted on that walk that her favourite story was about an angry man called Heathcliff who loved one woman to distraction.

Luc realised that all of Lisette's anxiety was connected with the safety of the mission, not her own safety. In l'Isle sur la Sorgue, her driving fear had been that she might never fulfil her role for London. Even now, her determination to face Kilian tomorrow was all about the mission. If he was ever going to get her out, he had to do so on her terms; let her believe the mission mattered.

'So how will you handle this?' he asked.

She smoothed her brow with her fingertips. 'I'm going to be forthright; I'll tell him about l'Isle sur la Sorgue. If I beat him to the punch by innocently offering the information, how can he consider me suspicious?'

'Well, that's certainly one approach.'

She gave a rueful smile. 'I don't have much choice. I know you'd like to argue the opposite, but frankly, to walk away now is unwise. It would be all the more suspicious. Can you understand that?'

Luc hated her in that moment for making perfect sense. He hung his head. 'You're right.'

Her eyes widened. 'You agree?' Luc smiled at her in response. Her tone became tender. 'Just for a second there, the angry maquisard faded away and I saw the romantic lavender grower who stole my heart.'

And in that moment all his resistance dissolved.

He reached for her. 'I can't bear the thought of losing you again,' he whispered.

She let him hold her for a long time before she gently pulled away. 'I have to be clear-headed now. I am Kilian's lover, and you are his spy.'

He nodded. He would bear this pain, and he would wait for Lisette to see out this part of her life on her terms. And when it was done – if they were both still alive – he would pick up the pieces and put what they had together again. '*Adieu*,' he said. There was nothing more to say.

She nodded. '*Adieu*.'

He kissed both her cheeks and then tenderly caressed her lips with his own before leaving.

As he emerged from Lisette's building he couldn't know that the German tourist on the other side of the street, seemingly taking a photograph of his wife in Montmartre, was actually focusing his lens on Luc. He snapped another photograph of him as he crossed the road and disappeared into the drizzle of a Paris evening.

30

The next day Kilian was waiting for Lisette on the Pont Neuf. Just yesterday he had stood here, wondering whether she was a spy. But now, as he watched her weaving her way towards him with that bright smile, he felt vaguely ashamed for having ever entertained the notion.

Loewe confirmed that she had gone home last night alone, eaten quietly and switched off her light at eight. This morning she had gone to work and had stepped out at lunchtime alone to pick up a few groceries.

Kilian had to smile as she waved happily at him while waiting to cross the street. She was so young, so beautiful, so German and so French. Why on earth would she want to work against him? He'd looked into her life this morning, calling up a few favours in certain offices. A few phone calls revealed exactly what Lisette had told him: she'd lived in Strasbourg, her parents had been killed in a car crash when she was seventeen. Her junior primary-school records checked out. And then there was Walter, the ultimate endorsement. How could she be the enemy?

In those last few seconds before Lisette arrived, Kilian wished he hadn't contacted Stülpnagel so impulsively. It was the right thing to have done, but he hoped it hadn't stirred up a hornet's nest. He should have waited. Well, it was too late for recriminations. Perhaps his new plan would ease his worries.

'Hello, Markus,' Lisette said breathlessly, and without any inhibition she put her arms around his neck and hugged him. She kissed him three times on his cheeks and impetuously embraced him again. 'You look a bit sad.'

'Do I? Forgive me. I was wishing I'd met you when I was thirty.'

'But that would make me fifteen,' she giggled. 'And I was entirely in love with Didier Badeau then, a sixteen-year-old chess player who made me weak at the knees when his hair would flop across his eyes.'

Kilian couldn't help but be amused. 'He could never have made you happy.'

She laughed. 'You're absolutely right. Thank you for inviting me here.'

'Did you think I wouldn't see you again?' he asked.

'No.' She grinned shyly. 'Isn't this spring weather glorious?'

'Yes, I thought we'd walk. A stroll along the Seine.'

'Perfect,' she said, linking her arm through his. They fell in step together and passed the *bouquinistes* that lined the banks – tiny stalls selling all manner of secondhand books.

'I love looking through all those old books,' Lisette said.

'Really? You're too young to have your head in dusty books.'

'Don't be condescending. I can enjoy old things. I like you, after all.'

He burst into laughter. 'How have you been?'

'I've missed you. Is that wrong, seeing as we barely know each other?'

He gave her a sideways glance full of tenderness and shook his head. He so wanted to hold onto this feeling; his world had been filled with grey for too long.

They stepped off the bridge and started strolling down the Left Bank.

Lisette asked, 'Have you heard the saying that the Left Bank thinks while the Right Bank spends?'

'Because of the Sorbonne, presumably?' he suggested.

'Yes. I suppose this area was filled with so many learned men – historians, philosophers, writers, teachers. I like this side. It has soul.'

'But you choose to live on the Right Bank?'

'What I can afford and what I like are often poles apart.'

He smiled, pointed at one of the bookstalls and they made their way towards it. They spent the next half an hour browsing in pleasurable companionship, brushing against each other now and again. He couldn't deny the connection that sizzled between them. He was too old for her, he kept telling himself. He couldn't deny that there was an age gap. But then another voice would whisper back: *so what?* He wasn't attached to another woman. He had nothing to feel embarrassed about as a single man with a young French lover. In his daydreams she was already his wife. It was an impossible notion.

Your days are likely numbered anyway, the invisible voice reminded. *So enjoy her!*

They finally found a café not far from Les Deux Magots, where they'd first met.

'Did you buy a book for yourself?' he said, noticing it in her hand.

'I bought a book, yes. But it's for you.' She handed it to him with a triumphant smile. 'Enjoy.'

'*Notre-Dame de Paris*.' He looked up. 'I like the work of Victor Hugo very much.'

'So do I. And as we've been walking in the shadow of the great cathedral, I thought it appropriate.'

'I'm charmed. Thank you, sweet Lisette.' He leaned over and kissed her, wondering whether she'd have to go without food for spending money on him.

'You've been so generous to me.' Then her face grew animated. 'Oh, I must tell you what happened to me yesterday.'

'Something happened?'

'Well, it's more that something happened to Walter, but it involved me.' She told him about an officer of the Gestapo paying Walter Eichel a visit, as though relating a tale of high intrigue.

He was astonished at her honesty, watched carefully for guile and found none. She spoke enthusiastically, laughing at the folly of the Gestapo. 'Can you imagine Walter's face when that horrid man stepped into his office? No, of course you can't. But let me assure you, Markus,' she said, dropping her voice to a whisper, 'that this von Schleigel embodies everything detestable about the Gestapo. Ugh.' She shivered.

'So his tale had no basis in fact?'

'Oh, he wasn't lying,' she admitted, grinning mischievously. 'I was arrested . . . I think – and I'm not sure, only because slippery von Schleigel barely spoke to me. He just locked me into a room and left me there to contemplate life for two hours. And then he let me go. But not before I'd casually let him know that Walter Eichel was my godfather. It was a ridiculous waste of time.'

This was it, Kilian thought. She was being honest, but would she tell him it all? He almost didn't want to ask. 'So why did he arrest you and then ignore you?'

Her eyes sparkled with amusement. 'I was travelling with a friend, Lukas Ravensburg, a German, who I'd known since schooldays. The Gestapo arrested Lukas, not me. I was caught in the crossfire, you could say.'

Kilian felt relief easing through him, dissipating the pain that had been skewering him. How could anyone look so gleeful if they had something to hide?

'That must have been frightening for you?'

She gave a casually dismissive gesture as she sipped her coffee.

'It was all a big misunderstanding. Von Schleigel had muddled Lukas with some resister somewhere in the Luberon. Anyway,' she said, looking bored with her tale suddenly. 'They let Lukas go soon enough, they apologised to me and I was on the next train to Paris. But it seems von Schleigel was worried I might create a problem for him with Walter, who has connections, as you know.'

Kilian nodded.

'Heavens! How arrogant von Schleigel is. He really believed I would spare him a second's thought and chat to Walter about him. Horrid man. I forgot him the moment I left Lyon.'

'And Lukas?'

'Hmm?'

'What happened to your friend?'

'Lukas? Well,' she began airily, looking up as she thought. 'He saw me off at Lyon and . . .' she shrugged. 'He was going back to Avignon, as far as I know.'

'And did he fall in love with you?'

She chuckled. 'Perhaps he did.'

'And you, Lisette?'

She gave him a wry smile. 'No, Markus, I didn't fall in love with him. He's a boy in comparison to you. But . . . I did lie to the Gestapo and tell them we were engaged. You can imagine Walter's surprise when the Gestapo man told him of my engagement.'

He feigned surprise. 'Why would you say you were engaged?'

'It was the fastest way to get both Lukas and me away from that vile place; I swear I could hear the scream of someone being tortured, Markus. It was . . .' Her expression became haunted. 'It was frightening, actually. Von Schleigel was grasping at straws, convinced that my Lukas and this resistance fellow shared vaguely similar features.' She looked away, distracted by the noise of laughter near the riverbank.

'Your Lukas?'

'What?' she said, returning her attention.

'You said *my* Lukas.'

He watched Lisette as her gaze softened. 'We were not lovers, Markus,' and the way she said it made him realise that she knew he was jealous.

He loathed how weak she made him feel. He genuinely felt like a possessive teenager. He would put a stop to it. He would call off Loewe today! And he would tell Stülpnagel that he'd simply been unbalanced by von Schleigel's insinuations. And he knew exactly how to end this tawdry episode.

He put his cup down and steepled his fingers. 'Lisette. I have to go away.'

'Oh,' she said, and an unreadable emotion flashed across her face. 'For long?'

'A few weeks maybe.'

'I see.' He watched her happy mood deflate. 'That's rather sudden, isn't it?'

'Not really. I've been putting it off. I can't any longer.'

She looked to be doing her best to hide her disappointment. It thrilled him. 'Berlin?' she wondered.

'Er, no, actually. Around France.'

'A holiday?'

He gave a snort. 'No, my dear. I am working. I have been promising to tour some of the key regions in France to speak with the clergy. It's part of my job to maintain relations between Berlin and the regional church hierarchy.'

'A holiday, like I said.' She grinned, regaining some of her humour.

'Well, I admit this is hardly work for a battle-hardened soldier. I'm sure it will be torture.'

'I feel terribly sorry for you, having to tour beautiful France. Take your punishment bravely, Markus,' she said. 'I will miss you, though . . . my battle-hardened man.'

He stared at her. He wanted to take her to his bed that moment, wanted to feel her naked limbs entwined around him. 'Will you?' he asked, his voice suddenly croaky.

'I can't get through an hour without you invading my thoughts. It's disastrous for work, for sleep. You've ruined my life!' she said jokingly, but neither of them laughed. 'And if I can't get through an hour, how will I get through several weeks?' Lisette looked down and fiddled with the scarf in her lap. 'I'm sorry —'

'Come with me,' he said, and suddenly everyone around them was invisible. Nothing and no one else mattered.

Lisette's eyes widened in surprise. 'What? How?'

'As my assistant. I need a good interpreter, someone amiable, charming. You're perfect.'

'But . . . the bank, I —'

'I'll speak with Walter. I can requisition you if I want, but that shouldn't be necessary. I'm sure he will gladly agree.'

He watched the light in her eyes catch aflame. 'You mean it?'

He nodded. 'I want you with me . . . need you with me.'

She surprised him by leaning across the table to give him a deep and lingering kiss. He was shocked to realise he felt no embarrassment; if anything, he lengthened her kiss by pulling her closer. He was utterly entranced by her.

'Take me back to your hotel, Markus,' she whispered.

He nodded, paid the bill and, without speaking, they walked arm in arm back to the Hotel Raphaël. Markus didn't want this moment to end, for in this magical instant he had never felt happier, never felt more in love. He'd admitted it: he loved Lisette. He'd never loved like this before, never felt this lightness in his heart . . . this unbearable, exquisite, all-consuming agony of desire and commitment.

And if this was love, he doubted he could ever tire of it; no wonder people wrote poetry and great novels about it. He led

Lisette up to his room and was pulling off his clothes the moment he closed the door behind them.

Later, sleepy in their tangled warmth, Lisette lay lightly on top of him. Their fingers were intertwined and she kissed his hand gently. 'I wish we could just see out the war like this.'

'Naked, you mean?' he teased.

'No. Sated and happy. I feel safe here in your arms, in your room. It's as though nothing else exists.'

'I'm sure driving through the French countryside won't be so bad. And we shall have each night together.'

'You make me feel guilty,' she said. He pushed back her hair and looked at her with questioning eyes. 'I mean, I'm being really spoiled. I'm very privileged, while the rest of my sort have to grind on.'

'You don't have a *sort*, Lisette. You are one of a kind, especially now that I know what you can do with that mouth of yours . . .'

She gasped and covered his mouth with her hand as he laughed beneath it. Lisette smiled self-consciously. 'That's our secret,' she whispered.

'Come on. Get up. I'm famished. You sap all my energy.'

She gurgled with laughter, and they reluctantly untangled themselves and began to dress. 'Oh, by the way,' she said. 'We're driving, rather than taking trains on this trip?'

'Yes.'

'Can we have a different driver to that man called Loewe?'

He looked up at her, surprised. 'Is something wrong?'

She shrugged. 'I'm not keen on the way he looks at me sometimes.'

'And in what way is that?'

'Oh, I don't know. Sometimes I get the impression he's watching me more closely than I'd like.'

Kilian blinked. 'You're imagining it.'

She shook her head. 'If I am, I'm not imagining my discomfort.'

'Well, don't worry about it any more. I'll request Klaus. He's ancient . . . at least forty-one. Will that suit?' he said, looking amused.

'Thank you. You're not going to fire Loewe, though, are you? I would hate for him to lose his job.'

'No. I'll just have him shifted while I'm away to a new department. Easily fixed.'

When Luc picked up the colonel later that night, he wasn't ready for what he was told.

'I'm glad you don't need me to follow Mademoiselle Forestier any more, Colonel, but may I ask why you're replacing me? I enjoy being your driver.'

'Yes, but Mademoiselle Forestier doesn't enjoy you, Loewe. Something about the way you look at her. Perhaps she sensed your surveillance.'

Luc knew what Lisette was doing and he could understand why. But going away with Kilian was dangerous. 'But I've barely exchanged more than polite salutations.'

'I will bring you straight back, Loewe, once we return.'

Luc chose not to push his luck. Besides, he had promised himself that he would no longer interfere with Lisette's plans. He had risked his own cover enough. He had family to find and lavender fields to plant again. And he had Lisette to love . . . if she would let him. But their love was in her hands now. He would no longer try to save her from herself.

'Yes, sir. How long will you be away?'

'Up to a month.'

Luc betrayed nothing, but his fears for Lisette began to grow. 'Safe travels, Colonel.'

'Thank you. Oh, and Loewe?'

Luc turned.

'Have you heard Lisette mention a fellow called Lukas Ravensburg?'

Luc felt the fear pulse through him. He shook his head. 'No, Colonel. Is he someone I should have come across?'

'Unlikely.'

'Where's he from?' How much did Kilian know?

'Not Paris. He's a southerner, apparently.'

Luc shrugged, his fear escalating. Had Lisette told Kilian this, or had von Schleigel? 'His name sounds German.'

'He is German. That's why I mention him. Anyway, keep your ear to the ground for me.'

Luc nodded. '*Auf wiedersehen*, Colonel.'

He went straight to Lisette's flat, hoping to ask her about Lukas Ravensburg. But he was too late. After being stopped a dozen times for being out after curfew, he found her flat empty. He knocked on Sylvie's door, hating to reopen that wound, but even Sylvie was nowhere to be found. His last port of call was Sylvie's letterbox; they used it as a means to pass each other messages. Right enough, there was a note for him:

Lisette left a message under my door saying she was going to be away for a month. She apologised for any bad feelings between us and wished me well. I watched a car pick her up a few minutes ago. An older man was driving so I presume you are not with her. She asked that I should tell you to stay safe, keep the seeds close (whatever that means).

I will be moving soon so I suspect we have no need to cross paths but I'll leave my address with Spiritualist. I'm sorry I didn't keep my promise, but then I suspect you're used to women falling in love with you. How odd that the one you fell for is in love with another. Hurts, doesn't it? Goodbye. S

He screwed the notepaper up in his fist and groaned.

PART FOUR

PART FOUR

Before Lisette departed with Kilian, she had managed to leave a final coded message at the café for Playboy. She advised London she would be away with the colonel and to not expect contact for up to a month. She hesitated before mentioning that part of her cover had been compromised, but assured that the integrity remained intact. She would report back as soon as she could.

After Kilian had spoken to Walter and arranged for her to be away, Lisette and Markus had left the city in mid-May. That day felt like just a moment ago. But here it was, already June. Where had the time gone? It had been lost in weeks of pure escapism. Lisette's one regret was that she hadn't been able to say goodbye to Luc before she left for the Loire Valley, but perhaps it was for the best.

Everything had happened so quickly between her and Luc, and going away had given her the physical and emotional distance that she needed to focus on her mission. She had never felt more confused – and at the same time so clear-headed. It was as though she were two people. One Lisette did love Luc, but the same woman did not regret asking Kilian to replace his driver, and refused – even in her quietest moments – to dwell on Luc. She found a place to set him aside in her heart, and played at being a translator by day and consort by night.

By London's measure, she was carrying out her mission perfectly: she had successfully infiltrated Kilian's life. But the truth was she had failed London miserably. She was none the wiser to whether any conspiracy plans existed, let alone whether Kilian might be actively involved. Her instincts told her that he was part of a plot, but hunches were not enough. And she could not hurry the process of extracting information. First she knew she must distance herself entirely from the Gestapo, from anything that connected her to the potential for espionage, and especially from Lukas Ravensburg.

And then there was Markus himself. The more Lisette got to know him, the more she realised that the danger Luc had spoken about was not the threat to her wellbeing so much as the threat to her heart. As each day passed, and especially as each night was enjoyed, her attachment to Kilian helplessly and unconsciously strengthened.

As their days drifted into weeks, working together, eating and sleeping together, she sensed him relaxing, beginning to trust her. She made a point of talking about every possible subject other than his work to put his suspicions to rest.

And he was in love with her. She knew that now. He had not said so, but she knew it as surely and as intimately as she knew the taste of his skin, the golden tips to his eyebrows, the laugh lines that appeared when he smiled. Even when he was happy, Kilian always appeared as though deep in concentration – assessing, analysing. Lisette never underestimated his ability to make sharp observations. Nevertheless, he loved her and his laughter reflected it. His pale, hungry gaze followed her faithfully, his mouth was hers, ever ready to seduce her with passionate kisses under cover of darkness.

In under five weeks she had achieved what many women had failed to come close to in years. Markus had even begun to open up about Ilse, his former fiancée. And the Markus whose heart Lisette had won was all passion; he was passionate about the men he had led, for Germany, for the arts – he was even passionate about chocolate. Most of all, he was passionate about her.

And that's what scared Lisette as they returned to Paris. It had been three weeks of running away from reality, and now both of them had to face occupied Paris again, with her red flags and rules, her salutes and constraints.

Late spring in provincial France had been magical. There had been much laughter together as they travelled through the picturesque countryside. Markus had even taken Lisette shopping, insisting on buying her some new clothes – summer frocks that showed off her figure. She'd opened up about her early life. It felt cathartic for Lisette to talk about her dashing father, her beautiful mother, their tragic end – she'd wept in Markus's arms for the first time since she'd been told of her parents' death, and he'd kissed away her tears. Lisette had realised with a mix of regret and sharp surprise that she had not guarded her own heart well enough; it seemed, without any awareness, she had steadily fallen for Markus Kilian. As they approached Paris, she felt a fluttering sense of panic at having to let him go. It was devastating to appreciate how important Kilian had become to her – and his love that was as stable as it was strong.

And for the first time her mission felt uncomfortable. Until now, the demands of the role had empowered her, given her drive and courage and the ability to cast inhibitions to the wind. She had discovered a new Lisette – one who was funny and mischievous, sensual and playful, and she thought this new persona would protect her true feelings. But Kilian, like Luc, had found a way beneath her shield and, through sheer force of character – his irresistible personality, his lovemaking, always surprising and generous – had navigated to her heart.

It was here where Luc resided; silent, patient, sad. It was here that she kept him safe, kept him hers, kept him alive, and as they entered Paris proper, she could swear that the fragrance of lavender was all about them.

'Do you smell that?'

'What, the rutabaga?' Kilian joked, although she could see he wasn't amused by his own jest.

'I smell lavender.'

'We left that behind in the south. It's your imagination playing tricks.'

But Lisette couldn't fight it, and her first sight of the Eiffel Tower brought back thoughts of Luc that she'd kept successfully separate for weeks. It also reminded her that she had little to show for her clandestine holiday, other than an aching conscience.

'What's wrong, my darling?' Kilian asked. 'You look pensive.'

'I wish we never had to come back here.'

'But Paris is so beautiful . . . and summer beckons.'

She decided to take the risk. 'I hate what this war is doing to all of us. Why can't someone just kill Hitler so we can all get on with a truce?'

She saw Kilian glance at the driver's partition, checking it was closed.

'Hush. Don't speak like that.'

'Well, you agree, surely?'

'I think a lot of people want to find a solution to achieve an end.'

'Talk plainly, Markus. If enough of us feel this way, then why isn't someone acting? What about the bastard who claims he loves Germany but keeps sending our young men to a senseless death?'

Kilian pulled down the jump seat opposite Lisette and moved into it to face her, effectively cutting off Klaus's rear vision. 'What has got into you, Lisette? This is dangerous talk. Remember where you are. Remember who you're with!'

'But you know it's true!'

'You know I do,' he growled.

'Then do something! You and your colleagues who want to

end this. Stop feeling oppressed and persecuted and so . . . helpless. *Do* something!'

His expression contorted into shock, the vertical line in his forehead deepening. 'I am, damn it!' he snarled, grabbing her wrists and squeezing them so tight it took her breath away. 'But leave it be.'

'I . . . I'm sorry, Markus.'

He twisted away, genuinely furious with her. 'I've said too much,' he muttered to the window.

She clutched at him, knowing she needed to sound clingy. 'Please, I just don't want us to end. I want this selfish life of ours to go on.'

He swung back, searching her face with that icy stare. 'But why should we end?'

'Because we're back here, back to the reality, back to the endless days of ration coupons. When the weather turns to autumn, I'll know the cold and hunger again. Men are dying by bullets, Jews are dying in prisons, babies are dying of malnutrition. And it's all one man's fault!' A tear escaped her eye, and it was not for show. 'We have to make it stop.'

His voice was brittle when he spoke. It was clear he was far from impressed by her uncharacteristic outburst. 'You're young, Lisette. And perhaps you're fraught – I blame myself for that – but I can't control your feelings in the same way that I can't help mine. What has to stop right now is today's erratic demands,' he said tightly. 'Our decimated army in the east is retreating so fast it's having to leave the injured behind. And still our leader refuses to acknowledge the defeat. His Operation Citadel in Kursk was lunacy. Hundreds of thousands of captured miles are being reclaimed by the Soviets and they are showing no mercy – nor should they, given what we've done to them even as we've been retreating. There is no pride left for the Wehrmacht now; we are nothing but barbarians under Hitler.' His voice was so taut she feared he might break down. 'Millions of our men have spilled their blood, for what?' He groaned. 'But those are my men, damn it. I can't begin to plumb the depths of my guilt that they die while I drink wine and make merry with you in the Loire Valley.'

He looked deeply into Lisette's eyes. 'I know we live here in a strange cocoon, but you do realise, don't you, that the British and Americans are threatening to land on French soil at any minute?'

Lisette played dumb, looking anxiously back at him.

'They'll take Calais any day.' Markus shook his head. 'I know you want more from me, but our lives are unimportant in the scheme of what is unfolding. You're a rare woman, Lisette – your humour, your nerve, your whole attitude to life. Don't let me down now. We've had enough self-indulgence.'

She felt a flush of shame as she realised she'd had to disappoint him in order to get what she needed. She wanted more, but she'd pushed him far enough today.

'I won't let you down,' she said, in a tone loaded with remorse. 'I don't know what came over me. Please forgive me.'

He searched her eyes, his voice gentle once more. 'Do you think I don't feel it too? Do you think I'm not dying a little inside that I have to give you back to Walter, to your horrible little studio, to your impoverished lifestyle? I too want this war to end. I want you to be mine, Lisette . . . as you've been mine these last few weeks.' He ran a frustrated hand through his neat hair. 'Damn it, I want you to be my wife!'

They both stared at each other, thunderstruck. The words reverberated between them, loaded with meaning.

'I'm sorry,' he finally said. 'That was . . . misguided.' He cleared his throat and slowly moved to sit alongside her again, took her hand. 'I know it's confusing you, Lisette.' He kissed her palm. 'Now, listen to me. I love you.' He fixed her with such a fierce gaze that she felt weak, and guilt pressed around her as though it were physical. His eyes were so ablaze with emotion they sparkled like aquamarines. 'But this is not the time to act upon that love. We can't escape where we are, the situation we find ourselves in, or who we are. For now, just know that if I survive this war, then I will ask you properly to marry me.' He paused, and looked down as he continued softly, 'There won't be a happier man on this earth if you say yes.'

Lisette's heart swelled with emotion, and she knew she had to respond. But all she could think of was how similar Markus's face was to Luc's. Did Luc know he looked so similar to her colonel? It was a punishment for her. 'Why do you talk of survival as though it may elude you? If the Allies take Paris back as they threaten, then you'll surrender and —'

'Be put on trial at the very least.'

She frowned. 'No, Markus. I —'

'Listen, it's irrelevant to speak of what may happen. We can but live in the present.' He kissed her tenderly. 'We are almost back at my office. You will wish me farewell, write those reports I asked you to compile and then deliver them by Friday afternoon. I cannot see you for a while.' He touched her arm gently. 'We must be resolute. My time will not be my own in coming weeks. I may even be sent out of France. But you have to be understanding. Go back to work, return to your life and wait. It may be months before we see each other again.' She looked startled. 'Or it could be days. I just don't know. But you have to be patient. Can you do that for me?'

She nodded, bewildered, but all the more anxious to know what he was hinting at. 'I know that you're seeing General Stülpnagel today and —'

He frowned. 'How do you know that?'

Lisette feigned innocence. 'I heard you speaking about it on the telephone yesterday.'

'But you were not in the room.'

'I know that, Markus,' she said, slight indignation in her voice. 'But one could hardly miss that man's booming voice when he announced the military commander's office in Paris had been reached.'

'But why should the general or my meeting with him interest you?' Kilian looked irritated.

So he *was* meeting Stülpnagel. She thought quickly. 'Well, I wanted to ask you to mention my name.'

'What?'

'I don't want to keep working at the bank. This time away has changed everything. It was never a permanent position anyway – just something to tide me over. I can hardly demand a role in your office, but . . . oh, it doesn't matter. If you'd prefer not to . . .'

His features relaxed with relief. 'I see. Well, I don't mind mentioning it.'

'Really? Thank you. Perhaps I could be a full-time translator – any department is fine.'

'Leave it with me.' Markus gave her a polite kiss goodbye on each cheek, mindful suddenly of Klaus opening the car door. 'I'll be thinking of you constantly,' he assured her quietly. 'I'll reach you.'

She nodded. 'I'll be waiting.'

'Klaus will take you home. Thank you for your help. You charmed the clerics, of course, like you charm everyone.'

'I'm glad I made a difference.'

'It would have been loathsome without you,' he whispered as he smiled. 'Say hello to Walter.'

'I'll miss you, Markus,' she said, as he closed the door and tapped on the roof. He lifted a hand in farewell and she watched him as the car drew away from the kerb.

Kilian wasted no time. In fact, he'd cut his trip short once the message had come through from Stülpnagel two days ago.

Kilian had begun the tour putting in a call to the general every few days as requested. They'd agreed that if there was no change to the status quo, they would discuss work details or make small talk about Kilian's trip. However, if Stülpnagel opened their conversation by asking him how the weather was, then that was Kilian's signal to get back to Paris urgently. It meant the plot to assassinate Hitler was moving to reality . . . and to a date. And yesterday the usual polite conversation had shifted. Stülpnagel's first question had been whether Kilian was enjoying some early summer sun down south, and Kilian felt his heart begin to beat at twice its normal speed.

He was surprised that Lisette had not questioned him about the sudden change in plans, but then she had shown no interest in his daily work other than her translation duties. However, her outburst in the car was certainly curious, and he was angry with himself for revealing what he had. This information was dangerous enough to send him and others before the firing squad. A loose mouth could incriminate dozens of men and trace a line all the way up the hierarchy to Berlin.

He closed his eyes outside the Hotel Raphaël and took a steadying breath as he watched the staff car depart. He trusted Lisette, and was convinced he could rely on her to keep her own counsel, but he didn't have time to ponder it further. He quickly changed and put through a call to Stülpnagel's department, leaving a message that he was back in Paris. Within minutes his call was returned.

'Welcome back, Kilian.'

'Thank you, General. It's been a while since I've seen you.'

'It certainly has. How about we meet to discuss those plans for the blessings?'

'Yes, sir. Where and when?'

'How about now? I'll meet you outside the Louvre.'

'Very good, sir. I'm on my way.'

Kilian arrived first with time to admire the grand surrounds of the Palais du Louvre, imagining all the people from history that had walked these flagstones. He recalled that Napoleon had once renamed the museum after himself and smiled ruefully. Hitler would do the same if he could. Stülpnagel didn't keep him waiting long.

'*Heil Hitler*,' Stülpnagel said half-heartedly. 'Shall we go in?'

'Why not?' Kilian replied. 'I'm ashamed to say that I have only visited here once since I arrived in Paris last year.'

'Nothing much to see anyway,' the general grumbled. 'Just a few sculptures. The curators have carried everything to chateaus around central France. I hear *La Joconde* is gracing someone's bedroom at the moment. Can you credit it?'

Kilian smiled wryly. He could believe it. The curators had transported countless artworks, including the *Mona Lisa*, out of the famous museum and its galleries for safekeeping. He wondered what it might be like to turn around in bed and see the Italian damsel's famous pensive smile upon him.

Their boots echoed through empty halls as they made their way to a deserted gallery of sculptures.

Stülpnagel paused to admire a sculpture of a Greek god, whose perfectly formed muscles were outlined expertly in the grey marble. He spoke without taking his eyes from the statue. 'We are close now. A few more weeks at most for everything to be in order. It will take place at the Wolfsschanze, I believe.'

'What makes anyone think they can succeed in the Wolf's Lair? I've been there. I'm sure you have too. It's too well fortified; security is a nightmare.'

'Have faith, Colonel.'

Kilian began to pace. 'Four failed attempts already. We must be mad, all of us. This man can't die,' he said, giving a mirthless laugh, thinking of von Gersdorff's desperate attempt to kill the

Führer in Berlin with delayed-fuse explosives in his pockets while he was guiding Hitler through an exhibition.

The general stared at him stony-faced. 'But at least brave men with conscience continue to try,' he countered.

'When, sir?' Kilian asked.

'It could happen at any time.'

'But surely there's a firmer date?'

'Not yet. July is our best option. The Wolffschanze is now our only option as Hitler barely appears in public, almost never visits Berlin any more.' He sighed. 'I will give you perhaps a few days' warning. Three at most, possibly only one.'

Kilian looked stunned. 'A few days?'

'You've won entire battles in less,' Stülpnagel replied.

'How will it be done?'

'I cannot divulge,' he said, then raised a hand gently. 'No, Kilian, this is not about trust; it's simply about protection. The less you know, the less you can be harmed. I told you before, if we fail, we need to leave behind people loyal to the cause . . . the next tier of resistance, you could say. You are integral to that tier. The Gestapo is closing in on all of us who conspire against the Führer. We're going to keep trying until we succeed, or until the last man dies trying. But if we do fail, your name will be unblemished. And you will have to regroup, find new loyal men and try again. Our army is in full retreat on the Eastern Front; we're fighting losing battles in Italy, and you know Calais is next. Time is running out for those of us who want to make peace.'

Kilian regarded the general gravely. He trusted this man, who had been in the army for forty years. He nodded.

'I haven't told another living soul in Paris what I just told you.'

'Then why me?'

'Because your job is to mobilise the army. I want them under your command so tightly that not a single officer answers to anyone but you. Do you understand?' he said in such a low voice that Kilian had to lean in close to hear.

'Yes, General.'

Stülpnagel moved to the next sculpture. 'I know you're admired. I know the men will follow you. You will secure Paris first and then France in readiness for a truce with the Allies.'

'I understand. But what about Karl Boemelberg? He's not going to let the SS and Gestapo stand by and do nothing. We can't just —'

'The head of the Gestapo here is someone else's responsibility. You do not need to concern yourself with the secret police or the paramilitary. Every one of them will be arrested once we know the target is dead and Valkyrie has been actioned from Berlin. Everything will happen in concert, but each has our individual roles to play. You know yours. Don't let anything get in the way.'

'I won't, Colonel.'

'Clear your diary. There are to be no distractions this month.'

'I'll be by my telephone day and night if necessary.'

'What about that French girl you were seeing?'

'She's half German, General.'

'I hear you took her away this last month to work alongside you.'

'She was my interpreter.'

Stülpnagel gave a wry laugh. 'Is that what they call it now? You're sure about her, Kilian?'

'She's given me no reason to think otherwise.'

The general began to walk towards the exit, smiling.

Kilian frowned. 'Am I missing something, General?'

'No, but I may send something over soon. It's of no consequence but it may help you see your life in a clearer light.'

'I have no idea what you mean,' Kilian replied.

The general grinned. 'No, I don't think you do. But it's not important. Stay focused. Keep her out of your life for now. I'm sure you've checked up on her – as have we. Await my call,' he said over his shoulder, striding out of the gallery and leaving Kilian standing alone and mystified.

———

The following night the first of the assault groups left British waters bound for the Normandy coast, and the morning after that – on 6 June – the Germans realised they had been duped when Allied airforces began bombing coastal batteries around Le Havre, nearly 320 kilometres from the anticipated invasion in Calais. Warships began arriving by mid-afternoon and within a couple of hours shelling started on the German fortifications. The first American landings on the beaches were underway by early evening, with British and Canadian landings an hour later.

Lisette was crowded with others in Montmartre around a radio broadcast from the BBC.

'D-day has come . . . under the command of General Eisenhower, Allied naval forces supported by strong airforces began landing Allied armies this morning on the northern coast of France.'

Some people cheered, others looked concerned, still others looked bemused, unsure of what it meant for France. It looked like their country would now be the final battlefield to destroy the Nazi stranglehold over Europe.

32

Markus had made no contact with Lisette for almost a month. She was still trying to contrive a way to meet with him, for surely whatever his clandestine activities were, they were now advancing. She had informed London that Kilian was involved in a plot to remove Hitler and she named the present military commander in Paris as a co-conspirator.

There was no sign of Luc. Lisette had left a message for Playboy asking whether he knew where the resister called Faucille might be. She'd heard nothing back, and the man in the café who changed his tea towels on their behalf was no longer behind the counter. Life was changing rapidly. Sylvie's apartment was vacant. There was no choice for Lisette but to break her own rules and go back to the safe house where she had first met Spiritualist, in the hope of finding out anything about Luc's safety.

She walked from Montmartre. The days were hot and sunny now and the journey was a pleasure, although there was no denying that a fresh tension had overtaken Paris. It wasn't fear, it certainly wasn't joy yet either, but there was a throbbing pulse of anticipation roaring around the streets as the latest news of the landings on the northern beaches filtered through radios and spread like a grassfire.

There had been plenty of private celebration when General de Gaulle installed a provisional French government at Bayeux after the landings, and just today Lisette had heard his victory speech broadcast from the town hall in Cherbourg.

Checkpoints were overly stringent in some areas and lax at others. She couldn't pick which it would be – it seemed all the usual protocols were being ignored. Lisette suspected that plain-clothes Gestapo were everywhere – she made sure to carry every relevant piece of ID she could, as well as stationery from the bank, and even the envelope addressed to her from Kilian, with the Nazi emblem embossed on the corner. Every little detail helped.

She was stopped twice en route, and both times was permitted to pass without many questions. As she approached the Avenue de Wagram she was especially careful. She knew that many of the buildings around this area had been requisitioned by the Germans, and it was forbidden to walk alongside one of them. She took the extra precaution of crossing the wide boulevards to keep clear of the white palisades and Nazi insignia. Two pedestrians nearby were being chased and manhandled, papers demanded.

She looked away and kept walking confidently until she entered Avenue de Wagram near the Arc de Triomphe. Her destination was number 87, a several-storeyed, grand Parisian building in the pale grey stone originally favoured in the late 1700s. Tall, gracious French windows opened onto tiny balconies of wrought iron above her as she knocked on the concierge's door. It was answered by a woman whom she thought she recognised.

'Bonjour, mademoiselle,' the woman said politely. 'What a beautiful morning.'

'It is.'

'How can I help you?'

'I come on behalf of Alexander,' Lisette said the password in French, evenly.

The woman didn't hesitate and replied with the corresponding phrase. Lisette smiled. 'Merci, madame.'

The woman let her in as though welcoming an expected guest. Once the door was closed, they both sighed.

'We can't be too careful,' the woman explained. 'Everyone is more watchful than usual.'

'You can sense that on the streets. Forgive me for coming without warning. I need to see Armand.' Armand was the codename for the leader of the Spiritualist network in Paris. 'Is he here?'

The woman nodded. 'You are fortunate. He's not around for long, though. You can imagine how things are escalating. Come. I will let him know you are here. What's your name?'

'Angeline.'

'Follow me. Coffee?'

'Only if it's no trouble.'

'Armand will have one too. He never pauses long enough, so I'll insist.' She showed Lisette into a courtyard where the sun had already crept in. Lisette sat and waited in the warm and reassuring sunshine. She wondered about Kilian – who he was meeting, what plans were being made – but once again caught herself moving from Kilian to Luc.

Choose! a voice in the back of her mind demanded. She frowned. No matter what her mission demanded, she had to know herself where her heart lay.

She imagined them both standing before her now, similar in appearance, Luc perhaps broader, Markus slightly finer of feature, certainly better groomed. She imagined Markus with his sardonic expression and pale eyes regarding her, saying little, looking confident, proud. Luc, meanwhile, had that haunted look. But the set of his jaw was firm, determined, and the bright blue of his gaze penetrated her defences, reaching her; knowing how to get deep inside her when she'd spent a lifetime building walls to keep people out.

'Angeline?' a man said and she jumped. 'Pardon,' said the unshaven, slightly dishevelled man before her, who she guessed was in his mid-thirties but looked older for his weariness. Nevertheless, he smiled openly and his voice was kind. 'I did not mean to startle you.'

'Hello, Armand. I'm sorry to call in like this.' She stood from the small bench where she'd been sitting against a sun-warmed wall and entered the cooler shadows of the courtyard.

'You are always welcome. It's been a long time.'

'It has. You didn't have tomatoes growing in those tubs last time . . . or parsley. How lovely it smells.'

'You look well. You are safe, I hope?'

'I am. I don't have to take as many risks as some others,' Lisette said.

'I won't pry. What brings you here?'

The assistant arrived with two mugs of chicory coffee, then left quietly.

Lisette blew on the steaming liquid. 'I'm looking for Faucille.'

'Ah. He is not here. I mean, not in Paris. To my knowledge he left the city last month. We haven't heard anything of him since.'

'Last month,' she repeated, her spirits plummeting. 'How long has he been gone?'

'I'm sorry, but I don't know. Manon saw him briefly in mid-May, and he told her then that he was leaving Paris the next day.'

'For where? Please, I have to know.'

'Angeline, you know how it is. We protect each other by giving out as little information as possible.'

'Armand, you know he's been watching over me, surely?'

He looked down and nodded. 'I'd heard.'

'He and I, we're . . .'

'What?'

Lisette wasn't sure what to say. It was a good question – what were she and Luc to each other? 'We're together,' she breathed, not knowing how else to describe their relationship, given her last few weeks.

He looked sad for her, and blew his cheeks out. 'Manon hinted that he was probably heading south.'

'What?' She hadn't expected that.

He put up a hand defensively. 'I can't say that's the truth. Nothing's certain.'

She put down her coffee untouched. 'Back to Provence?' Lisette couldn't imagine Luc would risk it, but maybe he would.

Armand shook his head. 'Central France, I suspect. That's where a lot of the action has been occurring. We're supporting the *réseaux* where we believe a lot of the German reinforcements can be delayed. I won't lie to you, Angeline. There's going to be some fierce fighting down there and a lot of the French resisters feel drawn to help.'

Lisette hadn't registered much of what he'd said. She was thinking about Luc, flinging himself into battle.

Armand touched her shoulder sympathetically. 'You'll hear from him soon.'

She gave a low sigh. 'Yes, I'm sorry. I just didn't get a chance to say goodbye.'

'On the occasions I did meet Faucille, I found him calm, utterly fearless – certainly dangerous – but far from reckless. His decisions are solid, and he takes precaution for others. You know that yourself, I'm sure. Faucille was determined to protect you.'

Lisette knew this, but to hear it from another person, to fully grasp the dedication Luc had shown her, caused her deep pain. Especially when she remembered how she'd turned on him, thrown his help back in his face, accused him of first abandoning her and then spying on her.

Looking at her behaviour now made her realise how self-absorbed she'd become.

'I'm sorry. It wasn't my intention to upset you,' Armand added. 'I thought you would want to hear this.'

She dug her fingernails into her palm to ensure her misting eyes did not betray her any further. 'No, no, I'm fine. And thank you. I did need to know this.'

'Angeline, Playboy did make me aware of the recent instructions that came through for you from London. It's my job to know. It's obvious your mission still has a high priority. Is there anything we can do to help?'

She shook her head. 'Stop the war?' she offered.

'We're doing our best,' he said, and they both smiled as the tension broke. 'You need to stay close to the radio every day. And while I don't know how long this house will stay safe, your dead-letter drop is untarnished. The café owner has also headed south to fight but he's left a sympathetic cousin in charge – you can feel safe there, and we know to contact you there.'

'Armand, my, er . . . role may go quiet for a while. Perhaps indefinitely.'

'I see.' He frowned.

'How can I help? Let me do my bit.'

He considered her offer. 'Well, all of us are involved in disrupting communications. We've got about fifty *réseaux* now covering every department of France. Paris is not so important. It's in places like Gascony and Auverge where the hard work will be done. How are you with battery acid?'

'What?'

He smiled. 'One of our best methods of sabotage for burning out cables.'

'Just tell me what to do,' she said.

'Visit the café daily. You'll receive a message. But Angeline, we have to be careful with you.'

'I understand. But even if you use me as a lookout, let me help.'

'All right. There may be something shortly.'

'I hear the telephone exchanges have been hit,' she said, remembering gossip she'd overheard. 'Sylvie?'

He grinned and stood, stretching in the thin sunlight. 'She single-handedly destroyed one exchange north of Paris that forced the Germans to switch to radio. It means Bletchley Park can listen in on their communications.'

'Is she all right?'

'I have no reason to believe otherwise.'

Lisette stood and kissed both of his cheeks. 'Thank you, Armand – not just for today but for . . . well, you know, being my rearguard. I didn't mean to take up so many precious hours of other people's time.'

'You've got Faucille to thank for that. I hope he comes back to you safely.'

'So do I,' she said, suddenly frantic to see Luc again. 'So do I.'

33

Luc had left Paris in the early hours of the morning after reading Sylvie's note. He didn't want to think it was her taunt that sent him hurtling from the city, but whatever it was, it was for the best. He had to get away from reminders of Lisette. By leaving the colonel's driving crew, he knew he was blowing any chance of getting close to Kilian again, but it was only a matter of time before the Gestapo closed in. It was better to get out of Paris, and he could be more help if he headed south, where the main activity was gathering pace.

The call to action was to stymie German progress at all costs. With the name Ravensburg openly circulating within the Gestapo, Luc opted to use Christian Loewe as his cover, especially as it permitted him to carry official German papers as a driver attached to the Paris-based military. Using the pretence that he was being sent south to drive back some high-ranking militia, he managed to get out of Paris on a gazogene bus for ten francs. Mont Mouchet was his target. This was one of the key regions to hamper the German advance from the south, and given that it was mountainous territory, it suited Luc well.

Overland, sleeping rough, mostly stealing food, sometimes lucky enough to be given a meal by a friendly farmer, Luc made his way first to Montluçon, but it was crawling with Gestapo. Buying a stick of bread and a small wedge of cheese, he felt out the owner of the grocery and took a risk. Luc wanted to know where it was safe for a maquisard to find the local Maquis, and there was no alternative. To his relief, the man with the long face and hangdog expression was Gaullist.

'Go to the viaduct at Garabit,' the grocer advised. 'If they want you, they'll find you.'

He did as he was told, surprised to find the local townsfolk on a twenty-four hour watch to prevent the Mont Mouchet Maquis, based nearby, from blowing up the only remaining road to Paris.

'They've already destroyed the stone bridges around the railways,' a local complained.

Luc had wondered at the people's stupidity. Did they really want the Germans having this easy access to Paris? He'd waited several hours before a man sidled up to him and nodded. Luc followed him, disappearing into the surrounding forest. There he had stayed for weeks, joining more than ten thousand Maquis in the region. German forces surrounded them but the Maquis leader kept his men calm, determined and useful, even without artillery. Missives were sent to London demanding weapons for this perfectly placed group of guerillas and they couldn't have come quicker.

On 18 June, set upon by a force of well-armed Germans, backed up by heavy artillery, the Maquis, making the best of the weaponry it had, went into battle at Mont Mouchet. The fighting began in the early morning and raged until darkness engulfed them.

Luc had little experience with guns. His skills with explosives had improved rapidly with his various sabotage jobs in Paris, but his exposure to real fighting was minimal. The reality of the assault was shocking; the noise alone disoriented him. Rather than shooting at the enemy, he quickly established himself as a messenger between groups of fighters. He was fleet but especially surefooted in the terrain. And Luc had a natural skill for understanding the lie of the land. He'd already got to know his way reasonably well around the region, and his excellent eyesight and speed meant he was able to keep up the lines of communication between the pockets of maquisards, as well as rescuing the fallen.

At one point during that terrible day, he had a man across his back and was dragging another by the arm up through the scrub, his gaze fixed firmly on a ridge, when he felt a bullet hit the man on his back. Using all his strength, he threw both men into a ditch behind a hillock; he nearly wept when he could find no pulse on the young maquisard he'd hauled up on his shoulders. The dead man was no older than nineteen.

'Don't take it too hard,' the second man said, seeing Luc's despair. He shrugged. 'We'd all rather die like this than working for the Boches in some stinking factory in Germany.'

Luc nodded at the grimy, weathered face of the injured man. 'Where are you hit?'

'Thigh, just above my knee. Not too bad. Here, take this,' he said, pulling a bandana from around his neck. 'Tie it round. Hard as you can.'

Luc did as the man asked, watching his companion suck in his breath as Luc pulled on the knot. 'All right?'

'I'll live to kill a few more if you hand me that boy's gun.'

An explosion rocked the earth below them.

Luc passed him the gun from the pocket of the dead man. 'My name's Luc. I used to grow lavender,' he said.

'Claude. I grew grapes and olives. Best vinegar, best oil in the south.' He grinned and the dried blood cracked on his face. Luc wasn't sure if it was Claude's blood or someone else's. It didn't matter. 'Thanks for the gun,' Claude said, adding, 'and if you can find some Pernod somewhere, I'll have that too.'

Luc laughed grimly. His attention was caught by another maquisard in trouble. Smoke was clearing and he could see more blood-soaked bodies sprawled on the hillside to his left. He counted three who looked to be dead but one was moving.

'Someone needs me, Claude.'

'Good lad. I won't forget you. Off you go.'

Luc leapt over the top of the ridge and began zigzagging his way across to the fallen. He could hear the injured man screaming now, and could see that he'd lost half of his leg. As twilight began to descend Luc could sense that the Maquis were fighting a losing battle.

He reached the man, who was no longer screaming; he wept quietly instead. He had lost too much blood – Luc knew he would not make it. He didn't know what he could do except lay down beside him and hold his hand. The man began to babble. He was from Limoges and was a worker in the ceramics industry. He had four children, a wife.

'Tell them I'm sorry,' he whispered close to Luc's ear. 'My name is Olivier Roussel.' He was younger than Luc had thought at first, probably barely thirty. His breathing was shallow and rapid. Luc pulled out a grubby handkerchief and wiped the man's face of blood. He looked like Laurent, with the same glint in his eyes, even though they were beginning to dull.

'Thank you,' he whispered. His politeness was achingly sad.

Luc ignored the whistle of bullets, the explosions of earth around him and the yells of dying men. He felt obliged to remain here until the man died.

Finally, Luc unwrapped his fingers from the dead man's hand and a deep sorrow permeated his soul. This battle felt hopeless, especially with aircraft strafing the region.

The French could not win – he knew that now – but for every hour they held the Boches pinned down here, it was another hour for their compatriots up north . . . another hour in which the Allies could fight their way closer to Paris. That was why they had to battle on here, but Luc was exposed. He needed to seek cover, get back to the main group and see if any messages had to be run through. He couldn't think about fatigue; none of them could.

Luc picked himself up, grabbed a sten gun lying nearby and ran through thick smoke. He had no idea what was coming at him; all he could do was head towards the higher ridges where he knew one of the main pockets of the Maquis were positioned.

He never made it.

The explosion erupted so close to him that it threw him up into the air. It felt like an eternity before he was flung back down to the ground, and in that space of time, where the sounds around him seemed to become muted, all activity halted. Smoke billowed and yet was still, men yelled but their faces were caught as though frozen. He could even see the flash of the guns – the flare in suspended animation – while he moved sluggishly, unsure of where he was in space, his mind blurry, his body numbed. Only one thought was clear – *Lisette*. Her name was a mantra in his mind, repeating. He was incapable of hearing anything else or forming any words or thoughts.

He mustn't die here. He had to get back to her.

Luc crumpled back onto the hard earth and lay lifeless as night finally closed in and the Maquis leader called his men into retreat.

Luc regained consciousness to the sounds of a donkey braying and chickens clucking. He was hot, parched and bright sunlight was bursting through the wooden slats of the walls around him. There was something soft behind his head but the ground was hard beneath him. He was lying in a shed, he decided.

He blinked, disoriented.

Someone grabbed his hand and when he turned he was confronted by a child. The lad's round, wide-eyed face was stained with smudges of grime, and the boy was peering solemnly at him through dark-blue eyes. Luc could focus properly now and noticed that the youngster's face was lightly freckled and he was missing his front teeth.

'You're alive, *monsieur*,' the child confirmed with a soft lisp.

Luc tried to talk but his mouth was parched. 'Water,' he croaked and the boy rushed away. When he returned he had an old woman with him. Her hair was grey and wrapped neatly in a bun, her clothes old but clean. She reminded him instantly – and sorrowfully – of his murdered grandmother.

The elderly woman urged her little companion to help Luc to lift his head.

'Drink, *monsieur*.' She gestured at the mug.

Luc gulped at the water. Nothing had ever tasted sweeter.

'Where am I?' he wheezed. 'I thought I was doomed.'

She chuckled in response. 'You are close to Pontajou. This is a farmlet, very isolated. It's about five kilometres from the fighting.'

'How did I get here?'

'Maquis brought you. A man called Claude was with them. As I understand it, they were leaving you for dead. But he put you on his back and dragged you to safety.'

'Claude,' Luc whispered. 'He was injured.'

'The bullet went through cleanly,' the woman assured him. 'He'll limp but he'll see it as a badge of honour. The Maquis held up the soldiers all day, most of the evening. There was another battle. Maquis lost that too but they did what was needed. Delayed the filthy Boches.' She turned slightly and spat.

'Where are they now?'

'Taking their reprisals over in Clavières and surrounding villages, we hear.' She said it wearily, with no malice.

Luc closed his eyes. 'I'm sorry.'

'You're safe here. We're on no map, and this barn can't be seen from the nearest track. We'll have good warning. You can run into the woods if need be.'

'Did they leave others?'

'You are all I could manage – with Robert's help,' she said, squeezing the boy's hand. 'But how are you feeling?'

He was so sore he couldn't tell immediately. He slowly tested his limbs and finally shook his head. 'My head hurts, my ears are ringing. To be honest, *madame*, every inch of me aches.'

'I imagine it would. But the angels were surely protecting you in such a battle. Claude said you were flung by an explosion.'

'Yes, I remember it now.' He instinctively reached to touch the lavender pouch beneath his shirt. 'Is Claude nearby?'

She shook her head. 'He couldn't risk it.'

'How long have I been here?'

'Four days.'

He was surprised. 'I won't stay long, *madame*. You have Robert to worry about.' He looked at the young boy.

She smiled. 'What is your name, son?'

'Luc Bonet.'

'Well, Luc, you must rest. Robert will stay close. He knows to watch you, and he far prefers that to his chores.'

Luc thought he smiled, but his world went dark again quickly.

It was mid-July before Luc left the farmlet. At his hosts' insistence he'd moved into the main house, a stone cottage that was bigger than it appeared, angling down the sloping land.

Marie, the old woman, had become a widow six months earlier. One of her sons had also died, fighting with the Maquis, and her second son – Robert's father – was doing his STO in Germany while his mother was working in Vichy. Robert did not see his mother for six weeks at a time but her sister dropped in on the boy and his grandmother once a month.

'Best you leave before Juliette pays her visit on Sunday,' Marie warned as she, Luc and Robert sat outside one day, Luc shaving himself with a small mirror and portable basin. 'She's not good at secrets.' Luc glanced at Robert, who was chatting to the donkey. Marie caught the glance. 'You have nothing to fear there,' she reassured him. 'He is far more reliable than his aunt. Plus she's looking for a husband, and you'd do nicely. You'll never get away to that girl of yours called Lisette.'

Luc stared, astonished, at Marie.

Robert laughed at his expression. 'You talk in your dreams, Monsieur Luc.'

Luc grinned. Robert had insisted on helping to lather up Luc's face with soap and now watched with great interest as Luc scraped the old blade across his raspy chin.

'He hasn't seen a man shave in far too long,' Marie said. 'He needs his father.'

Luc reached out for her hand. The skin was like leather on her palm, but it was parchment-thin on the back where her knuckles, misshapen and arthritic, gave her hands a gnarled look. He held that knotted hand to his damp face. 'He'll be home soon, Marie. Your family will be reunited and this wretched war will be done with. Just stay safe, and keep Robert safe a bit longer.'

She regarded his image in the mirror. 'Lisette must be missing you by now.'

He looked down at her hand and covered it with his own. 'I don't know.'

'Well, go and find out.' She gave a low chuckle. 'Women need wooing, Luc . . . even in wartime.'

He sighed, looked up at the stone cottage with its dark tiles and symmetrical windows, their flaking paintwork and the broken hinge on the wooden door. Marie was right. It was time to go. He would miss this little haven; it had kept him safe, given him time to heal . . . and not just physically.

'I regret having to leave.'

'I know. But you will come back one day. I'm sure of it.'

Luc nodded. 'Will Robert understand?'

'You and the boy have become close. But children are resilient. Don't worry on his account.'

Robert had finished chatting with the donkey he called Bernard, and now came skipping back to Luc, who stood bare-chested, towelling off the final dregs of soap on his face. Earlier, Robert had proudly given him one of his father's shirts to wear, and Marie had polished Luc's shoes and dusted his trousers, cleaning them up as best she could.

Now, Robert took the towel from Luc and then pointed to his father's shirt, hung on an apple tree nearby. 'Papa won't mind.'

Luc glanced at the grandmother again, with gratitude in his eyes. 'Marie, I will repay your kindness one day.'

The old woman made a hushing sound. 'We all do our bit. Robert's been wondering about that pouch around your neck. I must admit, I have too, but I told him not to pry. Is that from Lisette?'

He shook his head. 'My grandmother gave this to me. She believed that lavender possesses magic.' Robert's eyes widened as Luc spoke. 'She said I was to wear the pouch of seeds always, and it would protect me.'

The woman grinned. 'Grandmothers know best.'

'*Oui, madame.* I would never argue with that.' Luc walked to the tree and took the shirt, grimacing at the pain in his shoulders as he put it on. After recovering consciousness he'd discovered an egg-sized lump on his head, and his back was badly bruised even after weeks of healing. He knew how lucky he was not to have broken any bones. His head had only just stopped throbbing constantly, and sunlight no longer made him wince in pain.

He did up the buttons slowly, feeling the tension in the air twist at his heartstrings. Robert would not be happy at him leaving, and despite her smiles and wise words, he knew Marie would likely miss his presence and companionship too.

'I wish you would not go, Monsieur Luc,' Robert said sadly. He glanced at his grandmother, an apologetic look on his face.

Luc swallowed. He crouched down to be eye level with Robert. 'I promise that I will come back one day. I have an idea – do you have a sewing needle?'

'What for?' Marie asked.

'You'll see.'

Marie's face formed a question. 'Wait – I will fetch one.' She was back soon, and handed a needle to Luc.

'Watch,' said Luc. He dug the needle into his own thumb and squeezed the flesh until a bead of blood bloomed dark and shiny. 'Do you think you can do the same?'

Robert blinked at him, uncertain at first, and then took the needle and bravely nodded.

'It's called a blood oath. One we can never break.'

That won the boy's attention and courage. Without hesitation he took a breath and plunged the tip of the needle into his thumb, giving a soft gasp.

'You're very brave, Robert,' Luc soothed. 'Now squeeze it as you saw me do.'

Robert obeyed and soon had a matching bead of blood. He looked up at Luc. 'What now?'

'Now we place our thumbs together like this,' Luc said, winking at Marie as he brought his large hand next to Robert's small one. 'That's it. Our bloods must mix.'

Robert was entranced. 'Why?'

'Because you and I are blood brothers. That bond can't ever be broken.'

The boy pulled his thumb away slightly so he could peer at their blood, smeared against his thumb. His eyes widened even more. 'Monsieur Luc, our bloods are one.'

Luc nodded. 'I, Lukas Ravensburg, also known as Luc Bonet,

do solemnly promise to return to this place as soon as I possibly can.'

Marie touched his shoulder gently. 'Luc, you can never love a woman too much. Don't delay. Go to her. Marry her. Then bring her to visit.'

Luc offered them both final hugs and with food in a small sack, he set off looking surprisingly well presented. As he turned for a final wave, he realised his life had been nothing but farewells these past few years. But here he would return, he promised himself, as the teary six-year-old blew him a kiss and yelled, 'Don't forget me, Monsieur Luc! Don't forget your promise.'

34

17 July 1944

Kilian read Lisette's note again. It hurt to read it because it hurt to be without her. He'd read it several times now, frowning as he tried to imagine what she had to say to him that was so immediate despite his warning.

> *My darling Markus,*
> *I won't waste words. I love you and miss you desperately. And I need to see you. Just once, if that's all we can have. But it is vital I see you. I have something important to say about our parting conversation . . . I have something to offer you.*
> *Please see me. Anywhere, any time.*
> *Yours, Lisette x*

The last time he'd seen Lisette was just before the Allied landings at Normandy weeks ago. All the radio talk had suggested the port of Calais would be the target, but the Allies had pulled off an inspired trick.

The Supreme Commander of German Forces for the Western Front had been replaced: a sure sign of panic. Cherbourg had fallen, de Gaulle had set up a provisional government and General Doll-mann had died of a heart attack after the defeat at Cherbourg, although rumours were buzzing that he had committed suicide. It was reported that Rommel had been seriously wounded in

Normandy. Kilian shook his head. Germany's hold over France, its last bastion of power, was unravelling.

All of the bad news only made him feel more committed to his private cause. He wished the conspirators had achieved their aims earlier – they might have been able to wrest back an iota of dignity for Germany. But if nothing was attempted soon, the Allies would beat them to it and destroy Hitler. Then there would be no terms, no negotiation of a truce. As it was, he already felt it was too late. Attempts by the German resistance had failed so many times he didn't hold out much hope for this one, which felt like a last-ditch effort by desperate men, an honour-salvaging final gasp to topple the leader. Hitler meanwhile continued to spit out angry, nonsensical orders that depressed his generals and crippled his armies.

But Kilian knew his instinct to keep Lisette at arm's length was right. The Gestapo would just love 'interviewing' her. He'd heard one of their favourite ways of extracting information was by neardrowning suspects in a bathtub.

Lisette's letter was affectionate, but it wasn't a love letter – that was obvious. She was clearly being cautious. What could she have to say to him? Their last conversation had been strained. He shuddered to remember his allusions to the conspiracy, and that she might be involved.

All would be solved if he could speak to Stülpnagel, but the commander had been away and uncontactable. Kilian cursed his his lack of information once again.

As if the gods had been listening, his phone rang.

He snatched at it. 'Kilian.'

'Colonel Kilian.' It was the latest temporary secretary they'd sent him. 'I have a Lieutenant Colonel von Hofacker waiting to see you. Can I send him in? He said he just needs a few moments.'

His pulse quickened. 'Yes, bring him up, please.'

'Very good, sir.'

The line went dead and he stared at the receiver. This was it! Stülpnagel had said von Hofacker was the only other person he could trust. This was surely news that the assassination was about to take place. He steadied his breathing, put Lisette's letter in his desk drawer and smoothed his uniform.

There was a peremptory knock at the door and it opened. 'Lieutenant Colonel von Hofacker, sir,' his middle-aged secretary said, and showed in the man behind her.

'Ah, von Hofacker. You've brought those details I needed, I hope?'

'Colonel Kilian,' von Hofacker replied and saluted. 'Yes, sir. I have them here.'

'Come in, come in. Can I offer you something?'

'No, thank you, sir,' he said and they both smiled at the woman as she left.

When the door closed, Kilian breathed out silently. 'What news?' he murmured.

Von Hofacker grimaced. 'Two aborted attempts this month.'

He stared at the man, momentarily speechless. It was so quiet in the room Kilian was sure von Hofacker could hear his blood pounding. 'Why wasn't I told?'

'Things are happening so fast and so secretly, even we don't know.' Von Hofacker raised his hands in mock defence as Kilian's chair scraped back and the colonel stood angrily. 'I know, sir,' he continued, just above a whisper. 'I know this is not ideal and that you need warning.' He shrugged. 'We are equally frustrated.'

'Tell me what occurred.'

'The first attempt was earlier this month.'

Kilian's expression drooped. 'And?'

'The man involved deemed it unsuitable. It's easy to become frustrated, but neither of us is pulling the trigger. The moment has to be right.' Von Hofacker had cleared his throat and proceeded.

'There was another attempt.'

'When?' Kilian's voice rose and then lowered as von Hofacker glanced around nervously. 'Tell me,' he urged quietly.

'The plan was to kill Himmler as well, the rationale being that he might prove a bigger problem than the one we already have. Himmler did not attend the gathering as expected and so the plot was once again aborted at the final moment.'

'The man has more lives than a cat!'

'You may be right there, Colonel. You may as well know that a third attempt was planned today, but was once again abandoned when the Führer was called out of the meeting room suddenly. I have only just heard about it myself.'

Kilian had clenched his jaw with frustration. 'So what now?'

'More patience. We try once more,' von Hofacker replied.

'Will we have some forewarning this time?'

The man shrugged. 'The next attempt is in three days. The man involved is resolute. He will not fail.'

Kilian turned quickly towards the windows. He didn't know whether to be elated or terrified. Both, probably.

'Colonel?'

'I'm still coming to terms with the notion that I am committing treason,' he growled in a low voice.

The man joined him by the window. 'Sir, you are protected. You know we have deliberately kept you at a distance, for good reason. Once we know that it has been done, the general will order the capture and imprisonment of all SS and Gestapo in Paris immediately.'

'Do you need my help with that?' Kilian asked.

They were whispering even though they stood side by side.

'No, sir. You will act after that, and only when we're sure it's appropriate to do so. I will contact you.'

'And if I don't hear from you?'

'Do nothing. Preserve your cover.'

Kilian shook his head. 'Why can't we do it all at once, gather up Himmler's mob, mobilise the Army?'

'Layers of protection, sir. Please trust the plan.'

'All right, von Hofacker. Thank you.'

The lieutenant colonel nodded and opened his briefcase. 'The general asked me to give you this, sir.'

'What is it?'

'Cover – it's all contrived paperwork about church needs, security and so on.'

'Ah, good.' Kilian took it without interest and flung it down on his desk.

Von Hofacker paused meaningfully. 'He suggests you cast an eye over it, sir. It, er, well, it makes for some interesting reading.'

Kilian looked at him, puzzled, but the man turned away.

'Thank you again for seeing me at such short notice, Colonel,' he said in a measured tone.

'Good luck, von Hofacker.'

'Yes, sir. And to you.' He paused at the door. '*Heil Hitler*,' he said, and gave a mirthless smile.

Kilian mumbled the same in response, refusing to utter the words unless they couldn't be avoided.

Von Hofacker left, and Kilian knew no work would be done today, or for the next three days; not until the deed was done and Germany was free of Adolf Hitler.

He looked at the file on his desk that von Hofacker had delivered and gave an angry sigh. He flung open the side drawer and threw it in – he would look at it later, but first he wanted to sort out this business with Lisette.

He glimpsed at her note again. If this all went wrong, he might be arrested, executed. Could he go to his death without holding her in his arms once more?

He picked up the phone and buzzed his secretary.

'Yes, Colonel?'

'Can you connect me through to a Mademoiselle Forestier, please?'

'Of course, sir. May I have the details?'

He gave the bank's name. 'And make a reservation at that restaurant down by the water. The open-air one.'

'Oh, yes. I know the one, sir.'

He was impressed. She was working out quite well, this one. 'One p.m. today.'

'Very good, sir. Just hold while I connect you.'

He waited in the silence that followed. It took only moments. 'Colonel Kilian? I have Mademoiselle Forestier on the line.'

'Thank you.' He heard the click of his secretary's phone disconnecting. 'Lisette?'

'Colonel Kilian.'

His throat tightened at the sound of her voice.

'It's nice to hear from you,' she said carefully. Good girl. She wasn't gushing in case the secretaries liked to eavesdrop.

'Likewise. I wondered if you'd care to have lunch with me today?'

'I'd be delighted.'

He could hear in her voice relief and pleasure. He smiled, and gave her the name of the restaurant. 'Would one o'clock be all right?'

'Of course. I'll see you there.'

'We have much to catch up on.'

————————

As usual, Kilian was early. When Lisette arrived she looked radiant, far too pretty, and he was sure his heart faltered when he first glimpsed her dark hair. It had grown. She wore it in a ponytail, accentuating her youth. He imagined her untying it and those raven waves hitting her naked shoulders . . .

The maitre d' showed her to his table as Kilian stood, beaming helplessly.

'You look divine in that dress.' It was a pale floral one he'd bought her while they'd been travelling, which showed off her slender arms and figure. It was cut low enough that he was prompted all too painfully to remember what she looked like without the encumbrance of the soft cotton dress. He cleared his throat. 'It's my favourite.'

She didn't say anything at first, just gazed at him with a wide smile. Then she kissed him softly on the lips in her uninhibited way and whispered, 'It's so good to see you, Markus.'

He felt a fresh thrill of desire and quickly glanced at the head waiter who had approached. 'Please give us a moment,' he said, turning eagerly back to Lisette. 'How have you been? Although I needn't ask – you thrive on loneliness, obviously. Or maybe I shouldn't be so presumptuous. Perhaps you haven't been so lonely?' He cursed himself inwardly – now he sounded jealous.

She regarded him with a pensive smile. 'I've missed you every minute of each of the thirty-six days we've been apart.'

'You kept count,' he observed in a soft voice.

'I always keep count,' she said. 'You should know that.'

He looked down. 'Thank you for your note.'

'I'm glad it prompted this.'

'No. That's not the only reason I wanted to see you.'

'Good. For someone who claims to love me, you have a strange way of showing it.'

'Don't do that, Lisette,' he said, wounded.

'What, complain?' Her gaze narrowed. 'How hard do you think this separation has been for me, Markus?'

'As hard, I imagine, as it has been for me,' he answered.

'It's mysterious and uncomfortable.'

'You know I would not ask this of you without good reason.'

Her deep-blue eyes flashed anger at him. 'Then give me that good reason. I deserve it.'

A waiter was back, handing out menus. Kilian tried to look interested in the selection. 'The *sole meunière* here is unrivalled.'

She gave a wan smile to the waiter. 'I'll have the sole and some steamed potatoes, thank you.'

He looked at Kilian.

'Perfect,' he said. 'For two.'

'Wine, sir?'

Kilian shook his head. 'Water is fine. Lisette?'

She nodded and the man left.

'I didn't come to argue with you,' Kilian began.

'Neither did I. It was the furthest thing from my mind. In fact, I've been feeling like an excited schoolgirl since you called.'

He broke into a grin. 'Ah, there you are. I knew you were in there somewhere, behind that anger.'

She gave him a stern gaze before shaking her head and making a point of casting a glance around her surroundings, as they sat in the open-air restaurant in the height of the Parisian summer.

'What?' He frowned.

'This,' she said. 'What are we doing here? The war is coming to us. Paris is the jewel for the Allies. And yet here we sit and calmly order *sole meunière*, while the locals,' she murmured, pointing out towards the bank of the Seine, 'have never been more famished, more without, more despairing . . . and yet so excited that change is coming.'

His expression straightened and he became serious. 'And how about you? How do you feel?'

'What do you mean?'

'Are you happy about the landings?'

She looked taken aback. 'If I'm truthful, yes.'

'I see.'

They paused while their glasses were filled from a silver jug of chilled water.

'Don't we all want change, Markus?' she continued once the waiter had disappeared again.

He sighed. 'Yes. I wouldn't be honest if I didn't agree.'

She picked up her glass. 'To change, then . . . for the better.'

He clinked his glass with hers. 'I will certainly drink to that.' He smiled. 'No more angry words. You are even more beautiful than in my dreams. Summer suits you. Are you busy at the bank?'

'Not really. There's so much uncertainty now. I feel like we're all just shuffling papers around our desks. Did you ever mention me to General Stülpnagel?'

His eyes clouded. She wasn't going to leave it alone. 'Actually, he mentioned you to me,' he said.

She paused and looked puzzled. 'How come?'

'Word had got around of our trip.'

'Were you embarrassed by it?'

'Not at all. It was my idea.'

'Did he reprimand you?'

'I don't answer to Stülpnagel.'

'But you do respect him.'

'Yes, of course. I admire him. He is one of the old guard.'

'And you're caught between two worlds, is that right?'

Their meals arrived and were quietly set down.

'I suppose that's true,' Kilian answered, unfolding his napkin. 'Eat up. By the sounds of things, this may have to last you for a week.'

'And you shouldn't eat for another twenty-four hours.'

'Nor will I,' he said, smiling.

'You look thin, Markus. Are you eating at all?'

'Not much. And it has nothing to do with my routine. I have missed you, Lisette, but I am also a cog in the wheel of the German administration, and even though I do loathe it, I have my responsibilities.'

She cut into her fish. 'Even as you tell me this, I discount it for being dishonest. Mmm, this looks delicious.'

He put his cutlery down in surprise. 'Why do you say such a thing?'

Lisette swallowed, dabbed her mouth with the napkin and fixed him with a penetrating gaze. 'Young, not stupid, remember? You're lying to me.' She returned to her food.

It was Kilian's turn to stare. He watched her eat, wondering what to say next.

'Eat up. It really is delightful,' she said.

'Lisette.' She ignored him. 'Lisette! Explain yourself.'

'Markus,' she began in a hushed tone. 'Whatever you're up to, I know you're worried. Would you like to know what I think . . . really?'

He nodded, almost scared of what was coming.

'I think you're hatching something very dangerous with high-placed people. It's so secret that even I represent a threat. Knowing you, I can only think of one thing.' She shrugged. 'I'm guessing that you're up to something that undermines the Nazi hierarchy.' She was muttering in the lowest of voices but still Kilian looked around.

The waiter sidled up and startled him. 'Is everything all right with your meal, Colonel?'

When Kilian hesitated, Lisette said, 'It's delicious. Thank you,' and asked how the rich sauce was achieved.

When the waiter had left Kilian stared at her while she finished the last morsel on her plate.

'Who are you, Lisette?' he asked softly, stunned by her astuteness.

She looked at him, a baffled expression on her face. 'You know me inside and out. That's the problem. I'm trying to help you. But you just push me away.'

She reached for his hand but he pulled it back, placing his fork and knife together on his plate. His appetite had fled.

'Markus, listen to me. If I'm right, and you are part of something that is trying to bring about the very change that we raised our glasses to, then let me help.'

His gaze narrowed. She seemed to take his silence as his permission to continue.

'I can move with far more freedom than you. If I can prevent you from exposing yourself or making yourself vulnerable, then I want to. I can be a messenger for you.' Her voice dropped to a barely audible whisper. 'I can even be an interface to the Allies, if you need.'

He sat back, wiped his mouth. 'We're leaving.'

She looked surprised.

'Get your things.'

'But your food, your —'

'I said we're leaving.' He stood, found the maitre d' and explained that an urgent matter had arisen. He apologised and paid the bill, leaving a large tip. With his mind in tumult, he grabbed Lisette's arm and propelled her forward along the Seine.

'Markus, you're being rough.'

'Am I? Walk faster.'

They hurried in silence, him pushing her through the sunlit streets back to the Hotel Raphaël, not exchanging a word with her until he'd slammed the door in his hotel room.

He noticed she didn't look scared, and couldn't help but be impressed. But he was also angry, mortified and unnerved all at once. This was so much bigger than him. He could not care less about his own life but there were too many others involved in this conspiracy – and he'd be damned if his lover was going to bring the whole thing down.

'You look as if you could kill me,' she said, surprising him with her calm.

'That was very dangerous talk, Lisette. I'd like to know how you formed such an opinion of me.'

'All right. Your sudden secrecy while we were away, your touchiness at my mention of General Stülpnagel – even though you spoke to him regularly – your deliberate distancing from me, your weight loss, and now this behaviour. I've obviously touched a nerve.'

She was so poised he was curious. 'Do you not think such an accusation would touch a raw nerve in anyone in a public place like that?'

'Yes, but you're not offended by my suggestion – as most would be – you're mystified, and definitely angry.'

'You're very observant, Lisette. Very cool.'

'Well, then, those attributes should be put to good use, don't you think? I can move without the scrutiny that you are subjected to daily. Tell me how to help, Markus.'

'Why?'

'So I can keep you safe.'

'Safe from an execution squad?'

She blinked in consternation. 'I can keep the Gestapo from knowing of your involvement.'

'I doubt it. The Gestapo already has you under surveillance, from what I hear.' Had he been duped? It was time to rattle her composure.

It worked. Her shock was evident, ghosting across her face. She quickly adopted a neutral expression, but he'd seen it. He'd even noticed her clench a fist momentarily.

'So, I see Herr von Schleigel has been stirring up trouble for me.'

'Yes. He paid me a friendly visit.'

'Why didn't you say something?'

'Why would I? I had no reason to mistrust you. Was I misguided?'

She shook her head. 'Anything I now say just sounds incriminating.'

'Not really. The truth usually is the best course.'

'I haven't lied. I told you myself about von Schleigel.'

'Yes, you did. Did you tell me the truth about your time in Provence, though?'

'What do you think I might have to hide?' she asked, looking at him, aghast.

'This fellow called Ravensburg, perhaps.'

'I told you about him as well,' she replied reasonably.

He nodded, unbuttoned his uniform jacket. 'Yes, you did,' he repeated in a weary tone. 'Frankly, Lisette, that's all your business, which is why I've left it alone. But you don't follow the same protocol. You are poking your nose into my business.'

'I'm trying to help you.'

'You could get yourself killed!' he snapped.

'So could you. And then I'd rather be dead anyway,' she countered.

They were both breathing heavily now. 'It's too late,' Kilian said. 'There's nothing you can do.'

'Markus, just tell me. Tell me what you're doing.'

He shook his head. 'I want you to go.'

'No, Markus, please . . .' She reached for him.

He needed to be strong but he melted beneath her touch; it had been so long. He allowed her to kiss him and found himself responding. Before he knew it she was guiding him to the bed, unbuttoning his shirt, her sweet mouth all the while seeking his.

It took all his reserves of willpower to extricate himself from her embrace.

'I can't,' he said, frustration and weariness crowding into his voice.

'Why?'

'I won't endanger you. I really do need you to go now, Lisette.' He began to rebutton his shirt. She stood, looking confounded. 'And I won't be able to see you . . . not for a long time, not until . . .'

'Not until it's over?'

He nodded. 'And if you're a spy, then whatever you think I'm doing is playing right into the hands of the Allies. You could hardly complain. And if you're not a spy, then I know I'm keeping you safe. You have to trust me. You are stepping into an arena that I have no control over. You are best away from me right now, no matter which side you belong to.'

'Do you care?'

He shook his head. 'No. Because it doesn't matter any more. The war is as good as lost but some of us want to restore our honour in some small way; we'll find out shortly if we can. As for you, where you belong is irrelevant. If you've lied, I don't want to know about it. Because if I discovered that you'd been lying to me, I would hate myself for being weak enough to fall for your charms – and for what you promised in my life. Right now I can let you walk out of the door believing myself in love with you, and with the memory of our relationship intact. Whatever you are, Mademoiselle Forestier, leave me with my memories.'

He tucked his shirt back in and walked to the door, opening it before she could say any more. He steeled himself. He had to let her go. She reached for her bag and straightened her hair. Spy, friend, foe . . . he loved her more than Germany itself, and because of that he had to protect her from Germany.

'Am I never to see you again?' she asked in a small voice. Her composure had finally slipped; she looked heartbroken.

He took her hand, bent and kissed it, clicking his heels lightly, as he had the first time they'd met. 'Let's just say until next time. Farewell, Lisette.' He closed the door before she could turn and say any more.

Lisette left the Hotel Raphaël feeling lost. She walked, without direction, trying to make sense of what had just occurred. She had played her last card with Markus, driven by her mission and by her real desire to help him, to keep him safe. But it had failed. And all the time – stupidly – she kept thinking about the meal Markus had left at the restaurant; how many people might actually kill for such a meal? And would he remember to eat again this evening? He was looking so gaunt. Thoughts clashed in her head, and wouldn't let her return to the bank, to her flat, not even to the familiar streets of Montmartre. And so she walked aimlessly in the sunshine, clinging to her small bag and the overriding notion that she'd seen Markus Kilian for the last time.

Sorrow gripped her, fisting into her belly, making her feel nauseated. She didn't want to examine herself too closely. Underneath there was fear – not only that her mission might just have blown up in her face, but that Colonel Markus Kilian had just seen her for the impostor she was. Had she broken his heart? Had he broken hers?

They were over.

If only she could tell him that she'd never wanted to hurt him. How overworked that phrase sounded, and yet it expressed her genuine sentiments. How could she ever want to hurt him? She had compartmentalised her life so skilfully that she had discovered two Lisettes. One was pro-German but pro-peace, in love with a German colonel with an easy smile, a quick wit and a heroic approach to life. She had even daydreamed of a life for them in Germany, beyond the war. It was a life of privilege, where Lisette would rediscover her love of painting, perhaps plan a grand garden, entertain society people and mother a brood of golden-haired children with perfect manners. She told herself these daydreams were important in strengthening her cover; the problem was that Kilian had affected Lisette in ways she didn't want to admit to herself. She did fear for him, she did want to see him again . . . she did love him.

But then there was the other Lisette – the one whose heart was lost to a troubled, enigmatic lavender farmer, as damaged by loss as she was. It was his sorrows, his sentimental nature and his painful past as much as the truth of who he was that had first attracted her to him. He trusted her. And their shared adventure in the south had bound them in intangible ways. She didn't daydream about a life with Luc, or about having his children. She could barely bring herself to think about him because she was frightened that she'd already lost him to the war. He was probably fighting in the south, where men were dying by the hundreds every day. She felt sure it was her determination to put her mission first that had sent him south. It wasn't right that she felt this way – Luc made his own decisions, after all – but she felt the burden of guilt all the same.

She loved him. She'd been in love with him from the moment she'd first seen him, but hadn't realised until he kissed her . . . so tenderly, so full of grief, coupled with desire. Luc was exciting, dangerous even, while Kilian was measured, stoic. Both were courageous – and now they were fighting for the same side!

Choose! the voice she feared from the back of her mind warned again. *It will come to it.*

And she knew it was true.

Lisette looked up and found herself standing in front of the café on the rue Pergolèse. She must have walked in circles for more than an hour, for it really wasn't that far from where she'd left Kilian.

Inside, a woman was working behind the counter, a red tea towel over her shoulder. She was the owner's cousin.

'Café?' the woman asked in a bored tone.

'Thank you,' Lisette said. 'I'll just visit the bathroom.'

The woman nodded.

Inside the bathroom Lisette hurriedly wrote out a note on cigarette paper, explaining that her mission had been compromised – Gestapo was involved and she had to distance herself immediately. Within moments she was back at the counter, waiting for her coffee to be poured.

'Do you have a spare newspaper, please, *madame*?' she asked as she paid the woman.

'I'll check.' The woman walked to the end of the counter and reached beneath. 'It's yesterday's. Best I can do,' she said, looking away immediately.

'That's fine, thank you.' Lisette took her coffee to a table. There was only one other patron at the counter and he was far away with his back to her. She checked that there were no mirrors, nothing reflective around that he could be watching her in. Satisfied, she surreptitiously stuck the note into the newspaper and began her usual routine of flicking absently through the pages.

She was surprised to discover a note a few pages in for her. It was from Armand, and as he'd promised, he had a job for her. It seemed to jolt her out of her mist. Her fuzziness cleared as she sat and took stock of her situation; she couldn't stay in her flat any longer. In fact, she couldn't go home at all. If the Gestapo really had decided to put her under surveillance, then she'd be mad to tempt fate any more than she already had. She experienced a brief moment of regret for Kilian's birthday gown and her precious perfume, but she had to let those go. Thank goodness she had all her ID papers with her and her money. Her clothes, her small suitcase, were all that was left in the flat. She hoped the new tenant enjoyed her soap!

And her job – she could no longer work at the bank. Walter was already linked to her, and she couldn't drag him any deeper into suspicion. No, she would have to resign today, but she couldn't go back there; she would have to do it by letter or phone. She looked around. Was someone watching her now? Had her café been compromised as well? No, the woman would have found a way to let her know.

Lisette had lived in such a bubble of security since arriving in Paris that she'd never fully understood the anxiety of discovery. This is what it must feel like to be Playboy, she thought, who she'd learned often sent his messages to London from the woods, having ridden out miles on his bicycle, because he was rightly paranoid at being traced. This was how Sylvie lived, working in a place she would attempt to sabotage, and then moving quickly once her mission was complete, only to set up again and start on a new mission. This is how they all lived . . . Armand, Sylvie, Luc. Especially Luc, who had been forced to look over his shoulder constantly. Lisette felt suddenly humbled as she remembered that he had always looked over her shoulder too.

She'd had a lot of help, most of it without her knowing. Meanwhile she ate exquisite food, drank expensive liquor, dressed in fine clothes, wore Chanel No. 5 and even danced at a cabaret hall in Lyon one evening, arm in arm with Markus, as though she hadn't a care in the world.

Now she felt the panic; the pounding heart, the ragged breathing. But she trusted her training to kick in. Calm was her greatest friend. Think clearly, make sound decisions. Safety first and foremost. Yes, she had to move and make sure that she was not followed. She must go through the procedures she'd been taught. Look in shop windows for reflections, watch if there was anyone following her. Move erratically around streets – take big circles, backtrack . . .

There was no doubting that she'd uncovered a plot, but what and when, she couldn't say; all in all, she'd been useless, while other agents risked life and limb. She thought of Luc fighting, putting his life on the line for faceless strategists in London.

Oh, Luc, she thought to herself. *Stay safe. Don't give up on me.* And it was at this moment that she knew that she had chosen her path. She crumpled Armand's note and left immediately after handing back the newspaper.

Lisette knew what she had to do now, gratified at how the sharp threat of fear brought great clarity. Colonel Kilian had shown her the ultimate generosity when he showed her the door. He was offering her a way out of their relationship while keeping what they'd shared precious and intact. She would never be able to understand the swiftness and ferocity of their attraction, but Luc had been right – Kilian would put Germany before her but he was also protecting her. He'd stayed true to his cause. And now, while she still had the chance, she must stay true to hers. Her mission might be compromised but she could still play an active role for the Resistance. Redemption began tonight, sixteen kilometres from central Paris, with a small team of resisters and a railway line that needed disabling.

But first she had to get to the safe house.

35

Kilian sat in his office, as still as one of the sculptures in the Louvre. He'd met von Hofacker very early that morning in the park behind the Notre Dame Cathedral.

'Do we have a time?'

'I can't be specific. We think around midday, maybe early afternoon,' his subordinate had replied calmly.

Kilian was used to holding his nerve but he was also used to being in control of orders, making his own decisions; today he felt like a puppet with too many other people pulling the strings. 'Are my instructions the same?' He knew how often orders could be misinterpreted, and he wanted nothing left unchecked at his end.

'Yes, Colonel. Remain at your office and carry on as normal. If all goes as we expect, I will call you.'

Kilian had sighed and nodded. 'I will await your call.'

'Thank you, sir. Incidentally, the general did ask me to check with you about that other business.'

'Other business?' he'd frowned, looking puzzled.

For the first time since Kilian had met him, von Hofacker looked uncomfortable. 'Er, yes. The file, sir.' When Kilian still looked unsure, he prompted him again. 'The one I gave you in your office. It's not terribly relevant now, but even so, it pays to be careful.'

'Forgive me, von Hofacker. I do recall the file. Just a lot of useless paperwork, surely?'

'Not all of it, sir. Perhaps you'd like to take a closer look. My apologies, Colonel, but I am obliged to enquire whether you are still accompanied by Mademoiselle Forestier?'

'I am not,' Kilian had replied, icily. He'd momentarily considered reprimanding the man but held his tongue.

'Again, my apologies, Colonel. Please ... read the file. It is essential that you distance yourself from this woman.'

'Why?'

'We believe she may be a spy. All is explained in the file. The Gestapo has been alerted. Makes us look good. They are closing in on the conspiracy in Berlin, but we don't want them sniffing around in Paris.'

Stunned by the accusation, Kilian could only think about getting back to the office and ripping open the file.

And now he sat in his office, mute. The file had been more than enlightening – buried deep within the nonsense paperwork was a series of photographs. They were grainy, shot through a window, and there were moments when Kilian could almost convince himself that it wasn't Lisette and the driver he knew as Loewe kissing.

The clandestine surveillance had been arranged by Stülpnagel, who'd been as good as his word; Kilian remembered now that the general said he'd look into Lisette. Here were the damning results. At first he'd stared at them in a shocked stupor; how could she be with Loewe? She didn't even know Loewe. It didn't make sense! But the written explanation clarified the whole tawdry affair. Loewe was an impostor. Stülpnagel had no idea of this man's actual name but the real Christian Loewe had died years earlier. Lisette's lover had used well-forged papers to get himself employed.

Kilian closed his eyes in fury. This man was surely Ravensburg. They were working together, had infiltrated his life together, had been lovers behind his back. He felt nauseated. He'd told his secretary to not disturb him, and to hold all calls unless there was a message from General Stülpnagel's office.

And so for hours he'd sat silently in his office, pondering Lisette and Ravensburg. Loewe had spoken German like a native but his French was flawless too – a perfect match for Lisette as a spy. Were they working for the Allies? They had to be. But given that he, Kilian, was currently out to pasture, why had he been targeted? He teased at his question in his mind, remembering conversations, unravelling Lisette's story as he moved back through everything he knew of her.

Was Walter involved? No. He couldn't imagine it. And Lisette was always wary of inviting Walter whenever he'd suggested it. So she was using Walter as her cover, working at the bank to support her everyday life while she integrated into his. And he'd fallen for it. He truly loved her, and he couldn't imagine that she had faked her responses to him that well. And yet the photos showed her in a tight embrace with a handsome young man who reminded him of himself, fifteen years ago.

How could they stomach what they'd had to do? How had Loewe been able to watch him making love to Lisette in the back of the car? How could Lisette bear to have him kiss her and touch her; had she pretended he was Ravensburg?

Kilian had had enough experience with women to know a lie, to know when pleasure was feigned. He knew Lisette had feelings for him. It seemed that she had somehow learnt to separate her bizarre double life. Her carefree and relaxed manner while they were away suddenly made sense – there'd been no reason to pretend. No, she hadn't faked it, and two days earlier there had been real desperation in her face. Kilian believed she was genuinely trying to protect him from the Gestapo.

Lisette's offer to help Kilian was risky – she could keep the Allies up to date with the plot, yes, but she also put herself right in the Gestapo firing line. Was she doing it for him? He didn't know, but right now he hated her with passion for trying to coerce him, for lying to him, but especially for making him love her.

How tragic they all were. While war raged and plots were hatched, he was engaged in a battle of the heart.

Why Lisette and Ravensburg had chosen him remained a mystery, but that was academic now. They'd stumbled upon something much bigger than a disgruntled Wehrmacht colonel. He felt sickened by the notion that they knew of the assassination plot – he already was a traitor to his own country, but to release information to Germany's enemies was abhorrent.

He'd set fire to the incriminating photos in his wastepaper bin, as well as the equally damning notes. He had almost thrown her letter in but he held back – perhaps because there was already enough pain associated with Lisette. He couldn't bear to watch her words of affection burn, and perhaps deep down he still believed them. He tucked her note into his inside breast pocket, near the letter he still hadn't posted to Ilse; he'd been adding to it regularly. Now it would have a new entry.

Stülpnagel clearly didn't see Lisette as a genuine threat, which was a blessing. Frankly, it was too late for any of them to be worried, for the plan was in motion and no Allied spy would risk jeopardising any plan to kill Hitler. If London knew, then London would be keeping silent and holding its collective breath for news of the Führer's murder.

Kilian sat in full uniform – not so much as a button loosened – and waited for the call from General Stülpnagel's office to take command of the German army in Paris.

The order never came.

Morning had shifted to afternoon and Kilian watched as the shadows lengthened until his office was bathed in the softest of evening light. He wasn't tempted to ring von Hofacker. He didn't need anyone to tell him that irrespective of whether a bomb had detonated in the Wolffschanze, Hitler hadn't died today. What had gone wrong didn't matter to him. Nothing much mattered to him any more.

36

The next few weeks were a horrifying blur for Kilian. The bomb had been successfully detonated, but once again Hitler had miraculously defied death. Kilian wisely kept his head low, and though tempted to feign illness, decided it was better to work quietly, arriving at his office early and keeping his churning emotions hidden under a granite façade. Behind closed doors he'd held his head in despair. General Stülpnagel had mistakenly believed that Hitler had been killed in the blast, and had begun to arrest the Paris-based SS and Gestapo. He then had to release them when it was confirmed that Hitler was alive, and the evil chain of command intact.

By the time Kilian learnt the names of the plan's architects in Berlin, they had already been executed: shot by firing squad in the courtyard of the war ministry. Rumours followed later that their deaths were hastened by senior military figures to stop Hitler discovering other high-placed men who knew of the plot. But the Leader wanted revenge. Stülpnagel had been recalled to Berlin; on the journey he'd attempted suicide. Kilian held no hope for the general – he was sure Stülpnagel would be executed. The vengeance continued, reaching beyond Germany as a wave of arrests began in Paris.

Kilian calmly put his effects into order and awaited the arrival of the Gestapo. He heard through his secretary that Lieutenant Colonel von Hofacker had been arrested in connection with the assassination attempt. Kilian was convinced it could only be hours before they knocked on his own door.

But true to their word, it seemed that Stülpnagel and von Hofacker had kept Kilian's name out of it. It had been over a week now, and the arrests in Paris had dried up, although Kilian knew that dozens of men had been and were still being rounded up in Berlin, including their families and all known associates. Hundreds of people were accused of treason, and Kilian's jaw seemed to grind constantly as he thought of all the good men and women – so many innocents – who would die.

He had to keep his promise to his co-conspirators: protect himself and look to the future, although the Allies would surely break through the lines before another attempt could be made. Paris would fall to the British and the Americans. There would be no further attempt on Hitler from within.

Nevertheless, he carried on as instructed. He gave his secretary the file that von Hofacker had provided as a cover for their only meeting in his office.

'We'd better keep this in case the secret police need it,' he said. 'This is all I have in connection with my single meeting with Lieutenant Colonel von Hofacker.' He needed to distance himself from those involved in the attempt, but not lie outright.

'Yes, sir, although I don't think anyone from the Gestapo has any reason to visit us,' she said, with a sympathetic smile. 'And we certainly don't need to help them.' She took the file from him carefully.

He nodded quizzically. Was there another renegade on his staff? 'How shocking it all is,' he remarked, probing.

'It is, Colonel. I know you could have me thrown out for saying it, but even as a German national I do wish it would end.' They were alone in the anteroom to his office but still she looked around.

He found a smile. 'I couldn't have you thrown out, Aline, because after a string of secretaries who've been scared of me, you're the first who isn't.'

'It must be my age, Colonel.'

'You can keep me honest.'

'No, sir. I'm going to do the opposite. The secret police see suspicion in all of us. Your honesty could incriminate you, this office, me. Herr von Hofacker did not make an appointment, so there is no record of his being here. I don't think we need to provide any link to you or this office, no matter how innocent.' She tucked the file into a bottom drawer and quietly locked it. 'I'll destroy this.'

On 7 August General Dietrich von Choltitz, whom Kilian knew well and had fought alongside, was made military governor of Paris, taking over from the disgraced Stülpnagel.

On 11 August Kilian managed to meet with the new governor on the pretext of renewing their former acquaintance. It didn't take Kilian long to establish that the general had plenty of misgivings about his new post. Paramount among these was von Choltitz's determination to defy Hitler's latest orders to burn Paris down.

'The war is unwinnable,' the new governor admitted. 'But the Führer cannot be convinced. I'm told he's still screaming orders to divisions that have already surrendered. And now here's his latest demented plan. He's demanding a scorched-earth policy, but there's nothing to be achieved by destroying this city.'

Kilian could not help but be quietly reassured by von Choltitz's words. Both of them knew that if Paris burned, the insurgents would rise up, and no French partisan would be in the mood to take prisoners. They would kill every German they could lay their hands on.

Kilian had assumed they'd go down fighting, but it seemed that inactivity was von Choltitz's plan. Despite the now near-hysterical orders from Berlin to leave Paris a smoking ruin, the general was hoping that his delaying tactics would give the Allies enough time to take the city.

'I know I can trust you, Colonel. I'm going to communicate with the Allies and send an emissary. This must happen quickly.'

Kilian nodded.

The general continued, 'The sooner they reach Paris, the sooner I can hand it over. We won't get out unbloodied but the Americans and British are our best hope – the French Communists will likely want us all swinging by our necks from the Eiffel Tower.'

'If your plan is to prevent further bloodshed, sir, and achieve some sort of truce, then a negotiation must be opened with the French underground. I agree, Paris should be preserved and I'm happy to act as the go-between if that helps you,' Kilian offered. He couldn't care less about living or dying, but he wanted at all costs to avoid a massacre.

When Lisette turned up at the safe house, the network had rallied around her. And so began her life as a true Resistance fighter, sleeping by day and working by night.

Her first mission was as part of a group that blew up a railway track north of Paris. A few days later she was among the saboteurs who attacked subterranean cables between Frainville and Aulnay, melting them with battery acid. The following night she was part of a massive effort to sabotage the Villeneuve Saint-Georges line on the south-eastern fringe of Paris. The job was so effective that trains would be delayed for weeks. In the meantime she acted as lookout for a derailment, and sabotaged a bridge leading out of Paris.

Exhausted and in yet another strange flat in the early hours of one morning, she allowed herself a quiet weep. She wept for Markus Kilian and the look of shock on his face, and she wept for Luc, from whom no word had been heard. Lisette had asked daily but all she received was a look of sympathy, or a shaken head. Luc was gone. There'd been fierce fighting throughout southern and central alpine France and she truly believed he had headed right into the fray, rejoining his fellow maquisards. He could be lying wounded. He could also be dead.

She'd lost both of them. But then, she always lost those she loved.

Of all people to find her whimpering beneath her thin blanket that morning, it was Sylvie who touched her gently on the shoulder.

'That never helps,' she said.

Lisette was embarrassed. 'I know. It's my little indulgence as I don't have soap or shampoo.'

Sylvie grinned. 'I hear you've been doing some really good work.'

Lisette sat up and wiped her tears away. 'Thanks.'

'I also hear you've been living quite rough.'

'My cover was blown.'

'So the colonel gave you up?'

She shook her head. 'No, let's just say an old foe caught up with me. I'm not taking any chances.'

'That's the way to think. So you need a place to stay.'

'Everyone's being kind. I'll sort something.'

'I have a place set up . . . you're welcome to stay there,' Sylvie offered.

Lisette was astonished. 'Really?'

'I'm rarely there. It's a flat over in Bastille, more room than in Montmartre, but it's not as decent.'

Lisette was taken aback by her generosity and momentarily lost for words. Her hesitation amused Sylvie.

'We're all in this together, you know; what we fight for is all that matters.' Sylvie lifted a shoulder. 'Our petty jealousies and desires are irrelevant.'

She was right. Lisette felt humbled. 'It won't be awkward for you?'

Sylvie grinned again. 'Not for me. I'm French, remember? You've lived too long among those straitlaced British. And frankly, I think I got the best of Luc.' Lisette tried not to bristle as Sylvie continued. 'Besides, he's gone. We've both had our hearts hurt by him. But I know how to heal my wounds. It would be wise if you learned to do the same, including that tender torch you carry for your German colonel.'

Lisette's mouth dropped open. She could not believe Sylvie would be so candid.

'Yes, before you ask, it is obvious,' Sylvie said, smiling a little at her shock. 'He's the enemy, Lisette. Every time you think about the people who've died, the innocents tortured, the families and lives destroyed, the six years of hunger, fatigue, desperation, of the newborns who have withered at their mothers' breasts and the old people who fell by the wayside – when you think of that, you keep your colonel's uniform in mind.'

'He really wasn't —'

'He's a German officer. He's as guilty as all of them. Now, are you coming?'

Lisette nodded mutely and followed Sylvie to an apartment in the backstreets of Bastille. On the fringe of the eleventh arondisse-ment, it was a scruffy area of Paris, and while the studio itself was as neat as a pin, the surrounds were full of grubby cafés, greasy bars and dirty buildings. But Lisette couldn't have been happier. At last there was a bed to sleep in, running water, a few meagre supplies. Sylvie even gave her a dress.

'Sylvie, I —'

'Don't,' her friend warned. 'I'm not good with thank-yous. I promised Luc a long time ago that I'd look out for you. Let's just say I keep my promises.'

Sylvie slid into the booth of the all-night café in Pigalle, far away from Bastille. The streets were deserted, tension was rife. Inside the café, the smoke sat in a thick layer above the heads of patrons. She smelled old grease and cheap perfume that clung to the worn fabric on the chairs. But no one appeared to mind. There was a sense of anticipation. Voices were muted, but with an undertone of excitement. Change was coming to Paris.

Sylivie's companion lit the cigarette she was holding.

'It's the end, I tell you,' he said. 'There's a general strike happening tomorrow that will escalate tensions. I know resisters will mobilise against the Germans. They don't care any more about strategy or guerilla tactics. It will be out-and-out street battles before the Allies swarm in.'

She nodded. 'I heard something very interesting today,' she admitted, lazily blowing smoke to one side.

'What's that?'

'You know I'm in contact with quite a few of the *réseaux*?'

He nodded.

'Well, there's word that the new military command in Paris wants to talk.'

'Talk?'

'Negotiate.'

'What terms?'

'We don't slaughter German soldiers. They don't burn down Paris.'

'I don't believe it,' he said, knocking back a shot of anise.

'I'm telling you what I heard.'

'Who's leading these talks?' he demanded.

'Ah, now, that's what makes it interesting.'

'Don't tease me, Sylvie.'

'You deserve it. But you don't deserve my company.'

He laid his hand on top of hers. 'But I do appreciate it.' He hesitated. 'Is she all right?'

'Yes, Luc, she's all right. She's at the flat in Bastille.'

'You know, Sylvie, you try to hide it, but you have a big heart.'

She flicked off his hand playfully. 'Don't charm me.'

He stared deep into her eyes. 'I'm trying to thank you.'

'Why don't you see her, if you're so concerned?'

He looked away, out into the crowded café with its rows of near-empty bottles behind the bar. 'I can't. Not yet.' He looked back at her and she knew she was looking at a man who was in love – but not with her.

'After all she's done . . .' she began.

'We've all done things in this war we'd rather forget.'

'I haven't, unless I count falling in love with you.'

'I'm sorry,' he said.

She gave a small shake of her head, cross with herself for admitting that.

'Finish what you were going to say. About the middleman,' he urged.

'It's why I'm not sure you can avoid Lisette.'

He frowned. 'I don't understand.'

'The conduit is Kilian. He's asked for both of you.'

Luc's face was dark in thought as he sat at a park bench, watching a blackbird prospecting for insects in the grass. It wasn't yet five a.m. but it was warm and bright. 'Over my dead body. I won't help.'

Armand looked pained. 'Listen,' he said, his tone sympathetic. 'Paris is about to blow up. The gendarmerie, the Métro, it's all on strike today. The railways will follow. The Allies are almost knocking on the door, the Communist partisans want to take Paris before they get here and the Germans are packing up. We've got twenty thousand resisters surging now, howling for revenge. My job has been to arm those insurgents for this very moment, but now the real problem is avoiding a massacre in the streets. None of us want that. This new governor, this von Choltitz, he can also see the future. He's right to extend a hand. And as much as I hate to shake it, I think we have a responsibility to avoid the inevitable bloodbath by trying to work with the enemy.'

'It could be a trap,' Luc said, anguished.

Armand laughed. 'A trap? Are you mad? What's to gain? The whole German garrison manoeuvring to capture a young female operative on the brink of their own defeat?'

Luc looked sheepish. 'All right, all right, but I won't change my mind. This is Kilian trying to lure her back. I'm not going to give him a chance to hurt her in any way.'

'Have you talked to her?'

He shook his head. 'She doesn't know I'm back. I want it kept that way.'

'Well, if you'd talked to her as I have, you'd know that Kilian helped her. He made it easy. He all but threw her out of his life in order to keep her safe. Whatever he was up to was dangerous. She could have been caught in the same net.'

Luc brooded, staring out unhappily at the tireless blackbird.

'He specifically asked for her,' Armand pressed again.

'Well, he can't have her. He's not the one in a position to bargain. Don't you see, Armand? For the first time they're scared. They know it's over, they know their lives are hanging by a thread. They need to bargain. And while I agree we don't want all-out slaughter, and I certainly don't want to see Paris burning, he can't make this sort of demand. He can ask for our help and we'll consider giving it, but Lisette is not in the bargain.'

Armand sighed. 'All right, Faucille. I will pass it on. What about you?'

'He can have me. Where?'

'I'll set it up. Stay at Avenue de Wagram until you hear.'

'No, I don't want to be seen. I'll stay in Montmartre – I'm squatting at her old bedsit. I repeat, Lisette is not to know. Do you understand?'

Armand shook his head with pity. 'There are thousands of insurgents about to rise up from the shadows and hit the streets of Paris.' He began to count off on his fingers. 'Communists, liberalists, anarchists, students, academics, Roman Catholics and Protestants. Their hatred of the Fascists has united them. And somehow SOE is trying to arm these impassioned people while trying to control all that hatred. Believe me when I say that I have bigger things on my mind, my friend, than your curious love triangle.'

On the evening of 18 August, Luc waited by the entrance of the Jardins du Luxembourg. The night was as black as ink with only a vague wash of moonlight blanketed by clouds. Even so, he'd positioned himself behind a bush and watched the car approach. It was habit rather than real fear – he couldn't imagine any traps were going to be sprung at this point. Besides, he didn't truly believe traps were Kilian's style. The colonel, he was sure, would rather confront him face to face.

And no doubt that was part of this whole charade. Why else would Kilian have specified Luc and Lisette as his points of contact?

He could see that Kilian was alone in the back of the car. Did Kilian know about him and Lisette? If so, how? No doubt he'd learn soon enough.

The car slowed. He could see both Kilian and the driver looking out the window. It was time. If Kilian wanted to, he could have Luc killed and still attempt to negotiate with the Allies through the Spiritualist network. In spite of that, Luc took a deep breath and stepped out from behind the bush, casting his hopes against his measure of Colonel Kilian.

Klaus braked and Luc hopped in as the car kept rolling slowly. While he was still hauling the heavy door closed, Klaus immediately took off, speeding in the direction of the Place Vendôme. It was nearing four a.m. and Paris was silent, save the sound of their engine and the deafening silence in the car.

Luc turned to stare at his nemesis. 'Colonel Kilian,' he said evenly, his tone appropriately polite.

The Wehrmacht officer regarded him with a glacial gaze. 'Do I call you Ravensburg?'

Luc nodded. 'It's my name.'

Kilian closed the glass compartment between Klaus and the back seat, and turned to Luc. The confined space was thick with tension. Kilian was armed, although his hands rested quietly in his lap, and was in full uniform. It was impressive, and Luc could understand why any woman would throw him a second glance. He thought about Lisette in this man's arms. The images were still in his mind, and he could replay them time after bitter time; Kilian's hands on Lisette, Kilian's lips at her neck, Kilian's mouth on hers.

'You know he's a dedicated Nazi,' Luc said, his head gesturing towards Klaus. Luc was relieved his voice was steady.

'Yes. Germany is full of the wretched swine,' Kilian responded. 'I don't fear him, however.'

'Why? Because you think the connection you're making with the Resistance and the Allies might save your skin?'

'No, Ravensburg. I don't expect to survive this war. Frankly, given how it's all gone, given that I never agreed with it in the first place, given that I have committed treason against my country, I think death now is the best option.'

'To escape reprisal?'

'To find peace,' Kilian replied quietly. He cleared his throat. 'I requested Lisette be here. Is she . . . well?'

Luc's jaw tightened. Now they were getting to it. 'What you have to say can be said to me.'

'But you have no idea what I might want to say,' Kilian replied.

'Nevertheless, I chose for her not to be involved. Besides, I haven't seen her for a long time.'

That caught Kilian's attention. He glanced up, fixed Luc with his pale stare. 'How come?'

'I left for Mont Mouchet, to fight.'

'I envy you.' Kilian sounded wistful.

'I am a *lavandier*, not a fighter. If I survive, that's what I'll do again.'

'Then I envy you all the more. Tell me something, Ravensburg – and I give you my oath it will not be repeated —'

'The oath of a German officer about to give up Paris?'

Kilian smiled coldly. 'The oath of an honourable man.'

Luc nodded. 'Go on.'

'Are you also the Bonet that von Schleigel spoke of?'

Luc felt sorrow bleed again. He hadn't permitted himself to think about Wolf in a long time. 'I am. And I owe von Schleigel on a private debt. The day of reckoning will come.'

Kilian gaze narrowed. 'I sincerely hope it does.' He sounded genuine. 'Bonet is a Jewish name?'

Luc didn't want to talk about this, least of all with a German colonel. But there was something about Kilian. In another place, another time, they might have even been friends. 'I have Bavarian parents; my father died fighting for Germany, my mother died when I was born. I was born in Strasbourg but adopted by a Jewish family in the south of France, and raised as their son. I loved my family as you may love yours, and I watched the *milice* drag them away after beating my grandmother to death.'

'Do you know where they are? Perhaps I can . . .'

'I don't need your pity, Colonel. You asked me who I am. I've told you. As for Lisette, I refuse you access to her.'

'You are right to. I suppose I selfishly wanted to see her one more time . . . to apologise.'

'For what?'

'That's between her and me. Does she know we're meeting?'

Luc shook his head.

'Best kept that way,' and Luc heard a deep sorrow in the colonel's words. Kilian cleared his throat. 'To business, then. General von Choltitz is aiming to make direct contact with the Allies.'

'Go on.' Sylvie had been correct.

'He wants them to hurry up. He can't hold the German garrison entirely at bay. But you must know that he is trying to keep Paris as undamaged as he can. Hilter is howling for every bridge to be destroyed. The Luftwaffe wants to raze the key monuments. Von Choltitz refuses to sanction those orders. He will surrender the city peaceably to the Allies as soon as they can get to Paris, but the problem is your resistance forces. We can sense the mood; the insurgents will explode onto the streets any minute, and the German garrison will be forced to defend itself. Your people, your leaders, have to find a way to contain the rage for a while longer.'

'We can't protect you,' Luc growled. 'That would not —'

'We're not seeking protection,' Kilian snapped. 'I'm trying to prevent a slaughter on both sides. We're better armed, better equipped, better organised. On the run or pinned down, we're going to take a lot of your partisans with us, if it comes to an all-out fight in the streets. Take my advice – get through to your networks and contain the hysteria long enough for von Choltitz to manufacture some sort of truce. He's talking with the Swedish ambassador to Paris right now. I thought I could reach you and Lisette quicker to aid this. Can you at least try?'

Luc nodded. 'I'll try. But the Communist elements are very determined. They want to claim victory and take control of Paris before the Allies arrive.'

Kilian gave a scornful sound. 'History can write her pages however she chooses. But please remember that the soldiers will respond with strength if attacked. There's only so much von Choltitz can do in terms of holding off.'

'I understand. We'll do whatever we can. Where can I find you? Communication is going to become even more difficult as our people start to cut all lines.'

Kilian nodded. 'See what you can do. I'm at the Hotel Raphaël but I don't know for how much longer. Can I drop you back somewhere?'

'No thanks. I'm better off on foot.'

'Good luck, Ravensburg,' Kilian said. 'And thank you.'

'I can't make any promises,' Luc said.

'The fact that you're trying is enough.'

Kilian was surprising; Luc almost wished he wasn't a German officer. 'By the way, Lisette was right, wasn't she? You were part of the assassination attempt?'

'On the fringe, but committed to it, nonetheless.'

Luc dipped his head, almost in salute. 'Then we are almost on the same side.'

Kilian smiled ruefully. 'It's a pity we have to be enemies.'

Luc opened the car door. 'Well, we'll always have one thing in common.'

'Indeed. But there can only ever be one winner . . . in war as in love. I hope the best man won.'

'Only she can decide that.' Luc stepped out of the car and walked away.

37

The Resistance leaders were failing to contain the growing anger raging among the vast numbers of resisters. Meanwhile, the Communists began calling for a general mobilisation of all partisans, urging Parisians towards insurrection.

The day after Luc met Kilian, the first of the dangerous skirmishes began. Luc's thoughts fled to Lisette, but Sylvie had assured him she would stick close to her during these dark days of unpredictability. That Saturday the Prefecture of Police, a puppet organisation of the Nazi occupiers, surrendered to the Resistance and Colonel Rol, head of the Communist resisters, assumed full control of the uprising partisan fightback against the Germans.

It seemed there would be too many differences, too many varying agendas to achieve any sort of cohesion, but somehow General von Choltitz did bolt together a tenuous truce. Brokered through the Swedish consul-general, a temporary and fragile ceasefire was agreed by Saturday night. On Sunday Paris seemed to be on a rollercoaster as more and more strikes added to the tension. Skirmishes kept breaking out and by the evening the resisters occupied the town hall.

Kilian led troops to respond to the combat in the streets, despite the ceasefire. Loudspeakers from German vans demanded that weapons be put down, but Kilian knew the Parisian Resistance fighters, particularly the Communists, had smelt blood. They wouldn't stop now.

By Monday the ceasefire was being openly ignored by both sides and by midweek the resisters began to die in the hundreds as the superiority of the German fighting ability and equipment began to take its toll. Parisian streets were barricaded again, like the early days. Kilian felt sickened as he watched the unnecessary carnage on both sides, but he could no longer expect his men to show lenience; they had to defend themselves. He knew the Allies were just hours away from entering Paris and that von Choltitz would surrender Paris.

By Thursday, all the military high command and most senior German officers had retreated to the Hotel Crillon on the Rue du Rivoli or the Hotel Majestic, which was near the Raphael, to await the handover. Kilian, however, refused to join them. He was not a man who surrendered. He was glad that von Choltitz had saved Paris and glad that the end was close. And while he had no intention of taking some sort of last stand, he refused to cringe in a hotel lobby and await the enemy like a thrashed dog.

Instead he decided he'd get drunk. The last time he was drunk he'd been a young and irresponsible man, but today he felt so old he needed to drown his sorrows. He wanted to be out in Paris, in the warm summer night, perhaps with his boots off and feeling the grass of the Tuileries beneath his feet. He headed for the Ritz and grabbed a half-full bottle of calvados from behind the bar. The hotel was still crowded with Nazis, all awaiting the official word that Paris was no longer theirs, but he ignored them all.

As he left he heard a rumour that some of de Gaulle's forces had already entered the city ahead of the main column. It seemed Paris was to be liberated by the French after all. He smiled wryly, imagining the wrangling that must have gone on within the Allies to permit that.

He stepped outside warily. There was still fighting in pockets but the skirmishes had dissipated significantly over the past twelve hours. But he had no fear for his life one way or the other . . . all he could think about was drinking calvados and remembering a sparkly spring evening when a young woman had reminded him how good it was to be alive.

Somehow, he wasn't surprised to see Ravensburg leaning against a nearby tree. He'd had a feeling their paths would cross again.

'Not celebrating, Lukas?'

'Plenty of time for that, Colonel. What are you doing?'

'I'm going for a drink.' He shook the bottle in Luc's face. 'Care to join me?'

'Kilian, I think you should join your companions at the Crillon before it's too late.'

'It's already too late. And I don't want to be there. Anyway, go on . . . I'm ready for your rightful and perfectly understandable gloat.'

'I didn't come to gloat. I came to find Lisette.'

––––––––

Sylvie and Lisette had stayed off the streets for days. It was dangerous for anyone to be out on foot. But while the rest of Paris was awakening with joy that day, Lisette's morning had begun with a vague sense of gloom. She couldn't put her finger on it. She should be excited, she should want to rush out into Bastille and cheer like some of the other locals. But the prickly notion of foreboding had not dissipated as the hours wore on, and by the afternoon of Thursday 24 August it had deepened into anxiety. She'd never thought of herself as having a sixth sense but her instincts were screaming at her.

Sylvie was sitting on the window ledge staring out, a cigarette smouldering in her hand. She'd begun chain-smoking over the last ten days. Lisette never knew how or where Sylvie got the money to buy them, nor did she ask.

'Sylvie . . .'

'Mmm? Can you feel it?'

'What?'

'Paris stretching, reasserting herself. She's French again,' Sylvie said, pride rich in her voice. 'By tomorrow the Americans and the British will be marching down our streets . . . but we did this. The French reclaimed Paris.'

Lisette held her tongue. Sylvie should be allowed to savour this moment.

'Listen. Can you hear them?' Sylvie hummed a few bars of 'La Marseillaise' along with the distant revellers. There was sporadic gunfire in the wind, bursts of snipers. Lisette flinched each time she heard one, imagining another person had just died for their cause.

'Sylvie. Please be honest with me. Of all nights, this is the night to be frank.'

'What are you talking about, Lisette?'

'I want the truth.'

'About what?' Sylvie said, and then held up her hand as if about to swear an oath.

'I'm being serious.'

'I can see.'

'Have you heard from Luc?'

'Luc? Now, why would you ask me that?'

'It doesn't matter why. Have you heard from or seen Luc?'

'When?' Sylvie asked, flicking ash absently at an ashtray. She missed. Sylvie never missed.

Lisette's eyes widened. 'You have,' she said, aghast.

'I didn't say anything.'

'You don't have to. Where is he? Paris?'

Sylvie licked her lips. 'I'm not allowed to say.'

'Where is he, Sylvie?'

'He's in Paris. Now be done!'

'Damn you!' Lisette cried. 'Where?'

'That I can't say.' When Lisette came closer, murder in her look, Sylvie shrugged. 'I can't say because I don't know. I have no idea where he comes from or goes to.'

'How long has he been here?'

'Who knows?' She took a drag, then stubbed her cigarette out. 'I saw him nine, maybe ten days ago.'

Lisette looked even more stunned. 'Where?'

'Pigalle! He doesn't want to see you.'

It was like a slap. 'What is he doing?'

'You don't want to know.'

'Do I have to go and try to find him?'

Sylvie's eyes flashed with anger. 'Don't be ridiculous.'

'Because you made a promise to Luc that you'd keep an eye on me?'

'Something like that.'

'Well, fuck you both! I don't need babysitting.' Lisette started gathering up her few things.

'Where do you think you're going?'

'I'm going to find Luc myself.'

'They're killing each other out there.' Sylvie pointed towards the window.

'I don't care. I'm not going to sit in here with you smiling knowingly to yourself. You've been good to me, Sylvie, but thanks and good luck.'

'He's been with Kilian!' Sylvie snarled. 'Happy?'

If Sylvie had said Luc was on the moon, it would have seemed less fantastic. 'What?' Lisette asked, her voice small.

Sylvie's temper cooled as fast as it had flamed. 'Look, I don't know if he's with him now. I just know that he's been in contact with him.' She told Lisette everything she knew.

'Markus asked for me?'

Sylvie nodded. 'Yes. Personally, I think you have a right to know.' She shook her head, began lighting another cigarette. 'But Luc met with Kilian alone.'

Lisette groaned. 'And you think they're together now?'

'Honestly, Lisette, I don't know. And frankly, I don't think anything Kilian or Luc does right now is going to change a thing. By tomorrow morning the Champs Elysées will likely erupt to the sound of liberation. Nothing else matters.'

Maybe that was the case for Sylvie. Lisette nodded, then turned and left the apartment without another word.

'Lisette! *Lisette!*' Sylvie called after her. '*Merde!*' she swore and ran back inside to grab her bag.

───────

Sylvie found Luc where she expected, at Lisette's old flat in Montmartre. It had taken her hours to get there on foot, avoiding the pockets of fighting that were increasingly giving way to celebration. People weren't yet sure if it was over but there was a sense of triumph permeating the streets. Sylvie was increasingly resentful as she walked – Lisette was robbing her of the victory.

Luc was sitting on the stoop of the building. He was not alone. There were plenty of other people in the street, all collectively holding their breath, waiting for some sign that it was over.

Luc picked her out immediately as she approached. 'Sylvie?' He looked around to see if she was by herself.

'She's gone,' Sylvie said. She was exhausted and irritated.

'What do you mean?'

She gave him an exasperated glare. 'I babysat your lovesick girl as long as I could. But she's not a child, Luc; she gets angry like any of us when she's patronised.'

'What are you talking about?'

'She demanded I tell her. She knows about you, about Kilian.'

His initially bewildered expression turned quickly to anger. 'Where is she?'

'She ran off. I think she's trying to find you, but she thinks you're with Kilian right now. She's probably trying to find him.'

He didn't waste another word. Before Sylvie could speak again he stood and began to run.

Luc dodged and weaved through gunfire and celebration; some were already dancing in the streets, with music blaring and wine flowing. Girls were bare-shouldered in summer frocks and men had their shirts off, waving them over their heads, singing 'La Marseillaise'. Strangers kissed, children ran around, seniors brought out chairs and sat on the footpaths to watch the spontaneous festivities, as everyone tore down any Nazi signs or flags. Parents of newborns hugged and wept at the thought their babies would know peace in the world.

Paris was mad this evening.

Where would she go? Luc wondered. He'd headed to the Hotel Raphaël, but found no sign of her. Flashing his German driver's ID at one of the senior staff, he'd been able to establish that Colonel Kilian was not in his room or in the hotel. Lisette was in none of the public areas. He'd run on, this time to the colonel's offices. Again he'd used his identification papers to persuade someone to check whether the colonel was in his rooms. He was not.

Luc had racked his mind. Where would she go? Think! The bridge near the cathedral where she'd met Kilian, perhaps? No, too public. Where, damn it? Where would she think Kilian would meet him?

The Ritz? Possibly. The Ritz had resonance for her too.

He'd run, heedless of his shortening breath, to the Place Vendôme, scanning the great square for any sign of Lisette. And how was he to get inside a hotel that was teeming with Nazis on edge? He'd approached, half expecting a sniper bullet to hit him at any moment.

And then, as fate wove her wand, Colonel Kilian had pushed through the hotel doors carrying a bottle. Kilian had noticed him immediately.

'Not celebrating, Lukas?' he'd asked.

Lisette did not follow the colonel out of the hotel; Luc's heart skipped a beat. He had no idea now where in this vast city she was.

Lisette had run, madly at first. But then she decided where she was going and started to walk calmly. No one would shoot at her; she wasn't worried about that. She looked like an ordinary French-woman; her problem was the general anarchy in the streets. Angry, excited men were capable of plenty, and a lone woman was an easy target.

She'd walked in such a distracted mood that Lisette was almost surprised when she found herself on the Avenue Kleber and approaching the Hotel Raphaël. She was worried what she might find, yet at the same time anxious that she might not find what she'd hoped for. No one stopped her when she ran into the familiar hotel lobby and lifted her hand to the concierge.

The lobby was deserted but she could see the bar was full of Germans, drinking very quietly, smoking, hardly speaking. The res-taurant was the same. People found safety in numbers, but it seemed no one particularly wanted any companionship. She ran up the stairs to the room she knew; the room where she'd been able to shut off the world and pretend she was someone else.

She was wearing the floral dress Kilian loved. How ironic, then, that she was here in Kilian's hotel, in Kilian's frock, but look-ing for Luc. She wiped her clammy hands on the thin cotton as she took a deep breath and knocked on the door. There was no answer. She knocked again. Silence. Instinctively, she reached for the handle and twisted. It turned, and the door gave with a gentle click. To her despair, the room was empty.

She didn't know where else to go. They could be anywhere. They could be together, or they could be at separate ends of the city. She saw Kilian's dress uniform hanging in the wardrobe, and her mind was transported to her birthday, when he'd all but torn a button on that jacket when he'd ripped it off in his eagerness to be naked with her.

She reached for it, held it close. It smelled of Markus. Lisette sat on the bed, Kilian's jacket clutched in her lap, and gazed into space. She was too frightened for Luc and Markus to cry.

The sensible voice inside her told her there was no point in hurtling from one familiar landmark to another. So she sat very still, and waited for night to descend. It would blot out the sounds of distant sniper fire, of revellers, of the frigid quiet in the hotel and the light in this room so she didn't have to see his things any longer.

In the morning, life would seem different. She knew it. And by the morning Paris would be free.

38

Kilian stared at Luc with a narrowed gaze. 'What do you mean, *find* Lisette?'

'She's disappeared,' Luc said. 'I think she's trying to find us.'

'Us?'

'She believes we're together. I came to find you in case . . .'

'You thought she might come here?'

Luc shrugged. 'I tried your hotel and your offices.'

'Well,' Kilian said. 'Lisette is charmed. She will be safe, I promise you. She's far too sensible to run through the streets of Paris.'

Luc agreed. Lisette could be counted on to be cautious. Even if she had run away, he didn't believe she would be skittering through the streets.

Kilian cast him a glance and strode by him.

'Where are you going, Colonel?'

'I told you, for a drink. You're welcome to join me, but don't try and stop me.'

'It's dangerous tonight, Colonel . . . to be German.'

'Can't change who I am. Neither can you, my friend. You're as German as I am. Come, let's both salute the end of the Reich; the end of this devil-inspired reign, and the end of the mad Austrian who brought this down upon us all.'

'You were part of it,' Luc said accusingly.

'Yes, I was. Come walk with me, as we talk.'

It was clear Kilian's mood was unpredictable. In spite of Luc's jealousy of the time Kilian had spent with Lisette, he didn't want to see the man die. He fell in step.

'You're right,' Kilian continued. 'I am part of it. I never liked it, but I was a man of duty. I am a soldier.' He gave a choked laugh. 'Sounds so pathetic now.'

'Don't expect my sympathy,' Luc said.

'I'm not asking for it. I don't believe any of us deserves it. However, some of us tried to change how it was.'

'And failed.' They had reached the Tuileries. Twilight was upon them, but the smell of smoke still hung in the air. Paris was not burning as Hitler had hoped, but bonfires of joy were flaring around the city as German flags and uniforms burned in celebration. The moon was out, bathing the gardens in a haunting light. And it was a balmy evening. Summer did not care whether war raged or peace prevailed.

'Kilian, this is not a wise place to be.'

'Scared?' the colonel asked.

'Only for you.'

'Don't be. I'm armed, remember.'

Luc wasn't impressed. A pistol against an angry mob was no defence. He watched as Kilian removed his boots. 'What are you doing, Colonel?'

'Beneath this extraordinarily pleasing moonlight, I plan to feel the warm summer grass beneath my feet and try to remember happier times in Prussia, when life was simple.'

'You can't blot out what your country is responsible for.'

'Oh, but I can try, Ravensburg. I have to try.' Kilian took a slug of the calvados and offered the bottle to Luc. Luc shook his head.

'Oh, come on. A sip between the vanquished and the conqueror.'

'I did nothing.'

436

'You won her, Ravensburg. I was no match for you.'

Luc hadn't realised they were discussing Lisette. He watched the colonel, normally so neat and smart, now dishevelled and barefoot, walking around the grass swallowing his second slug of brandy.

'She loves this, you know.' Kilian waved the bottle. 'Calvados. Make sure you always order it for her.'

'No. It will remind her of you.'

Kilian offered the bottle again. 'Come on, Ravensburg. Let's drink to Paris, to saving the city from Hitler's flames.'

Luc reluctantly took the bottle. 'All right, I'll drink to that.' Kilian looked delighted as Luc swallowed the shot, the apple brandy burning. It was powerful. He'd drunk calvados with his father in Paris, a memory that prompted thoughts he couldn't examine now. He watched Kilian swig from the bottle.

'You plan to get drunk?'

'Thoroughly.'

'Is that how you want the world to see Colonel Kilian tomorrow – drunk, bleary-eyed, staggering around?'

Kilian just gave an enigmatic smile. 'Let me offer you some more.'

Luc shook his head and Kilian swung around, yelling something into the night, before swigging again from the brandy. No doubt he'd been drinking all day, and it was catching up with him. He was swaying now.

'Had enough?' Luc asked.

'No. I can still think.'

Luc sighed and looked around. There were bursts of gunfire audible, but they seemed to be a long way off. The sounds of celebration were drifting across the Place de la Concorde from the Champs Elysées. Soon people would be out and about, leaving the safety of their neighbourhoods for these more salubrious areas, normally frequented by the Germans.

He could almost imagine the column of triumphant French, British and American troops arriving, being kissed by the women and cheered on by the men. But even amid this happiness, Luc thought of all of the tens of thousands, perhaps hundreds of thousands, of men, women and children who'd perished – including his own family. France should be weeping for the loyal citizens it had lost – in battle and in the camps, from Drancy in Paris through to the Polish work camps. He shook his head to clear those thoughts; there would be time enough for that scrutiny.

When he looked up, Kilian was dancing, moving slowly on the grass with his eyes closed.

'Come on, Colonel,' Luc said.

'I'll never dance again,' Kilian slurred. 'I'll never hold a woman again.' And as he turned around to say something else, Luc caught movement out of the corner of his eye. He grabbed Kilian just as a small band of youths rounded a bend in the gardens. It didn't take much guesswork to see that they were looking for trouble.

'What have we here?' one asked. He couldn't have been older than fifteen, with a baby face and floppy dark hair. He was waving a revolver.

Luc scanned the eight or so lads. The boy with the gun was the eldest; most looked younger and very unsure of themselves. Their nervous glances kept darting to their leader.

'All right, lads. No trouble, eh?' Luc said in a strong voice, holding up his hands to show he was unarmed.

'It's a Nazi!' one of them yelled.

'No, no, you've got it wrong,' Luc said. 'Do I look Nazi? I'm Maquis!' He'd taken care that morning to put on his maquisard pin, shaped as a double cross. 'Look,' he said, flicking back his collar to reveal it. 'I am French, like you.'

'We're talking about him!' the boy with the gun roared.

'Him? Don't be daft. He killed the owner of that uniform

earlier today. He's celebrating. Look, we stole this bottle of brandy from one of the hotels. Want some?'

The leader faltered, not quite convinced, but it was obvious he was interested in the liquor.

'Give them the bottle,' Luc urged Kilian.

The colonel seemed to come out of his hazy thoughts and realise what was occurring. To Luc's horror, he withdrew his pistol, cocked it and levelled it at the boys. 'No one gets my calvados,' he said – in German.

The group reacted as one in instant alarm. Luc could see the leader's hand trembling.

'Do you even know how to shoot that thing?' Kilian asked in French.

'He's a Boches!' the leader screamed.

'Yes, I am, boy,' Kilian snarled. 'But he is not. My companion here is exactly as he says. He is a loyal Frenchman. He is a brave maquisard who has captured me, and probably brought me here to kill me.'

'Is that right?' the youth asked Luc.

Luc could see the other boys backing away. He knew there was fire in Kilian's eyes and his pistol was trained straight on the boy's heart. He wouldn't miss, either, despite being drunk.

'What's your name?' Luc asked the visibly shaking leader.

'It's Didier,' someone answered for him.

'Put the gun down, Didier,' Luc requested, gently. 'I'll explain everything.'

'Did you lie?' Didier demanded. 'Are you Maquis and is he German?'

'Didier,' Kilian said, suddenly reasonable. 'Let me prove it.' He turned towards Luc and without another word, fired his pistol at him.

Luc found himself on the ground, so shocked he couldn't speak. His eyes were on Didier, who looked equally stunned.

'Now, Didier,' Kilian continued. 'Are you ready to use that or are you a coward, like all the other French who let us take over your country?' Luc couldn't believe Kilian was baiting the boy.

'Kilian, don't!' he tried, wincing from the sharp pain that now ripped through his torso. He wasn't even sure where he was shot. He didn't care.

Kilian wasn't listening. 'Just a bunch of cringing cowards. And now you're letting the British and the Americans rescue you. You can't even fire a gun when you've got —'

A shaking Didier pulled the trigger and Luc yelled in despair as Kilian dropped beside him. Immediately the group of youths ran off into the night, perhaps as shocked as he was.

Luc looked around frantically for help. There was none. The moon had gone behind a cloud and no one walking on the path might even see the two bodies on the ground.

Luc understood now that he'd been shot in the shoulder. There was blood and pain, but his mind was on Kilian. Would Lisette blame him? He dragged himself across the rough path to where Kilian lay silent.

'Kilian. *Kilian!*'

'Ah, but that hurts, doesn't it?' the colonel groaned.

'Why did you do it?' Luc demanded.

Kilian laughed weakly. 'I've been wanting to shoot you since I saw photos of you kissing Lisette.'

Luc grimaced. 'Well done.'

'I'm a good shot. You'll be fine. And it served its purpose.'

Luc did a quick scan of the colonel; in the ghostly moonlight the blood looked ominously dark. There was too much of it. Kilian was dying.

Luc pushed an angry hand through his hair, lost in frustration and increasing desperation. He had to find help. 'You got yourself shot deliberately. We could have —'

'Shut up, Ravensburg, and listen,' Kilian ordered, breathing with difficulty now. 'Let me say what I have to. I doubt there's much time.'

Luc became quiet.

'Everything's easier this way. I don't have to face being taken prisoner or going on trial . . .' He sighed. 'A bullet is so much cleaner and I have to tell you, Didier wasn't a bad shot.' He coughed. 'I think it's done the trick.'

'Listen, Kilian . . . Markus —'

'I said, be quiet. You're going to have to love her for both of us, because heaven knows I don't go to my death happy that she's yours. But I know that she's with the one she loves. She chose you.' He winced, gave a groan. 'I need you to . . .' He began pawing at his pocket but his head fell back, exhausted from the effort of holding pain, shock and death at bay.

'What?' Luc said, putting his ear closer to the dying man's mouth. He reached to where Kilian was gesturing and dug inside the blood-soaked jacket. He felt paper and realised it was an envelope, which he slid out.

Luc cradled Kilian's head on his uninjured shoulder. They lay side by side, like mates – more like brothers, in truth, for they were so similar.

'Already addressed,' Kilian struggled to say. 'Send it for me, when this is all done.' He grabbed for Luc's shirtfront. 'Promise me,' he urged in a growl of pain, his pale eyes haunted in the low light.

'I promise.'

'Now, give me a final swig of that calvados. Let me die with the taste of someone I love on my lips.'

Luc reluctantly tipped a small dribble of the brandy into Kilian's mouth.

'Thank you,' the colonel whispered, as he ran his tongue over his lips. '*Bonsoir*, Lisette,' he breathed. 'So much prettier to say farewell in French, don't you think?'

The question died with him as Kilian's eyelids closed. Luc lay with him a little longer beneath the soft moonlight among the gardens, choked with emotion.

39

Lisette woke to the sounds of cheering. She was disoriented at first, and then realised she was still in the Hotel Raphaël; she'd fallen asleep on Kilian's bed and slept deeply.

There was no indication that anyone had disturbed the room through the night. Kilian's jacket was still lying across her, like a blanket. She stood, made an effort to clean and tidy herself in his bathroom. When she emerged she looked presentable, and the frock she'd been wearing didn't look as creased as she'd feared. She looked in the mirror and pinched her cheeks, but even she could see how slight she'd become. The good food and good living of her weeks away with Markus had not lasted, and the weight had fallen off her since she'd returned to Paris. Dark circles had appeared beneath her eyes, and her cheekbones stood out starkly. Markus would be appalled at the state of her, but in truth she looked no different to the other famished people of Paris.

Lisette took a deep breath. It was time to go. She didn't think she'd ever see Kilian again, but she'd accepted that long ago. Now she had to find Luc. She needed to return to places he knew. Montmartre, perhaps? She couldn't face going back to Bastille and Sylvie right now.

Yes, she would go to Montmartre. She wanted to go to Sacré Coeur – the place where she felt most at home in Paris. She could leave a note on her old apartment door. Luc would find it – if he was looking for her. And he would come to her at the church.

At least it was a plan. And it was one that comforted her in her fractured state. But this was no longer about SOE or a mission. It wasn't even about the war. It was simply about her heart. Life had become complicated, and she had compartmentalised her life, but she needed to realign now. And the voice in her head was right. She had chosen. Lying in Kilian's hotel room, beneath his jacket, with his smell on her and his sheets beneath and the memory of him engulfing her, Lisette knew she had to let him go. He was her mission, and she *did* love Markus. She hadn't expected to, certainly hadn't wanted to, but he was a force, and in a different life they would have been more than lovers. Markus loved her, that could not be denied.

A small sob escaped her. She hated herself, and she hated London for turning her into this person. Markus was such a good man. If he'd been born British, he would have been hailed an Allied hero.

For the first time since that day more than twelve months ago when Captain Jepson recruited her, Lisette felt ashamed. Until now it had always been about striking back at the enemy, sabotaging the machine from within. Except Markus was the enemy. She felt the tears on her cheeks and hurriedly swept them away. No tears!

If only she could tell Markus that what they had shared hadn't all been a lie. Could she ever explain it properly? Yes. She would like to tell Markus of her love for Luc – an equally good man. Luc he had stolen her heart before she and the colonel had met. But it was too late now. Too late for recriminations and apologies.

She hung Kilian's jacket back in the wardrobe, straightening it carefully and lingering for a moment in farewell. She would never see him again – she was sure of this. Lisette held the sleeve against her cheek before giving it a kiss.

'Goodbye, Markus,' she whispered, then she closed the wardrobe door and left his room.

Armed Germans moved around in the lobby. They were likely

preparing to surrender their weapons and themselves, but not to an angry band of trigger-happy men. She wondered how many of those French outside had joined the Resistance once they knew that the Allies were close. She wondered also at how many were former collaborators, now looking for protection in the ranks of the brave.

She wasn't concentrating as she walked quickly through the lobby, keen to remove herself from the gathering Germans. She stepped out the door and was shocked when one of the men pacing outside yelled, 'Her!'

Lisette looked up, startled.

'She's one of them,' the voice said.

'One of their whores!' another called out.

She stopped dead, watched the angry men approaching. 'What?'

A man gripped her arm. He was old but he was strong. Unshaven and jeering, he stared at her. She could smell liquor on his breath but he didn't seem drunk.

'Hello, whore,' he spat in German.

She opened her mouth in dismay. 'I'm French,' she explained.

'Worse! Slut!'

'Shame on you, whore!' came the catcalls.

No amount of protest or explanation was going to change anyone's mind. She was dragged down a side street, aware of a small crowd of people following, jeering, calling her names. Not all men, either. Women and even children were among the mob.

'Where are you taking me?' she demanded.

No one answered her. And she simply wasn't strong enough to twist away. Even if she had kicked and fought her way free from the older man, there were ten, twenty others who'd grab her. Lisette knew that to struggle now would be to invite a beating; it was wiser to cooperate. It would pass.

She became slightly disoriented as she was roughly pulled

along, and saw that she was being directed towards another mob, far larger. There was a carnival atmosphere, lots of clapping and cheering, and she was pushed through the crowd until she emerged to see a small line of women waiting with their heads bowed. Lisette felt a sharp twist of fear at the sight.

She had no one to shield her. These strangers would vent their rage, and they would have fun doing so. The women knew they could not escape that rage, in the same way that a tethered goat knows there is no escape from the blade.

———

Luc had stayed with Kilian for a few hours. He was surprised at the deep despair he felt that the colonel had given his life so cheaply and so deliberately. He told himself he should be thrilled, and yet all he felt was sorrow; it reminded him of how he'd felt kissing his grandmother's cold face, how he'd looked upon Wolf's ruined body and accepted another loss. He didn't want it to feel the same, but it did.

Luc gently unclasped Kilian's stiffening fingers from the Walther P38 handgun. He checked the chamber. It was empty. He hung his head in fresh dismay. So Kilian had left the hotel with only one round in this gun. Luc felt sure that it had been intended for Kilian himself, but instead he'd shot Luc to save Luc's life. Kilian had needed the young French boy to pull that trigger.

Luc straightened Kilian's arms and took the trouble to pull back on his socks and boots as best he could. He even straightened the man's hair. He didn't want to think what would happen to the body if it were discovered by French freedom fighters, but that was no longer his concern.

He looked at the bloodstained envelope in his lap. It was addressed to someone called Ilse Vogel, which he could now just read beneath the lightening sky. Luc tucked it into his pocket; he'd post it as promised when the inevitable madness died down. It was the least he could do.

He slipped Kilian's pistol into his trousers, beneath his shirt. He checked the colonel's pockets; there was some money, a single cigarette and a lighter with his initials engraved on it. Luc dropped the lighter and money into his pocket with the letter. He didn't like the idea that Kilian's corpse would be looted, even though he wanted none of the man's possessions.

'Despite what you thought, you were a formidable adversary,' he said quietly to Kilian's still face, his heart heavy. He sensed that the world had lost a good man. Once again he was struck by how much Kilian reminded him of himself in appearance. He sighed, squeezed Kilian's hand and then stood.

He'd all but forgotten about his own bullet wound until now, but the exertion of standing had awoken it. The bleeding had stopped but it was still very painful. He took off his shirt with difficulty and assumed that the bullet had passed cleanly through his shoulder. No bones seemed to be shattered. He touched the pouch hanging from his neck and smelled a faintest waft of lavender. His seeds had survived this long, and if his grandmother was right, they still protected him . . . even from bullets. He would need to get the wound cleaned and dressed; it might even require stitches. But for now he ripped his shirt tail to form a makeshift bandage.

'Goodbye, Colonel,' he said softly in German.

Luc took off and didn't look back, running out of the Tuileries through all the haunts once again, just in case he stumbled across some lead on Lisette.

As he approached the Hotel Raphaël he noticed crowds of people loitering outside. His sleeve was grabbed by a man standing in the leeway of the building.

'Excuse me.' The man looked nervous.

'Yes?'

He glanced at Luc's shirt, still damp with his blood. 'I . . . er . . . I work . . . worked at this hotel,' he whispered.

Luc frowned. 'What is it you want?'

'Some hours ago, you asked me about the young lady.'

Luc hadn't recognised the man out of his uniform. It was the concierge.

'After you left, she came.'

Luc's eyes widened. 'She did?'

The man looked around furtively, and Luc pulled him back behind a corner of the building. 'What can you tell me?' He started digging in his pockets for money.

'No, no,' the man protested. 'Perhaps you should get to a hospital, sir.'

'What about Mademoiselle Forestier?'

'I did see her last night – she was looking for Colonel Kilian.'

Luc's jaw tightened. 'Where did she go?'

'Up to his room. And I think she must have stayed because I saw her again this morning, but . . . but —'

'What?'

'They took her.'

Luc stared at the man quizzically.

He pointed. 'Not that long ago. That's what everyone's waiting for here. Either to see Germans dragged out, or their whores and collaborators.'

Luc's expression clouded, like a gathering storm. He understood.

'Down there,' the man said, pointing again. 'They're teaching a lesson to all the French women who associated with the Boches.'

Luc ran, following the sound of a jeering crowd.

———————

Lisette refused to weep. It didn't win her any sympathy, but this was not a crowd in the mood to show compassion anyway. She'd discovered that the girl next to her was a waitress who worked in a café popular with the Nazis.

'I was friendly, yes,' she whimpered to Lisette, 'but I'm married, *mademoiselle*. I have a baby. I needed tips.' She dissolved into tears. The woman behind her was far less emotional.

'Hooligans,' she said. 'You see that man with his blade?'

Lisette nodded, watching it being waved around.

'He's a collaborator. I know Remy Jocard. He's spent years sliming up to the Nazis, passing on information, fingering people to the Gestapo – most of them innocent. He's a pig! And look at him now, pretending to be offended by us. I cleaned their hotel, that's all I did, trying to keep body and soul together for my family.' She spat at her feet.

Lisette gritted her teeth. There were calls from some of the men to strip the women, run them through the streets with swastikas painted on their breasts. Still others were calling for calm.

It was Lisette's turn to be paraded in front of the crowd. The young mother had just been led away, her humiliation complete. But Lisette, at least, deserved the crowd's contempt. She had fraternised with a German colonel, accepted his gifts, become his lover; if only she could explain that she was a spy. Lisette was shoved roughly to the centre of a makeshift stage and she didn't resist. There was nothing to be gained. Besides, she felt too weak to fight back. She couldn't remember the last time she'd eaten. She wasn't sure whether the crowd was moving or whether she was swaying; Lisette felt a sudden light-headedness. She didn't want to faint. Not now. Not yet.

She wasted no time. 'This man's name is Remy Jocard. He is a collaborator! I know, because I've seen him fraternising with the Nazis,' she yelled loudly, happy to lie on behalf of all the other women.

The man grabbed her and slapped her. 'Shut your filthy mouth, Nazi whore!'

The blow hurt but she managed a sneer even though she was now dizzy. 'Boches-lover!'

The crowd murmured.

'I'll do you properly, bitch!' he threatened.

'You'll do her fairly, Jocard, or perhaps you'll be answering to this same crowd,' a new voice said. It was an older man, and as Lisette watched him she realised it was the maitre d' from the magnificent restaurant at the Ritz. She nodded at him, remembering how he'd enjoyed her praise.

And so it began.

Lisette was forced to sit on a small bench. This was a merciful relief. She clutched her bag close to her belly as she heard the dislocated sound of scissors hacking roughly at her shoulder-length hair. Her tormentors threw some of the dark lengths into her lap and the crowd cheered. She looked forlornly at the hair that her father had loved, her mother had plaited, that Kilian and Luc had caressed.

And now a new sensation began. Lisette felt the barber's blade begin to scrape against her scalp. Her remaining hair fell away in chunks around her, looking as dead as she felt inside. Jocard was rough and she felt the sting of the cuts he carelessly inflicted.

The trauma continued and the only way she could escape was to go inside her own mind. As though separating herself from this scene, she felt her spirit dislocate. She could see herself sitting on the bench, her eyes downcast, her lips thinned and resolute. One man held up her chin so the crowd could see her face, while Jocard shaved off her hair in clumps. She watched it all from a distance.

'You wouldn't want to draw any more blood on this girl, Jocard,' her supporter warned.

Jocard mumbled beneath his breath but she didn't feel the blade slice into her scalp again as the last of her black hair fell away and the crowd – most of them, anyway – laughed and cheered at the newest *femme tondue* in the popular justice sweeping France during the liberation.

Lisette let her breathing slow and deepen as best she could and let her mind transport her to a field of lavender. The bees buzzed around her, the stalks tall and strong, their purple flowers level with her face. She could smell their perfume.

And in doing so she could smell Luc.

――――――

Luc ran headlong into the crowd. He pushed through the mocking throng and shouldered his way painfully towards the front, his shoulder bleeding freely again. He arrived in time to see Lisette raise her shorn head and look directly at him with large, vacant eyes, almost violet in the light. She could have been a young boy, she looked so waif-like. Her summer frock hung loosely on her frame.

The worst thing, though, was the thin rivulets of blood that ran from her shadowy scalp past her ears and down her neck.

'Lisette . . .' he whispered, his voice choked before his anger arrived. 'Get away from her, you thugs!' he roared.

As Luc pulled free Kilian's gun, women began to scream. Everyone backed off as Luc brandished it; he suspected he had murder in his eyes, and felt fortunate that the gun held no bullets.

'Get your filthy hands off her,' he warned again, aiming the gun at the *tondeur*.

'You can have her,' the man taunted, seemingly unafraid. He dragged Lisette to her feet and pushed her in front of him.

'This woman is as Maquis as I am!' Luc yelled for all to hear. 'She has spent the last year trying to help free this nation. What were you doing?' He levelled angrily at one woman and pointed the gun. She nearly fainted. 'Or you, *monsieur*!' he said, swinging around at another man who shied away. 'What were you doing to save our country?'

'*Monsieur*,' said another man carefully. 'Take your woman away. You look as if you've shed enough of your own blood. We don't need any more spilled here.'

'Hypocrites!' Luc spat. He shoved the *tondeur* aside before he lifted Lisette into his arms, ignoring the protest from his shoulder and the blood that now wet her dress.

He put her hands around his neck, laid her warm, bare, bleeding head against his chest and watched as she wept. 'I smelled the lavender, Luc. I knew you'd come for me.'

Ignoring the tears streaming down his own face, Luc pushed through a much quieter crowd, carrying Lisette like a precious bird. He hadn't been able to save anyone he loved, until now. But he had kept her safe.

Luc walked as far as he could with his wounded shoulder. And then he placed Lisette on a small cot in the apartment in Montmartre, lay down beside her and held her still and silent until the evening closed in and darkness carried them both into welcome, peaceful oblivion.

40

Lisette woke up with a start and looked around, momentarily disoriented as she took in the familiar surrounds of her old flat and Luc lying next to her awkwardly on her single cot.

It was the blood she reacted to first.

'Luc,' she called. '*Luc!*' She was shocked to discover that he'd been shot. Her frantic pawing reopened the wound and fresh, bright blood seeped onto her fingers. *How? When? Why?* Kilian sprang to mind but she dismissed the thought. Luc needed help immediately.

She reached for his clammy forehead. His whole body was burning, and her dress was damp with his perspiration. It was a warm morning but Luc was shivering. She prayed he wasn't dying. The bullet itself may not have claimed his life, but infection could.

She had no choice but to find help – and she knew where to go. She was dirty, bloodied and confused but she ran out of her flat and down the stairs, feeling the strange sensation of wind on her bare scalp. This was her old stomping ground, where she still had friends.

She almost cried with relief to find the kind doctor she knew at home, and he wasted no time hurrying to her flat, generous enough not to mention her baldness.

They both bent over Luc, who was still hot but whose feverish murmurings had dissipated. The doctor examined him carefully.

'The bullet went through his flesh cleanly. Your young man has no smashed bones, and the bullet left no debris. I've cleaned and drenched the wound with lavender oil, and stitched it as best I can. It will have to be re-dressed regularly. Can you do that?' the doctor asked.

'Gladly.'

'I've left some fresh rags. And then just keep it in the sling. It will be sore and stiff for weeks, perhaps permanently.'

'The stitches?'

'Out in two weeks. You can do that too, but use plenty of oil, and sterilise the blade or scissors in boiling water, scrub your fingers and douse them with the the lavender oil. Infection is the enemy.'

She nodded. 'Thank you. How much do —'

He waved a hand at her testily. 'You owe me nothing, *mademoiselle*.' He glanced at her head. 'I think you've paid your debt to France.'

Lisette looked down. 'I deserved it.'

'You're not a collaborator, are you, child?' he said.

'No, doctor. I am a British spy.' His mouth opened and she watched understanding ghost across his face. 'Hush. Don't tell anyone else,' she pleaded.

He smiled. 'And you were part of that liberation. I'm sorry,' he said, glancing again at her head.

She scratched her scalp. 'It will grow back.'

'Use the lavender oil on those cuts. It works wonders. I'll stop by and see your patient tomorrow. Call me if his fever worsens, but I suspect it will break later today.'

And it did.

When Luc woke, she was seated by the bed.

'Is it really you holding my hand?' he asked in a croaky voice.

She smiled, reaching for the cup of water she had readied. 'In heaven I would have hair. So I'm afraid you're in Montmartre.'

After he'd drunk thirstily his head flopped back on her pillow and he lifted her hand to his lips and kissed it gently. 'Nowhere I'd rather be.'

Lisette laid her head on his chest and wept silently as he stroked her bare scalp.

———

Days stretched into weeks as Luc got stronger. He winced when he moved but he never complained, and what had begun between them as careful, gentle caresses moved into longer, tighter embraces until one evening Luc pulled off his sling.

'I've had enough of that,' he said, throwing it across the room.

'But, Luc, you have to —'

'It gets in the way,' he griped.

'In the way of what?'

'This,' he said, and pulled her onto his lap. 'I want to hold you with both arms.'

She grinned, relaxing into him. 'And what else?'

'Feeling you with both hands,' he said and cupped her breast, kissing it through her thin blouse.

Lisette gasped quietly and grabbed at his hair, pulling his head back so she could kiss him, long and deeply.

'Take me to bed, nurse,' he demanded when they finally broke apart, breathing rapidly. 'I'll let you do anything you want to me.'

'Anything?' she repeated. She began to laugh as he picked her up with a wince and placed her on the single bed, rolling gently on top of her. He kissed her scalp but she shied and shifted away.

'I like bald women,' he insisted. 'I always have.'

Now she laughed tearily. 'Don't, Luc. It's hard to look like this.'

'Like what? Like a beautiful woman? Most women would give a limb to look like you, Lisette. Even bald you're exquisite. So let me enjoy every inch of you.' As he pushed himself against her she could hardly fail to feel his desire.

Their laughter resounded through the apartment block and out the windows onto the street where it was drowned out by the loud celebrations.

Finally their laughter succumbed fully to lust as they explored each others' bodies and desires, joining together completely. With a gasp of pleasure, Lisette dug her fingers into Luc's back as they found a slowly escalating rhythm that became their private music.

Over the next dozen days they lived and laughed and made love in the tiny flat . . . and fell in love again, deeper than either had thought possible. But on the thirteenth morning Luc woke up and looked at Lisette in a way that he hadn't in a long time.

'What is it?' she asked, a chill bringing goosebumps to her flesh.

'I have to go to Avenue de Wagram. We need to find out what's happening.'

'Don't, Luc. Let's just forget —'

'Listen to me,' he said, stroking the velvety stubble on her head. 'I saw Sylvie yesterday.'

Lisette bristled.

'She dropped by for five minutes to pass on some news,' he reassured her. 'She told me that there's an SOE office set up and they're waiting for their agents to check in.'

'I have never been happier than I am at this moment,' Lisette explained, touching his cheek and then his heart, where a small pouch of seeds still sat next to his skin. 'These kept you safe for me. Let's just remain safe and stay here.'

But Luc was adamant. 'The war is not over, my beautiful Lisette. I want to get you out of Paris. I must know you're safe . . . or none of this was worth it.'

'Then take me to Provence. We'll go to your old home in Saignon where —'

He shook his head. 'I can't.' He looked at her with intensity. 'Please understand. I can't. Not yet.'

'Don't make me go alone.'

'We have to get you out of Europe. You need to be debriefed. It's time, Lisette. You've done your bit. I want you away from all danger.'

'No, Luc. I'm not going anywhere without you. I'll only go if you promise that you'll return to England with me.'

It was an enormous request, but the truth was he couldn't imagine a day without her now. And it didn't matter where, so long as it was away from all the painful memories.

He nodded, and her face burst into a smile. They sealed their bargain, making love so tenderly it rendered him weak. He would never need any other woman again.

—————

As they prepared to leave the apartment the following day, Lisette had asked him the question Luc had been dreading.

'Luc, I want to know about Markus Kilian. You were talking about him through your fever. I want the truth.'

He'd known he'd have to face the retelling at some time. If he were honest, he was surprised it had taken her this long to bring it up. But he suspected that Lisette had deliberately pushed Kilian aside in her mind so they could have this time alone, together, in love, and without Kilian's name so much as uttered between them. But no matter how much they'd pretended, he'd been there – in the room with them, sharing their bed with them. Luc knew it was right to tell her, and he hoped with all of his heart that it would be cathartic for both of them.

'All right,' he said, swallowing.

Lisette looked frightened. She sat down on the bed and he sat next to her, taking her hand and cupping it between both of his, as if he could protect her from what he needed to say.

'Kilian died on the night of 25 August.' He felt her hand rip from his as she covered her mouth in anguish.

'You're sure?' she gasped, her eyes wet with sudden tears.

He nodded. 'I was with him when he took his last breath, and I stayed with him through the night because . . .' He shrugged. 'He deserved it.'

She wept quietly.

Softly, gently, he told her everything that had happened. He spared her none of the detail.

'It was peaceful, you say?' she asked tearily when he'd finished.

'Yes, utterly. He died smiling and sipping on calvados because it reminded him of you.'

'Thank you for looking after him at the end.'

'He was very hard to dislike.'

She dried her tears on her sleeve, sniffing hard. 'Markus would have made a terrible prisoner of war anyway.'

'He never had any intention of being taken. The bullet was meant for him, not me.'

Lisette slipped back his shirt and kissed his scar. 'Then he'll always be with us. But I love you, Luc. You never have to wonder; it was always you.'

41

Lisette gazed at Luc. 'All right?'

They were sitting in an anteroom of the Hotel Cecil on the Champs Elysées, where SOE had set up its makeshift Parisian headquarters.

He nodded. The sight of her bald head still shocked, and caused people to turn and stare, and it irritated him how their journey had attracted so much unnecessary attention. People assumed Lisette was a Nazi collaborator, but fortunately, she no longer cared. Some people even spat at them as they walked, but she held her head high.

'They can't hurt me any more,' she had assured Luc.

Now Lisette was watching him from the seat opposite. 'Ready?' she whispered.

A woman approached and introduced herself briskly with a warm smile as Vera Atkins.

'Oh, my dear.' She embraced Lisette, hugging her long and hard. 'How brave you are.'

Lisette touched the soft fuzz on her scalp. 'One day soon there'll be no sign that any of this ever happened.'

As he listened Luc didn't want to think about the internal scars, though. Not visible but permanent. He prayed that Lisette would escape unscathed.

Vera's eyes were gentle as she turned to Luc. 'And you must be the man we've only known as Faucille.' Her French was flawless.

'Lukas Ravensburg,' he said, for the first time feeling his name to be right. 'Luc,' he added.

'Well, I know a lot of us feel that we're very indebted to you, Luc, for all you've done to help our agents . . . for all of us who knew we could trust you.'

'Thank you, *madame*,' he replied.

'Well,' she said, smiling broadly. 'There's someone behind that door just bursting to add his thanks to mine.'

Lisette smiled. 'Colonel Buckmaster?'

'One and the same. He can't wait to see you both. We've got all your paperwork in order. I've organised for the two of you to travel to England at the end of the week, if that's all right? We'll arrange the formal debrief there.'

As the trio approached the door of the suite, one of the British agents from the Spiritualist network stopped Luc, looking relieved and delighted to see him.

Vera paused, stepping back to talk to Lisette while the two men exchanged news. 'All of you have been through too much together,' she said. 'I love watching everyone's faces light with joy when they see an old friend, and know they've made it.'

Lisette realised it must have been tough on people like Vera, never knowing if they were sending their agents to their deaths.

Vera cocked her head slightly. 'He's very handsome, your masquisard,' she said, and winked. 'Tell me, what was Luc before he joined the Maquis?'

'Oh, he was a lavender keeper. And if I have my way, that's what he'll become again,' Lisette replied.

They left for the Sussex coast aboard a large fishing boat from Calais. On board was a mix of returning soldiers, civilians and a few agents, none of whom they knew. It was a clear day; Luc stared gravely at the French shoreline disappearing.

'Are you all right?' Lisette asked, leaning into his body.

'I never thought I'd leave France. I love this country.'

'I do too. But I'm hoping you may love England too. It's close enough that we can always come back to France.'

After two hours they sighted land.

'That's Beachy Head,' she said, pointing to the cliffs, tying her headscarf a little tighter. The wind had a nip in it. Days were cooling. Soon it would be autumn.

'England,' he breathed, almost in disbelief.

She squeezed his arm. 'We'll find somewhere quiet to live. We'll start again, Luc.'

He nodded sadly. 'I miss Provence.'

'I promise we will go back.'

'One day. Not yet. But some day I'll take you back to Saignon and we'll walk through my lavender fields, where my seeds come from.'

'We'll plant some lavender fields for you . . . in memory of your grandmother. I love you, Luc. I love you enough to go anywhere at all with you. So long as we're together, I'm happy. But we have to start somewhere. Why don't we give Sussex a try? A new beginning for us both.' She looked at him and he saw her love reflected in her dark-blue eyes, as well as her hope for a family of her own.

'Yes. A new beginning,' he said, pulling her close and kissing the top of her head reassuringly. Luc had to wonder whether this rugged northern landscape, so far away from Provence, would ever compete with the soft purple beauty of his wild French lavender.

He would try, for both their sakes. He would become the lavender keeper again and, in so doing, keep the memories of all those he loved alive.

ACKNOWLEDGEMENTS

The inspiration for this story came from reading about Bridestowe Lavender Farm in northern Tasmania. It's one of Australia's quiet secrets and true success stories. Go visit sometime – it's not far from Launceston – and marvel at what its present 'curators', Robert and Jennifer Ravens, are achieving with their purple meadows first sown by the Denny family at the turn of the last century. Be warned: like Europe, there's only a few short weeks in summer (late December/early January) in which to see the Ravens' lavender at its most breathtaking. Their enthusiasm for this novel was evident from our first telephone call a couple of years ago – my sincere thanks to them for their wealth of both historical and contemporary information as well as their brilliant support. All power to you, Robert and Jennifer, as you forge ahead with Bridestowe as a world leader in pure lavender oil production.

There was so much to learn about the Second World War before I felt comfortable to use it as a backdrop for a story. I've lost track of the articles I've sifted through, the documentaries I've watched, and the tower of books I've read just to be able to get a snapshot of the time in my mind. However, I was determined to keep this tale focused on my triangle of characters and what was happening in the microcosm of their lives, rather than trying to wrestle with the bigger picture of world war and all of its theatres and political machinations.

Even so, as small as that focus is, this book has many to thank, beginning with the folk at Penguin for giving me the scope and opportunity to explore my tale. And when I realised that my story-telling was too big for one volume, the editorial team magnanimously allowed me to work with two. So there is a second book, which I'm pleased to say I've almost finished drafting. It will certainly be on its editing journey by the time you read this. So, my gratitude to the very caring Bob Sessions and Gabrielle Coyne for their largesse, and to my editor Ali Watts for her insight, friendship and gentle guidance on the long haul. Also to Arwen Summers for helping me to pare back that big final edit. Thank you all, and of course to the wider family of Penguins in sales, marketing and contracts – you are always so supportive.

My thanks to the gentle, generous Blanc family of Saignon for their hospitality during our stay in Provence, and to villagers Christine Bourdin, Liliane Jenselme and Alain Blanc for sharing their memories of wartime Saignon. Also my thanks to Jean Girou, historian and Catherine Richards from the office of tourism, both in Cavaillon. Particularly, though, my thanks to Severine Henin and Laurent Crotet for taking us into their family and for their wonderful generosity . . . but especially for your friendship, Sev.

David Harrison, a UK-based historian, became a precious resource of knowledge on the Special Operations Executive of the War Ministry, bringing alive an era and inspiring me to write about brave people like Francis Cammaerts, Vera Atkins, Maurice Buckmaster, et al. I felt as though I knew them – thanks, David. You were an absolute rock.

Although I have done my utmost to ensure research accuracy of time and place, any errors that may occur are mine alone. Plus, I have taken a few liberties – which is a novelist's prerogative! – including suggesting that the pure *lavandula angustifolia* grows around Saignon, when it more likely needs an additional 300 metres of altitude to thrive.

Thank you to my French class for keeping me in the mood, to Isabelle Pernot in Lille for so many helpful translations, and to Jack Caddy for letting me use him in my story. Fly safe always, Jack!

Thank you to Pip Klimentou for all the fast and furious reading of drafts and for your generous friendship always. A special nod to the latte gang, who round off my writing weeks with fun and laughter each Friday – even when I'm overseas with your lovely messages so I don't miss out on the gossip . . . I love Fridays!

Finally, boundless love and thanks to Ian McIntosh for his help with all the research, ordering, purchase and marking up of so many reference books; for letting me roam London, Paris and beyond to gather the material for this book; for taking me to Provence to see the lavender in full bloom in that precious three-week window; and for braving the Holocaust halls in London and Paris with me during that harrowing time of research; for carrying my bags, for reading behind me, for understanding and accepting all the lonely times when I've been lost in the 1940s; but especially for my beloved coffee machine that got me through some big writing days.

Fx

ALSO BY FIONA McINTOSH

THE FRENCH PROMISE

The Lavender Keeper story continues

It's 1950, and Luc and Lisette are building a new life on the south coast of England, away from the traumas of war. But Luc remains haunted by private promises that remain unfulfilled.

When Luc finally learns the tragic fate of his family, his resolve breaks, and Lisette knows that unless drastic measures are taken, their marriage will not survive. They cast their fate to the winds and sail for Tasmania, hoping to build a new life and new lavender fields on the other side of the world.

Australia exceeds even Luc's hopes and dreams, but just when life is settled, the family is hit by tragedy again. Old demons resurface to haunt Luc, and he decides to return to Europe – for only then can he fulfil the promises by which he has been bound.

Don't miss the dramatic conclusion to the romantic adventure *The Lavender Keeper*.

Read on for a sneak peek...

I

Luc liked this time of the day – when only the fishermen were up – and especially this spot on the South Downs, leading onto Beachy Head, the highest cliff in Britain. He shifted his gaze from the uninterrupted view of the town's sprawl and its long shingle beach to where he could see one of the fishing boats heading in. Behind it, like a welcoming party, was a flock of gulls, their wings beating furiously as they wheeled, dipped and powered forward, depending on where the next treat of fish cast-offs would be flung as the men busily gutted their catch.

Luc could smell the fresh haul now; the years had not blunted his almost freakish ability to pick out individual aromas. Even now he could separate the salty, mineral notes of the fish from the ancient, earthy smell of coal fires burning in hearths of the houses below him. If he concentrated hard enough, he fancied he could even pick up a whiff of the darting rabbit in the distance that shared this dawn with him, stirring the grasses and kicking up dust.

The cries of the excited birds were carried on the chilled wind that chased through Luc's still-bright hair, ruffling it from his forehead and then instantly blowing it back again. He pushed away the yellowy-gold hank that had fallen across his face and then gave up fighting it. He had given up fighting altogether, unless he counted the rows with his wife. Lisette deserved so much better. How had she come to terms so quickly with her losses, her life's

469

changes, while he yearned for the past? There were moments when he felt there was nothing to fight for any more, and on those bleak occasions he had taken to digging his nails into a scar he carried on his wrist. Its memory of the wound he'd sustained at Mont Mouchet reminded him that he'd survived not only his injuries but the hail of bullets and storm of bombs, when so many other brave souls had not. He remembered the young father who'd taken his last breath speaking of the family he loved as Luc had held his hand so he wouldn't die alone. Luc couldn't remember his name, didn't want to; it only added to his self-loathing that he'd somehow slunk away from France's suffering to let others bear her pain.

France had prevailed, however. The Nazis – those that the Allies could round up – had been put on trial, the leaders and abusers executed. In the meantime soldiers had been repatriated, families reunited, and life postwar was beginning to form a more solid shape across Europe.

But Luc had still not shaken his guilt.

It had been nearly seven years since the liberation of Paris and they'd sailed away from France in a fishing boat that landed them on the shoreline of Hastings on Britain's south coast. He desperately hadn't wanted to leave his country but he couldn't admit that to anyone, and in 1944 with the decimated German army retreating, the wounded animal was still dangerous and all he could think of was getting Lisette away to the relative safety of England. Her superiors had demanded it, reminding him that this British spy's clandestine missions were behind her.

They were both injured emotionally but as Lisette had often reminded him, 'Show me someone in this war who isn't.' It was her way of countering her pain – all of it connected with the loss of Markus Kilian – a colonel who had been her mission, become her lover and at some point taken part of her heart too. He was still struggling to come to terms with what had happened. In fact, both of them found it easier not to mention Kilian at all.

And as the weeks had stretched into months until the German surrender, the loneliness of the Scottish Isles where they'd retreated to help Lisette finally bounce back from her wartime experiences, but Luc had never stopped pining for his homeland.

In summer the Luberon of Provence was hot and arid, carrying on its breeze the scent of lavender and thyme. In the cooler months, its villages would pulse to a different perfume of olives giving up their precious oil and the yeasty smell of grapes being crushed. Around his own village he would wake daily to the smell of fresh baguettes baking and in spring the blossom from the expansive orchards surrounding Saignon would litter the ground.

He was a man of the Alps, of unforgiving terrain, with its white winters and multicoloured summers and farms dotted here and there. But he was trying so hard, for his new family's sake, to become a man of the coast . . . of pebbly beaches with drifts of seaweed, and of tall, elegant houses, standing in a line on the seafront. Provence was a motley of brightly painted houses, where shutters of blue and yellow punctuated walls of ochre or pink. But in Britain's south it was a monotone palette; the large terraced homes favoured walls the colour of clotted cream and were framed by shiny black doors and iron railings. He couldn't deny the quiet formality of Eastbourne where they now lived; it didn't shout anything . . . it simply whispered a weary sort of elegance. He missed the loud colour and even louder voices of the French.

It was only up here – on the desolate cliff tops, far away from real life – that Luc felt at home. He could never hide that truth from Lisette: she knew that from up here on a clear day he could look out across the English Channel and see France.

Luc wrinkled his nose at the sour smell that was reaching him from the boat and blinked at the sunrise just breaking over

Eastbourne pier. Shadows of clouds stretched across the lightening sky, while a finger of orange across the horizon pointed firmly at France.

Here is where you should be, it baited.

But he couldn't return to France. Not yet. His wounds still felt too fresh. He thought of the friends who'd given up their lives to bombs, bullets and the collaborator's accusing nod. He thought of the villages destroyed all over France and the generations it would take to restore them. But mostly he thought of the family he had lost: parents, sisters . . . his beloved grandmother, whom he'd cradled in death and whose talisman he now wore. Her pouch of lavender seeds was a constant reminder of all that had been taken from him – people, lifestyle, livelihood. The few lavender heads inside had long since withered but if he closed his eyes and inhaled, there was still a faint perfume of Saignon.

One day he would return.

He'd written to the International Tracing Agency in Germany a few years back. He'd been thrilled to learn that the ITA had been set up by the Red Cross in 1946 to help people find their missing families, and expressly for the purpose of helping the Jewish people with answers and news of those who had suffered genocide at the hands of the Nazis. There had been two exchanges of letters with the ITA to date. It was more than a year since he'd heard back. But the silence was curiously comforting; as long as the organisation kept him waiting, there was hope.

He forced himself not to dwell too long or too often about his lost family because the darkness of it was toxic. It was his burden, not Lisette's. His challenge was to build a normal life for Lisette and Harry, now three. Luc hoped he'd teach him French as he grew – it would be so easy for them to speak it at home. Right now, though, the echoes of war were still ringing in everyone's ears so to be speaking in any language other than English was madness. He'd worked hard to become fluent. Lisette was a chameleon; she could override the lilt of her French accent with a southern English manner of speaking and was quickly losing her Frenchness in favour of fitting in completely. He'd never shake his accent, but no one bar Lisette and a couple of people at the defunct War Office would ever know the truth behind the brave French Resister who'd aided the Allied war effort.

It had been the new Defence Ministry's idea, at the debriefing, to change his true surname. Luc had to agree that with a name as German as Ravensburg, their new life would never work. But Bonet, the adopted Jewish surname he'd accepted as his own for a quarter of a century, was no longer his name either. He couldn't pinpoint when during the war he'd emotionally left it behind but he knew why. It was always a borrowed name, bestowed with love by the Jewish family that had given him a life and a home. To take Lisette's name didn't feel right either. It was Lisette who'd suggested shortening his real name to Ravens. It had the right ring of truth to his proper name but would not attract negative attention.

Lisette had refused to hide or justify her role as a British spy in France, getting beneath the German command using the oldest cunning known to man – the honey trap. Instead she had agreed to hole up in a lonely cottage on a remote island in the Orkneys for sixteen months, seeing out the war, until her once-shaved hair reached chin length again and she returned to Sussex to marry Luc in her grandparents' local church. Once married, Lisette didn't want to leave southern England, but there was no way Luc could agree to life in London or even a large, busy town. She'd tried a new tack, suggesting positions on the south coast.

'I'm a farmer . . . a specialist grower,' he'd argued, when she'd told him about a job as a postman in Worthing or a carpenter's hand in Rye. He'd lost track of the number of suggestions he refused. Her patience with him only darkened his mood because each time he shook his head meant another few months of living off her savings. She never complained. Lisette was not without means but that was not the point. Luc wanted to support his family, yet every time she gave him the opportunity he turned away from it. It was a vicious cycle that stole his sense of worth and independence.

Eventually a job as a lighthouse keeper at Beachy Head bubbled to the surface. Luc remembered that day well; it was the first time in years that he'd felt a weight lifting from his shoulders. Here at last was the loneliest of jobs in the most remote location. Luc had leapt at it and loved the smile it had returned to Lisette, knowing their future was being secured in Eastbourne where her parents had hoped to live.

Lighthouse families were provided accommodation but the cottages were based on the Isle of Wight and Lisette was having none of that. While she was prepared to live alone for two months at a time, she had refused to be separated, with him on the mainland, her on an island again and Harry not seeing his father for such long periods. Instead she had dipped into her inheritance and rented them a small cottage in the Meads – sitting atop Eastbourne proper.

'Luc, if you squint a bit, you could trick yourself that it's hilly Provence, couldn't you?' she'd said excitedly one warm afternoon as they'd strolled across Beachy Head, Harry suspended between them, holding a hand of each parent and lifing his legs from the grass, giggling his pleasure.

He should have said yes. Should have given her a hug and thanked her. Instead honesty had prevailed and did nothing but damage, especially as he had muttered his wounded retort in French. 'Place is about emotion; one loves somewhere not just because of how it looks but because of the way their heart reacts to it.'

The hurt had instantly shadowed across Lisette's face. 'Luc, you've got to snap out of this. For Harry's sake, for my sake! This is our home now.'

The reality of her sentiment had only deepened his personal crisis.

When Luc took the time to examine the chaos in his mind, he believed his discontent stemmed from his sense of impotency to fulfil promises. He had promised himself he would find his family, or at least find out what had happened to them. He had promised to return to central France one day and see young Robert and his grandmother, who had saved his life and nursed him back to health. Robert would be about twelve now, and Luc had to wonder whether Marie was still alive. Who would be looking after that sunny, sweet child who'd bravely cut his thumb to share blood with him? 'I'll come back,' Luc had promised, but years had passed.

He had also promised to find a German who had inflicted perhaps the greatest wound when he forced Luc to murder an old man he loved as a father.

Then there was the silent, wounding despair that ate away at him day and night in not living up to his promise that he gave his beloved grandmother that he would be the keeper of the lavender; that he would never let its magic die and that he would plant it again one day.

'It will save your life; give you life,' she had said often enough in that singsong way of hers.

Perhaps the lavender's magic had kept them safe, but where was that magic now?

The single promise he'd fulfilled was the one he'd made to his enemy. Markus Kilian had been an enigma. As a decorated and beloved colonel in the Wehrmacht, he represented everything Luc despised. But strip away the uniform, the status, and Kilian embodied all that Luc admired in a man. Kilian had lost his life protecting Luc but both of them knew the sacrifice was ultimately for Lisette . . . and her safety. Luc knew Kilian had hated the Nazis but he had loved Germany. When he died, it was with Lisette's name on his lips, a genuine and respectful smile for Luc, and an unblemished record of patriotism. It could so easily have been Luc bleeding out in the Tuileries Garden that terrible night as Paris was liberated.

As the colonel had counted his life in minutes, Kilian asked Luc to post a letter for him upon his death. It had taken Luc a long period to do so, choosing the right time when letters wouldn't be seized by the Allied forces. At the end of 1945 he had bought a British stamp and posted Kilian's bloodstained letter within another envelope to Ilse Vogel in Switzerland. He'd accompanied the letter with a note of his own, written in French. He could have written it in fluent German but that was too risky. He'd never heard back from Miss Vogel and didn't expect to.

Luc knew he shouldn't, but he frequently wondered how often Lisette thought about her German lover. When thoughts of them together crowded his mind he'd come here to the cliff edge – where far too many people willingly stepped off – to let the wind blow the jealousy away. For he had made promises and needed to keep them . . . sometime, somehow, but not yet.

Luc stood, stretched and licked the salty film from his lips. The sky had brightened considerably. If he walked back around the headland he'd see the old Belle Tout lighthouse that had been decommissioned at the turn of the century. It was a wonderful old building on the highest part of the cliff face. If Luc had worked there, he could have gone home each night, cuddled his son and kissed his wife, but the lighthouse had proved ineffective. When sea mists gathered or low cloud descended, the craft would sail perilously close to the cliffs.

The new red-and-white-striped lighthouse that had been built out to sea was his place of work now. He rotated shifts with two others to ensure the bursts of light every 20 seconds were visible beyond 25 miles out to sea. Today was the first day of a two-month posting for him. Leaving Lisette and Harry was becoming harder with each new eight-week shift. As his son grew, Luc realised he was missing out on milestones: Harry's first smile, his first tooth, his first strangled attempt at a word. It had been 'Daddy', according to Lisette.

He preferred the midnight-to-0400 watch most of all, when it was silent and dark . . . and lonely. His life in the lighthouse was a perfume concoction of brass polish, petroleum gas oil and lubricating oil . . . and paint, of course. Three keepers sharing a confined space meant the smell of men spiced the air too. His watch hours flew: winding the lens clock, checking that the burners were pricked out, that the fuel tanks were stocked to keep the light burning constantly through the night. He was happy to tackle whatever needed to be done.

When he was off-duty, every third day, and if the weather was being kind and the tide was out, he would scramble over the rocks and their tiny pools of crabs, and make his way across the exposed wet sand and onto the smooth pebbles. He'd take a few moments – even by torchlight if it was still too dark – and find Harry some special pebbles, before he leapt up onto the seafront proper.

Sometimes, if things were slow, he could sneak a lift back in the relief boat and make a quick dash up the steep, looping pathways to the promenade. He'd all but run the short way home to startle Lisette with a surprise visit, desperate to cuddle his wife and son for the daylight hours. She'd always turn misty-eyed to see him as he lifted her up and twirled her around in his arms. And they'd not let each other go, other than to lavish Harry with kisses and hugs, stories and playtime. They'd have eight hours together and then he'd be running back down to the front, braving the treacherous rocks again to make his shift.

Meanwhile Lisette loved their life and could only improve it if Luc were with her every day. She was making new friends by the week, was a member of two women's groups and was talking about doing some amateur dramatics. And Harry, of course, gave her life its new focus.

Luc wished he could solve his problem of dislocation. There was a gulf they couldn't fully bridge and it was called the English Channel.

'Let's move back to France, then,' Lisette had said a month or so earlier. 'Perhaps you'll be happier there.'

'No. You've built a life for Harry here.'

'He's a child, Luc. He'll adapt. He's half French.'

'German too,' he'd snipped.

She'd cut him a dark look. 'Let it go.'

He'd nodded but they'd both known he was lying; he couldn't let it go.

'Listen, Luc. Let's get some professional help,' she'd suggested softly. 'There are psychologists who can —'

'I'm not having anyone poking around in my mind. No, Lisette. I'm not mad.'

Her gaze had narrowed then. 'I know, Luc. But you are maudlin.'

'Everyone is! A war has just finished. Everyone's lost someone.'

'No. Everyone is not behaving like you; quite the opposite, in fact. Everyone else is looking forward. There's a sense of optimism. Yes, we've all lost someone but we don't wear that pain like a badge of honour.'

He hadn't understood her turn of phrase but he'd grasped the meaning. 'And I do?'

She'd given him the saddest of smiles – a mixture of gentle disdain but also pain. 'Every waking moment, Luc. It's as though you won't allow us to be happy.'

Won't allow us to be happy . . . he heard the echo of her words in his mind. And she was right. He was holding them back; him and his bleak mood and his unfulfilled promises.

He sighed. This existence couldn't last, not with Harry growing and increasingly needing his father around, but that thorny issue of what next should be left for another day's soul searching. As he stood, dusted himself down, the brighter light picked out a small silhouette in the distance. A youth? He was staring over the edge of the cliff as if looking for something, his breath curling in white smoke. From what Luc could tell, the man didn't even have a coat on or scarf. Who went walking in April without being rugged up properly?

'He'll catch his death,' Luc murmured to himself, unaware that for once he was using a proper English idiom.

As a gull gave a mournful cry over the beach Luc realised that this was precisely what the fellow intended. He wanted to catch his death . . . he was planning to jump.

'Hey!' Luc shouted and then whistled loudly in the way that Harry was practising hard to master. He ran full pelt at the figure, who'd whipped his head around to search for the intruder. Somewhere in the back of Luc's mind he knew experts would disapprove of his approach, but he knew a thing or two about contemplating one's own death and about what the demons in a dark mind could achieve with their infernal whisperings.

'Stop!' the fellow yelled back, holding up a hand. It was only hearing the deeper voice that Luc realised it was a man, not a teenager.

'You stop!' Luc hurled at him, not breaking stride until he was within a few yards. Then he slowed, feigned breathlessness, his hands near his knees. 'Give me a moment,' he gasped, winning some precious time.

The newcomer was distracted and Luc, as he straightened, got a better look at him. He was small, maybe five foot six, tops. He was likely in his late twenties, perhaps early thirties; clean-shaven, dark, short, combed and oiled hair with a neat parting. Even the tie he wore over a pressed white shirt was knotted neatly at his throat.

He obviously planned to be found dressed and ready for his own funeral. Luc noticed a walking stick on the ground nearby. The man had been crying; his eyes glossy from his tears and his nose bright red from the stinging cold.

'Leave me alone!' he said.

'My name's Luc,' Luc replied, pronouncing his name the English way.

'I don't care.'

'What's yours?'

'I'm not telling you.'

'It's the least you can do.'

'What?' The man frowned.

'I can save the police a whole lot of time if I can give them the name of the man splattered below.'

His eyes widened with fear. 'Shut up!'

Luc gave a small gust of scorn, covering the step he took nearer by waving his arms at the man. 'Make me.'

'You're twice as big as me.'

'And then you're a cripple, of course,' Luc said, nodding towards the walking stick.

'You bastard!'

'*Oui, c'est moi.* Luc, the French bastard.'

'Yes, I can tell you're foreign.'

'Why? Because an Englishman would politely let you jump? Mind his own business?'

'As a matter of fact, yes!'

'No, because like you he would be a coward,' Luc baited, taking another step closer now. He was just steps away from being able to poke the fellow in the chest.

'Coward?' the man railed, his voice high and angry. 'Listen, mate, we didn't hand over the keys to London. You French just gave Hitler a very warm welcome, didn't you, and expected the English to save you.'

The well-worn insult barely cut. But Luc sat down suddenly, pretending that all the stuffing had been punched out of him. He sighed, dug in his pocket for cigarettes. He didn't smoke but in order to fit in he habitually carried around a pack. His co-workers had cottoned on soon enough and curiously liked him more for the pretence.

'Cigarette?' he offered.

The man nodded, looking resigned, and Luc was careful to flick the pack over. When he flung over a box of matches, he inched a bit closer while the man was distracted. Luc held a cigarette between his lips but didn't light up and his companion didn't notice.

Luc watched him take a slow drag, his fingers trembling in the chill, which he let out with an equally slow sigh. 'I'm Eddie. Edward, my mother calls me.'

'Why?'

Eddie blinked. 'Because that's what she christened me.'

Luc grinned. 'No, why die now?'

Eddie looked startled at the directness of the question.

'That was your intention, wasn't it?' Luc said, carefully putting it into the past tense.

Eddie nodded, took another drag. He was shivering. 'My wife and new baby were killed in the bombings. We were living in the East End – couldn't afford much else – and Vera, well, she liked her job at the War Ministry. She was a good secretary, was our Vera. Her mother looked after our son when he came along – she lived with Vera while I was away. We called him Harold, after my dad, who died in the Great War.'

Luc swallowed at the mention of his son's name, but suddenly nothing in his world smelled good. Even the taste of Eddie's tobacco at the back of Luc's throat was bitter.

'It was her day off, apparently,' Eddie continued, unaware of Luc's discomfort. 'Her friend told me they were going to take the youngsters to the zoo but Harry woke up sickening so they stayed home with her mother . . . and died.' Eddie's voice shook. 'Direct hit. All three gone. Them and a few other families.' He gave a mirthless, shrugging laugh. 'I was at the Front and all I lost was the use of my leg.' He banged on it. 'Useless bastard thing it is.' He startled Luc by picking up the walking stick and with surprising strength hurling it over the edge of the cliff. Luc watched it fly through the air, heard it clatter below them somewhere and hoped it was symbolic . . . that Eddie's fire had burned to cold with that gesture. 'I've tried to make a good fist of it, Luc, really I have. But without Vera . . .' He trailed off, looked away. 'I never got to hold my boy. He was blown to smithereens, not even six months old. I had nothing to bury. I can't even visit a grave for my family. They're just gone. It's as if they were never there.' He began to sob. Luc no longer waited, shifting to hold Eddie's shaking shoulders. He remained silent until Eddie's tears were spent. 'I don't want to live without them.'

'Vera wouldn't be very proud of you, though, if you threw your life over this cliff, would she? You said she was good at her job, loved her work?'

Eddie nodded.

'That meant she was brave – going to work each day, risking the Blitz, and why? Because she believed that every little bit she contributed was keeping you safer. That one day you'd come home to her.'

'But I didn't. She wasn't there. All I got was a telegram, a glass of brandy with my commanding officer and a slightly earlier release.'

'But you did come home, Eddie. That was what Vera wanted. She kept you safe in her mind but not for this,' Luc said, pointing to the cliff. 'You'd make a mockery of her, giving your life cheaply, when you survived the war, dodged all those bullets and bombs.'

Eddie smiled sadly. 'Not all of them.'

'Well, the useless leg makes you a hero. She'd want you to enjoy the peaceful England that you both fought for. You owe it to her, Eddie. In her honour, find a way through this. There's work for men like you and although it doesn't seem so right now, there's a happy life to be lived if you forgive yourself for surviving and forgive Vera and Harry for dying.'

I am such a hypocrite, Luc thought at that moment, hating himself.

Eddie's tears began to fall again. 'I don't feel strong enough . . .'

'You are, though. Think of the men who didn't make it. Live a little for them. Live . . . because they gave their lives so you could.'

The advice was easy to give . . . he could hear the sense in his words; why couldn't he drink some of his own tonic?

Eddie nodded. 'When you say it like that, it does feel cowardly to end it all.'

'It *is* cowardly to end it all. It's far braver to live.'

'I thought that's why you were here too,' Eddie admitted.

'To jump?' Luc looked incredulous.

Eddie shrugged.

'No,' Luc said, feeling the pinch of goosebumps pucker on his skin in silent alarm. Is that how he'd appeared? Desperate? As bleak as Eddie?

'No,' he repeated and shook his head firmly. 'I'm just a grumpy French bastard who likes his own company.'

'No wife?'

He nodded, feeling a needle of embarrassment. 'I have a beautiful wife and a son.'

'Then what the hell are you doing up here, man? What wouldn't I give for the same!'

It was Luc's turn to nod, to feel ashamed. 'I was just on my way home.'

'Then go home,' Eddie said. 'Don't worry about me. The moment has passed,' he said, standing awkwardly and holding out his hand. 'I'll go to the pub where it's warm and drown my sorrows hopefully.'

Luc stood and offered a handshake in farewell. 'How will you go?'

'I'll limp.' He grinned, then lifted a shoulder in resignation. 'I won't jump, I give you my word. Not today, anyway.'

'Don't go to the pub. Come home with me.'

His companion looked at him quizzically.

'Come and have a home-cooked meal, get warm, meet my family – my son's called Harry too. He's three.'

Eddie shook his head. 'Too hard. I'll get upset.'

'No, you won't. You'll have a happy time. I have some excellent whisky, too. Come on. It will be good for you to be with a family.'

'So I'll know what I'm missing?' Eddie said, not fully able to hide the bitter tone.

'No, so you'll know what you have to look forward to.' Luc squeezed his companion's hand. 'Never reject a Frenchman's offer . . . it's bad luck.'

'Really?'

'No, I made that up but it sounds good, eh?'

A smile ghosted faintly beneath Eddie's sad façade. 'You sure your wife won't mind?'

'Lisette? She loves company. She'll be impressed I have a friend to bring home.'

'Don't tell her how we met.'

'Of course not.'

'It will take ages for me to get down without my stick, you realise that?'

Luc bent over. 'Get on my back.'

'You're joking, right?'

He shook his head. 'I used to do this in the war over far tougher ground than this. Come on, it's cold and my wife gets cranky when I'm late.'

Eddie frowned. Luc beckoned impatiently. Finally Eddie shrugged and clambered onto Luc's back and they set off, feeling ridiculous, but Luc's stride was long and purposeful and he was grateful suddenly for Eddie's arrival into his world that reminded him how fortunate his own life was.

Luc took a final wistful look at France, which he could now clearly see across the stretch of water, and comforted himself with the pretence that it was not old fish or seaweed he could smell on the salted breeze, but the perfume of wild lavender.

ALSO BY FIONA McINTOSH

NIGHTINGALE

**'Love comes out of nowhere for most of us,
when we least expect it.'**

Amidst the carnage of Gallipoli, British nurse Claire
Nightingale meets Australian Light Horseman Jamie Wren.
Despite all odds, they fall deeply in love. Their flame burns
bright and carries them through their darkest hours, even
when war tears them apart.

When Jamie encounters Turkish soldier Açar Shahin on the
bloodstained battlefield, the men forge an unforgettable
bond. Their chance meeting also leaves a precious clue to
Jamie's whereabouts for Claire to follow.

Come peacetime, Claire's desperate search to find Jamie
takes her all the way to Istanbul, and deep into the heart of
Açar's family, where she attracts the unexpected attention of a
charismatic and brooding scholar.

In the name of forgiveness, cultures come together, enemies
embrace and forbidden passions ignite – but by the nail-
biting conclusion, who will be left standing to capture Nurse
Nightingale's heart?

A breathtaking novel of heartbreak and heroism, love and
longing by a powerhouse Australian storyteller.